KATE LANDRY
HAS A PLAN

BOOKS BY REBEKAH MILLET

BEIGNETS FOR TWO

JULIA MONROE BEGINS AGAIN

KATE LANDRY HAS A PLAN

⤜ BEIGNETS FOR TWO ⤛

KATE LANDRY HAS A PLAN

REBEKAH MILLET

BETHANYHOUSE

a division of Baker Publishing Group
Minneapolis, Minnesota

© 2025 by Rebekah Millet

Published by Bethany House Publishers
Minneapolis, Minnesota
BethanyHouse.com

Bethany House Publishers is a division of
Baker Publishing Group, Grand Rapids, Michigan

Printed in the United States of America

Library of Congress Cataloging-in-Publication Data
Names: Millet, Rebekah, author.
Title: Kate landry has a plan / Rebekah Millet.
Description: Minneapolis, Minnesota : Bethany House Publishers, a division of
    Baker Publishing Group, 2025. | Series: Beignets for two
Identifiers: LCCN 2024031567 | ISBN 9780764240966 (paper) | ISBN 9780764244575
    (casebound) | ISBN 9781493448951 (ebook)
Subjects: LCSH: New Orleans (La.)—Fiction. | LCGFT: Romance fiction. | Novels.
Classification: LCC PS3613.I56265 K38 2025 | DDC 813/.6—dc23/eng/20230327
LC record available at https://lccn.loc.gov/2024031567

Emojis are from the open-source library OpenMoji (https://openmoji.org/) under the Creative Commons license CC BY-SA 4.0 (https://creativecommons.org/licenses/by -sa/4.0/legalcode).

Cover design and illustration by Mary Ann Smith.

Author is represented by The Steve Laube Agency.

Baker Publishing Group publications use paper produced from sustainable forestry practices and postconsumer waste whenever possible.

25 26 27 28 29 30 31   7 6 5 4 3 2 1

JESUS, YOU WENT AND DID IT AGAIN.
THANK YOU FOR THIS STORY.
THANK YOU FOR NEVER GIVING UP ON ME.
THANK YOU FOR YOUR PEACE IN THE MIDST OF TRIALS.
AND THANK YOU FOR BEIGNETS.

1

THE BRIDE'S BOUQUET ARCED THROUGH THE AIR, targeting me like a deployed missile. I stepped back at the last second, letting it smack the ground at my feet. Gasps echoed all around as if I'd committed the vilest of sins. One of the bridesmaids, drowning in peach chiffon, swooped up the floral arrangement, brandishing it high as though she'd won a coveted prize.

I wanted to tell the woman the bouquet meant nothing. That even if she got engaged and made it to a month before her wedding day, her happily ever after still wasn't guaranteed. Instead, I swallowed my sour grapes and continued to the edge of the courtyard that lay behind my café, Beignets & Books. Thanks to the bride delaying the start of the wedding by forty-five minutes to change the color of her toenail polish, I was late picking up my adopted niece, Hayley. I hated being late. To make matters worse, Hayley wasn't answering her phone.

A cool mid-February breeze traipsed through, rustling the leaves of the ancient live oak canopying the outdoor space. I cinched my coral cardigan, covering the matching sleeveless sweater beneath. A dark gray pencil skirt and black heels completed my professional appearance. I reached Penny, a college student who'd started as a hostess years ago, moved on to waitress, and now additionally acted as my right hand during special events like this one.

"I need to fetch Hayley from the library." I adjusted my hold on my purse. "Can you keep an eye on things until I return?"

Penny, with her thick brown hair pulled into a sleek ponytail, cast a wary glance at the temperamental bride. "Of course. All that's left is the second line?"

"Yes."

As if on cue, the trumpeter from the live band moved forward, playing a loud, high call to the guests. Everyone stopped in their tracks, responding with the customary shout of "Hey!" The rest of the jazz band joined in, continuing the festive melody of Joe Avery's "Second Line." The bride and groom were handed umbrellas decorated with tassels and sequins. They danced and walked, jutting the parasols above their heads. Guests grabbed napkins, waving them as they followed the couple in what I described to out-of-towners as an untamed version of a conga line.

"I've got it covered, Boss." Penny gave a mock salute.

"Thanks." I hurried through the side gate and into my bright blue Honda Civic (Consumer Reports top safety pick). At five in the evening, the sun barely clung to the sky. I pulled from the driveway and whispered a prayer for God to carry me through the rest of the day. A wedding was one thing. A bridezilla another. But a wedding with a bridezilla in the climax of Mardi Gras season?

Had this been any other time of year, I would arrive at the library within ten minutes. But St. Charles Avenue had already been barricaded for the parade due to start in half an hour, forcing me to the back streets. Back streets crammed with cars parked bumper-to-bumper against the curbs, rendering the narrow roads harder to maneuver.

Using the Bluetooth connection through my vehicle, I called

the library, ending up in the librarian's voice mail. "Hi, Mrs. Gail. It's Kate. I'm running late, and I'm so sorry. This day has been a doozy on every level. A bridezilla, Mardi Gras . . . and all that brings."

I came upon a group donning coordinated Mardi Gras shirts, their thick horizontal stripes of purple, green, and gold impossible to miss. They moseyed down the middle of the street unaware—or not caring—that they blocked traffic. I ground my teeth, two seconds from honking the horn. If only I knew how to safely rev my engine. Or could conjure Inspector Gadget. *Go, go gadget cattle prod.* "This world is full of *people*, Mrs. Gail, which you well know." Since we both worked with the public, we'd commiserated over the years. My uterus cramped, wanting to add its two cents. "Plus, it's the heaviest day of my period. I'm totally going to use the remedy you told me about."

Two of the guys lagging at the rear of the oblivious bunch paused, lowering the large ice chest they carried. One of them opened the lid and snagged a beer. *Oh no you don't!* I honked, hating how polite my car sounded. The men didn't even notice. What I needed was a horn with different settings. A mild toot to scare squirrels and butterflies, a strong warning blast for emergencies, and a medium honk for situations like this. Or for when screen-addicted people hadn't perceived the red light they sat at had turned green.

I caught a glimpse of myself in the rearview mirror and the all-too-familiar worry line stretching vertically between my auburn brows. I pressed my index finger to what I'd dubbed the Crease, trying to smooth it away. Hayley wasn't supposed to leave the library alone, but at thirteen, she'd been steadily pushing her boundaries. What if she'd slipped out when Mrs. Gail had been in the bathroom or distracted? *Mrs. Gail!* I was still on the phone with her! "Sorry for rambling. I should be there in a few minutes. Please don't let Hayley leave. Thank you." I disconnected.

Miracle of miracles, the group moved from the street and onto the sidewalk. I hooked a right at the corner and eventually came to the nonbarricaded section of St. Charles Avenue. Another minute and I'd be there.

I whipped into one of the handful of parking spots reserved for the library, elated the paradegoers had obeyed the library-only parking signs. In the 1940s, the historic estate and large plot of land it sat on had been willed to the public library system. It had also been Hayley's favorite place since I'd taken custody of her at the tender age of two.

Unlike other homes on the grand avenue, this mansion, with its Romanesque architecture, leaned toward a darker, imposing quality. Heavy rock-faced stone and round masonry arches dominated every aspect. Hayley had referred to it as a castle when we'd first started coming each week. She'd even gone through a phase of wearing princess costumes on our visits.

Major roof damage caused by a hurricane had led to the entire interior being gutted and remodeled for function with a cheery modern feel.

I opened the front door, gaze scanning for Hayley, and came to a screeching halt. Behind the library's reception desk sat Micah Guidry. Or at least, I was ninety-five percent sure it was him. The last time I'd clapped eyes on him had been our high school graduation, two decades ago. He'd always been striking with those deep green eyes.

A warm itch broke across my skin. The years had been good to him. I smoothed my skirt at my hip and pulled my shoulders back. Would he think the same of me?

His gaze met mine, his lips curving into a surprised smile. Lips that had knocked my Keds off in seventh grade. Lips that had tasted like pineapple Life Savers. "Kate Landry." His low voice held the slightest scrape.

The itch morphed into a tingle, and a faint quiver rolled through my stomach. "Micah Guidry."

He eased to a stand, his desk chair rolling backward. "How've you been?"

"Good. And you?"

"Good." He scratched behind his ear, the pencil in his hand barely brushing against his tidy, golden-brown hair.

"I'm picking up my niece."

"Redhead, yea high?" He lifted his other hand (no wedding ring) at chest level, drawing my attention to the firm planes beneath his hideous Hawaiian shirt. Yup. The years had been good to him. But not his style. What grown man walked around sporting palm trees and pink flamingos? At least the short sleeves accentuated his biceps.

I mentally pinched myself. *What's wrong with you?* "Yes. That fits her description."

"So she's . . . Claire's daughter? You adopted her?"

I nodded.

His features softened, and he set his pencil on the desk. "I'm sorry about your loss."

"Thank you." Despite the eleven years since Claire and her husband Adrian's death in a sailing accident, unexpected reminders of their passing in moments like this still stung. Though not as bad as they used to. I was just relieved Hayley wasn't nearby. Reminiscing about how great they both were was one thing. Discussing their actual deaths, another.

"I would have attended the funeral, but I was living in Colorado at the time." His earnest stare held on mine. That action alone was so different from most people, who looked away when Claire entered the conversation.

"You stayed there after finishing college in Boulder?"

"I did." His brow tweaked. "I see you're still good at remembering facts."

And steamy first kisses. Stop that! Where was this coming from? It had to be the chaos of Mardi Gras wearing me thin. Had I run into Micah Guidry a month from now, my reaction would be that of the rational forty-year-old adult I normally was.

Micah's head tilted.

Oh. It was my turn to speak. But nothing came to mind. How was that possible? If there was one positive thing my upbringing had instilled in me, it was never being thrown for a loop. Or at least not showing it. Striving for indifference, I slipped on the Landry Mask. Some mothers passed down family recipes of filé gumbo or crawfish étouffée to their daughters. Mine had gifted me with lessons on emotional camouflage.

Movement sounded from above and to the rear. Hayley's black-and-white-checkered Vans came into sight, plodding down the stairs from the second floor. My tension lessened at laying eyes on her, even if was just her feet.

Micah cast a glance in Hayley's direction, then returned his attention to me. "I moved back a few weeks ago."

"And you're a librarian?"

"I am."

That made sense. Growing up he'd always had a book in his hand or could be found in the school library. "You're now working here? Has something happened to Mrs. Gail?"

"She's fine, but her brother in Arkansas had a bad fall. She's taking a leave of absence to care for him. I'm filling in until she returns. Or I find a permanent position."

I gnawed my lower lip. He'd be here for a while. Here, where Hayley visited several times a week and regularly volunteered, which meant I'd have to see him again. "I'm sorry I'm running late to pick up Hayley."

"You're not late."

I glanced at the huge clock on the wall made up of books with numbers in their titles. Oversized hour, minute, and second hands accommodated them. The short hand pointed to a novel titled *Five Days in Skye*, the long hand to a children's board book called *Two by Two*. "You should've closed ten minutes ago."

One corner of his mouth hitched. "You're still a stickler for punctuality."

I slightly narrowed my gaze. "I'm going to take that as a compliment."

"As it was intended." His smile broadened, a gleam in his eyes emphasizing his amusement.

Hayley had stalled at the first landing, bringing her toothpick legs clad in jeans into view, as well as her drooping backpack. Her head bowed over her phone, her thumbs tapping at the screen.

"Would it make you feel better to flip the *Closed* sign?" He inclined his chin to the door behind me and the sign hanging on it, facing the wrong way.

Warmth invaded my cheeks. "I see you're still a stickler for . . ." *Where, oh, where had my brain slunk off to?* "Books." *So lame.*

"I'm going to take *that* as a compliment." He crossed his arms, causing one flamingo on his shirt to appear as if it sniffed the butt of another flamingo. "I'm guessing you're still anti-books?"

"No." Slight annoyance shadowed my tone. I wanted to reference the publications lining the walls of my café, but I didn't want to initiate Micah Guidry visiting my establishment and flustering me on my home turf. Though those books were all nonfiction, and Micah had always preferred made-up stories.

"You don't know what you're missing."

In a blink I was back in seventh grade, the pressure to experience a first kiss growing rampant among my friends. Like having to get a Swatch watch. And a Swatch guard. Talk about useless protection. "I seem to remember you using that line on me once before."

Micah's mouth pursed in a combination of shamelessness and delight. He rubbed his jaw, his fingers bristling against his five-o'clock shadow. "It wasn't a line then."

Heat swept up my neck.

He paused mid-brush. "You still blush."

I stiffened, cursing my tell and my pale skin that highlighted it. "And you're still brash." Though that wasn't exactly true. Micah had just always been forthright. Or maybe that was what we now called not having a filter. I eyed Hayley, silently imploring her to get off her phone and hurry.

"How about a truce?" Micah's goading expression had transformed to one of repentance. Sort of.

"I didn't realize we were at war."

His eyes crinkled at the edges. A blinking light on the desk phone caught his notice. He nodded at the front door. "I bet it's a madhouse out there with the parade coming." Holding the handset to his ear, he pressed a button on the phone's base.

Hayley slunk down the final steps. Her red flannel shirt looked like it'd been filched from Paul Bunyan's closet. And an oversized sweatshirt was tied loosely around her waist, as though it could slip off any moment, tangle her legs, and send her plunging to her death. Adding to the likeliness of that scenario, her focus lay on digging through her schoolbag.

I clenched my keys in my hand. She knew the dangers of not paying attention when going down stairs. I'd created a song that we sang together when at the age of four, she'd insisted on taking the stairway on her own from our second-floor residence above the café. *"Hold the railing, look with your eyes, then there won't be a tumbling surprise."*

"Looks like I missed your call," Micah said.

I blinked back to the present. "What?"

14

His athletic body hunched over the phone, listening intently. *Oh no.* The rambling voice mail I'd left for Mrs. Gail.

My stomach plummeted. I scowled at Hayley, who moved like an inmate walking to the electric chair. I headed for the front door and opened it, hoping to elicit a quicker stride from my niece. "See you around." I'd tossed the hasty farewell over my shoulder, one foot out the door.

"Kate," Micah called from behind.

I stilled. Hayley crossed the threshold, nearly dragging her book bag, the straps brushing over my feet, gathering a million germs.

He lowered the phone, mischief twinkling in his emerald eyes. "My sister swears by Advil and Pop-Tarts."

I held in a breath in timing with two beats from the wall clock. "Thank you." My tone relayed two different words: *shove it.* I flipped the sign on the door to *Closed* and left.

2

I WOULD HAVE TO AVOID MICAH GUIDRY for the rest of my life. It was the only rational solution. Because there was no way I could face him after that humiliating voicemail. I sighed, rubbing the Crease. Hayley and I drove our way back through the chaos I'd just fought through.

She sulked, something she'd become proficient at. "I could've walked home."

"Not with all this Mardi Gras melee happening."

She tucked her long, pin-straight, light-auburn hair behind her ears, bringing her pale, delicate features out from hiding. The past year her choice of clothing had changed dramatically. Gone were soft feminine colors and frilly accessories. Little by little, she'd gravitated toward what could only be considered hobo apparel. "Even when it's not Mardi Gras, you won't let me walk back and forth. Or take the streetcar."

"Because there are serial killers and drug dealers and . . . teen-nappers out there."

"If you let me get a dog, I'd have protection."

Here we go again. Hayley had begun an aggressive campaign for a dog several months ago. I didn't have time for a dog, or even a fish. And as much as she'd said she'd take care of it, I—

like all the parents that had gone before me—knew her promise would end up broken. "You can't bring a dog into the library."

Her slender fingers tapped across her phone screen at warp speed. Steel-gray polish coated her nails. *Sigh. No more pink sparkles.* I knew what was coming next as she'd become predictable in her quest for a dog. She was connecting via Bluetooth to my vehicle's speakers.

Within seconds, Sarah McLachlan's "Angel" filled the sedan. In researching pet adoption, Hayley had discovered the ads from the '90s, including the song from the old heart-wrenching ASPCA animal cruelty commercials.

When her desire for a pet had first surfaced, we'd had a detailed discussion of why we couldn't have one. And by discussion, I meant her staring daggers at the wall while I listed a multitude of reasons. As a result, she'd begun pulling away from me. Our conversations had dwindled to one- or two-word responses on her end and then her holing up in her room. At that time, she'd also initiated psychological warfare. Other than the "Angel" song, she'd leave the TV in the living room paused on commercials showcasing emaciated canines of every variety.

I'd read in a parenting book to ignore this type of behavior. And so that's what I'd done. Ignored the commercials and gritted my teeth through each beautiful note of Sarah McLachlan's now irritating voice.

I parked in my driveway, leaving a foot of space between my front bumper and the iron gate to the courtyard. Hayley bolted from the car before I'd killed the engine. I switched the music off and tipped my head back against the seat, a weary sigh escaping.

Hayley skirted the brick wall of the courtyard, avoiding the staff working to return the area to normal. Her slender shoulder brushed the year-round landscaping framing the perimeter. She made her way to the outdoor stairs leading to our residence, which occupied the second floor of the house that had been my grandma's Garden District mansion. The café occupied the bottom of the Greek Revival estate Mawmaw's family had bought in the 1920s.

Up Hayley trudged, except this time she held the railing. A small victory.

I exited my car and entered the courtyard, where blessedly, Penny directed the last of the lingering wedding guests to leave through the restaurant. The tablecloths had been removed, and the event tables were being deconstructed by the extra staff I'd scheduled to serve food and drinks. They'd stow them and the folding chairs in the storage shed.

I slowed as I passed Penny. "You're a godsend."

"I know." She flashed a smile and collected a pile of linens our supplier would pick up for laundering.

Taking the steps to the wraparound porch, I continued through the back doors of the café, depositing myself into a short hallway. The aromatic scents of freshly brewed coffee and fried dough greeted me. If I kept straight, I'd land in the main section of the restaurant, where I should go and check on things. There was always something to check on. The murmuring of customer voices intensified, along with dishes clattering.

I took an abrupt left, unlocked my office door, and closed it. A few minutes alone wouldn't hurt. I dropped my keys and purse on the desk, made a pit stop in my private half bath, and then collapsed in my cushioned leather chair and peeled my heels off. My toes exhaled in ecstasy.

My gaze drifted to a framed napkin on the wall. An eighteen-year-old napkin that had been pulled from a dispenser at Café Du Monde, where I had been waitressing at the time. It was actually my last day waiting tables, as I'd landed a job in the café's corporate office. Mawmaw's will had been read several days earlier, and my sister and I were in a state of shock. During one of my breaks, Claire and I had sat at a corner table.

She was twenty-one, I was twenty-two, and the reading of the will had sealed our future.

It had also shoved a bigger wedge between us and our parents. Mawmaw had bequeathed everything, including her home and hefty bank account, to us. We'd decided that day to open our own restaurant and documented it on the napkin. A café honoring Mawmaw and the things she loved: her beignet recipes and books. We'd signed the napkin as though it were a solemn oath.

I swiveled my seat, the overhead lights reflecting off another frame. This one protected a piece of paper with several goals Claire and I had crafted—after the napkin contract—and again signed for added emphasis.

The first goal, opening the eatery, we'd accomplished together five years later. Having completed culinary school, and with an intense passion for food, Claire had become the chef, managing the back of the house. My business degree and experience from working my way up through Café Du Monde positioned me as general manager, running the front of the house.

But then Claire and Adrian had died two years later. And everything, *everything,* had changed. A small ache throbbed in my throat. *Chin up. Chin up.* I stood and approached the enclosed timeline, focusing on Claire's looping signature and our game plan, which had been a saving grace. It gave me purpose. Something tangible to complete when the world felt out of control.

Outside my office window, I spied the bride-and-groom second-line umbrellas propped against the base of the two-tiered fountain. I tried for a deep, cleansing breath . . . and failed. Turning away, I slid my fingers across my desk and nudged the mouse. My computer awoke from its slumber, the monitor revealing the desktop wallpaper of the Grand Canyon. The machine automatically loaded a different picture of vacation destinations every few days. Of places I longed to visit. Places out of reach. For now, anyway.

I reclaimed my chair and logged on to Facebook through the café's business account. In the search box, I typed in three words, *Ryan Comeaux Georgia.* Bracing myself, I clicked the search icon.

Checking my ex-fiancé's personal page was a guilty pleasure I only indulged in annually, which happened to fall during Mardi Gras season, which encompassed the anniversary of our breakup.

Was this tradition unhealthy? Absolutely. But finding his single relationship status unchanged over the years had been a small consolation prize. Several Ryan Comeaux's loaded, and I perused the profile pictures for the handsome, irksome face of my ex. My gaze halted on the screen. *Bingo.* There was Ryan, another year older, and his smile just as full. I hovered the cursor over his grin and clicked hard, as though I could somehow knock his front teeth out. He'd always had his personal page set to public viewing, but I never looked beyond the only thing I wanted to know. And there it was again. The *S*-word holding strong.

Vindication hummed through my veins.

Considering my own single status, it was an ironic victory. But remaining unattached was a choice for me, hewed from harsh reality. Ryan had been a colossal mistake. One I'd never make again. I logged off and rolled my neck, working out the tension trying to seep in. My heart nudged me to slip into the cool evening air and pray. I didn't always find answers in praying, or instant peace, but I knew God heard me. And there was something about verbally talking to Him, getting my thoughts off my chest, that helped lighten the load.

Beyond my window, a breeze stirred the leaves of the oak tree, beckoning. I always felt closer to God when speaking to Him outside. I stifled a snort. As if He didn't have X-ray vision and couldn't see me just fine where I sat now.

Hayley ghosted past on the porch. No doubt the parade had drawn her outdoors.

I slipped my heels back on and exited my office. Instead of walking through the café, I eased out the back door, taking the porch around to the front, the route Hayley preferred.

The setting sun had made way for darker evening skies, the streetlamps following suit and flickering on. A trace of BBQ smoke hovered from one of my neighbors. Soft white light from the side windows of the restaurant poured out, and a melody of drums and horns saturated the air, becoming louder with my advance.

Sure enough, a high school marching band strutted down St. Charles Avenue. A thick crowd lined the street, swaying and clapping to the up-tempo music. A woman on the sidewalk danced, pulling a purple, green, and yellow feather boa from her neck, waving it above her head.

Mardi Gras was a blessing and a curse. Great for extra business with the influx of tourists, but the chaos and additional details involved with running the café during parades was a hassle. Thankfully, with the three-foot iron fence bordering my corner lot, I had a bit of control over the revelry and people trampling my property. Normally, the gate was open, welcoming customers to walk right in and take the path to the front entrance. Not so during parades.

Jonathan, another college student who worked as a waiter the rest of the year, now manned the gate in his seasonal role as the beignet bouncer. I'd learned long ago that with the café smack-dab on the parade route, most people viewed my establishment as nothing more than a public restroom.

Therefore, in the midst of parades we switched to a reservation-only policy and marked those patrons with plastic wristbands. No reservation, no wristband, no admittance. Customers also didn't mind paying a convenience fee for enjoying the festivities from our restaurant, and the use of its bathroom.

The floodlights from the house revealed Hayley on the front lawn, within the enclosure, snapping pictures with her phone. Only one other couple remained inside the fence. No doubt most of the patrons preferred to be closer to the street, where all the action was. Hayley had removed the sweatshirt from her waist, her flannel shirt hanging on her slim frame like a deflated parachute. I'd gone through the same phase when I was her age. Despising my skinniness and how other girls were developing while I remained as flat as a sheet of plywood.

I hadn't had the option of trying different clothes to experiment with, or to hide under. No, my mother would have sooner died than allow her daughters a say in anything, even in clothing. Thank goodness for Mawmaw. She'd secretly taken us shopping and let us keep those purchases at her home and wear them when we stayed over. It wasn't that I'd aspired to don something scandalous like a tube top and Daisy Dukes. I'd just wanted a choice.

I stopped next to Jonathan. "How's it going?"

"Good." He wore the laxer of the uniform shirts employees had a choice of, pairing the white logo T-shirt with jeans. "Everyone with a reservation checked in, and most of them are out in the crowd." He inclined his chin toward the throng.

"Perfect. If you need a break, let me know."

"I will." He lowered his voice. "And don't worry about Hayley. I'm keeping an eye out." Fortunately, Jonathan was a vigilant brother to three younger sisters and understood my protective streak with Hayley.

"Thanks."

The roar of a tractor's motor increased, towing a float decorated as a Viking ship. Shouts of "Hey!" and "Throw me somethin', mister!" erupted from the crowd. The masked riders aboard the faux ship threw beads, trinkets, and plastic cups. Several small frisbees sailed from the float to paradegoers.

Hayley neared the fence, waving her hands, her attempt at

catching anything unsuccessful. The float rolled on, and her attention shifted to the sidewalk. A man perched a few rungs up on a wooden parade ladder. A child's seat—similar in design to one on a shopping cart—was attached to the top, where a toddler sat above the throng. The father pointed to the float making its way to them.

I stepped off the concrete walkway, my heels sinking into the sod, and stood next to Hayley. "You used to love sitting in a parade ladder."

"I did?"

I nodded. "Your mom, dad, and I would take turns manning it."

Her brows knit together. "I don't remember that. But I do remember the year we dressed up as dalmatians on Mardi Gras Day, and I kept stepping on your tail."

Ah. That had been two years after Claire and Adrian's passing, when she'd been in prekindergarten.

"Wouldn't it be fun if we had a real dalmatian and dressed up like that again?"

I snorted. "Nice try."

Another float rode by, this one bedecked as a dragon, the scales lined with thousands of lights. Hayley's gaze remained on the father and daughter. The toddler was gently tossed a small stuffed animal, to her great delight. A bittersweet smile curved Hayley's lips.

Invisible fingers pinched my heart. "I can dig up the pictures and videos from those parades with your parents. If you want to see them."

Her gaze slid to her phone. "That's okay." She opened her texting app and scrolled through it.

The advice of the childhood therapist I'd sought after the accident came to mind. *"Offer the past, but don't push."* Pulling in a low breath, I redirected my attention to Jonathan. He shook his head, talking to a man on the other side of the gate who faced away from me. A broad-shouldered man donning a flamingo-themed Hawaiian shirt.

No. How was this possible? I'd gone two decades sans Micah Guidry, and now I'd seen him twice in the span of thirty minutes? I quickly calculated my evasion possibilities, then eyed Hayley. Despite my petite stature, she was still too small to hide behind. Dashing to the front entrance of the café was a no-go. Especially with my hair like Rudolph's nose. It'd give me away in a blaze of copper. *Darn you, floodlights!*

I eased around Hayley, using her as a barrier, and crouched, pretending to fiddle with my heel. Maybe her oversized hobo shirt would shield me. After a moment, I leaned, peering past Hayley's legs, and found Jonathan alone. I exhaled, my muscles relaxing. *Thank You, God.*

"Lose something?"

The question had not come from Hayley. My molars ground together as I faced forward.

Micah squatted on the other side of the fence, a playful, knowing glint in his dark green eyes.

Sarah McLachlan.

3

ONE OF MY HEELS SANK INTO THE GRASS, tipping me off balance. Perfect. Now my body matched my brain.

Micah, still with the humorous shine in his eyes, nodded to the gate, silently asking for entrance.

I bit the inside of my cheek and made my way to Jonathan, giving the okay to allow Mr. Flamingo in.

As Micah stepped through, the shouts of the crowd behind him escalated again with a double-decker float rolling by. Beads flew from it, several catching on the branches of the two massive live oaks standing sentinel before my home. I swallowed a groan.

He turned, following my line of sight. "Not a fan of the beads?"

"No, I'm not." Goodness knew beads from previous years still clung to the higher branches, the sun bleaching out their color. They dangled year-round like discarded loops of floss.

Micah slid his hands into his pockets. "Seeing you earlier had me thinking of your grandma's house, and wondering . . ."

"You fought through the mess of barricades and crowds to take a peek at my grandma's house?"

"I'm renting a place on Chestnut Street, not far from here."

What? Chestnut was part of the route I speed walked three times a week. A perfect route I'd mapped out with smooth sidewalks, shady trees, and no barking dogs.

He studied the house and scrolling columns, the wooden sign hanging from a decorative iron post on the front lawn. "You turned her home into a café?"

"I did." My lungs expanded at the awe in his tone. "Well, Claire and I did."

"Are my eyes deceiving me, or is that *books* in the name? You sell books too?" He edged toward the entrance, excitement in his features, as though something wonderfully new to discover lay inside and he didn't want to wait another minute.

"No." I kept my feet planted. "I don't sell books. They're part of the atmosphere."

"Would you mind showing me around?"

I glanced at Hayley, who texted feverishly with someone. Rationally, I was ninety-eight percent sure it was her best friend, Emma. But irrationally, my thoughts stuck on that two percent. What if a meth dealer had randomly texted her, offering a free high? Did they still work that way? Giving free drugs the first time to get kids hooked? Not that Hayley would take them up on their offer. But what if they'd disguised the opioids as Skittles? I'd always taught Hayley never to accept candy from strangers. But still. I rubbed the Crease.

"If you're too busy, I can come back another time," he said.

"No." I lowered my hand. I didn't want Micah returning and seeking me out. If I could douse the curiosity radiating from him, he wouldn't need to come back. At least not to find me for a tour. He would become a regular customer. No special treatment. And I wouldn't have to worry about battling the sensation that my feet stood on unsteady ground, like I was attempting to stand on a raft in the middle of a pool. *Good grief.* How could a kiss from seventh grade still affect me this way? Was it because it was my first kiss? Or the best kiss I'd ever had? Ryan had kissed like an octopus devouring its prey. All hands and sloppy.

He shifted. "No, I can't come back, or no, you're not too busy?" A dash of teasing coated his tone.

My gaze trailed up to his face. To his strong, stubbled jaw. Eyes vibrant and piercing. If I were allowed only two words to describe him, I'd choose *ruggedly handsome*. In my heels, he stood a smidge taller than me. I wouldn't have to break my neck to kiss him like I had with Ryan's skyscraper height. Would Micah still taste like pineapple Life Savers?

Kate! I broke eye contact, my pulse rattling. *Pull yourself together!* Mardi Gras. This was all Mardi Gras's fault. I just had to hold on three more days. Like the rest of New Orleans, I would return to normal after Fat Tuesday. Clasping my hands before me, I recalled his question. "I'm not too busy." I cast a glance at Hayley and then Jonathan, who inclined his head, letting me know he'd keep watch on her.

Micah opened the front door, the bell above jingling. With the patrons outside in the thick of the festivities, the restaurant lay empty, save for Mrs. Adélaide. She enjoyed the parade sights from one of the window tables. Our oldest customer in age and loyalty, her smooth, Cajun French accent held the same broken dialect as Mawmaw.

"Hey, Mrs. Adélaide," I said. "Enjoying the view?"

"Oh, *oui*." The wrinkles bracketing her smile deepened. "So much to see. De floats. De people. Especially dem *bébés*."

I couldn't help but return her grin. I'd come to learn people-watching was her favorite pastime. But with the raucous crowds and dimly lit sidewalks, I'd need to ensure someone walked her home when she was ready to leave.

Micah closed the door, cutting off the revelry noise from the parade.

Penny stood at the hostess stand, offering a pleasant nod as she answered the café's phone.

"Wow." Micah paused, his face tipping up to the sixteen-foot ceilings, his gaze trailing along the intricate white moldings, rosettes, and supporting scroll brackets. In this main section, the lightness of the cream-hued walls had been a must with the only natural light coming in from the two front windows. "It's completely different but still the same."

"We tried to keep as much in place as possible." Up-tempo jazz, set to a low volume, tinted the background.

"You moved the stairs." He gestured to where a grand staircase had once connected the top and bottom levels.

"We needed to in order to open this central area and provide privacy for the second floor."

His brow quirked.

"That's where Hayley and I live."

"You live here too?"

I nodded.

He considered that and stepped across the white-oak floors to the first room running along the side of the main dining space. "This was your grandma's front parlor." He paused in the archway separating what now housed the sports-themed room. Four round tables filled the spot. Life-sized cutouts of Eli and Peyton Manning stood in the corners, the shelves lined with books on the history of the Saints, as well as the other New Orleans–based teams.

He moved to the chefs' room, which had originally been Mawmaw's library. It had been pared back to now hold a few tables for customers, and a shelf with cookbooks by local legends like Paul Prudhomme, Leah Chase, and Justin Wilson.

"Her books are in each room." Sweet satisfaction curled beneath my ribs. "We wanted to incorporate as much of her as we could."

"Are her beignets on the menu?"

"They are."

A fond smile spread across his face. "I loved her beignets.

That was one of my favorite parts of Mardi Gras Day, when she'd open her doors and cook all day long."

My breathing slowed, memories flickering. Claire in the kitchen, right there at Mawmaw's elbow, learning and trying different recipes. Me playing hostess and keeping my mom from bickering at my dad in front of others, including Micah.

Micah crossed the main area, weaving between tables, and entered the music-themed room.

I followed, pausing at the threshold. Only Harry Connick Jr., in the form of a cardboard replica, occupied the space. Several strands of Mardi Gras beads hung around Harry's neck. "You were the only one from school who came to Mawmaw's party every year." My voice had gone soft. Even Ryan had only made an appearance once despite the fact we'd dated all through high school. Ryan had preferred spending the day with his friends in the French Quarter, an entirely different atmosphere from the tamer gathering at Mawmaw's. Another warning sign of his character I'd ignored.

Micah scanned past the tables and fireplace to the rear wall. "The dining room used to be open to this space."

"Yes. When we renovated, we took it over to expand the kitchen."

He returned to where I stood, again taking in the main room.

The front bell jingled, the ruckus from outside slipping in, along with Hayley. Veiled curiosity marked her face as she glanced between Micah and me. She didn't break her stride though.

"Hayley," I called.

She paused in her trek, halting next to the hostess stand.

Penny left her post to check on Mrs. Adélaide, giving us privacy.

I straightened the business card holder atop the stand, containing cards with the café's social media accounts and QR code. "Did you know Mr. Micah and I pretty much grew up together?"

Hayley's large round eyes stared back, unblinking. She almost resembled a character from one of those odd anime shows she'd become interested in.

Micah edged forward. "I went to school with your aunt and mom. Elementary through high school."

Hayley's gaze zipped to Micah.

"Though your mom was a grade younger than me and your aunt, of course," he said.

Hayley held him in her stare, her expression unreadable. "Is Mrs. Gail coming back to the library?"

Ouch.

Micah didn't flinch. "I was told she'd be back in a few weeks, but that could get extended."

A beat followed. She moved to leave.

"Hayley," I said.

She stopped.

"It's not polite to just walk off when you've been talking to someone."

"Sorry," she mumbled to her shoes. Her eyes rose slowly, shifting from Micah to me. "Bye."

Micah fought a grin. "See you around."

"I'll be up in a bit," I said to her retreating figure.

She vanished through the back door.

A low sigh loosened from within. "Once upon a time, I was the cool aunt." I grabbed a menu from the hostess stand and motioned to an open table in the back corner.

Micah took the seat across from mine. "Has it been a tough transition with Hayley?"

I nodded, handing him the menu. "Claire was effortless at being a mom. But me?" I shook my head.

"So that never changed?" He set the menu aside.

I blinked, confusion rocketing through me.

He winced. "That didn't come out right."

"No," I lightly chided. "It didn't."

Penny paused her approach, but I waved her forward. She took our order and left.

"I apologize." He rested his elbows on the table and bit his bottom lip in endearing awkwardness. "What I meant to say was . . . well, back in junior high, you were the only one not to dress their flour-baby for that home ec project." His brows lifted, and he smirked. "Or even name it."

"Goodness." I leaned back in my chair, covering a chuckle with my hand. "I'd forgotten."

"I didn't. It was kind of hard not to. That poor naked sack of flour."

Penny arrived with our drinks.

Micah's gaze remained on me. "You just shoved that baby into your backpack the entire week."

Penny slowed her motion of setting Micah's steaming coffee before him.

I raised my hand as though swearing an oath. "Let the record show it wasn't a real baby."

"Oh." His eyes widened, swinging to Penny. "No, it wasn't a real baby."

"Good to know." Penny placed a cream server on the table and a decaf café au lait before me. She stepped away smiling.

I returned my attention to Micah. "That was the only assignment I didn't ace my entire time in school."

"No doubt it still irks you." Faint lines creased the corners of his eyes. "Miss Perfectionist."

I wrinkled my nose at him.

He added cream to his coffee and stirred. "I'll never forget that same week when we were put in the church daycare."

"That's right." A light laugh escaped. "Real baby interaction was part of the assignment."

"You basically stood in the corner in horror."

Penny exited the kitchen and placed Micah's plate of original beignets on the table before retreating. The scent of freshly fried dough wafted. Micah lifted one of the puffy square-shaped pastries. Powdered sugar dusted the dessert. He took a bite, the crispy outside giving way to the soft, airy middle. His eyes slid shut with a moan.

I couldn't help the pride blooming within. Especially with receiving approval from someone who'd basically grown up on Mawmaw's beignets.

He chewed and swallowed. "I'm surprised Café Du Monde hasn't put a hit on you."

"There's enough business to go around for everyone." I sipped my decaf, savoring the rich chicory, appreciative of how Penny had prepared it exactly how I liked it. "I never did thank you for stepping up that day in the church nursery."

He shrugged and devoured another bite. "Did you ever get over your baby phobia?"

"It wasn't a phobia. It's just . . . I'd never interacted with babies. Or kids for that matter." I slid my napkin-wrapped silverware to the side for them to be reused. "I've never had a desire to have my own children." Which meant I'd rarely paid attention to them, other than sending pitying glances to over-whelmed parents in the toy aisle at Walmart and rejoicing in my decision to remain childless.

His chewing slowed, his gaze turning thoughtful. Too thoughtful.

It unsettled me. I shifted my regard to the windows. "But Claire, she'd always wanted children. When she got pregnant, I was ecstatic. We'd been in the midst of remodeling"—I mo-tioned to the restaurant—"and immediately decided she and Adrian should live above the café to make life as easy as possible for her." When Claire's husband couldn't make it to a doctor's appointment, I went. I threw her the best baby shower (after extensive research). "I watched her belly grow every day. Was there when her water broke and for the birth."

Micah wiped his mouth with his cloth napkin. "I was fortunate to make it in for a week after the births of my niece and nephew to help Renee."

Renee, his sister. "How old are they now?"

"Eighteen and nineteen."

"Was that your first time around a baby? Other than that doomed Sunday in childcare?"

A smile touched his lips. "Yes, and it was overwhelming. Renee's husband was stuck overseas on duty, and my dad had little experience with babies. He basically learned with me."

I nodded. "With Hayley, I learned how to change diapers and that babies needed burping. And that babies cried. A lot. And peed and pooped. A lot."

"And spit up a lot."

"Right? But despite that, I was thrilled to babysit." I held up a finger. "After taking CPR classes."

"Of course." He sipped his coffee, his wry grin disappearing.

I leaned forward, lowering my voice. "But I was equally thrilled to retreat to my quiet apartment, where I wasn't responsible for keeping another human alive." Slowly, I turned my cup on the saucer, the porcelain grating. "Two years of blissful aunting passed." My hands slunk onto my lap.

"And then the worst happened." His heavy tone bore so much compassion in that one sentence.

My throat thickened, a sense of encouragement pushing my emotions to the surface. "In one fell swoop, I lost my sister and best friend, and Hayley lost her parents." My lungs squeezed, and I stared at my coffee. "I'd been babysitting, right upstairs, when I got the call. In a state of brain fog, I buckled Hayley in her car seat, drove to a bookstore, and purchased everything they had on raising children."

"And you moved into Claire's place above the café?"

"Yes. I didn't want Hayley losing the security of her environment." And there was no way I was letting my parents obtain custody. Thankfully Claire's will had rendered that process easy.

Her wishes had been clear I receive sole guardianship of Hayley in the event of her and Adrian's death. Funny how having horrible parents made you want to protect your children from them too. Or from having your own children at all.

"All you've done sounds very maternal to me."

I reached for the container at the center of the table, holding varying sugar packets, and straightened them. "She's breathing and healthy. But I have no idea what's going on in her head. She doesn't talk to me anymore."

"She's a teenager. That's normal."

"She's not a normal teen." My eyes met his. "She lost her parents. And she's being raised by someone missing a maternal gene."

"You're selling yourself short. The way you flew into the library earlier could rival any paranoid helicopter mom I've seen."

Lightness eased into my heart. I studied Micah, perplexed at how I'd spilled my guts to him so easily. Maybe it was our shared history, and he was a connection to Claire. A connection I hadn't had in ages. Or maybe it was his mesmerizing eyes and how he looked at me like I was the only person in the room. Or in the New Orleans metropolitan area. The air thinned, and that traitorous tingle broke across the skin at the back of my neck. *God, please don't let me blush.*

The front door bell jingled, and two women entered, both wearing the café's reservation wristbands. They made their way into the music room, where Natalie, another waitress on shift, followed. Their entrance popped the bubble of . . . whatever it was that had been building.

Micah's throat bobbed. He moved his empty plate aside and reached for his coffee.

With a low exhale, I eased back in my chair. "This has been way too one-sided. Between that voice mail I left and this conversation, if I ever run for a political office, you'd have enough ammunition to annihilate me."

One edge of his mouth lifted. "Would it make you feel better to have some dirt on me?"

I snickered. "Of course."

"Okay." He set his cup on the saucer with a clink. "Our senior year of high school, I was the one who toilet-papered your house."

My jaw unhinged. "My mom hates you!"

"Your grandma supplied the toilet paper."

I gasped a laugh. "You know, I had a feeling she had something to do with it. My parents did too."

He gave a shrug that came across as equal parts sheepish and wicked.

"So after high school you took your toilet-papering skills to Colorado?"

He nodded. "Graduated from college and got married."

Hmm. His lack of a wedding ring brought two scenarios to mind: divorced or widowed. "And you stayed in Colorado?"

"I did. After a few years of marriage, my ex-wife and I realized we weren't . . . a good fit."

A red flag hoisted. "I'm sorry to hear that."

His lips rolled inward with a head bob, his gaze falling to the table. It seemed Micah could be filtered when it suited.

Breaking solemn vows over not being "a good fit" felt like a glib description. Was he sugarcoating his role in their breakup? Or had his wife done something unforgiveable? The red flag in my mind rippled in the wind. "Do you have children?"

"No. So I spoil my niece and nephew. An upside to moving back here."

"There's always a silver lining."

He nodded, but something in his expression gave the impression he didn't wholeheartedly agree.

4

FILLING IN FOR A HUNGOVER EMPLOYEE was not how I'd wanted to start my day. It was Ash Wednesday, a.k.a. the day after Mardi Gras. I always knew who my dependable employees were based on today. One of the waiters for the first shift had shown up with bloodshot eyes and reeking of booze. I'd sent him home and gone into action, prepping the front of the house, and then stayed on shift since opening at eight. Steadily, for the last four hours, we'd had customers of every variety, from beloved regulars to tourists with flights to catch.

Penny glided past me, pushing through the swinging door connecting the main dining room to the kitchen. It whooshed shut behind her. Dishes and silverware clattered to my right, the busboy on duty clearing a nearby table.

Standing at the server station in the back, I waited for the computer to generate the bill for my final customer. Thankfully, it had been Mrs. Adélaide. I strummed my fingers on the small connected printer. I should have been in my office double-checking the payroll checks that had been delivered against the data I'd submitted to the company that processed our payroll.

The antique gilded mirror on the wall above the computer revealed a middle-aged woman who'd gotten little sleep thanks to Hayley's BFF, Emma, staying over. My auburn hair lay limp, the edges nearly grazing my shoulders. Maybe I'd do a conditioning treatment tonight. I pressed the Crease and swore I heard it scoff as it puckered right back up.

"Name one good thing." The words echoed through my mind in Claire and Mawmaw's voices. We'd tossed the mantra at each other when one of us was looking at the glass as half-full . . . of sewer water.

I rolled my neck. *One good thing. One good thing.* Okay. Emma's mom had picked up both girls this morning, and she'd be hosting a sleepover tonight. With school out all week for the Mardi Gras holiday, it was nice having another parent share in keeping the kids busy. Another *dependable* parent, who was vigilant about making sure no one snuck out in the middle of the night or was trying to acquire a body piercing instead of innocently hanging out at the mall.

The printer finally clicked and clacked, spitting out the receipt. I ripped it free and returned it to the leather billfold, along with a pen and Mrs. Adélaide's credit card. A second good thing came to mind. I hadn't seen Micah since Saturday. The day he'd learned of my horrendous period, and I'd learned of his murky divorce. *Gracious.* I adjusted the collar of my button-down café shirt. I'd gone for comfort today, pairing the top with casual capri pants and slip-on Skechers. A waitress apron looped my waist, the pockets holding an order pad and pen.

I dropped off the billfold to Mrs. Adélaide, exchanging good-byes as my phone rang its generic tone. I pulled it from my pocket and read the screen. *Trisha Freemont.* I answered, holding my hand to my other ear to hear over the restaurant noise. "Hello."

"I found the perfect property." Trisha's bright voice carried through the line. We'd met at a business mixer several years ago, and she'd declared if I ever sold Mawmaw's house and gave her the listing, she'd change the names of her children to mine.

I retrieved my keys from my pocket, unlocked my office door, and stepped inside to beautiful silence. "Are you calling from the future? Riding shotgun in a DeLorean with Michael J. Fox? Because I've told you I don't have the money for a second location right now."

"I know the timing's not ideal," Trisha said. "But as soon as I saw this property, I knew I had to tell you. It's in the French Quarter."

"I can't afford the French Quarter." I pinned my phone between my ear and shoulder, untying my apron.

"This one's not so out of reach. It's a rare one story. On Royal Street. It was a French café that closed ages ago."

I stilled. "The Vieux Carré Café." The words rasped from my lips.

"That's it."

Claire had adored the spot. Whenever we'd visited, she'd slipped into if mode. *"If we owned this place, I'd fill that antique bakery display case with . . ."* and *"If we owned this place, I'd paint those French doors to the courtyard a softer green."* Claire had even snuck into their kitchen once for a peek and returned to our table with more if-dreams.

My gaze drifted to a photo of the two of us. The candid, taken by Adrian, rested on the bookshelf behind my desk. We'd been in Jackson Square, eating fresh pralines and people-watching. Claire had been laughing unabashedly at me. An elderly woman had stopped and rubbed the top of my head for good luck (something natural redheads endured from older generations). Claire had loved the French Quarter. The eclectic colors of the buildings, the energy floating in the air. She'd dreamed of a location in the heart of that. The snapshot blurred, my throat thickening.

"It's not on the market yet," Trisha prodded.

In moments like this, I really missed my sister. Missed the way her brain worked, the way she evened me out. Considered things I didn't. Had her accident not happened, I'd walk right into the kitchen and pull her into this call. I could just imagine the excitement she'd exude. Working to swallow, I rubbed my nose with the back of my hand. But I had her, in a way, through the plans we'd made. My focus moved to our goals hanging on the wall. The first two had been completed. Opening the café and renovating the courtyard for special events.

The final task, launching another location, was closing in. I had six years to achieve it on the timeline Claire and I had crafted. The loan from the courtyard would be paid off, and we'd have some breathing room before applying for another one to invest in expanding. But it wasn't supposed to be for another six years. Five years to carefully plan and prepare. Financially and mentally. And another year to execute that plan and officially open.

"Once this property hits, it won't last." Urgency infused Trisha's tone.

My pulse increased, pounding in my ears. Every beat urged to hurry-hurry-hurry. But somewhere within the rush, an echo of caution murmured. I closed my eyes, drawing in a breath, gathering my thoughts.

A ding sounded from my phone, signaling an incoming text. I switched Trisha to speaker and found the message she'd sent. A picture of a building filled my screen. One that Claire had loved. One that wasn't too big or too small. One that was just right. "Goldilocks," I whispered, voicing the word Claire and I would use when describing perfection. Like when she'd refine a new recipe and the first time I'd held Hayley.

"What?"

"Nothing."

Hurry-hurry-hurry palpitated through my veins again. The fear of losing this opportunity pushed that faint warning away. At the very least, I could look at the space. Looking never hurt, right? "How soon can I see it?"

Several hours later, I stood on the sidewalk of Royal Street. Although the Vieux Carré Café appeared to have been abandoned for quite some time, charm still filled her. A sweet little brick structure in the midst of larger, mixed-use buildings. Her cream-painted façade contrasted with the other structures in their burnt oranges, steel blues, and varying maroons.

Intermittent traffic flowed down the narrow, one-way lane, bringing the squeal of brakes and exhaust fumes. I bit the inside of my cheek. Customer parking would be a problem here, but that issue plagued all of downtown New Orleans.

A woman exited the clothing boutique next door, a shopping bag in hand. I took in the other storefronts on the ground level, their businesses touting antiques, art, and jewelry. My gaze tipped up to the residential dwellings occupying the second and third floors of those buildings, their balconies overlooking the street. Intricate, wrought-iron railings trimmed their outdoor spaces.

The slate sidewalk beneath my feet glistened from the brief shower that had fallen earlier. My reflection in the glass doors to the café looked back at me, my expression mirroring the mixture of eagerness and uncertainty tumbling through my stomach. I'd changed into a caramel A-line skirt, beige sweater set, and heels. I smoothed a hand through my hair. If the owners of the building happened to be here, I wanted to make a good impression.

Trisha approached, waving a hand. A wide red belt cinched the waist of her flowing black dress. "She's special, right?"

"Unfortunately, yes." And for deeper reasons than Trisha knew.

She laughed, unlocking the front door and stepping in. "Let me find the switches."

Dust motes caught in the natural light issuing through the

windows, and the stale air held a trace of ground coffee. No doubt what had been their signature blend. I closed the door. The lights flickered on, and my heart pinched. *Oh, Claire.* I moved forward into the empty space, taking in the exposed brick walls and teeny-tiny black-and-white hexagonal tiles on the floor. The low ceiling emitted a familiar coziness.

Behind me, the front door creaked open. "Knock, knock," a man's voice called.

I turned. Horrible, detestable shock gripped my throat. Ryan Comeaux, my ex, stood in the entranceway.

"Sarah McLachlan," I swore lowly to myself.

Ryan had always reminded me of a nongreasy version of Matthew McConaughey. Right down to his rascal smile. Oddly enough, he didn't appear surprised to find me here. Had he watched me enter?

"It's good to see you." Southern charm still oozed from him.

My ribs squeezed, as if every emotion were tightening behind them, vying for room. Regret, betrayal, and as much as I hated to admit it . . . loneliness. Though not a loneliness I wanted *him* to fill.

"Who do we have here?" Trisha emerged from the back, walking past the beautiful, antique bakery display case Claire had loved. She held her hand out to the scoundrel, and they shook.

"Ryan Comeaux," he answered. His tailored navy suit fit him to perfection, his pale blue button-down matching his eyes.

I took note of his bare ring finger and cleared my throat. "An old acquaintance."

One of Ryan's brows quirked.

Trisha's eyes gleamed with all sorts of questions. But thankfully, she was too professional to voice them.

I returned my focus to Ryan. "Why are you here?"

"So you're not together?" Trisha's tone revealed her confusion.

41

"No," I said.

The front door opened once again, and a stout man in slacks and a polo shirt entered. He introduced himself as Ryan's real estate agent.

A sour taste filled my mouth.

That spark in Trisha's demeanor shifted.

I settled my attention on her. "I thought this place wasn't on the market yet."

"It's not." She tossed a glance from me to the scoundrel and the scoundrel's agent. "Excuse me a moment." Stepping away, she pulled out her phone and began tapping the screen.

Ryan's agent did the same, opting to make his call outside.

Great. That practically left us alone. Me and the man who'd dumped me a month before our wedding. Without an apology. A man who also appeared to be interested in this very property. Questions abounded, but I wasn't going to give Ryan the satisfaction of showing any interest. Narrow French doors set in the wall overlooked a courtyard. The ones Claire had wanted to repaint. I moved toward them.

Ryan beat me to the side exit, reaching for the aged brass knob. The door slightly stuck as he opened it. He scooted back to let me pass. If only his public chivalry matched his private one. If only I hadn't wasted all those years blindly in love.

Moving past him, my arm brushed his. I inwardly cringed at the contact. How could I have once craved his touch? I stepped down and into the cool, fresh air. A layer of pollen and grime from a southern magnolia tree coated the ground. The concrete would need pressure washing, and the overgrown landscaping a trim. But the iron railing separating the space from the sidewalk and Royal Street was fabulous.

Ryan followed. "I take it you're expanding the café?"

I lifted one shoulder, grateful for his cluelessness about Claire's attachment to this place.

He snickered.

"How long have you been back in town?"

"A few days. I'm partners with Paul Rodgers now, and we're looking to open a second restaurant." His flashy name-dropping tone begged for a reaction.

I kept my features neutral. Paul Rodgers was the latest hotshot chef on the Food Network. And this would be their second venture?

When Ryan had broken up with me, he'd left New Orleans for a new job, managing a swanky eatery in Georgia. He now studied the mature magnolia tree, and I studied him. His drawn eyes hinted at a restless night's sleep. Or perhaps a lifestyle of restlessness. *Not my concern.*

Eleven years had passed since I'd seen him in person, but it felt like yesterday. I'd been standing in my living room, and he'd hovered near the front door, his declaration reverberating through me. *"I can't do this. This isn't what I signed up for."*

It had only been three months since Claire had died. Hayley had been two and potty training. She'd stood at my legs, her little arms reaching up, grasping my shirt. "Need to make!" Numbly, I'd lifted her, holding her on my hip. Ryan had walked out the door, and Hayley had peed on me. The next day I'd bought Pull-Ups, and he'd moved to Atlanta.

"So I'm just an *old acquaintance* now?"

I returned my focus to the present. "Would you prefer I referred to you as something else? Copycat Coward, perhaps? Or my personal favorite, Runaway Ryan?"

His features tightened, and he sidled past me, his shiny loafers avoiding the long-dead magnolia blooms that had dropped.

I took in the outdoor space and eyed the length of the modest building, something not quite adding up. "This place doesn't seem big enough for a restaurant of Paul Rodgers's proportions."

"Yeah, well . . ." He bent forward, scrutinizing a section of the railing. "We're planning a more intimate establishment for this project."

Intimate. *Hmpf.* Which no doubt meant *expensive.* I returned inside and found Trisha and the other agent talking near the front entrance. Ryan shadowed me as I surveyed the meager kitchen and bathrooms, both of which needed upgrading, putting this venture even further out of my reach. But the dining area and courtyard were perfection. I snapped several pictures with my phone to torture myself with later.

Trisha glanced at me. "What do you think?"

Ryan butted in, motioning to the floors. "It's a total gut job."

My heart flinched. *The adorable hexagonal tiles!*

He gestured to the rear. "All of that needs to come out for a bar."

The bakery display case Claire loved!

"And we'd need to raise the roof."

The cozy, curved ceiling!

His agent nodded. "It's not a historical building, so none of that should be a concern."

"We'd only buy it because of the location," Ryan said. "And the courtyard. Though that would require a full overhaul too." He moved to the French doors, eyeing the magnolia tree. The one Claire and I had sat beneath the day she'd snuck into the café's kitchen to scope it out.

I stifled a gasp. Despite my memories, a tree that size in the French Quarter was such a rarity. It seemed like pure wickedness to remove it. If I hadn't known better, I'd suspect a long red tail with a pointy end hid in the backside of his pants.

Ryan turned, his gaze traveling the range of the space. "Modern, sharp lines. We need to keep to the aesthetic of our brand."

Which was the opposite of Beignets & Books, and the ambiance of this city.

"Why open a restaurant here if you don't want it to feel like the French Quarter?"

Ryan assessed me for a prolonged, uncomfortable beat. "I have to say I'm surprised you're looking to expand." He loosely held his hands behind his back, an air of arrogance flavoring his tone. "Didn't you recently complete an expensive renovation on the courtyard at Beignets & Books?"

My lips parted. "Are you spying on me?" Plus, how dare he talk down to me! And in front of others!

"Maybe I am." His irritating smile held a blend of toying and challenge. As if he had the liberty to flirt with me.

My body tensed, my pulse running wild. I jutted my chin to the courtyard. "Looking to copy my work again? Being in your forties now, I thought you'd be past that."

A muscle in his jaw twitched.

That's right. I went there. He wouldn't have graduated from high school or college with the GPAs accredited to his name without me. He'd even copied my career path, convincing me to help him get the internship I'd wanted with a prestigious New Orleans restaurant group.

He scoffed with a shake of his head. "If you took out a loan for that exterior renovation, the timing would mean you can't afford this place. Not unless you went into further debt, which I know you'd hate."

Ire singed beneath my skin, but I kept the Landry Mask in position. During my entire relationship with Ryan, he'd gotten what he'd wanted. Manipulated and used me. And I hadn't realized how smooth he'd been until after we'd split. I looked him square in the eye, fire blazing up my spine. "You have no idea what I can afford. And unlike you, I don't need a business partner to write the checks for me."

He blinked, three times in rapid succession.

With that I left, Trisha silent at my side. Our heels clicked across the sidewalk, blending in with traffic noise. We turned the corner, and my bravado fizzled like the last bit of Silly String struggling to leave the canister. "He's my no-good ex-fiancé."

"I didn't know you were engaged."

45

"It was a lifetime ago." I slowed my pace, my car coming into view parked against the curb.

Trisha tucked her phone into her purse. "I have a no-good ex-husband. If I had the money for that building, I'd loan it to you."

Hands on my hips, I pulled in several deep breaths. Had the previous ten minutes really happened?

"The good news is the seller is a bit of an oddity. She's letting agents show the space, but isn't allowing offers until after the Fourth of July."

The Fourth of July? That was over four months away. But at least it somewhat lessened the urgency of rescuing the place from Ryan. "Sounds like she wants to ensure there's a bidding war."

Trisha nodded. "But it gives you time to see if you can make an offer."

"Or start a GoFundMe under the name Sticking It to My Rotten Ex."

"I'll contribute." She flashed a smile with her departing wave. "I'll be in touch."

"Thanks." I sighed and continued on to my car, my attention halting on the bumper. A new magnet stuck to it. One I hadn't noticed before because I'd been walking away from my vehicle when I'd arrived. A decal with a cartoon canine declared, *Life is better with a rescue dog.*

5

"HAYLEY'S UPSTAIRS HATING ME." I pressed the Crease.

My best friend, Julia Reed, sat across from me at a wrought-iron table that Friday evening in the courtyard. "If your kids don't hate you at some point in their lives, you did something wrong."

I chuckled without humor.

We were in the midst of our long-standing weekly date. The crisp February air provided a welcomed contrast to our steaming decaf café au laits and beignets. The floodlights from the house lit the area and the three-tiered fountain anchoring the space.

Yesterday, Hayley had returned from her sleepover. The night she'd been gone I'd discovered her latest tactic for getting a dog. I'd snuggled into bed, turned on the TV, and discovered our DVR had been filled with canine-oriented shows of every variety. *Pit Bulls and Parolees*, *The Wizard of Paws*, and a plethora of dog competitions. I, in turn, added *The Dog Whisperer* (starring neurotic canines) and *Cujo* to the listing. She'd retaliated by setting up camp on the sofa and playing a marathon of ASPCA commercials on the television via YouTube. Hours of quivering, emaciated dogs. Talk about torture.

Julia wiped her mouth with a cloth napkin. Light caught and sparkled on her year-old engagement and wedding rings. At forty-one, she held a slight resemblance to a brunette version of Alicia Silverstone.

For a little over a decade now, Julia had been a gift from God. We'd met at a Grief Share group counseling program at our church. She'd been struggling through the abrupt loss of her husband and raising two young boys on her own. We'd instantly bonded.

"Is she still clamming up on you?" Julia asked.

"Yes. The only thing she talks about is getting a dog. Other than that, zilch."

"Well, you do have more than your red hair in common."

"Meaning?"

"Meaning your stubbornness."

I shot her a look.

One corner of her mouth twitched. "Or maybe *determination* is a better word."

"I'd like to point out my *determination* helped your products become the number one seller at Nancy's Naturals." With assistance from her newlywed husband, two collegiate sons, and me, her small side business of homemade, non-toxic cleaners had taken off. For which she'd been extremely grateful.

Her face scrunched. "Let's move on to a different topic. One that avoids you tossing 'I told you so' at me for the millionth time. Anything new happen this week?"

The beignet in my gut churned as Ryan came to mind. Would it be wrong not to mention him? After all, he could be classified as *old*. An old mistake that had returned to bite me in the butt. An internal nudge prodded. As though an invisible finger pointing out that thought as the lie it was. I scraped in a breath. "I saw my ex on Wednesday."

She leaned forward, eyes bulging. "Are you serious?"

"Was Zacchaeus a wee little man?"

"Why are you just now telling me? Where did you run into him?"

I sipped my café au lait, stalling, and set the cup on the saucer with a faint click. "I was viewing a building."

She gave me the mom look. Like I'd devoured the last Ding Dong and left the empty box in the pantry. "Has some distant relative I don't know about keeled over and blessed you with their fortune?"

"No."

"Then why torment yourself by looking to expand now?"

"It's a unique property." Which was an understatement.

"That you can't afford."

My scalp prickled. Julia was right. But what stung the most was that her words echoed Ryan's. Which also meant he was right. And he'd been dead-on correct that I hated being in financial debt. The stress of potentially defaulting on one loan was difficult. But the thought of having two loans looming? The world didn't hold enough Tums.

She shook her head. "I'm glad you can't afford it. You need to slow down, not gear back up again."

I pulled my lower lip between my teeth.

Her gaze narrowed, no doubt her sharp mind working. "Please tell me you're not considering going to your parents for the money."

Ever so slightly, I raised a shoulder.

She lifted her gaze to the moon with a groan.

"First, I'm looking into a city assistance program. My parents are a backup plan." I rubbed the Crease. "I hate the idea of going to them, but . . . Claire adored that location. She would daydream about it." I lowered my hand. "That's where I saw Ryan. He's interested in the spot too, and I can't stand losing it to him. I've already given up so much to that man. He was so . . . arrogant. And he wants to suck all the life and charm from the place. All the things Claire loved about it."

Her expression softened. "Regardless, hate is not a good motivator."

"He didn't ask about Hayley."

With a blink, she stiffened. "Maybe hate is a good motivator. What is he? A sociopath?"

"No. He's just a thousand percent selfish."

"What a bullet you dodged there." She studied me, her brows drawing together. "How are you feeling after seeing him?"

"Angry." I tossed my napkin on the table. "At him and myself for how I let him use me. How I allowed myself to be so vulnerable."

"That's understandable. But do you really want to go into further debt? Make yourself beholden to your parents? Would Claire? I seem to remember you giving me wise advice about thinking things through, looking at all the angles, and praying on them."

Boo. She had me there. Why was it always easier to give advice than to follow it? I stared at the fountain, not wanting to see reason. The faint rumble of a streetcar moving down St. Charles Avenue carried over the mansion.

"What other secrets are you keeping from me?"

Micah catapulted to the front of my brain. My gaze darted from the fountain to the live oak to the back doors of the café. "Did you want another order of beignets?"

"No, thank you," she said sweetly and leaned forward, dropping her tone. "Now spill it."

I dragged in a breath through my nose and released it, resignation stooping my posture. "There's a temporary librarian filling in."

"And . . ." She rested her elbows on the table, interlacing her fingers.

"He happens to be a . . . sort of a childhood friend. We attended the same school and church from kindergarten through high school. Though we never hung out socially." My gaze glided across the mansion. "But he did always come here every year for my grandma's Mardi Gras Day parties."

"Well, that's nice."

"He was also my first kiss."

"Ew." She leaned back. "I bet that was awkward seeing him again. First kisses are the worst."

"Not mine," I mumbled.

She perked.

Shivering schnauzers. How could I have let that slip?

"What's his name? Does he give you the zings?"

Landry Mask. Landry Mask. "Micah Guidry." I folded my discarded napkin a little too carefully.

She inhaled a gasp more appropriate for a TV melodrama.

Ugh. I held up my hand. "I honestly think my reaction to him was the stress from Mardi Gras." I picked at invisible lint on my sweater. "A Mardi Gras sickness."

She eyed me skeptically.

And she was probably a smidge right in doing so because I couldn't help but imagine that Micah had only improved in the kissing department. Especially with those manly arms of his. And his firm chest. And the air of confidence that swirled around him.

A knowing smile stretched Julia's face. "The way you're blushing, I think you still have that illness. Perhaps it's a type of lingering Mardi Gras fever?"

I tipped my chin up. "As a woman in my forties now, it could very well be a hot flash."

"Or a Micah flash. Has Hayley been to the library this week?"

My chin lowered. "No."

"She's had the entire week off and hasn't visited her favorite place?" One of her brows quirked.

"We've had a lot going on." I nudged my plate aside. Hayley had asked to go today, but I'd given her busywork in the café and paid her for her time. "But she's going tomorrow." My cheeks warmed again at the thought of seeing Micah.

Julia tossed me a smug grin. "I think your Mardi Gras fever is back."

6

SEVERAL TIMES A WEEK, Jesus and I held a prayer-cardio session. In keeping with that schedule, the next morning I'd dressed for exercise and now stretched in the courtyard. It was six thirty, the rising sun slowly ushering in the day. A chill sharpened the air, making me grateful I'd pulled on an LSU sweatshirt over my long-sleeved tee.

The squeak of the iron gate cut through the quiet. Mayté entered, a tote bag hanging on her petite frame, her chef's coat peeking from beneath her jacket. "About to do your power walk with Jesus?" Despite living in the United States most of her life, her Cuban accent remained strong.

"I am."

"Everyone show up for the morning shift?"

"Yes, thank goodness."

Mayté continued her path to the rear entrance. Though small in stature, she ran the back of the house like a five-star general. Order and respect ruled in her kitchen. Plus, she understood food cost percentages, labor rates, and waste numbers. Ten years older than me, she'd attended culinary school with Claire, stepped in when Claire had gone on maternity leave, and then came back after her death. Mayté was the epitome of a blessing.

In the midst of losing my sister and my life crumbling, she'd been there. Steadfast.

I finished loosening my arms and rolled my shoulders. "How are you this morning?"

She traversed the steps to the porch and opened one of the French doors. "Ready to kick another day in the shins." The door closed behind her.

I smiled. Was that a Cuban expression or just Mayté being Mayté? I widened my stance, stretching the muscles in my legs. Bending at the waist, I came face-to-face with an enormous glob of bird poop. I winced and straightened, surveying the brick pavers around me for any other droppings. I checked the bottoms of my tennis shoes and then carefully walked the area. Several more gifts had been left. *Great.* At least the fountain and lone wrought-iron table-and-chair set had been spared.

I tilted my head to the branches of the live oak. In the past we'd had a problem with squirrels and some pesky mockingbirds. Both of which had been chased off with the help of our inflatable owl, whom Hayley had dubbed Sir Neville Hooter. It seemed Sir Neville would be called up for duty again.

I retrieved my phone from the zippered pocket on my running pants and accessed the notes app to update my to-do list. The last thing I needed was poop raining down on our next special event.

My email icon showed one new message had been delivered. I opened it to find a pitiful dog staring back at me. "What in the—" I scrolled back up, reading the subject line: *Welcome to the Creole Poodle Rescue Newsletter.* A scathing mutter tripped past my lips. My gaze shot to the second floor, to Hayley's bedroom window, and narrowed.

Jesus would hear an earful about her during this morning's workout.

Three puffs in. Three puffs out. My quick stride across the sidewalk matched my strategic breathing rhythm. Crisp air moved in and out of my lungs. An old pickup truck rattled past, and the corner of Chestnut Street came into view. The street Micah now lived on. My breathing pattern hitched. Not a big deal. Not. A. Big. Deal. Chestnut was super long. Micah may not even live on the portion I speed walked. I hadn't noticed any for sale or lease signs recently, so most likely he resided in another section. Plus, he had that red flag. I remembered his voice as he'd said, *"My ex-wife and I weren't a good fit."* How would he have finished that sentence if he were being totally open?

"My ex-wife and I weren't a good fit . . . because I'm a serial cheater."

I certainly didn't want a man like that in my life. Or Hayley's.

Thank you, Jesus, for rational thinking.

I regained my breathing tempo. Puff-puff-puff in. Puff-puff-puff out.

Homes with varying architecture lined the way, from simple Acadians to detailed Victorians. Their bold colors added to the character of the neighborhood. Deep yellow, pumpkin orange, turquoise. Parts of this area were like an exploded Crayola box. Some houses sported iron pickct fences, sectioning their meager front lawns. The crepe myrtles that provided shade in the hotter months now lay bare, morning dew and spider webs clinging to their scraggly branches.

Half a block ahead a man wheeled his garbage can to the curb.

Puny poodles. It was Micah.

My lungs tightened, wheezing my three puffs in, and I stalled. A renegade band of tingles erupted within. *No!* If my Mardi Gras theory held true, this attraction was supposed to have disappeared along with all the tourists. When the street sweepers had rolled by the café, I'd imagined them gathering my hormones right up with all the discarded beads and litter. But instead, it was like fertilizer had been sprinkled on them.

Maybe his divorce hadn't been about cheating at all. *"My ex-wife and I weren't a good fit . . . because we couldn't agree on the thermostat setting."*

Hadn't I just thanked Jesus for rational thinking? Pull it together! Micah was only a guy. Wearing jeans and old-school Adidas. And another ugly Hawaiian shirt. Plus, he was a rule breaker. It was the wrong day for trash pickup. I purposefully walked on non-garbage days so I wouldn't have to smell the waste. My breath misted up, as if my body were sending unapproved smoke signals to catch his attention. I clamped my mouth shut.

Options. Options. I could turn around. He hadn't detected me yet. Though I hated allowing him to disrupt my routine.

He set his can at the end of the driveway and turned, doing a double take. A smile spread across his face as he lifted his hand in greeting.

My belly fluttered. Fluttered!

I continued on my regular exercise path (a partial victory), stopping on the pavement a few feet before him.

"Morning." His shirt boasted palm trees and coconuts. A slight improvement from the flamingos.

"Good morning."

"You found where I live." He motioned to the peach Creole cottage behind him.

My lips twitched. He dwelled in the most feminine home on the block. If all that peach wasn't enough, the trim, door, and full-length shutters were painted mint green. Estrogen oozed from the place. "I wasn't looking. You just happen to be on my walking route."

"Really?"

"Yes, really." I eyed his trash can.

He nudged the can with his toe. "Is something wrong?" A tease infused his words.

"No." I unzipped and rezipped the pocket on my upper thigh holding my phone.

The edge of his mouth quirked. "The way you're evil-eyeing my garbage, I'd say there is."

"Well . . ." I tugged the hem of my sweatshirt, sliding it over my hips. "I realize you've been gone a long time, and I don't know what they do in Colorado, but here, it's an unspoken rule not to put your trash out until garbage day."

He fought a smile.

"Or leave your can out all week."

A twinkle lit his deep sage eyes. "Is that so?" He retrieved a set of keys from his pocket and moved to an older model Jeep Wrangler at the curb. Didn't he know Jeeps were prone to flip? He opened the passenger door of the gray death trap and reached inside for a cardboard box full of VHS tapes.

I lifted my chin. "It is."

"You're still a rule follower." He shut the door with his elbow.

"And you're still a rule bender." Shifting my weight, I beseeched my brain for a snappier comeback and perused the contents of the box in his arms. "That's an interesting selection of entertainment you have there." The video covers on top revealed tapes like *Anne of Green Gables* (the best version, with Megan Follows), *Gone with the Wind*, and the original *Sabrina*.

"I just came from my dad's. We've been clearing stuff out. They were my mom's."

Oof. An invisible punch socked me in the gut. He'd lost his mom to cancer the summer before ninth grade.

He altered his hold on the box. "It's how we spent our time throughout her treatments. It was easier to watch chick flicks than to talk."

I swallowed, all intentions of teasing him gone. "It's nice you had that time together. Though I wouldn't call *Gone with the Wind* a chick flick."

He gave a self-deprecating snort. "Definitely not."

"I bet I've seen all of these." I reached into the box, lifting a copy of *Roman Holiday*. "Claire and I had regular movie nights with my grandma." Though Mawmaw's preferences included lots of Alfred Hitchcock. Hence my disdain for birds of any kind.

A sharp breeze blustered through, ruffling the short sleeves on Micah's shirt. He shivered.

I released the movie and stepped back. "You better head inside before your coconuts freeze."

His brows shot north.

"Your shirt!" Heat burst up my neck, erupting into my cheeks. "There are coconuts on your shirt!" I squeezed my eyes shut and shook my head. "I was trying to be funny."

He chuckled. "Mission accomplished."

"I'm leaving now." I pointed down the street. "To where you can't witness me die of mortification." With a wave I walked away, Micah's laughter trailing after me.

Pure embarrassment kept me warm the remainder of my power walk and left me with oodles of nervous energy to scratch off the next item on today's to-do list. I stood on the sidewalk in front of the café beneath the two live oaks. Donning work gloves and operating a manual pole tree trimmer, I carefully navigated the branches, targeting my enemies one by one.

Good-bye, beads. Like plucking a stubborn eyebrow hair free, instant satisfaction flowed at snipping each one and watching the Mardi Gras souvenirs drop to the ground.

Pieces of beads in varying colors and sizes littered the grass, sidewalk, and edge of St. Charles Avenue. I'd set out bright orange traffic cones to keep people from parking at the curb and having their vehicles pelted.

With the sun out on this cloudless day, I'd shucked my sweatshirt long ago, sweat permeating my skin. My shoulders and arms burned like the dickens. It took several clips to get the really tangled suckers down—the category most fell into. *Ignore those aching muscles. Your shoulders will look amazing. You won't have to do arm exercises this week. No sirree. No push-ups for me.*

Only a handful of beads remained within reach since the pole barely extended to sixteen feet. I'd have to wait for the weather to knock the higher beads down. Or pray God would make me blind to them.

Steady traffic zoomed by, along with streetcars bustling with passengers. I hooked a Krewe of Rex official parade bead into the lopper section of the trimmer and pulled the connected rope, guillotining the nuisance. *Not-so-long live the king.* The keepsake fell to the ground, the medallion on it clinking against the pavement.

"Need some help?"

I cringed at Ryan's familiar, masculine voice. *You've got to be kidding me.*

Had I not already experienced the jarring reality of his return to town, this moment may have pummeled me. I hated that I'd need to be on guard now. That he could pop up on me unannounced and unwelcomed, like a pointy chin hair.

It was a Saturday morning, and yet he'd dressed as though going to a casual business meeting. Slacks, loafers, long-sleeved button-down beneath a sweater vest. It seemed at some point he'd started shopping at the same place as my dad.

My wrist had begun aching fifteen minutes ago, my upper body exhausted from hefting the pole, but there was no way I'd let him help. I clipped another bead, imagining it as one of his fingers. "Why would you want to break your lifetime streak by helping me now?"

He stopped several feet away. "I was hoping we could be friends. Keep things civil."

I scoffed and lowered the pole, giving my screaming muscles a reprieve. "I'm holding a saw. The fact I haven't decapitated you yet shows how civil I'm being."

"You never used to be this . . ."

I lowered my sunglasses, leveling him a warning glare.

A smirk appeared on his face. "Fiery. And you look nice, Kate. Really nice. I didn't get a chance to tell you the other day."

Another thing he hadn't done the other day? Offer a long-overdue apology. And seriously? Was he hitting on me? A streetcar slowed to a stop, its wheels grinding against the rails. The back door folded open and Jonathan, a.k.a. the Beignet Bouncer, exited. He waited for a pause in traffic before crossing the street. Offering us both good-mornings, he gave Ryan a smooth once-over and turned his attention to me. "You need help?" Did he mean with getting rid of the beads or Ryan?

"Thank you, but I'm all right."

He nodded and made his way into the café.

I pushed my glasses back up and resumed my work, hefting the tree trimmer and hooking another bead. If Ryan truly wanted to help, he'd grab the rake propped against the iron fence and start gathering the debris.

"Are you going to put in an offer on the Vieux Carré Café?"

I yanked the rope, snipping the bead. "Are you harassing everyone who's interested in that property?"

"Are you going to answer my question?"

Yank, snip.

He kicked a bead from the sidewalk into the grass. "This morning I was having breakfast at Café Du Monde in Jackson Square and remembered how you'd worked there, and how you and Claire had signed and framed that napkin."

Yank, snip. I hated how he casually mentioned Claire. Like he, the person who'd abandoned me shortly after her death, had any right to utter her name so nonchalantly.

He thumbed his ear. "And then I remembered the plan y'all had concocted and framed. How carefully you'd thought out everything financially. And how your grandma's will had a stipulation her home could never be used as collateral."

The pole slipped within my grasp, and I fought to keep hold. Unease wound through my core. I lowered the tree trimmer.

He held his arms behind his back and cocked his head, all smug-as-you-please. "A loan substantial enough to buy that property would require collateral. And to avoid a collateral loan, you'd have to have a partner I don't know about, which you'd hate. Or your parents are backing you, which you'd hate even more." He studied the mansion with a shrewd eye. "This all means you can't afford to expand right now. Which means you were just window-shopping." He projected his voice, as though reinforcing his upper hand. "Seems kind of rude to waste your agent's time like that."

A heated twitchiness spread through my extremities. I hoisted the pole and positioned the saw to the base of a branch hovering above Ryan's ego-inflated head.

He shifted out of range. "Turns out you have a lot of your grandma in you."

"That may be the nicest compliment you've ever given me. Good-bye, Ryan."

He grinned and said good-bye, strolling back the way he'd come. Probably to crawl down the closest sewer drain for a shortcut to his home in Hades.

I snipped the last bead within reach and lowered the trimmers, laying them on the ground. Taking up the rake, I began bullying the beads into a pile. Aggravation punctuated my movements. How could I have wasted so many years with that man? The rake's tines scraped over the dormant sliver of lawn and grated against the sidewalk. "'Just window-shopping,'" I muttered, impersonating Ryan.

The heap of debris grew, leaves and blades of brown grass getting caught up in my fury. The calluses on my hands screamed for a break, and I finally complied.

Releasing the rake, I stretched my trembling arms and shoulders. My gaze meandered over Mawmaw's mansion, from the peaked shingled roof to the massive white columns. The curtains along the second-story windows were closed. Goodness knew what Hayley was up to.

I shook my head and continued my perusal. At least with the cooler temperatures I wouldn't have to mow the lawn for another month or so. Like all Southerners, the grass shriveled up with any bit of cold that hit here. I took note of the ceilings on the wraparound porches. The palest of blues coated them (a New Orleans superstition I only honored because of Mawmaw and her fear of evil spirits). They'd need a refresh soon. With the soaring ceiling heights, the project stretched beyond my capabilities, which meant shoveling out a lot of money to a professional. The ever-present weight on my shoulders increased.

A long breeze swooshed through. And as I'd done so many times as a child, I closed my eyes and concentrated on the rustling leaves above, imagining the ancient oaks were speaking to me. A light and fruity fragrance kissed my senses, and I opened my eyes, taking in the snapdragons flanking the entrance gate. They instantly lifted my mood, their delicate orange-and-yellow blooms swaying in the gust.

I pulled in a deep breath and redirected my thoughts to where they should've been all along.

God, you know how much Claire loved the Vieux Carré Café. Plus, it's a spectacular location. I paused, stretching my back muscles and sighing. *It seems too good to pass up.*

A notification chimed from my phone. I fished my cell from the pocket of my running pants and unlocked the screen. A reminder from my calendar app about tonight stared back at me. My stomach sank. It was a monthly occurrence I loathed more than my period.

Dinner with my parents.

7

"I HATE SAD SATURDAYS," Hayley muttered.

"Me too." I rang the doorbell to my parents' home in Old Metairie, an elegant suburb on the outskirts of New Orleans. Deep, somber chimes rang, setting the tone for the evening. Several years ago, we'd officially named the last Saturday of every month, our standing dinner appointment with my parents. "Name one good thing."

Hayley effused a long-suffering sigh only a teenager could manage. "The desserts."

"You sound like your mom."

Her lower lip rolled in, her gaze plummeting to her feet, as though realizing she'd actually conversed with me on a topic that didn't involve getting a dog.

"My one good thing is this will be over in a few hours." And I could feel my parents out for a loan. Or at least begin dropping breadcrumbs about the potential expansion. They were my plan C. My plan A was the New Orleans Redevelopment Authority. I'd reach out to them for a meeting, hoping to utilize their Small Business Grant Assistance Program. Plan B was a federal SBA loan, as long as it didn't require using Mawmaw's

63

mansion as collateral. In her will, Mawmaw had been adamant her house not be lost because of a forfeited loan.

"If we had a dog waiting for us at home, that would be something to look forward to."

I smothered a sigh and turned, surveying the shallow front lawn.

This plot of land had been the site of my childhood residence. But twenty years ago, when the next-door neighbors had listed their place for sale, my parents had snatched it up and demolished both homes, right along with my and Claire's memories (not that there were many happy ones). I think that was partially why Mawmaw had willed her mansion and belongings to us. She didn't trust my parents with them.

Now sat a monster of a house, where just two people resided. The only things remaining from our early years were the trees near the street. Ones we hadn't been allowed to climb, which was torture since live oaks were the best kind for scaling. Especially on a road with little traffic.

The doorknob twisted, much like my stomach.

My mom appeared, wearing a tweed skirt suit she'd no doubt purchased from Saks Fifth Avenue. Mama hadn't been a religious person, save for Christmas Eve and Easter Sunday. But she faithfully attended Saks every Saturday. And dragged Claire and I along up until our late teens. It was her version of church, except instead of grape juice for the Lord's Supper, they gave her champagne to sip while she shopped.

Mawmaw once said that my mom's parents, who passed before I was born, had died on purpose to escape my mother. I believed it. But just about every Sunday morning Mawmaw picked Claire and I up for church. It had irked Mama, but not enough to risk her objecting for fear of exclusion from her mother-in-law's will. I never knew if it was the threat of public shame of them being cut out or the fact that Mama wanted more money to sit in their already fat bank accounts. In the end, they'd still been excluded from receiving anything from Mawmaw's estate. Because of that jilting, Claire had started our monthly dinner gatherings as a hopeful way to mend our relationships.

Mama scanned me and Hayley, her Lancôme-colored lips pinching to one side. The style of her dark auburn hair was an exact replica of Nancy Reagan, circa 1981. The greens and browns in the tweed suit complemented her pale complexion. Though I'd bet her personality tonight prickled more than the fabric. Her low heels (yes, she wore heels at home, even when she wasn't expecting company) completed her polished appearance.

Mama's silent inspection continued.

I fought the urge to squirm beneath my simple teal wrap dress and flats. Hayley remained mute beside me, having donned black slacks and a dove-gray sweater.

Mama's hazel gaze met mine. "You're late."

"Only by ten minutes. There was an accident on the interstate."

"We'll have to go straight in to dinner."

Well, that was another one good thing. We'd missed the appetizers and strained conversation portion of the evening.

Our footsteps echoed against the marble floors as she ushered us past their formal living room, Daddy's study, and into their opulent dining room.

Daddy stood from his seat at the head of the long table, looking like he'd just returned from golfing with the president. "Girls." His greeting was much warmer than Mama's, his unusually casual outfit no doubt annoying her. Every month she wanted everyone dressed as though we were posing for a Christmas card.

Hayley and I took turns kissing Daddy's cheek and taking our assigned seats. The table could have easily accommodated twelve, but was only set for four, forcing us to sit across from one other. Somewhere in this elaborate mansion sat eight chairs that belonged in this room. Eight chairs that would be hefted back by their poor maid after we left.

Mama took her seat, snapping out her cloth napkin and laying it over her lap. She rang the bell next to her silverware (yes, a bell), signaling her personal chef (yes, a personal chef) to begin this torturous meal. "You'll have to excuse your father's appearance this evening."

"You look great, Daddy, like you got some sun today."

My father had always been a doppelgänger for Michael Douglas, which he loved, especially when Michael Douglas had snagged Catherine Zeta-Jones. He sipped amber liquid from his scotch glass. "Thank you. And I didn't have time to change because we got held up at the last hole."

"The last hole or the club bar?" Mama muttered to the ornate crown molding.

Daddy took another sip of his drink. Before retiring, he'd been a cardiothoracic surgeon, always at work or on call. Nights and weekends he'd be swept away without a moment's notice, which never bothered him. If anything, it had been the opposite. I never could blame him for not wanting to be home, where Mama was. But I *could* blame him for being an absent parent and a doormat to Mama. When Claire had moved out, she'd asked him why he stayed, and he'd simply said that Mama made life easy for him. All he had to do was go to work. Disappear into a challenging job he desperately loved. She took care of everything else.

"How did you play?" I asked.

He gazed at his scotch glass. "Better than yesterday." If Mama was a member of Saks' congregation, upon retirement, Daddy had become a dedicated deacon at the neighborhood golf club.

Their latest personal chef entered, wearing a white coat and carrying a large tray. He placed a plate before each of us, only

Hayley and I thanking him, and left. From the scent of Tabasco and cinnamon, I knew it was a sunburst salad. And since Mama dictated every meal, it was her doing. My neck stiffened. I lowered my fork, ready to remind her, once again, that spicy foods upset Hayley's stomach.

Hayley caught my eye, shaking her head imperceptibly.

I raised my brows. *Are you sure?*

She gave a slight but resolute nod.

I sighed and forked a bite of baby lettuce, spearing a cranberry that would've been soaked overnight in port wine. The explosion of tastes was instant. Sugary juiciness with a hint of heat.

Daddy chewed and swallowed. "How's business?"

"Good." I sipped water from my crystal goblet, sending up a quick prayer over the breadcrumb I was about to drop. "I've actually come across an interesting opportunity."

Daddy's expression held intrigue, Mama's leeriness.

Hayley stopped pushing her uneaten salad around, her full attention on me.

I set my water down. "There's a property in the French Quarter that's coming on the market soon." Playing it cool, I took another bite of our first course. A contradictory texture of smooth blue cheese and crunchy sliced almond.

Hayley resumed fake eating.

"You're looking to expand already?" Daddy cut through his salad, his knife grating against the fine china. "Isn't your money tied up in the courtyard?"

"It is."

Mama gave Daddy a knowing look. She had always controlled everything in this house. Claire and I when we lived here, my dad, their money. Would she offer a loan, or watch me squirm until I asked for help?

Mama dabbed the corner of her mouth with her napkin. "Then it seems you've *missed* an interesting opportunity."

Watching me squirm it is.

She continued. "I told you renovating the courtyard was a colossal waste of money. People don't like eating outside with the heat and bugs. You run a respectable café, not a BBQ."

I muffled a scoff. As if there was something wrong with BBQ restaurants. "I only use the courtyard for special events."

Daddy shifted in his chair. "You invested into something you're not using all the time?"

"Special events are picking up." *Sort of.* "And those catered parties lend themselves to controllable costs, which means a high profitability."

Mama sniffed, and her gaze caught on her plate. With a scowl she grasped her bell and rang it.

Oh, heavens.

The chef reappeared, uncertainty in his features. "Ma'am?"

"Is this Stilton or gorgonzola?" Mama gestured to her dish. Her tone gave no indication as to which cheese was the correct answer.

"Stilton, ma'am."

For a beat, her gaze narrowed further at the poor guy, his job resting on which form of blue cheese he'd served. "Very well." She dismissed him with a condescending wave.

I had a feeling when this chef was fired, he'd steal her bell like the last one had.

Mama placed a piece of the cheese in her mouth, concentrating on her bite as though she still didn't believe her cook.

Hayley accidentally knocked a cranberry off her plate and quickly returned it.

It was just enough to turn Mama's attention her way. "Hayley, how are your grades right now?"

"Good, ma'am," Hayley answered, low but clear.

Mama leaned forward. "What does 'good' mean? What's your GPA?"

Hayley avoided direct eye contact with her, as though she were a dangerous monkey.

I straightened, pitching my voice. "She's doing great in school. She turned in a really fascinating social studies project on Hurricane Katrina."

Mama waved that praise away, her unrelenting stare on Hayley. "What's your GPA?"

Hayley lifted a slim shoulder. "Average, ma'am?"

Although her usage of ma'am with Mama was a sign of respect, it also bore a sign of the tense formality between them. The only times I'd *ma'am*'d Mawmaw had been with a simple yes or no answer.

Mama rang the bell and projected her stern voice toward the kitchen entrance. "Next course, Andre."

Andre arrived in a flash, removing our salads and replacing them with pork tenderloin, roasted potatoes, and brussels sprouts. He refilled our drinks and vanished. Hopefully to search the classifieds for another job.

Hayley took a tentative bite of potatoes, relief washing over her features. She shoveled in another morsel, chewing while cutting a portion of meat. Daddy followed suit, quietly eating his meal.

Mama pointed her fork at Hayley. "Average grades would be Cs." She flipped her gaze to me. "You need to push her. Get some tutors." Her stare returned to Hayley. "Your mom's grades started waning in high school until we got her a tutor. She graduated with a 4.0."

Claire had graduated with a 4.0 *and* a stomach ulcer.

Hayley stilled, studying her untouched brussels sprouts. And seriously, who served brussels sprouts to their grandkid?

I clenched my fork and knife, striving to maintain an unaffected voice. "Her grades are fine."

"What about extracurriculars?" Mama's regard swept over each person at the table. "Colleges look at extracurriculars."

Releasing my grip on my utensils, I switched to strangling the napkin on my lap. "She's in seventh grade. College isn't on her radar yet."

"It was on your radar at her age."

Because it was my ticket to moving out of here.

Daddy rose and refilled his scotch at the bar cart.

Mama returned her attention to Hayley. "Are you in any clubs? Or student council?"

Hayley's big blue eyes lifted from her plate to the floral centerpiece, and she shook her head.

Mama sighed. "Hayley, do you think you can grace us with more than shaking your head and two-word answers?" Mama stared at me while she pointed this question. Another jab at my subpar parenting.

"Yes, ma'am. I'll try," Hayley said.

I stopped strangling my napkin and took up my utensils again, the desire to bear weapons surging. "You need to take it easy."

Mama pulled a face. "How is she supposed to develop her social skills unless she contributes to conversations? Participates in clubs?"

"There's nothing wrong with her social skills," I said. "Hayley has friends, helps out at the café, volunteers at the library."

"The *public* library," Mama muttered, sipping from her goblet. "One can only imagine the cast of characters there."

Micah came to mind. I'd avoided seeing him earlier by staying in the car and texting Hayley when I'd arrived to pick her up. Pretty soon it would be obvious I was steering clear of him. Especially since—thanks to the embarrassing period voice mail I'd left—he knew I'd forged a somewhat friendship with the former librarian.

"Kate, stop rubbing between your brows," Mama scolded. "It's unladylike." She turned her gaze to Hayley. "Hayley, you're wearing the same thing as last month. Why don't you wear any of the clothes I've given you?"

"Mama," I cautioned.

Hayley had worn the most conservative of her wardrobe. She'd even donned a pair of flats she loathed. It'd prompted my change from heels to flats in a show of solidarity. She was completely appropriate for dinner with her grandparents. And uncomfortable. And she'd done it for them.

Mama scrutinized Hayley. "You're so scrawny."

"Mama." Even I heard the warning growl in my voice.

Mama continued. "At least the outfits I gave you would accentuate the positives of your body."

Hayley, still invoking the dangerous monkey rule, stared at her vile veggies.

"Mom." Heat, having nothing to do with hot flashes or a hot man, raced through me. I gaped at Daddy, wishing, not for the first time in my life, he'd come to my rescue.

He met my gaze.

Vulnerability encircled my heart, squeezing tighter and tighter. *Choose me this time. Choose Hayley.*

A sad emptiness overtook his expression, and he dropped his sights to the table.

My heart withered, my eyes growing hot. After a lifetime of him being a coward to Mama, it was foolish of me to hope it'd be different this time.

"And your hair," Mama said to Hayley. "Do you own a brush?"

I shot to my feet. "We're finished here."

"Katherine, really." Mama all but rolled her eyes.

"You're being rude." I dropped my napkin on the table.

"*You're* being rude," she said. "Sit down."

If I didn't sit, I'd ruin any chance of a loan. My plan C would be destroyed. But unlike my parents, I believed some things were worth more than money or taking the easy route. I looked at Hayley. "Let's go."

With our dramatic exit complete, I pulled my parent's front door shut behind us and took a breath of the cool night air.

Hayley leaned into me, her thin arm wrapping my waist. "Thanks."

Wonder struck, and a gust of love so deep and full and true surged. How long had it been since she'd hugged me on her own? A year? I knew that was expected with teens, but I hadn't realized how much I'd missed all of those childhood snuggles until this very second. I returned the gesture as we took the walkway to my car. "Anytime, kiddo."

8

THERE HAD BEEN A MURDER in the courtyard. The following Monday, Sir Neville Hooter lay on the ground, ripped and deflated. It was just after lunch, and I'd ducked upstairs to grab some Advil. My muscles still ached for relief from working that tree trimmer on Saturday. I'd secured the bottle as Sir Neville had snagged my attention through the kitchen window.

Like a homicide investigator, I now hovered over the deceased's body, scanning for clues. Dozens of small nicks covered Sir Neville's face. One of his eyes was completely missing. Larger slashes marred his torso. It must've been a cat. Didn't cats play with toys? And didn't cats loathe birds? Sir Neville checked both of those feline perp profiles. I straightened and surveyed the perimeter's brick wall. A cat could've easily gotten in and out of the courtyard and climbed the tree.

As my gaze scanned to where I'd fastened Sir Neville to the lowest branch near the trunk, I caught the slightest movement on an overhead limb. My eyes slowly tipped up-up-up, the hairs on the back of my neck rising.

There sat a parrot. A *huge* parrot. I scrambled backward. The lime-green creature had to be the length of a ruler. It watched me from the branch above Sir Neville's lifeless body.

Watched me with its big creepy bird eyes. A line of bright teal marked its right cheek. It raised one of its feet, and within its claws lay Sir Neville's eye. I gasped. "Murderer." I flapped my arms, the pills in the bottle rattling. "Shoo! Shoo!"

The beast remained unmoved.

The café's back door opened, and Mrs. Adélaide ambled out. "Everything okay, *cher*? I was on my way to de bathroom and saw you flailing."

"That parrot"—I pointed—"killed our owl."

Mrs. Adélaide shuffled to the edge of the porch, squinting and scanning the great oak. "Oh." Her eyes widened and then tightened to slits. "I know dis bird. *Cést fou.*"

"He's crazy?"

"*Oui.* He took up in my magnolia tree. Made such a mess." She raised her fist to the animal and muttered a long sentence in pure Cajun French, her throat emphasizing the curse words with a vengeful rasp. She turned to me. "You have a gun?"

I blinked. "Um . . ."

"Tomorrow, I'll bring mine."

Images of the movie *Stop! Or My Mom Will Shoot* flashed before me. Especially with her helmet of powder-white curls and thick glasses swallowing her lean face. She gave major Sophia Petrillo vibes from *The Golden Girls*.

"That won't be necessary." I took the steps up to the porch. "But thank you. Let's get you inside."

I shot one last evil eye at the butcher, and ushered Mrs. Adélaide into the café. She made her way to the bathroom, muttering "*Cést fou*" several times. I cast a quick glance over the main dining room and found Ryan waiting at the hostess stand.

Sarah McLachlan.

Suspicion surged in my gut, looping and knotting.

He removed one of the café's business cards from the stand, sliding it into the pocket of his black slacks. His eyes met mine. He smiled.

My grip on the Advil tightened.

Behind Ryan, the front door opened, and Micah entered.

Mangy mutts. Who else would show up that would make this moment any more awkward? My gynecologist?

Micah, whose shirt featured pineapples donning sunglasses, noticed Ryan first. Open displeasure coated Micah's features, as though he'd stepped in dog poop. *Interesting.*

Ryan followed my line of vision, turning. His countenance hardened. *Doubly interesting.* Had they not liked each other in high school, and I'd missed it? They shook hands and exchanged a few words, Ryan giving Micah a once-over with an air of snootiness. The hostess interrupted them, leading Ryan to an empty table. Maybe I'd arrange for a plate of beignets with extra powdered sugar to be dropped on the lap of his black pants.

Micah made his way to me, a slight frown darkening his handsome face. "I'd like to talk to you about something, but if you've got plans right now"—he nodded in Ryan's direction—"I can come back another time."

"No, I don't have plans with anyone. Especially not him." I tossed a sneer in Ryan's general vicinity and motioned Micah toward my office. "I'm hoping this is a good something you want to talk about."

He followed, his expression shifting to a partial smile. "It falls somewhere in the middle."

We entered my office, and I shut the door, then rounded my desk to my chair. My forgotten extra foam latte waited. At least it would be cold enough to down the Advil with.

Micah took one of the guest chairs, his attention absorbed by the bookcase behind me. Instead of books, pictures of Claire, Hayley, and a hodgepodge of Hayley's arts and crafts from elementary school filled the shelves.

Between the possibility of Mrs. Adélaide packing heat on her next visit and Ryan's appearance, my temples pounded like they held an angry drummer captive. Well, I could obliterate that one problem. I shook out two pills and downed them with a long sip of tepid caffeinated goodness. A foam mustache clung to my upper lip. With zero napkins and Micah enthralled with Hayley's kindergarten rendering of a streetcar, I licked it away.

Only Micah wasn't staring at my décor anymore. No, his gaze tracked the movement of my mouth.

My breaths slowed, sharp energy charging the air.

He quickly averted his stare, a muscle flexing in his jaw, as though he were frustrated with himself.

Had my office shrunk? And who had stolen all the oxygen? I needed clarity. Stat. Something to squash the electrical current thrumming under my skin that he kept evoking. Clearly his ugly clothes weren't a strong enough deterrent. If anything, the pineapples on his shirt only thrust memories of our junior-high kiss into the forefront of my mind. *Oh, that kiss.*

"My ex-wife and I weren't a good fit . . . because I'm a cat hoarder, and she was allergic."

Though I didn't spy a single cat hair on him. But at least I'd returned to rational thinking. Not a single man since Ryan had sparked this strong of a reaction. I'd had little flickers here or there. But nothing powerful enough to jump-start my long-dormant heart when it came to romantic feelings.

"Do you have that sweater set in every color?"

I snapped from my thoughts and ran a hand down the long sleeve of my navy cardigan. "Do you raid Magnum P.I.'s closet every morning?"

His green eyes twinkled. "I'm on my lunch break. And I've found kids are more open to me when I dress like this."

"Oh." My posture wilted. "That makes sense." And it was . . . endearing. *Nope. Don't fall for it.* Other than the gigantic red flag flying above his head, he drove a flip-prone vehicle. "So what did you need to talk about? I'm guessing it's not my wardrobe."

One side of his mouth hitched. "No, it's not about your clothes. Over the weekend the special events room at the library

76

had a pipe break in the ceiling. The water damage is enough to where they're renovating the entire space, which means it's off-limits for now. Which leads to canceling the spring events."

My heart sank a little, and several special events Hayley had attended passed through my mind. For one, she'd created her own picture book about alpacas that had been added to the library's shelves for others to check out. Though that had been years ago, the book remained on a shelf to this day. I'd even spied Hayley looking through it last month. For another event, she'd dressed as a favorite fictional character (Susan from *The Lion, the Witch and the Wardrobe*). And then there'd been a scavenger hunt that had taken place on the library's property. She'd animatedly talked about it for days after.

"They're reallocating the funds for the spring events to offset the renovation fees. But if I can find another location to hold the gatherings at no cost to the library, I have approval to promote them as official events. I was hoping we could move them here, to your courtyard."

The proverbial needle scratched across the vinyl record. "Here?"

He held up his hands. "Just until the renovations are complete. The goal for now would be one event a month, for the next three months. My concern is if they die off altogether, they'll never start again. I've got snacks and basic supplies covered. But I don't have enough funds for a location."

Suspicion once again crept in, winding through my stomach. Maybe it was Ryan's reappearance bringing my old insecurities of being used more easily to the surface. And if so, good! I needed the reminder. "What's in it for you?"

He flinched.

Okay. Perhaps he wasn't like Ryan.

"Nothing's in it for me. I'd just hate for these kids to lose the events they love. Events that give them something positive to be a part of."

Unmistakable conviction percolated, and then swelled from

within my core. *Oh, God, I don't have time to host library functions.* Or have the courtyard looking like a daycare when potential clients dropped by to consider it as a venue. Regardless of my hesitations, the sensation to say yes to Micah persisted. My attention drifted over my desk to the treasured catawampus pencil holder Hayley had crafted out of popsicle sticks when she was five. At a beloved library function no less. I pulled in a breath and released it. "I'll think about it."

"Thank you." He rose to leave, an easy smile forming.

I stood to escort him out.

"You won't have to do a thing, if that's what you're worried about. My girlfriend's great with parties and kids, and she's volunteered to help."

Shock rippled through me, leaving me unable to move. *Landry Mask. Landry Mask.* All I could manage was to nod like a bobblehead doll.

He opened the door and paused on the threshold, his hand on the knob. "Would you like this closed?"

Another bobble-head nod.

"Thanks again." He shut the door.

I sank into my chair, mentally chastising myself for being so pitifully taken by surprise. Of course he had a girlfriend. He was a gorgeous man who'd chosen a profession that helped others. A profession that put him in the line of single moms who could see how great he was with children. Or grandmas with eligible daughters who could see how great he was with children. Even beyond the library, he was out there in the world with his athletic physique and laid-back personality. And his pineapple kisses.

Apparently, the big red warning flag I'd imagined rippling in the wind when it came to Micah and his divorce hadn't mattered to someone else.

For the next twenty-four hours I engaged in a tug-of-war with God. I now sat in the back corner of the courtyard on a small bench tucked into my favorite prayer spot. A vine of pink jasmine ran up the brick wall behind me, reaching for the waning sun, its plump blooms on the verge of bursting free. I'd dropped Hayley and her friend Emma at the library after school, along with some snacks. Emma's mom had offered to bring Hayley home when she picked up Emma, but I'd declined, knowing I had to talk to Micah. To either grant his request or reject it.

I inhaled a hint of sweetness from the jasmine and relaxed my tense shoulders. Ignoring that pressing from God always proved futile. Because in the end, I knew the only peace I'd feel would be giving in to what I should have done. And I never regretted surrendering to His promptings.

"God, you know this timing isn't good. I can't have a million kids swarming the courtyard. There's bound to be casualties." I gazed at the tiered fountain, the lush landscaping that had finally filled in every nook and cranny. "And Micah seems kind of free-spirited. What if he reads them a medieval story, and they build catapults?" I could almost hear Mawmaw's vintage French doors shattering. See the newly sprouting tulips getting squashed.

"And if I'm being honest, despite the fact that I'm not looking for a relationship, it would've been a smidge easier to say yes to a *single* Micah Guidry." I glanced down at my beige heels. An ant carrying a leaf from the vine crawled along the pavers. Closing my eyes (and my running mouth), I sought God. The persistent conviction I'd been feeling swelled. I sighed, tipping my face skyward, catching sight of the murdering parrot in the oak tree. "Cést Fou," I growled, shaking my fist at it like Mrs. Adélaide had. "God, since I'm giving in with the library events, do You think You could do something about that bird?"

Ten minutes later, I exited my car at the library. Traffic whizzed by, but all I heard was Micah's voice from yesterday. *"Do you have that sweater set in every color?"* My outfit today was purely out of spite. Slim-legged trousers and a feminine pinstriped blue shirt that hit at my elbows. *"My girlfriend's great with parties and kids."* Well, there was nothing I could do about that remark. I knew he hadn't meant it as a dig. That it had only been to ease my concerns and help his cause. But man oh man, I wished I hadn't confided in him on my past feelings about children and my fear of lacking parental skills.

I hauled open the historic wood door, and my gaze instantly latched onto Micah. A jolt of awareness shot through my belly. He sat behind the reception desk, his brows furrowed at a computer screen. His Hawaiian shirt featured volcanos. Appropriate for the heat erupting within me that hopefully wouldn't tattle through my cheeks.

His attention shifted to me, and his olive-colored eyes transformed from pensive to . . . pleased.

My internal lava chamber bubbled. *He has a girlfriend. And a red flag.*

"You just missed Emma's mom."

I nodded. *He's pretending to be happy to see you because he needs your help.*

That lava in my stomach quelched.

Movement at the far end of the reception desk garnered my attention. Nellie, Mrs. Gail's assistant—or, really, I guessed Micah's assistant for now—stood there, silently working. Donning disposable gloves and a slight grimace, she made her way through a stack of hardbacks, transferring them to a book cart. Years ago, Nellie had taken on the job in an effort to help with her germaphobia. Nellie cleaned the now-clear counter with a disinfectant wipe and then pushed the cart toward the back, disappearing into the area that had once been a grand dining room. It now housed the nonfiction section.

Micah rounded the desk, stopping a few feet before me. Leaning in, he lowered his voice. "Has she always been like that?" The scent of pineapples wafted with his nearness.

Whimpering whippets. Was I having a delusion? Was this some sort of cruel trick because I now knew he was forbidden fruit? I hushed my tone to match his. "Nellie hasn't talked to you?"

He shook his head. "I'm guessing she has a problem with germs?"

Biting the inside of my cheek, I readjusted my purse strap on my shoulder. It wasn't my place to disclose Nellie's phobia.

Realization dawned on his face, and he rubbed his forehead. "That's why Mrs. Gail left instructions that it was my responsibility to go through *all* returned books. And the drop box."

I quirked a brow. "I can see Nellie wanting to avoid children's books for obvious reasons." I mimed picking my nose. "But the others?"

His hand slid from his temple to the back of his neck. "Unfortunately, boogers aren't only found in children's books."

I recoiled, clutching my throat. "I didn't think it possible, but you're making books even less appealing for me."

"I hate to break it to you, but you have a café full of books the public has access to."

"Uh-uh." I held up my hand like a school crossing guard halting traffic. "The majority of people ignore them. Plus, they don't leave the premises."

He folded his arms with a smirk.

"Moving on." I widened my eyes, emphasizing the end of that subject. "We're getting off topic."

"We have a topic?"

"We do."

"Does it involve you crushing the hearts of the library's patrons? Most notably the hearts of kids and teens?"

81

Most notably, one teen in particular. "If it were only *your* heart that would be crushed, then my decision would've been easier."

He chuckled. "Which means you're letting us use the café?"

"I am."

His smile skyrocketed.

My heart twinged.

"Thank you. So much. I have just about everything pulled together for the first event. It's an *Alice in Wonderland* theme." He leaned across the desk, grabbing a copy of the book. "There'll be a Mad Hatter tea party in the courtyard with these crazy decorations hanging from the tree above the tables, then croquet in the yard in front of the café—"

"What?"

"I even found some lawn flamingos at my dad's place we can set around the course."

Talk about a confirmation of my fears. Children with mallets? Smacking wooden balls? Not adhering to proper croquet rules? I could just hear a window—or four—shattering, and see the café sign on the front lawn being treated like a piñata. A shudder rolled through me. "You never said anything about using the front of the café."

"Well, I was hoping . . ." His brows slowly rose, no doubt in an attempt to be charming.

"No. Absolutely not. And this is exactly why I'm only agreeing to this if I'm in charge of everything." I crossed my arms. "And I do mean everything."

His mouth pulled to one side, contemplating.

"Take it or leave it."

"You still like total control." Faint lines fanned at his eyes. "Reminds me of that group science project in tenth grade."

"The project where you questioned and pushed at each of my suggestions?"

His head tilted, highlighting the strong angles of his jaw. "The project where you acted as a dictator instead of an equal?"

"This isn't a high school assignment, Micah. It's my place of business. The sole income for Hayley and me. I have to ensure nothing jeopardizes that. My customers expect a certain atmosphere, and I can't risk losing them to another restaurant. Or missing out on potential business."

"I understand. It's just . . . these library events are supposed to be fun."

I scoffed. "I can be fun."

"Kate, even your exercise is exact and controlled."

"Excuse me?"

"Three times a week." He marched in place, pumping his arms, miming my speed-walking motions. "Same pace, same route."

"Stalker!"

"It's not stalking when you're going right past my home like clockwork."

Interesting. So last Saturday he'd known I'd be walking by. Had he timed his appearance to run into me, or was it coincidence? "According to the American Heart Association, speed walking is the most practical way to achieve the recommended thirty minutes of low-impact cardio three times a week."

He held my gaze, a sparkle of amusement in his eyes.

I sighed. "You've brought us off topic again. Are you agreeing to let me be in complete charge of the events at *my* café?"

"Will you at least wear an Alice costume?"

I nailed him with a glare.

"The Mad Hatter?"

My glare narrowed to a pure scowl.

His lips twitched. "With the way you're looking at me, I think the Queen of Hearts would be better suited for you."

I snatched the book from him and set off to find Hayley.

9

"WHAT'S THE AGE RANGE FOR THIS PARTY?" Julia scanned the courtyard of Beignets & Books and the round tables and chairs I'd
hauled from the storage shed. Each was set for four.

"Toddlers to teens."

When she'd asked if she could help with the first library
event, I'd pounced on her offer. And that first event would begin
in exactly thirty minutes, at one o'clock. With the cooler temps
of mid-March still cooperating on this Saturday afternoon, and
the overcast skies lending a hand, we were poised for perfect
outdoor-party weather. And since naptimes generally occurred
after lunch, the timeframe seemed a smart move for children to
arrive after having worn themselves out elsewhere.

We stood next to the fountain, which I had turned off so it
would pose less of a temptation to the younger attendees. My
water feature would not be used as a wading pool. Or a sink.
Or a urinal.

"Hmm." Julia's face scrunched.

"What?"

"Well, it seems kind of formal for kids, especially from what
I remember taking the boys to when they were little. But we

went to a different library than yours. Does your library lean to the fancier side?"

A slow churn started in my gut. Although Micah had doled out a plethora of suggestions over the past two and a half weeks, the only one I'd taken was a tea party. And some of the supplies he'd gathered for the arts and crafts activity. Julia's opinion only confirmed my second-guessing that had begun this morning when Hayley had helped set everything up. Her reaction to the paper teacups and saucers hadn't been the delight I'd experienced at finding them online at a deep discount. She'd frowned at the subdued floral-themed sets and made a comment about the tea party in the book being whacky and bizarre.

"No, our library isn't fancy." I laid a hand against my middle. "I thought it might be refreshing to be a little more . . ."

"Formal?"

"Refined." Or maybe *reserved* was a better word. "My goal is to evoke a calm environment and discourage any inklings of roughhousing. You know how much it cost to remodel this courtyard." I moved to one of the tables and smoothed a wrinkle in its cream tablecloth.

"I do know. And I think it's great you're doing this. It's nice to see this area getting used more."

Hadn't Daddy made a similar—though derogatory—remark about not using the courtyard all the time? At another table, I adjusted one of the folding chairs. In addition to the teacups, saucers, matching plates, and napkins, the center of each table held a tiered tray of cupcakes a local bakery had donated and dropped off earlier.

"It's a lovely setup," Julia said.

"Thank you." I tipped a leery gaze to the oak's branches. "Any other sightings of Sir Neville's killer?"

"Not since the murder."

"Is it still leaving you presents?"

"Oh yes," I sighed. "Today marked day twenty-two." My morning routine now included hosing escalating amounts of bird poop from the pavers. Never had I thought one parrot could produce so much waste. What was its food source? A Taco Bell dumpster? "What makes it worse is I feel like it's watching me." I slowly scanned the tree, a slight shudder crawling over my skin.

"Is Mrs. Adélaide still talking about bringing her gun?"

I pressed a finger between my brows, rubbing. "She hasn't mentioned it since last week. Apparently, she hasn't been able to locate a purse big enough to fit her weapon to get it here."

"What's she got? A shotgun?"

I dropped my hand with a shrug. "As long as she keeps showing up only toting her little cross-body wallet, I'll count that as a blessing."

"So what's the plan with all this?" Julia tucked her phone into the back pocket of her fitted jeans. She'd paired the dark denim with a flowy sleeveless top, highlighting the tone in her arms. Her active job as a housemaid helped maintain her fit shape.

"The plan with all this" was to keep the library events alive and hence, keep Hayley happy. For her to witness me championing something she loved. And possibly redirect her obsession with getting a dog. For at least one day anyway. I glanced up to her bedroom window, where she was probably strategizing her next move. Would it be another car magnet? Another newsletter subscription? I shook my head. "I figured we'd start with Micah—"

"The man whose kisses you still dream about."

I gasped, my jaw hanging for several heavy heartbeats. "Julia. Reed. Is that why you volunteered? To meet Micah?"

She suddenly became very interested in one of the blooming azalea bushes. "Maybe it's a little bit why."

I kept my gaze lasered on her. "Julia."

She turned, a sly smile forming. "Maybe it's *a lot* why I volunteered."

An exhale burst free. "This isn't like you. You're not a meddler."

"When it comes to the people I love, I am."

Her declaration softened my irritation. "Well, prepare to be disappointed."

Her head tipped sideways.

"Micah has a girlfriend."

"Oh." Her expression deflated. "I'm sorry."

I waved a dismissive hand. "It's not like I was interested anyway."

One of her brows rose. "Who's the one trying to lie now? Other than your ex, Micah's the only man you've ever freely spoken about. That's huge. And I'd like to point out you blushed while doing so."

"And I'd like to point out his mysteriousness about the reason behind his divorce."

"Maybe she cheated on him. That's not exactly something a guy wants to share."

A possibility I'd thought of. I moved to a different table, adjusting plates and teacups that did not need adjusting.

She shadowed me. "So you're really not interested in him? You're completely recovered from your Mardi Gras fever?"

"Mm-hmm."

"Mm-hmm, indeed." Heavy skepticism coated her words.

I skirted to another table, unnecessarily tweaking its place settings too. Now was not the time for a love-life discussion. "As I was saying. Micah will read a portion of the book, then we'll move on to making hats, which is where you come in." I swept my hand toward the well-organized arts and crafts worktable, where the kids would create themed paper hats. I'd purposely removed the bottles of glitter Micah had included in the bin he'd given me. Didn't he know glitter was the devil's confetti?

I'd also replaced the glue with scotch tape, and the regular crayons and markers with washable versions.

Julia took in the setup, nodding. "Cute. Do you have another activity for the teens?"

"No." Uncertainly once again flared in my stomach. "As long as there's food, they should be happy, right?"

"That's how my boys worked at that age." Her two sons now attended college out of state.

I scanned the table settings, biting the inside of my cheek. Hopefully Micah had secured enough for everyone to eat. The kitchen would be busy with our usual Saturday business. I couldn't impose on them if we ran out of food. Or absorb the extra cost.

"It's going to be great." Julia injected a little too much perk into her tone.

"I plan to play the movie too. That's a guaranteed hour and fifteen minutes of keeping kids still and quiet." I indicated the portable projector and screen normally used for weddings and anniversary parties as a way for the couples to show a loop of favorite photos. "I have everything required for a successful library event. Refreshments, a book reading, and an activity." I made a checkmark in the air with each item listed.

"And how long is this event?"

"Three hours."

She loosened a low whistle. "Three hours of maintaining a calm environment full of children." She winked. "You may need to pay me in more than beignets."

The back doors to the café opened, and Micah emerged.

My traitorous heart pitter-pattered. *Stop that.* He has a girl-friend. And a red flag from his divorce. A huge, unknown red flag.

A beautiful blonde made her way out behind him.

The pitter-pattering ceased. Sydney Dupré. The church sec-retary. *She's his girlfriend?* My heart shriveled.

Sydney wore jeans and a T-shirt with a stack of books on it that read *bookaholic*. With her golden hair and voluptuous curves, she was a gorgeous woman.

A gorgeous woman who loved books.

I rubbed the Crease. There was no competing with that. *Chin up, chin up.* I didn't want to compete anyway. Still . . . I shifted my shoulders and tugged the hem of my white Beignets & Books button-down. I'd left it untucked for a more casual appearance and paired it with burnt orange capri pants and flats. So basically, I looked like an upside-down Dreamsicle. Except even a Dreamsicle had more shape.

"From your reaction, that must be Micah." Julia's low voice snapped me from my shock. "Sydney's his girlfriend?"

"Looks like it." I waved at them, trying to pull the Landry Mask in place.

"Hey, girl!" Julia called, recovering from her own bout of surprise. Julia and Sydney worked closely together on the church's ministry with cleaning homes for the elderly.

Micah and Sydney descended the porch, and the sensation that I was dropping enveloped me. Very appropriate for an *Alice in Wonderland* party. But as I hit the bottom of my rabbit hole, reality struck. Sydney was Micah's type. The only thing Sydney and I had in common was our age. And Jesus. We couldn't have been more opposite. I irrationally felt like reverting to my fifth-grade self and stuffing my bra with Kleenex.

Well . . . This would make it that much easier to banish any zings or thoughts of him as being more than a friend. My vulnerable heart was once again safe. Plus, I wouldn't have to speculate any longer about the real reasons behind his marriage ending. My final theory would have to rest on them not agreeing on the thermostat setting. Or his wife having turned out to be a serial killer. And she'd one day escape prison, so whoever Micah was in a relationship with risked getting murdered.

"Thank you for coming," I said to Sydney, then introduced Julia and Micah. They exchanged handshakes.

"Thanks again for doing this." Micah's gaze skimmed the courtyard, his smile slightly fading. No doubt at the lack of pink lawn flamingos and gawdy decorations hanging from the tree. Though Sydney had been a surprise, his Hawaiian shirt was not. It featured the faces of Lewis Carroll's characters.

"You're welcome." I tucked my hair behind an ear and attempted to avoid looking directly at him. At his attractive face. His strong, clean-shaven jaw. Was I smelling pineapples again?

"How do y'all know each other?" Julia motioned between Sydney and Micah.

I tried not to gawk at my best friend for being so uncharacteristically forward.

Sydney fidgeted with her purse strap. "We met at church about a month ago."

My gaze swung to Micah. "You go to my church?" The surprise in my voice rang clear.

"If it's the same one as Sydney, then yes. Started when I returned to town." He slid his hands into his cargo shorts. "I've been attending with my dad on Saturday evenings."

"Ah." Julia jutted a thumb back and forth between us. "We attend on Sundays."

He nodded as his phone trilled. Pulling it from his pocket, he glanced at the screen, his forehead furrowing. "Excuse me, I need to take this." He moved away, aiming for the back wall, taking his tanned and toned calf muscles with him.

Ugh. This would've been so much easier if he'd had scrawny chicken legs.

Julia turned her vivid eyes on Sydney. "Are y'all dating?"

My mouth popped open. The woman was like a bloodhound set loose on a fresh prison escapee.

"Yes." Sydney seemed mesmerized by Mawmaw's mansion

and the outdoor space, her gaze absorbing everything. "Your place is so beautiful."

"Thank you," I said. With Sydney distracted, I shot Julia a *back off* look, and returned my focus to Sydney. "I appreciate you coming."

"I'm happy to help wherever you need me." The sincerity in Sydney's offer resonated.

Sigh. Sydney Dupré was too genuine of a person to dislike. Which I'd already known from the handful of times we'd interacted at church. "Well, I've got Julia manning the arts and crafts. Maybe you could keep an eye on the side gate." I gestured to the back left corner. "To ensure little ones don't slip out unattended. Oh, and I set a refreshment table for the parents over there too. And a drink dispenser for the iced tea. If you notice it running low, it'd be great if you could let me know."

"Sure thing." Sydney headed to her assigned post, her long blond hair billowing out behind her. Like a full-figured Rapunzel.

The back doors flew open, and a harried woman with a minibus of kids under the age of nine emptied onto the porch. The children beelined for Micah, stampeding between the tables as though they were bulls in the streets of Pamplona. "Careful!" the lady hollered after them.

Micah ended his call in time to offer high fives and fist bumps to each of the boys and girls.

"They're early." I glimpsed the time on my phone, the muscles in my neck tensing.

The kids lost interest in Micah and started darting through the courtyard in different directions. The woman who'd brought them collapsed onto a chair at one of the tables, not seeming to care about keeping an eye on her brood. She helped herself to one of the cupcakes. Those were for the children! *Go, go gadget cattle prod.*

Micah approached, pocketing his cell and following my line of vision. "Easy now." Too much teasing dusted his words.

Julia piped in with a conspiratorial grin. "I didn't think Kate would be the one breaking her own calm-environment feel."

Before I could shush either of them, another wave of kids and parents sailed out the back doors. "It's not supposed to start for another twenty minutes."

"Yeah." Micah shrugged. "People always show up early. Especially when food's involved. I'd planned to be here sooner but got caught up at my dad's before picking up Sydney."

I bullied the Crease. "It would've been nice if you'd told me."

"Sorry." A slight wince puckered his face. "I figured you'd been to enough of these things with Hayley to know."

"We always arrived right on time."

He snickered. "Of course you did."

I tried to tamp down my glare at him. Tried and failed.

He fought a smile. "Where's Hayley?"

"Probably lining my bedroom walls with pictures of emaciated Chihuahuas."

Julia chuckled.

Micah glanced between us. "Am I missing something?"

I shook my head. "Hayley most likely won't make an appearance until Emma does."

"Hmpf." His lips pursed. "I figured she'd be down here running everything. She seemed pretty excited about the event being here."

"She did?" That was news to me.

Several kids circled the fountain like sharks. Another child ducked beneath a table, rattling it and the tiered serving tray sitting atop it.

I quickly took the stairs up to the porch. "Excuse me!" I called out in a loud teacher voice, clapping my hands.

Everyone's attention turned my way. Micah came to stand beside me.

"Hello, and welcome to today's library event. The tables here in the middle are for the kids so they can be closer to the activities we have planned. Parents, if you're comfortable with letting your child sit by themselves, we have a section for you in the back corner." I motioned to the area, and Sydney waved with a lovely smile.

My heart withered.

Another swell of parents and older kids made their way out and down the steps, filtering to the sides.

"Before we take our seats and get started, I want to review a few rules."

A collective moan echoed from the younger guests.

"Number one." I held up a finger. "The fountain is off-limits. It's filled with chemicals that could kill you."

The children closest to the water feature backed away with wide eyes.

Micah gave a muted snort.

I nailed him with a scowl and lowered my voice. "Chlorine is toxic."

I redirected my attention to the crowd. "Rule number two is no running. And no climbing in the gardens or any of the trees." *Oof.* I sounded like my mom.

A little boy around eight years old raised his hand.

He was instantly my favorite child here. I pointed to him. "Thank you for raising your hand. What's your question?"

"Rule number two is actually three rules."

Several snickers erupted. Including from Micah.

My mouth slanted. Okay, maybe that kid wasn't my favorite. "Rule number three, er, the last rule, is to remember this is a place of business. Even though we're outside, we need to use our inside voices."

Micah shifted, scratching the back of his neck.

I reached for the copy of *Alice in Wonderland* resting on the porch railing and handed it to him.

"You good now?" His dark green eyes twinkled.

I lifted my chin. "Yes."

He turned to the group and pitched his voice. "It's so great to see all of you here today. We've still got a few minutes before we start, so feel free to find a seat or visit the bathroom, which is inside." He motioned to Mawmaw's beloved antique French doors.

I envisioned kids running in and out, slamming them. Roughly handling the precious vintage doorknobs. Leaving the doors propped open wouldn't do. The last thing I needed was a fly infestation in the café or the A/C leaking out. Maybe I'd take up residence there, acting as a doorman.

I moved toward them as Penny poked her head out. Bad news loitered in her eyes as she neared. "The internet's down."

Mangy mutts.

"Is something wrong?" Julia approached.

"The internet's out." I turned to Penny. "Did you try rebooting the router?"

"Yes. It didn't work."

Julia's attention slid from Penny to me. "What's that mean for everything?"

"It doesn't affect the café," I said. "Our ordering and payment system runs on an on-site server."

Penny pushed her ponytail off her shoulder. "And the program will store all the credit card swipes and process them once reconnected to the internet."

"That's good," Julia said, infusing a super-positive Mary Poppins tone. "So it's not a big deal."

I moved from pressing the Crease to massaging my temples. "I can't stream the movie."

Julia's expression plunged, as though her Mary Poppins umbrella had been hit with buckshot.

"I already called our service provider," Penny said. "Everything looks fine on their end. They said it must be an internal issue."

Ugh. "What about our local tech people?"

Penny gave a brisk nod. "I left them a voice mail and sent an email through my phone. But since it's the weekend, I'm not sure how responsive they'll be."

Deep breath in. Deep breath out. "Thanks, Penny. I appreciate it."

With an encouraging smile, she departed.

Another round of caretakers and kids poured into the courtyard. Too many to keep track of. *God, You've multiplied fish and loaves of bread. How about cupcakes?* A little girl darted inside, slamming the French doors, the glass panes rattling. I flinched and switched back to rubbing the Crease, knowing it would be in full pucker mode. Scanning the area, trying to come up with a viable solution to fix the movie problem and the possible shortage of food, my sights paused on Micah at the base of the stairs. Gone was his earlier teasing façade. Concern emanated from his jade gaze.

He neared, pausing midway up the steps. "You're looking a little pale."

"The internet's out, which means we can't stream the movie."

"Well . . ." His stare descended to the book in his hands. "We'll come up with something to fill the time. We could play charades." His eyes veered up to mine, a sparkle chasing away the unease that had just been there. "Or I could go get those croquet sets. I know how much you loved that suggestion."

An unexpected blip of lightness broke through at his goading, easing the clamp of my molars. "N. O."

His answering smile barely contained his chuckle.

The audacity! "This isn't funny."

Tucking the book under one arm, he rubbed his jaw with his free hand. "It's also not the end of the world."

"He's right." Julia touched my elbow. "Let me call Wyatt and see if he can help."

"Wyatt!" Hope soared from the depths of my rabbit hole. "That's right! He's a technology whiz!"

Micah edged up the final step. "Who's Wyatt?"

Julia held her phone to her ear. "My single and handsome brother-in-law." She waggled her brows at me. It hadn't been the first time she'd expressed her desire to set me and Wyatt up.

I smothered a sigh. *Here we go.*

10

I WOULD HAVE MADE AN EXCELLENT SOLDIER. Three hours and fifteen minutes later, I still stood at my post at the French doors. Approximately twenty children from ages four to fourteen had initially shown up. Micah had publicly thanked me, rallying a round of applause that quickly died with my reviewing the rules once again. And adding in being careful with the French doors.

After getting the lowdown on the itinerary, most of the older kids had fled. Hayley and her BFF Emma had deemed the tea party too uncool to participate in. They'd retreated to my prayer nook in the back corner, where the massive trunk of the live oak provided a barrier. Even now, they sat shoulder to shoulder, their heads tipped over their phones. *Sigh*.

Micah's words from earlier ghosted through me. Had Hayley really been excited about today? Thinking back, the only time I remembered her showing interest was on the drive home from the library the day I'd agreed to host the event. She'd ridden in the passenger seat, flipping through the book, and asked what I was planning. I'd been too dazed by Micah's wild suggestions that I'd responded with an "I don't know yet."

Oh no. I cupped my forehead, my eyes sliding shut. Why hadn't I seized that moment to include her in all of this? I should've asked for her input from the get-go. This could have been our chance to do something together. Something other than bickering over a dog. And I'd wasted it. Returning my gaze to Hayley, a heavy dullness weighed in my chest. Claire wouldn't have botched this. Even Micah had picked up on Hayley's interest. My throat grew thick, defeat and guilt duking it out in my midsection. I'd failed.

I'd viewed this event as a task to work through as quickly and painlessly as possible. *Huh.* Micah had also been correct in pointing out my need for control. Though it irked me to admit it, that science project we'd worked on together in high school had been better because of him challenging me. Maybe God had aligned our paths again for a similar reason. I skimmed the courtyard and spied Micah crouched next to a table, talking to a little girl with glasses. He wore a hat he'd created with no less than three sets of rabbit ears. *So ridiculous.* But like earlier, another blip of lightness broke through, easing that weight on my chest.

Despite Micah's best efforts to make the arts-and-crafts activity fun, only a few preschoolers actually donned their creations. I'd thought hat making would keep the boys and girls occupied for forty-five minutes. I'd been wrong. With the movie still a no-go at that point, Micah had rallied everyone for another session of reading, changing his voice for each of the characters, using sweeping arm motions and over-the-top expressions. At least he'd garnered some chuckles.

Thankfully, Julia's brother-in-law, Wyatt Reed, had arrived and fixed the internet problem before Micah's voice had given out. I'd tried to pay Wyatt for his services, but he'd turned me down, only accepting an order of beignets as payment. I scanned the area and found him standing on the fringes. Though he'd repaired the glitch, he'd stuck around. Probably to ensure the issue didn't return until the event had ended. In his early forties, Wyatt was the epitome of handsome. Tall, dark hair, solid build. But after meeting him at Julia's wedding last year, we hadn't hit it off. Even if my heart had been open to the idea of dating, he held a quiet reservedness that seemed impenetrable.

The movie wrapped up, and I took in the sullen faces of the handful of children who'd been forced to stick it out. *Sheesh Louise.* Several kids had laid their heads on the tables and were dozing. I pursed my lips. Maybe only serving iced chamomile tea had backfired. But I hadn't wanted to introduce caffeine of any kind. On the plus side, their parents appeared happy not to be chasing them around.

I gave up my station at the French doors, descended the steps, and slumped onto a chair next to Julia, who sat alone at the arts-and-crafts table. Beneath the remains of the hat-making activity, dots and smears in varying marker colors covered the tablecloth. Thank goodness it was disposable.

Julia adjusted her Cheshire Cat hat. "Did you slip Benadryl in the food?"

"At least my courtyard is still in one piece."

"And your murderous bird didn't make an appearance." She snickered. "Between him and your killer fountain, it's a wonder anyone survived."

I straightened. "In my defense, if a kid had scooped a cup of water from the fountain and drank it, they would've gotten sick."

"Fair point." She fought a smile.

I gathered the crayons within reach, placing them in a Ziploc bag. The whites, browns, and grays lay ignored, their points as sharp as the day they'd rolled off the Crayola assembly line.

Julia followed suit with the markers. "When did you find out Micah has a girlfriend?"

My motions slowed. Reflexively, the Landry Mask stood at the ready to slip into place. But this was Julia. Eleven years ago, she'd been the one person who'd seen me at my worst. To the outside world, I only mourned the passing of Claire and

Adrian. No one dared mention the humiliating death of my relationship with Ryan. But Julia had known I also grieved the loss of my almost-marriage. Of what I'd thought my future was going to be. "A few weeks back. But I didn't realize it was Sydney until today." I glanced across the courtyard to where Sydney spoke with one of the parents. "She's perfect. Just look at her."

"No one's perfect." Julia snapped a cap onto one of the markers. "According to Sydney they're not dating seriously."

My attention zipped to my nosy best friend. "You asked her that?"

She lifted a shoulder, adding the marker to a Ziploc bag. "Not directly but yes. They're still in that getting-to-know-you phase."

"Doesn't matter." I abandoned the crayons and collected the scraps of paper that had been snipped from the hat creations, wadding them into a ball.

"Because you're not interested anyway."

"Exactly."

Julia added the final marker to her bag and sealed it. "They don't seem lovey-dovey. I haven't seen them hold hands. Or sneak in a kiss. Not even a peck."

I stopped pummeling my makeshift stress ball. "Not everyone is pro-PDA like you and your husband." I tossed the paper into the nearby garbage can. *She shoots, she scores.*

"I'd like to point out that though this event has been a total snoozer for the kids, it's been extremely entertaining on the adult level."

I surveyed the other grown-ups. Most of them had taken a seat and zombied into their phones. Except for the first mom who'd showed up. She'd spent her time scarfing cupcakes and trying to weasel free beignets.

Julia leaned in, as did the Cheshire Cat sitting atop her head. "Wyatt's been watching Sydney, and Sydney's been eyeing the dessert trays with what appears to be extreme longing."

Glancing in their direction, it did appear that though Sydney and Micah were in a conversation, her vision was locked on a plate of the remaining cupcakes. And then, on the edge of the festivities, Wyatt lingered. With the way he glanced Sydney's way, maybe he hadn't stuck around to ensure there weren't any other technical difficulties.

Julia tapped my forearm. "Do you want to know who Micah's keeping tabs on?" The Cheshire Cat must've sunken its claws into her brain because the mischief in her tone made the answer clear. And ridiculous.

"You're wrong." I returned my attention to cleaning up, collecting the safety scissors. "Besides, that all sounds like a love triangle. Or a love octagon. And, no, thank you, to any part of it. I have too much on my hands with Ryan popping up on me like Whac-A-Mole. And there isn't a hammer big enough to clobber his inflated head."

"Ryan's been here?" Her eyes widened. "At the café?"

"Twice. His first visit was to purely irritate me about the Vieux Carré Café."

She removed her hat, placing it on the table. "When was this?"

"The same day as the dinner from hades with my parents." Which had led to me recombing through my finances and considering a withdrawal against my 401(k). Or hocking my nonvital organs on the black market. In the end, I'd decided to stick to plan A. I'd completed a mountain of paperwork for the New Orleans Redevelopment Authority and scheduled a meeting with them. "The second time he showed up I didn't even talk to him. He just ate and left. And was a skimpy tipper." I dropped a pair of scissors into the storage bin.

"Do you think he's trying to rekindle things?"

I blinked, the idea spreading over me. Was he? He *had* been a little flirty. Plus, his lack of a wedding ring and Facebook relationship status marked him as unattached. But . . . no, the evidence of our history kicked that possibility to the curb. I still had Hayley, who he'd yet to inquire after. And the only interest I had in Ryan involved him experiencing excruciating pain. "I think he views me as competition, and he's trying to get a feel for what he's up against."

"Or he's trying to get a feel on *your* feelings for him. What if he regrets what he did and wants you back? You're gorgeous and loyal and kind—"

"Not to him."

"I'm just saying that could be Ryan's motive. Or side motive. You'd be a fabulous catch for any guy, including Wyatt." Julia returned her gaze to her brother-in-law.

I snorted. "You transitioned to that brilliantly."

She gave an unrepentant shrug. "There's really no hope for Wyatt? He's so great. As a former Green Beret, he can handle anything from espionage to home repairs."

"Didn't you just speculate about his interest in Sydney?"

Her mouth scrunched.

"No matter." I held up a hand. "Wyatt didn't give me the zings the last time we met, and he doesn't give me the zings now."

Julia nodded solemnly. "The zings are very important."

Of their own volition, my eyes sought and found Micah, making his way over. He stopped a few feet away and slid his hands into his pockets. "Julia, I wanted to thank you for your help today."

She waved him off, pushing to a stand. "I was happy to. Can I get y'all anything from inside? I'm going to grab some coffee."

Micah and I both declined.

Julia took a step away, then paused. "Micah, when I told you we attend church on Sundays, I forgot to mention we go to the second service. It starts at eleven o'clock . . . you know . . . if your dad ever wants to try a different time. And we sit on the left side of the sanctuary. In the middle."

Good grief, was she going to drop a location pin tomorrow when we were in our seats and text it to him? And *hello*. He has a girlfriend. Regardless of Sydney expressing her and Micah's relationship as not being serious, they'd still DTR'd. Plus, that huge red flag rippled above his head.

"Thanks," Micah said to her. "I'll let my dad know."

Wearing a satisfied expression, Julia departed.

Micah moved her folding chair, putting additional space between us before he sat. He slipped off his six-eared rabbit hat, revealing a full ring of smooshed hair and a mark from the paper across his forehead. "Do you have a dead body under this table?" He lifted the tablecloth, peering below.

"What kind of question is that?"

He eased back, the seat creaking beneath his weight. "You look guilty."

Guilty of illegally crushing on you. I picked up a worn orange crayon. Its paper had been peeled, its tip a dull nub. Into the bag it went.

Micah added a tape dispenser to the arts-and-crafts bin. "I wanted to thank you again too."

"And rub the disaster in my face."

"No." One corner of his mouth lifted. "Well, maybe a little." He collected the remaining rolls of tape.

A dramatized gasp broke out from Hayley and Emma's direction. They were in their own little world over there, when they should've been a part of the happenings over here. My gaze wafted to the table before me and a rough outline of a small hand traced in purple marker. "Something you said earlier has been nagging me."

Smile lines fanned the corners of his eyes. "Just like old times."

"I'm trying to pay you a compliment."

"Using the word *nagging*?"

I fought an eye roll. If the Lord had dropped Micah momentarily onto my path for a reason, I'd need to pray for extra patience. "You said Hayley had been excited about today."

He nodded.

"Apparently, I ruined that excitement." As if on cue, Hayley and Emma abandoned the courtyard, making their way upstairs. I swallowed a sigh. "I've also been thinking how this was not a memorable event for these kids. Not like the ones Hayley had growing up. And today is certainly not one she'll think back fondly on in her old age."

Micah's stare remained channeled on me. Quiet. Absorbing.

I shifted in my seat. "I think I'm ready to concede to you handling the next function here."

He studied his hands, a gentle smile spreading across his face.

Bewilderment sprinkled over me. I'd expected him to whoop with triumph or toss a tease my way. Was his brain too busy, already spinning with ideas for the following party? "I'm still not allowing croquet. Or catapults that launch hard projectiles."

His gaze rose, connecting with mine. "What about catapults that launch soft projectiles?"

I huffed a laugh.

The credits on the movie began rolling, rousing the remaining children from their seats.

Micah reached for an overlooked marker. "What if we plan the next event together, with Hayley?"

"That would be . . ." Too many sensations fluttered through me, no doubt playing across my features. Hope, relief, possibility. "Perfect. That would be perfect." *Goldilocks.*

Pushing to his feet, he chucked the marker into the bin and unleashed a devastating smile . . . aimed at Sydney, who headed our way.

God, other than extra patience, can You send some Bubble Wrap for my heart? Just in case.

11

THAT MONDAY I WOKE TO THE SOUND of something far worse than
an alarm clock. It was the sound of puking.

I bolted from bed and across the hallway to Hayley's bathroom, my bare feet slapping against the wood floors. Wearing
a Zelda T-shirt and pajama pants with dogs of various breeds,
Hayley retched, her slight body bent over the toilet. I gathered
her hair back. "It's okay."

She moaned, crumpling to her knees and heaving again.

With my stomach twisting in solidarity, I frantically searched
the countertop for a hair tie. Instead, I found an explosion of
beauty products. Eyeshadow and lip gloss in varying colors
scattered one side of the sink. An open compact of powder,
blush, eyeliner, mascara. The other side packed with gels, foam-
ing mousses, and a flat iron.

There. An elastic with a knot of Hayley's red hair entangled
on it.

Holding her tresses with one hand, I stretched, reaching
with my other for the band and grasping it with my fingertips.
Gently, I fastened her limp locks into a low ponytail. "Do you
feel cold?"

Another moan and round of vomiting.

Discarded towels—that Hayley hadn't laundered this past weekend like she was supposed to—covered the floor. I stepped over them and opened the linen cabinet next to her sink. Only one clean washcloth remained. After running it under cool water, I wrung it out and draped it along the back of her neck. Her shoulders spiked, and she shivered, sinking to her butt on top of another heap of used towels. The pallid color to her face did not bode well. I placed the back of my palm to her forehead. *Warm.* I leaned over, placing my lips to her forehead. *Hot. I knew it.*

In the kitchen I grabbed the ear thermometer from the medicine cabinet and a cup of water. Back in the bathroom, I took her temperature, eliciting my own groan at the results: 101.5.

"Here." I rested the cup in her hands, wondering if she could even hold it.

She swished and spit into the toilet.

"Have you had any diarrhea?"

She shook her head, looking more pathetic than the dogs in those ASPCA commercials.

"I'm guessing you picked up a virus."

Another moan. She handed me the cup and lumbered to her feet, me hovering at her side. She made an attempt at brushing her teeth and took a tentative sip of water. Holding her elbow, I ushered her to her room. At the threshold, Hayley's talent for creating her own wall-to-wall carpeting continued. Except instead of towels, a mixture of clothes greeted us. Plaid skirts, T-shirts, jeans, pajamas, socks. We trudged through them to her bed, where I tucked her in, only covering her with a sheet since she was running a fever. If I gave her Tylenol, would she be able to hold it down? I glanced at the clock on the bedside table. *6:05 a.m.* The pediatricians' office didn't open until eight.

I set her water on the nightstand and returned to my bedroom, grabbing my phone.

Mayté answered after several rings. "Everything okay?"

Dishes clattering and small appliances roaring permeated her background, the morning prep well underway for when we opened in two hours.

"Hayley's sick."

"Sorry to hear that." Unease blended within her tone. "But you're both banned from the café."

Despite the situation I smiled at her directness. It was one of the characteristics I adored about her. "I agree. The last thing we need is the staff or customers getting sick. I've got my laptop, so I'll process payroll from up here." And hopefully I'd have time to review the previous month's financial statements. My meeting with the New Orleans Redevelopment Authority was Friday, and I wanted to ensure I was prepared to have my best shot at one of their grants. Making an offer on Claire's dream café location felt so close. My own stomach churned, and it had nothing to do with Hayley's current condition. "If you need anything, let me know."

"We'll be fine. Especially with Penny on the schedule. I'll make my abuela's chicken noodle soup for tonight's dinner and leave it at your door. It'll fix Hayley up and keep you healthy too."

"That'd be perfect. Thank you."

Unlike me, Mayté loved to cook and was talented at it. Shortly after Claire's death, she'd been horrified to discover Hayley and I had been living off takeout, frozen foods, and peanut butter sandwiches. We'd struck a deal for her to prepare us meals utilizing the café's kitchen. Mayté had free rein over what she made us for dinner, and I compensated her for it. For the two days a week Mayté was off, we survived on our own. Or had leftovers since Mayté tended to make bigger portions before her time off from the café.

At 7:55 a.m. I dialed the doctors' office. For the record, I was a pediatrician's nightmare. I'd quickly gained that status the first year of custody over Hayley. Mild fevers, colds, tummy aches that could have been appendicitis, allergies that could possibly be a cold that could possibly lead to pneumonia. I called for everything. Overkill? Most likely. But Hayley's well-being rested solely on me. There was no way I'd let her or Claire down. And as far as being a nuisance to the doctors' office, I'd also periodically dropped off treats as a thank-you for putting up with me. After a multitude of rings, a generic message came on, stating they weren't open yet, and to head to the ER if it was a true emergency. I disconnected and called right back.

At 8:05 a.m. they finally answered.

"Hi." In that one word I heard the edginess in my voice. "My thirteen-year-old's throwing up and running a fever. I'd like to bring her in."

"There's a stomach bug going around." The receptionist spoke with bored indifference. "That's probably what she's got. It just takes waiting out. Does she have any other symptoms?"

Was she about to give me the brush-off? I needed answers beyond a guess at her illness based merely on two symptoms. I needed to know exactly what I was dealing with so I could come up with a game plan. "Um, she's very weak." Technically I *had* helped her back to bed. "And she has a fever. Did I mention that?"

"What's her temperature?"

"102." I winced. Yes, I'd rounded up. But it was a perfectly acceptable thing to do. Even the Louisiana Department of Revenue rounded the dollar amounts on the café's sales tax forms. Plus, Hayley's normal temperature ran low.

The tapping of a keyboard came across the line. "Can you bring her at one o'clock?"

My shoulders sagged, my grip on the phone loosening. "Yes. Thank you."

The stomach bug had turned out to be the flu. Despite an answer to her illness and instructions of fluids, fever meds, and rest, my anxiety had only festered. Everything I'd given Hayley Monday and Tuesday had come right back up. Water, Gatorade, bananas, crackers, Mayté's soup. To keep her from living at the toilet, I'd positioned my gumbo pot next to her in bed. At least it'd gotten some use. One saving grace was her fever subsiding. But that relief had fallen way to the fear she was dehydrated.

Julia, who was in North Carolina visiting her boys at college, suggested contacting the pediatrician and asking them to call in a prescription for antinausea meds. The worry monster clawing at the lining of my stomach somewhat eased its scratching at that suggestion. But not enough. I'd convinced myself a phone conversation wouldn't suffice. By late Tuesday afternoon I'd packed Hayley and the gumbo pot into the car and toted her to the pediatrician. They'd reassured me she wasn't dehydrated and had prescribed antinausea medication.

We now waited in the drive-through line at Walgreens. This evening we were supposed to be having a brainstorming session on the next library function with a hot and not-so-single librarian. I'd count that postponement of extra time with Micah as a tiny silver lining. As time to get my still lingering Mardi Gras fever under control.

Speaking of lingering illnesses, I peered Hayley's way. With her eyes closed, she rested her head against the passenger-side door. Her pale auburn lashes contrasted to the dark circles beneath them. Her slumped posture radiated she had all the strength of soggy French bread. This was by far the sickest she'd ever been. And despite that, for the past thirty-four hours of persistent vomiting and hardly any sleep, she hadn't complained. Not once.

She was so much like Claire. I pulled in a deep breath and couldn't help but smile at the thought.

Hayley straightened with a grimace. I shifted the gumbo pot on her lap, and she leaned over it, dry heaving for a long minute. Strands of her hair had escaped her ponytail, and I tucked them behind her ear. "Thanks," she whispered weakly, then returned her head to rest against the door.

Despite Hayley's onset of teen moodiness, she was a good kid. A good kid who'd been dealt a lousy hand in life. Steady pressure built in my chest, pain jabbing at my heart. She was a good kid who had never given me real trouble of any kind. A good kid with one set of rotten grandparents and another set who'd long ago gone to be with the Lord. A good kid who hadn't disobeyed a single rule I'd put in place. A good kid who never asked for anything.

Well . . . that wasn't exactly true.

I gazed at her, my throat swelling with emotion, and squeezed out the words I knew I'd come to regret. "You can get a dog."

It seemed the miracle drug for beating the flu was the promise of a pet. By the next morning, Hayley had springboarded back to health. Thursday and Friday we'd resumed our regular routine. Saturday, though, we had not.

I exited the parking lot of the animal rescue center, positive we had just adopted a naked mole rat. The volunteer at the shelter had assured me it was a hairless Chihuahua mix. Their best guess labeled the critter as part pug. I still wasn't convinced it was of any canine classification.

Hayley sat in the passenger seat, snuggling the creature, cooing to it.

I shook my head. I'd planned to navigate her toward a really, really, really old dog. Like two paws in the grave. Or one of those mature, trendy dogs with three legs everyone had nowadays. We could've named it Lieutenant Dan. But her heart had latched onto a puppy. A puppy! I'd had zero dog experience as a child, which meant a puppy was worse. Topping it off, this animal was ugly. Hideous. A face only a mother could love. And apparently not even that, because its mother had rejected it.

Hayley cuddled the pale rat against her neck. "I'm naming her Precious."

I cringed and came to a stop for a red light. "From *The Hobbit?*"

"No! Because she's so precious. Look at her." She tenderly extended the quaking dog toward me. Eyes the size of Ping-Pong balls. Ears like a gremlin. Skin the palest of pinks. Several scraggly strands of white hair poked through its wrinkled hide.

I fought a shudder. At least Precious was small. She wouldn't take up much room or require a lot of food. And any accidents she had would be small too.

"Well?" Hayley's ginger brows rose expectantly.

The light turned green, and I accelerated through the intersection. "For the next library event we could do a *Lord of the Rings* theme. She could be a prop."

Hayley shot me a look, nuzzling the dog to her chest. "Don't listen to her, Precious. You're beautiful. Yes, you are."

I rolled my eyes. At least Hayley was talking to me . . . well, mostly to the dog. Regardless, I'd take that as a win. And after yesterday, I needed one. My meeting with the New Orleans Redevelopment Authority hadn't gone well. The Vieux Carré Café didn't meet the zone location requirements of their target areas for their Small Business Grant Assistance Program. It was time for plan B. I'd now focus on a federal SBA loan. As a woman-owned company, hopefully it could give me some extra points with securing one. And hopefully without using Mawmaw's mansion as collateral. I rubbed the Crease. Darn that clause in her will.

"Why won't she eat?" Hayley sat on the kitchen floor, her brows pinched. Precious, with a slight tremor I was beginning to think was permanent, sniffed Hayley's socked feet.

I occupied a barstool at the island, trying to hide my scowl as I surveyed the receipt from our trip to PetSmart. It was long enough to be the tail to a kite. "Like every living creature, she'll eat when she's hungry."

After adopting Precious, we'd stopped at PetSmart. I'd strode through their doors with the intention of purchasing six items: a crate, leash, collar, food, and food-and-water dishes. We'd ended up with a ridiculous number of things for a dog barely weighing two pounds. One of those items? A toothbrush. For a dog!

"But she hasn't eaten all day. She's got to be hungry." For the millionth time, Hayley positioned Precious before her bowl. A tiny pink bowl more fitting for a hamster. Precious stared at the dry puppy kibble, her long, skinny rat tail shaking between her hind legs.

The thinnest thread of sympathy stitched into my heart. "She's probably stressed. Today's been a big change for her."

"Oh." Hayley leaned back, pondering. "She could be like you. You don't eat when you're stressed."

I blinked. When had she noticed that tendency of mine?

Precious's head lifted, and she released a string of whimpers. Hayley scooped her up, and she quieted. Great. We had a puppy who was arm spoiled. Just like Hayley had been as a baby.

That night brought zero sleep. One of the rules I'd implemented with getting a dog was when we slept, the animal would reside in a kennel in the laundry room. Precious had railed against that decree, her whimpering cries leveling up to full-out, earsplitting wails. It was as though the dog pound scene from *Lady and the Tramp* had been playing on repeat. How could such a small creature make so much noise?

Hayley had shuffled into my room around two in the morning, begging me to let her free the dog. That she'd keep a close eye on it in her bed. Exhausted and a little queasy, I'd relented.

Several hours later that mild queasiness had morphed into deep nausea. I now lay in bed, hoping it would pass. Hoping for a little more rest. It was Sunday. The only day the café was closed. The only day I could sleep in. The sun's rays crept through my blinds, welcoming the day and taunting me. My stomach twisted and lurched. I threw the covers back and sprang from the bed. My foot landed in something soft and warm. *No.* I gritted my teeth. *No way.* I glanced down and sure enough, dog poop squished up between my toes. Yesterday's thread of sympathy for that rat snipped in two. Holding down the contents of my stomach and a curse, I hobbled on my heel to the bathroom and hurled.

12

SOMEHOW, I'D SURVIVED SUNDAY. An enormous help was Hayley completely taking care of Precious, even cleaning the gift the dog had deposited by my bed. But by the next morning, I was certain the Grim Reaper had left me a calling card at my new address, the toilet.

Thank goodness Emma's mom was on carpool duty today. She'd picked Hayley up and would bring Hayley home after her and Emma's time at the library after school. Our quick exchange of texts had revealed that the flu had wreaked havoc on their family last week. A piece of information Hayley had neglected to tell me.

I sat on the cold tile floor in my bathroom, sipping Gatorade and trying to muster the strength to return to bed. A clammy chill crawled across my skin. With a groan I reached up for the digital thermometer on the counter. Took my temperature twice. Both readings confirmed my fever-free status. Yesterday I'd ran the identical temps Hayley had. And like Hayley, the fever had subsided quickly. A good thing since I hadn't been able to keep any meds down. Or liquids. Clearly I'd caught the same flu strain. I had all her symptoms and a new level of sympathy for what she'd gone through.

Resting my aching back against the bottom cabinets, I picked up my phone from the floor and composed a group text to Mayté and Penny. I was supposed to cover the hostess shift this afternoon. And process payroll. They both replied back that they had everything covered. After thanking them, I leaned over the toilet and hurled again.

Precious's cry pierced the air. Crated in the laundry room, she wasn't a happy camper. But there was no way I could look after her. Plus, being caged when we weren't home was her future. At least until she was potty trained. Had this been a normal Monday, she was right where she'd be anyway. Her whining continued. Incessantly. I cleaned myself up and dragged my body to bed, hoping the rat-dog would have mercy on me and hush so I could sleep.

Ping.

I startled at the sound of a text hitting my phone. Through a groggy haze, I rubbed my eyes, peering at my alarm clock on the nightstand. *3:00 p.m.* I patted the covers all around me, unearthed my cell, and confirmed it was still Monday. Thanks to Precious, I'd only drifted off for twenty minutes. A message from Emma's mom previewed on my screen.

Elise

Slight change of plans. Something's come up
and I can't bring Hayley home from the library,
but Jacob will. Just wanted you to know.

No flashed through my brain in bold neon, and I pushed myself to a sitting position. My last encounter with the sixteen-year-old came to mind. I'd been dropping Hayley off at Emma's house. Jacob had grunted a "'Sup" by way of greeting as he'd climbed into his sedan. White earbuds had clogged his ears and shaggy hair had covered his eyes. If those driving hindrances hadn't been enough, the kid had peeled out of their driveaway like he drove a getaway car, nearly clipping my bumper. I wouldn't trust him piloting Hayley in a go-kart in an enclosed track, much less a real vehicle on real streets. A blip of energy from somewhere deep within pumped through my dehydrated veins.

I texted a nice thank-you-but-no-thank-you and sunk back into my pillows.

An hour later I slogged down the stairs, lugging the gumbo pot. Humid wind swirled around me, the skies completely masked in dark clouds. A bolt of lightning zigzagged in the distance. I flinched. Looked like we were in for one of our infamous pop-up thunderstorms. My strength drained with each step. *You can do this. Once you get to the car, you'll be okay.* I'd regain my vigor after sitting a beat. I reached the landing as a deep rumble of thunder broke across the atmosphere. The live oak's branches swayed above me, leaves ripping free and twirling in the air. Hopefully I could make it to the library and back before the rain started.

I shuffled past glob after glob of bird poop on the ground. "Cést Fou," I grumbled, despite my raw throat. "I hope lightning strikes you." In my car, I shoved the pot to the passenger seat and cranked the engine. The radio instantly filled the silence, squawking the Emergency Alert System notification. A tornado warning had been issued for all of Orleans parish. *Great.*

I caught my reflection in the rearview mirror and blinked. Was that . . . lice? I leaned closer and picked one of the white dots, realization dawning. Darn those new towels! They'd only been through one wash and were still shedding little fuzzies. *Ugh!* I didn't have enough time or energy to pick them all free. I shifted the car into reverse, my stomach lurching. I reached for the gumbo pot, hoping the queasiness would pass. What else could possibly go wrong in this moment?

My *low gas* indicator light flipped on.

Sarah McLachlan.

With hardly any vehicles on the streets due to the weather, I made it to the library in record time. I pulled into a parking spot and cut the engine to save gas. After texting Hayley that I was here and to hurry, I leaned my head against the window and slid my eyes shut. That was much better. I could do this. I just had to get home. Hayley could help me up the stairs. Maybe I'd lie on the floor in my walk-in shower. At this point it wasn't like I was vomiting food. And lying in a shower seemed more sanitary than next to a toilet.

Tap-tap-tap. I lifted my head (when had it gotten so heavy?) and glanced up to find Micah peering through the window. Concern and a sense of urgency layered his features.

He pulled on the door handle to no avail. A crease formed between his brows. "You need to get inside." His voice muffled through the glass.

"I'm sick." I massaged my throbbing temples. "Just send Hayley out."

He shook his head. "We're under a tornado warning." He tried the handle again. "Unlock the door, please." His *please* wasn't so much a pleasantry as an impatient request.

I hit the unlock button.

He immediately opened the door. Warm air and the scent of impending rain barreled in. "You need to get inside. Now." The wind pulled at his hair and T-Rex Hawaiian shirt, highlighting the flatness of his stomach.

Gracious. Speaking of dinosaurs, he had that Chris Pratt–*Jurassic World* vibe. One hundred percent smoldering intensity and protectiveness. I angled away, raising my hand to cover my mouth. "I have the flu. I don't want you catching it."

"If you don't exit that car, I *will* toss you over my shoulder."

I dropped my hand, indignation sparking within. "You will not Rhett Butler me!"

In one fluid motion, he leaned in and across me, and un-clicked my seatbelt. "Start moving, Scarlett."

He'd done it so fast I hadn't had the chance to protest his action. Or enjoy the sensation of his body being in such close proximity. And was that cinnamon I'd smelled? *Stop that. He has a girlfriend. And was possibly divorced because he hates children.* No. That wasn't right. He wouldn't have become a librarian if that was true.

Lightning flashed along the opaque sky, and I flinched. Micah stubbornly held his ground, waving his hand at me to hurry.

With a grunt of annoyance, I yanked my keys from the igni-tion, grabbed my purse and the pot (thankfully empty), and maneuvered out of the car. My tender stomach rolled. *Lord, please don't let me puke in front of this man.*

Micah took my purse and keys but left the pot in my care. "Remind me never to eat anything of the gumbo or soup variety you've prepared." He shut my door, and we made our way up the concrete path to the entrance.

"I'd have to actually cook to do that."

Thunder boomed and the clouds broke, a steady stream of warm rain showering down. I hurried as fast as I could, which wasn't saying much. Still, Micah stuck to my side. By the time we'd ascended the three steps to the covered porch, the strength I'd built up sitting in the car had vanished. I placed the pot on the ground, ready to take a seat next to it.

Micah looped my purse strap over his shoulder, grabbed the pot, slid an arm around my waist, and all but carried me forward.

Hayley opened the door, her eyes wide and lips pressed in a grim line. "You look terrible."

"I'm fine."

She closed the door behind us and took the pot from Micah.

He continued half-toting me past the reception desk and toward the rear of the massive mansion. "The back hallway's the safest place for us. No windows. And it's an interior structure."

"Where's Emma?" I spoke the words over my shoulder to Hayley.

"Jacob picked her up," she said. "She's home."

Micah adjusted his hold on me. "It's just us and Nellie."

Nellie, who loathed all germs. I groaned. We turned the corner and a hallway stretched before us. Nellie stood at the far end, not looking one bit pleased, and I had an inkling it had nothing to do with the tornado warning and everything to do with my current state of sickness.

Micah released his grasp, and I shivered from the loss of his body heat.

Nellie stiffened.

"I don't have a fever. I'm just cold because I'm wet." I glanced down at myself. *Oof.* My vintage Jazz Fest T-shirt clung to my frame, highlighting the fact that I wasn't wearing a bra. *Of course.* Not that I had much in that department anyway. But still. I took the gumbo pot from Hayley, using it as a shield.

Nellie flattened her back against the wall.

"It's empty." I tilted the pot for her to see.

Micah darted into a room off the hallway.

The pot became too heavy to hold, and I set it down, crossing my arms over my chest with another round of shivering. What was the A/C on? Fifty? I took in the goosebumps dotting my arms and my legs. They ran all the way down to my—*Oh no.* I had on two different socks *and* shoes. Hello, Punky Brewster.

I glanced up and found Nellie continuing her open, negative assessment of me. Slowly, I raised one of my feet to my butt to hide my fashion faux pas, standing like a flamingo. I quickly lost my balance. *Forget it.* Who cared at this point anyway?

Micah returned with a Hawaiian shirt, a bottled water, and a folding chair. As he handed me the shirt, he edged closer, examining my hairline.

"It's not lice!"

A gasp came from the other side of the hallway. "I'm just going to . . ." Nellie fled several paces, opened a door that revealed the world's smallest supply closet, and shut herself in.

With a sigh, I tipped my head back in defeat.

Micah and Hayley exchanged barely contained chuckles.

"I bought new towels." I raised my voice for Nellie to hear. "And they're still shedding."

Micah unfolded the chair and set my purse on the floor next to it with the water.

"Thank you." I gladly lowered onto the seat, my body feeling like it was weighted with sandbags.

"I've never seen her this sick," Hayley said to Micah.

"Are you sure you don't want it?" I held up Micah's dry shirt to him. He was as drenched as me. From his T-Rex to his brown slacks.

He lifted a staying hand. "I'm good."

I slipped the enormous shirt on and buttoned it up, inhaling a clean and crisp scent.

Micah turned, giving me privacy.

Beneath his tent of a shirt, I maneuvered my soaked top off. This entire moment couldn't have been more opposite from that scene in *Flashdance*. "You can turn back around." I draped my wet shirt on the rim of the gumbo pot. At least my nausea had subsided. Now if only I could gain my strength back.

Another cycle of thunder detonated, the walls vibrating.

Hayley inched closer to me, her fingers moving across the screen of her phone. "The radar says the storm should be past us soon."

"The warning expires in ten minutes." Micah leaned against the wall and then thought better of it, frowning at the water mark his shoulder left.

The wind yowled its force in an unrelenting siege. *Lord, please keep us safe. And everyone at the café.*

Hayley lowered to the floor, her attention still on her cell, flipping through pictures she'd taken of her dog. "Precious must be freaking out."

I continued my prayer. *And for Hayley's sake, please protect Precious. But definitely not that evil bird.*

"Have you been drinking and resting?" Micah shifted from one foot to another, studying me.

I shrugged, too exhausted to verse the truth. I was resting as much as one could with a puppy determined to drive me up the wall, and a business no one else could run but me. Well, that wasn't quite true. Mayté and Penny had handled everything today. Hopefully there weren't any issues with payroll. I'd only showed Penny how to do it once before. But I did have step-by-step instructions printed. And she knew where they were. But I hadn't told her about double-checking the physical checks when they arrived tomorrow. Or how to double-check the amounts on the paychecks that had been direct deposited.

Micah stepped forward and gently pinched the skin on my hand. "I think you're dehydrated." He took the bottled water and unscrewed the top, handing it to me.

"Thank you, Dr. Guidry." I tilted my face up, holding eye contact. "But I'm fine."

He inclined his chin for me to drink. I obeyed, taking a tiny sip, hoping it stayed down.

He scrutinized my mouth. "Your lips are dry."

"Maybe my lips are always dry." I set the water at my feet and rubbed an ache at my temples.

"They're not," he said. "They're usually . . ."

Oh my. Oh my. I slowly lowered my hand.

Pink bloomed in his cheeks, and he retreated a step, his attention landing everywhere but on me.

If my mouth still wasn't so parched, I'd swallow. I glanced Hayley's way and was relieved to find her obliviously sucked into her phone.

121

Micah cleared his throat. "When this storm passes, I'm taking you to the ER."

"I don't want to camp out at the ER for hours on end. And I don't want you around me any more than you've been."

"I already had the flu last week."

I narrowed my gaze at him.

He held up his hand in a Scout's honor gesture. "It made its way through my jiujitsu class."

Jiujitsu? "You take karate?"

He scoffed. "Brazilian jiujitsu is *not* karate."

"Whatever you say, Mr. Miyagi."

One edge of his mouth tipped up. "I thought I was Rhett Butler."

A sigh slipped free. "You're many things. Including a first-kiss thief."

His brows rose.

Hayley's head popped up like a meerkat.

Terrified terriers.

Her entire face lit as though she'd heard the juiciest piece of gossip.

Why oh why had I said that? Maybe my flu was really an advanced case of that Mardi Gras fever. "It was in seventh grade."

"And it wasn't a stolen kiss." Micah crossed his arms, the amusement in his deep olive eyes a contrast to his stance.

A sly grin spread across Hayley's face. "*I'm* in seventh grade."

My head pounded. "Don't remind me."

13

AGAINST MY WISHES, we'd piled into Micah's deathtrap Jeep. With the tornado warning over, he'd held to his word. And his full tank of gasoline trumped my empty one. We dropped Hayley at home and now drove to an emergency clinic (my compromise over going to the ER). He hooked a quick right onto St. Charles Avenue.

I gripped the handle above my door.

"Sorry." He eased off the gas. "You look so weak. I just want to get you there."

"Please be careful on the turns. Jeeps are prone to flip."

He pulled a face. "I've never flipped my Jeep."

"Doesn't mean it can't happen." My queasiness revived, and I readjusted the pot on my lap. *You will not puke in front of this man. Focus on the live oaks lining the street. The regal mansions. The clearing skies. The fact we weren't decimated by a tornado.*

Mama's personalized ringtone of the *Jaws* theme song emerged from my purse. Since I was already suffering, it couldn't hurt to add to it. Or really, to be done with this convo so I wouldn't have to ring her back later. I answered.

"You missed dinner Saturday night." Her agitated voice filled my ear.

My grasp on the phone tightened with what little strength I had.

"We sat there like fools," she said. "Waiting and waiting. No call. And no call yesterday either. I raised you better."

I noted the *I* she'd used, not *we*. At least we all clearly understood Daddy's nonrole in our upbringing. "Do you not remember how our meal ended last month?" The words scraped past my dry throat.

"Oh, Katherine," she pooh-poohed. "It wasn't a big deal."

We hit a pothole, the jolt intensifying my nausea.

Micah cringed and mouthed an apology.

I eased in a calming breath, willing the sickness to subside. "It was an extremely big deal. We're not coming back until you promise not to be a bully."

"A bully?" Her tone pitched.

The water Micah had made me drink twisted in my gut. "I have to go." I dropped my phone in the center console and leaned over the pot, the seatbelt pulling against me. I heaved, angling my face to shield Micah from having to actually see anything. The poor guy. He'd had to listen to my period voice mail and now this. This was the stuff of husbands, not old friends becoming new friends again.

"Katherine?" Mama's squawk came through the line. "Katherine?"

My stomach rolled again, and I dry heaved, leaning the side of my face on the pot's cool rim. A sheen of sweat broke out across my skin, the pounding in my skull unbearable.

"Mrs. Margaret?"

I blinked, lifting my head. Micah had my phone. My belly cramped again for an entirely different reason.

"I'm Micah Guidry. I went to school with Kate and Claire."

Oh, how I loved that he'd included Claire. Would Mama

remember Micah from Mawmaw's annual Mardi Gras gatherings?

"I'm taking Kate to urgent care. She's got a bad case of the flu." A beat of silence. "Yes, ma'am." All emotion bled from his tone. "Good-bye." He returned my cell to the cupholder, a muscle clenching in his jaw. "She hasn't changed," he muttered.

Even if Mama hadn't remembered Micah, he certainly remembered more than her name. I wiped my mouth with my damp T-shirt still draped on the other side of the pot. "Well?"

He regripped the steering wheel. "She said being sick doesn't excuse rude manners."

⚬—⚬

I woke to the sensation of being carried. I opened my eyes just enough to realize I was cradled against Micah's firm chest and stomach. He toted me across the shadowed courtyard. Too exhausted to put up a fuss, I leaned my head on his shoulder and attempted to be helpful by gripping his neck.

"It's all right. I've got you." His warm breath fanned my ear. His arms banded my back and my bare knees.

I tried to remember getting in and out of his Jeep, but my brain felt like it floated inside a lava lamp. The last thing I recalled was receiving an IV and a cocktail of meds for the nausea and headache. And something to relax me. The doctor had been adamant about lots of rest. The floating sensation moved in an upward motion. I cracked my eyes again, noting the floodlights had been turned on. How had he made it so quickly to the stairs?

"We're almost there," he said.

Thoughts jumbled through my foggy mind. At the clinic, Micah had taken care of everything. Talking to the receptionist. Filling out the forms. All I had to do was sit there. What a luxury that had been. Had I even thanked him? In my current state of loopiness, I wasn't sure. If I had, it seemed grossly inadequate for all he'd done. Maybe I'd give him a discount at the café, like I did for on-duty police officers. My eyes drooped shut, and I strained to reopen them. I could custom-order him a Hawaiian shirt with beignets. Or one with naked mole rats. Another slow blink. Naked mole rats wearing Hawaiian shirts. I snorted. Man, my eyelids were impossibly heavy. I had to tell him . . . something before I fell asleep and he left. Mawmaw had always said compliments were the best gifts. Smart and caring came to mind. Though that sounded too schmoopy. My nose brushed against his collar. *Keep it light.* I surrendered to closing my eyes and dragged in a deep breath, taking note of his crisp scent. "You smell like clean sheets . . . and muscles."

A soft chuckle vibrated from his chest. "Go to sleep, Kate."

I bolted awake from a dream in which my rear end had made contact with a wet toilet seat in a public bathroom stall with no door. Thank goodness my aching bladder had kept that nightmare from continuing. Sunlight leaked through the blinds, my alarm clock reading *9:09 a.m.* Peering over the side of my bed to the floor, I verified the all-clear and stood. And slightly swayed. With my arms out for balance, I lumbered on wobbly legs to my en suite.

With my business done, I lingered before my sink, gathering my bearings. It was Tuesday, right? Thankfully the nausea had retreated. I was just sore all over. And weak.

Not a sound emanated from within the house. I retrieved my phone from my nightstand and checked Hayley's location through our tracking app, finding her at school. She must've gotten a ride with Emma. And, considering the quietness, had possibly slipped Precious some Benadryl.

Returning to the bathroom, I studied my reflection in the mirror. Hair a mess, eyes swollen. Said puffy eyes widened as my gaze traveled south to a Hawaiian shirt and no bottoms. Gasping, I yanked up the hem, relief flooding in at the sight of my shorts. *Oh no.* My empty stomach dropped, and I grasped the counter's edge, revisiting yesterday evening in vivid detail. Throwing up in Micah's Jeep. Him talking to Mama. Carrying me. The clean-sheets-and-muscles compliment. Micah tucking me into bed with Hayley hovering at his side. Maybe my nausea really wasn't gone. I peered up at my face, my cheeks blushing with the truth, and shook my head. I was an in-control, mature, responsible woman. Yet somehow, in the presence of Micah Guidry, that all disappeared.

Piddling puppies. Would he tell his girlfriend what had happened? My head tipped back. Of course he would. He'd done nothing wrong. I'd have to apologize to him *and* Sydney Dupré. A deep sigh pushed from my lungs. Well, if he'd needed any incentive to end a reviving friendship with me, last night had provided it in spades. There was no saving face at this point. At least it wouldn't be hard to put distance between us since we'd both be doing it. We'd get through these library events, and that would be that.

After a shower and donning a tank top and pajama shorts, I all but tiptoed from my room, not wanting to make a sound and alert Precious to my presence. She'd be residing in a crate in the laundry room, positioned on the other side of our house, near the guest bathroom and bedroom. Adjoining those spaces were our open-concept living, dining, and kitchen areas.

Sunlight poured in through the three sets of French doors overlooking the balcony and St. Charles Avenue. Like the café below, a wraparound porch ran the perimeter of the second floor.

From the fridge I grabbed a cold Gatorade and placed it on the white marble island next to a box of saltines. The breakfast of champions. The front door opened, one manly hand on the knob, attached to an even manlier arm. I screamed, raising my hands in self-defense.

The door widened farther, revealing Micah, cradling Precious. She trembled and whined against his chest. "Sorry." He released her. "I thought you were still asleep."

Precious scampered to me, but I stood frozen, my heart sprinting beneath my ribs. "How'd you get in?"

"Hayley gave me the spare key." He held it up as proof and set it on the end of the kitchen counter, along with the leash and poop-bag dispenser. An inner glow lit his green eyes, and he inclined his chin at me. "What were you going to do there? Poke my eyes out?" He moved to the sink, washing his hands.

It did in fact appear as though that was my self-defense move. Both my hands were raised, pointer and middle fingers poised, ready to gouge my attacker's eyes. I lowered them, the rush of adrenaline leaving me exhausted. "I've always heard to go for the eyes and the groin." Precious shook at my bare feet. I reached down and patted her wrinkly, bald head.

Micah dried his hands on a kitchen towel, his expression turning grave. "You should know I have also learned the ways of the Three Stooges." He positioned his hand sideways off his nose in the classic eye-poke block.

I wanted to smile, but guilt stole the reaction. And then I remembered I was braless. Again. I snatched Hayley's hoodie jacket hanging on a barstool, slipping it on and zipping it up. Thankfully it was one of her Paul Bunyan pieces. Abandoning the Gatorade and crackers, I made my way past the dining room table to the leather sofa. "Thank you for . . . everything. I'm sorry about what I said last night. It was out of line."

He waved me off, setting the towel on the island. "You were pretty out of it."

"Still. I'll apologize to Sydney." I eased onto the couch, the leather cool beneath my thighs, my leg and back muscles grateful for a reprieve from being on my feet for just that short span of time. I pulled a cream throw pillow to my chest.

Micah squatted to pet Precious, his brows pulling together. "You'd do that?"

"Of course. Why? Haven't you told her?"

"No. And I don't plan to."

My gut twisted.

"My ex-wife and I weren't a good fit . . . because I kept inappropriate secrets."

Precious trotted off to her water bowl, her puppy toes silent against the wood floors.

Micah pushed to standing, his gaze resting on me. "Sydney and I broke up last week."

All of the air sucked from the room, my thoughts swirling. *Landry Mask. Landry Mask.* Who had done the breaking? Julia had said Sydney appeared casual about their relationship. And if Micah had dumped Sydney, wouldn't he have phrased his declaration that way? "I'm sorry to hear that."

He gave an automatic nod, but his forehead wrinkled, and he moved his attention to the dining room table and the books Hayley had checked out of the library.

Was he nursing a wounded heart? The way he'd smiled at Sydney at the last event would support that assessment. Perhaps Sydney had learned the truth behind Micah's divorce, and it'd been too much. *"My ex-wife and I weren't a good fit . . . because she discovered my secret wife and children, and I got busted on a live* Maury *episode."*

"Got a headache?"

"Hmm?" Oh, I'd been smooshing the Crease. "No. I mean, yes. I mean . . . everything aches." I brushed my wet bangs from my eyes.

"Which is why you should be resting." He crossed his arms,

bringing attention to his biceps and the plain white T-shirt he wore. Basketball shorts and tennis shoes completed his ultra-relaxed ensemble.

"I'm resting." I half-heartedly motioned to myself. "Part of me thinks I may be dreaming right now. You're not wearing a ridiculous shirt."

One corner of his mouth twitched. "I guess it takes being near death for *you* to slum it."

My shoulders stiffened. "There's nothing wrong with a professional appearance. One never knows what the day will bring or who you could run into." An actual piece of advice from Mama I'd followed that had proven valuable time and again. My lower backed throbbed, and I shifted to a more comfortable position. "Can you grab the Advil? It's in the cabinet over the microwave."

He moved through the kitchen, quickly finding the medicine. Such a strange sight for a man to be stirring around naturally through my space. It'd been years since another guy had been up here. And he'd been a plumber. Micah set the pills on the counter. "Emma's mom picked up Hayley this morning. I waited with her in the driveway to make sure she got off to school all right."

Oof. I could just imagine Emma and Elise's reactions to Micah being here so early and the impression that gave. Hopefully Hayley had given a detailed explanation. I winced. Well, not too detailed considering she now knew Micah and I had kissed forever ago.

"Elise will bring her home after school."

"That was sweet of you to look out for Hayley, but you didn't have to come over that early."

"I didn't." He grabbed a glass from another upper cabinet. "I was here all night."

Surprise struck me silent, that huge detail slowly absorbing into me, overdosing with concern for Hayley. It was the first time a man had ever slept here, other than her dad.

Micah filled the glass with the Gatorade I'd abandoned. "Hayley was pretty freaked last night when I carried you in. With you being knocked out, it didn't seem right to leave y'all. So I offered to stay, and she jumped on it."

I began breathing again, my posture wilting. Poor Hayley. She'd never seen me like this. But at least she'd been okay with Micah staying the night. That was a huge relief. Regardless, I'd talk to her about it. And that seventh-grade kiss with Micah. She didn't need to be getting any ideas in her head.

Micah handed me the Gatorade, set the Advil on the coffee table, and cast his gaze over the room, the Monet print on the wall capturing his attention.

What would I have done without him? Driven myself to urgent care, puking along the way? How would I have gotten home and up the stairs? My circle of close friends consisted of Julia, who was out of town. It wasn't like I could call my parents. And Mayté and I had always kept our relationship on the professional side.

The shadows beneath Micah's eyes spoke of his lack of sleep. Had he been checking on me all night? I couldn't remember the last time someone had taken care of me. I'd had to power through on my own the past decade. If I hadn't felt well or was tired from nursing Hayley through a sickness like the previous week, there was no one to tag team. In those hardest moments, prayer and God's strength had carried me. And it seemed God had intervened yesterday in a new way, exactly when I'd needed it.

Emotion steadily built within me, pressing against my ribs. "Thank you again. For everything. I . . . ." Rubbing the tip of my nose, I tried clearing my throat.

A small smile spread across his face. "You're welcome." He pointed to my Gatorade, silently reminding me.

Holding the drink to my lips, I took a few cautious sips, afraid the nausea would return. Precious pawed at my feet, but I was too tired to bend over and give her attention.

Micah moved to the kitchen, returning the Gatorade bottle to the fridge. "Mayté left some sort of casserole, if you're hungry."

"You talked to Mayté too?" I set the glass on the coffee table, on a coaster Hayley and I had made at school in second grade, during a Dad's Day event.

He nodded. "When Hayley was leaving this morning. You're still banned from the café, and now I am too." His eyes twinkled with humor. At least he wasn't offended by my chef's bluntness. And hopefully the woman didn't have the wrong idea about Micah. "Mayté said everything's under control downstairs."

Pursing my lips, I garnered my strength, shifting to stand.

He lifted a staying hand. "She also said if I catch you trying to do any work, that I'm to hide your phone and laptop and tell you she won't cook for you anymore. Only Hayley."

A soft smile emerged at Mayté's bossy care. Maybe my relationship with her wasn't totally professional. I slumped back into the sofa. Despite the aching heaviness in my body, my heart felt lighter. My gaze shifted beyond the French doors to the branches of the live oaks. I'd never had two days completely off from the restaurant. A day here or there. But never a true temporary alleviation of duties. My emotions rebubbled to the surface, and I blinked them away with a yawn, my attention returning to the room.

To the very single man loading my dishwasher. A single man with a genuine heart. Though, Ryan had had a genuine heart once. Or at least, I'd thought he did. Cold reality swept through, sharpening my wits. I may have been single the past eleven years and bore all the weight and responsibilities, but I hadn't had the worry of being used. Or not loved enough for life's curveballs. And I certainly had the smarts not to get involved with a man who wasn't a good fit with his ex-wife because he wasn't a Dolly Parton fan. *Nah. Scratch that.* Everyone adored Dolly.

Micah closed the dishwasher with a click and turned my way.

I stifled another yawn. "I appreciate all you've done. Truly. But you can go now. I'm fine."

One of his brows rose. "Are you?"

Precious relentlessly scratched at my toes. I hefted my feet to the couch and slumped sideways into the cushion, resting the side of my face against the leather. The hairless pup continued harassing me, standing on her hind legs, pawing at the sofa.

"No," I cautioned sternly. She whined.

"The doctor said you needs lots of fluids. And rest."

"Which I'll get."

Precious unleashed a high-pitched wail.

Micah's other brow lifted. "Are you going to be able to bring Precious up and down the stairs every few hours for her to do her business?"

I groaned. That was an obvious no. I was ninety percent certain I'd only vacate the couch for emergency purposes. Another yawn escaped. "I'll put her in her crate until Hayley gets home."

"Where she'll cry and keep you awake." He opened the box of saltines on the island.

I hated his correctness.

He pulled a sleeve of crackers free. "I already took the day off from work. I've got nothing else to do."

Be still my heart. Wait! No! Do not be still! Be the opposite of still! Be moving! Be on a pogo stick! "You didn't have to do that."

He shrugged. "Nellie was more than happy to cover for me."

"Nellie." I cringed. "Do you think she'll get a restraining order against me?"

"You don't think she already has one?" He opened the wrapper to the crackers and held them out to me with a wry grin. "Eat something. I'd like to get your strength up before I leave with Precious."

14

THE CRICK IN MY NECK roused me from sleep. I shifted from lying on my side to my back, my face unpeeling from the leather of the sofa. Ugh. I rubbed my sweaty cheek. Sunlight bathed the living room. Shielding my hazy eyes, I glanced at the entertainment center and the clock residing on one of the shelves. I concentrated enough to make out it was one. My stomach growled. Before dozing off I'd eaten a few crackers and drunk a glass of Gatorade. And, hallelujah, it had all stayed down. Maybe I was ready for some of Mayté's casserole she'd left this morning.

Slow footsteps sounded, and Micah emerged from the hallway leading to my and Hayley's bedrooms. A prickle of suspicion darted up my spine. He held Precious in one arm and a folded newspaper in the other. And where were his shoes? Had he removed them to go into stealth mode?

"I thought you were going to your place." My voice proved thick with sleep.

"I was, but . . . after you dozed off you looked cold, so I got you a blanket." He set a wiggling Precious down.

She scurried toward me and stopped next to the sofa, her enormous googly eyes beseeching me, as though insisting I acknowledge her presence. As I reached over for a head pat, her rat tail swished. Easing to a sitting position, I cleared my voice. "Thank you." But that still didn't answer why the man had come from the direction of our bedrooms. Had he been snooping?

"I was going to use the blanket from your bed, but I realized you'd slept in your puke clothes all night."

I winced. That had to be the worst way to be referenced by a single, attractive man. Or really, any human being with a beating pulse.

"So I stripped your bed." He jutted a thumb behind him toward my room. "And laundered everything. I was just putting it back."

"You washed my things?"

"Only bedding and towels." He held up his hand. "I know better than to wash a woman's clothes and bras and . . ."

I tensed. *Please don't say panties.*

"Delicates."

I exhaled a low breath, massaging the ache in my neck. "Thank you, I think."

He altered his weight from one socked foot to the other. "All of this is to preempt you from getting mad at me."

Using my palms, I wiped the sleep from my eyes. "What did you do? Turn all my white bedding to pink with a rogue red sock?"

"No. When I found the blanket, it led me to your secret stash of Twinkies." He unfolded the newspaper, but it wasn't a newspaper at all. "And tabloids."

"*What?*" I glanced down at my lap and discovered Maw-maw's afghan. A bolt of heat shot to my cheeks. Normally, the colorful blanket resided in an antique trunk at the foot of my bed, concealing the contents of the chest. Of all the blankets in the house, he'd found this one? I gripped the cro-cheted cover, fighting the impulse to yank it over my head and wait for my flaming blush to dim. Or for the sock-footed sneak to leave.

"In my defense, a corner of the blanket was peeking out of the trunk. Practically waving at me." He mimed a limp wave.

"In *my* defense, those tabloids are my grandma's."

One side of his mouth tipped into an annoyingly endearing grin. "But you've read them, right?"

Why was it so hot in here? With all these holes in Mawmaw's blanket, it shouldn't be this hot. I pushed the sleeves up on Hayley's hoodie I still wore and ripped the blanket off my legs. Precious pounced on the edge of the cover hitting the floor. "I haven't read them all."

He held up a periodical in each hand, both from the '80s. A copy of the *National Enquirer*, featuring the latest Elvis sighting. And *Weekly World News*, highlighting Bat Boy. My cheeks flamed afresh.

His smirk slid into a chuckle. "You haven't read them all *yet*."

Avoiding his stare, I focused on Precious, full-out gnawing on the blanket. "No," I scolded, pulling the cover away. She latched onto it with a growl. Maybe she was part pit bull. I hoisted the puppy with one hand, and her ferociousness disappeared, along with her hold on the afghan. I moved the blanket out of reach and placed her on the floor.

Micah eyed me expectantly, making it clear he wasn't letting his discovery go. Maybe he was part pit bull too.

I curbed a sigh. "I flip through one from time to time, in my grandma's honor." And as a more tangible reminder of her. How many times had I found her browsing those pages at her kitchen table during her afternoon café au lait? Remarking on Elizabeth Taylor's latest marriage and divorce. How she couldn't wait to try La Toya Jackson's meatball recipe that had been printed in one edition. Or reflecting on David Hasselhoff's beach body. These tabloids were a unique part of her. The equivalent of having a bottle of her favorite perfume and taking a whiff every now and then. Plus, the stories were so ridiculous I couldn't help but smile when reading them.

His mouth scrunched to one side, playful skepticism brightening his eyes.

"At least they're not riddled with boogers."

"I obviously gave you a bad impression of library books. They're not all riddled with lagniappe."

"Ugh." I cringed. "You've been living up north too long. Lagniappe is only in reference to *good* free things. Extra fried shrimp on a po'boy. Additional time on the carousel at City Park."

"Extra time spinning isn't a good thing."

"Any more talk of puke clothes or spinning or boogers and my appetite will officially be shot."

He perked. "You're hungry?"

I nodded.

After heating up Mayté's breakfast casserole, Micah and I sat across from each other at the dining room table. Thankfully the scent of eggs, red bell peppers, and onions hadn't turned my stomach. Several tentative bites in, and I was hopeful I'd hit a turning point in recovering. Precious snoozed at my feet, picking the worst possible place to get accidentally stepped on.

Micah's utensils scraped against his plate as he cut another forkful. "Why the stash of Twinkies? I mean, I understand hiding the tabloids. That's pretty embarrassing."

I nailed him with a glare.

He chewed and swallowed, playfulness toying in his eyes and at the edges of his mouth. He was too charming for my own good.

I nudged a square of onion with my fork. "Growing up, my mom didn't allow junk food. So Mawmaw would sneak me and Claire Twinkies, and we'd hide them in our rooms. Even when I lived here with Mawmaw during college, I still kept a box in my bedroom."

"You lived here with her?"

"For four years." I lifted a shoulder. "She was having health issues and needed help."

His fork paused midway to his mouth, his eyes widening. "You were her caregiver?"

"It wasn't me alone. A year later, when Claire turned eighteen, she moved in too."

"What was wrong with her?" He returned his uneaten bite to his plate.

"COPD. She tried hiding it from us, but we'd noticed it progressing for a while. Doing anything simple, like walking to the bathroom, left her exhausted and wheezing. So instead of going into a dorm, I came here. Against Mawmaw's wishes, of course." I rolled my eyes, fondness for her warming my chest. "But it wasn't like she was going to kick me out."

Micah leaned forward. "What was it like caring for her?"

I pulled in a lungful of air, wishing those final years had been ones filled with positive memories, like the rest of my life with Mawmaw had been. "The beginning wasn't so bad. But her last year on this planet was hard." My breathing slowed. "She'd started having episodes of mental confusion, so we had to hire someone to watch her when we were at classes." Thank goodness Mawmaw had the money to afford that help. "And then nights and weekends, Claire and I scheduled our work shifts so one of us was always home with her." That time was also when the cracks in my relationship with Ryan had surfaced. He hadn't been a fan of the caregiver role I'd taken. Of my attention shifting away from him. His reactions and the strain on our bond should've been a warning flare blazing across the sky.

I stared at my plate, the heavy tug of the past trying to drag me back into its grim clutches. "But Mawmaw became less mobile, and the physicality of caring for her began wearing on us. Changing diapers, both of us carrying her to the shower. Eventually we couldn't manage that and had to do sponge baths." Oh, how she'd hated being fussed over with those cleanings, her delusions bringing out a combative side impossible to reconcile with the woman we'd known all our lives. "Hardest of all was the emotional toll of hearing her struggle for each breath, especially when a cough gripped her." My eyelids grew hot, my throat scratchy. "I try not to think of it because it triggers so many bad memories."

Micah had grown still, his gaze steadily on me, a pinch between his brows.

"Being a caregiver like that . . ." I slowly shook my head. "Watching someone deteriorate, day in and day out. It's heartbreaking." An aching dullness gathered beneath my ribs. "And not just for the person who needs care, but for those who help them. The emotional strain. I hated those years for Claire. She should've been out, being young and having fun." Thankfully after Mawmaw's death, Claire had bounced back quickly. I, on the other hand, had repressed my own inner wounds for her sake.

Micah stared at his hands resting in his lap, his lips slightly pinned together.

I grimaced at having brought on a conversation so full of gloom.

Sarah McLachlan.

Especially with his mom having gone through a battle with cancer. My fingertips flew to my temple. "I'm so sorry. I didn't mean to be thoughtless."

He blinked, his stare fastening on mine. "You weren't."

"But I was. I'm sure you went through something similar with your mom."

He waved me off. "Her situation was completely different.

139

She didn't need constant care like your grandma, or have mental or mobility issues."

"I'm still sorry."

"You have nothing to apologize for. I promise." He picked up his fork, finishing his meal. "So the Twinkies are a tradition?"

I nodded. "They help me feel closer to her. To the good memories."

"Along with reading her old tabloids." One side of his mouth quirked, a genuine twinkle returning to his eyes.

My tense muscles eased. "It's not like I'm buying new ones. Once I'm done with hers, that's it." I managed another bite of the casserole.

"And then you'll give books a try?"

I shrugged and swallowed. "Stranger things have happened."

He moved his empty plate aside and reached for the periodical featuring Bat Boy. After flipping a few pages in, and a moment of reading, he snorted. "This is terrible." Turning another page, he rested his elbow on the table. With a restrained chuckle, he continued reading and rubbed his chin, his fingers grating his stubble.

Based on the varying times of day I'd now seen him, it seemed he shaved every morning on work days. Did he prefer a beard? Did he remain clean-shaven to appear more approachable to kids, like the way he wore Hawaiian shirts? Was his stubble coarse or soft? Would it leave a burn against my skin after kissing him?

Whoa! Pull it together.

The girlfriend issue may have disappeared, but he was most likely nursing an injured heart. Which hit too close to home. Did I really want to entertain the thought of opening myself up again in that way? To being vulnerable? No. No, I did not. Besides, he still had that divorce red flag rippling above his head.

My gaze drifted to the *National Enquirer* on the table. The marketing quote from their old commercials played through my mind, *"Inquiring minds want to know."* Hadn't Micah and I reached the point of asking personal questions? He'd witnessed me throw up, as well as being drugged and braless and making inappropriate compliments about his muscles. He'd spent the night. Walked around in his socks. Discovered my guilty pleasure. He also knew about my insecurities with Hayley. And my dreadful periods. Though that last item had been uncovered accidentally. *Sheesh.* Not even Ryan had known that.

God, what do You think? Do You keep putting this big question mark about Micah in front of me for a reason? Or is it none of my beeswax? Perhaps finally knowing would be for the sake of our budding re-friendship. To put us on equal ground. And as Hayley's guardian, shouldn't I know more about the man who'd been dropped into her world? Even if his position at the library was temporary? I studied his face. His strong jaw. The slight crook in his nose, giving him a rugged appeal. He'd broken it in high school, during a football game, and had had two black eyes for a week. I chewed the inside of my cheek.

"My ex-wife and I weren't a good fit . . . because she flossed at red lights, and tossed her floss picks out the window."

I released my fork against my dish with a light clink. "Can I ask a personal question?"

His attention rose from the tabloid, a tentative smile following. "How personal? Are you wondering about my opinion of Bat Boy and if he'll use his powers for good or evil?" The tentativeness in his features snitched on his diversion effort.

Something within me nudged to press on. "I'd like to point out that since we've become friends again, you know way too many private things about me."

"Including your appreciation of the way I smell."

Warmth spread up from my neck, too fast for me to slip the Landry Mask in place. This time he'd pulled out his deflection A game and had swung for the fences. Maybe now wasn't the right time to satiate my inquiring mind. I picked up my glass and sipped the water, hoping the chilled beverage would help alleviate the heat in my face.

He eased in a breath and released it, his playfulness falling away. "What would you like to know?"

I eyed him for a moment, the space between us growing thick with uncertainty.

"Go ahead." His tone encouraged, carrying the weight of an almost calm resignation.

The nudge in my chest returned, reassuring. I set my glass down. "What happened to your marriage?"

He didn't appear surprised by my question. Not one bit. With his lips sealed in a tight line, he dipped his jaw. His gaze turned inward, reflective. "My ex-wife and I began trying for a baby right away. We'd both wanted a huge family."

Uh-oh. The casserole in my stomach started a slow churn.

"After two years of being unsuccessful, we decided to get checked out, fertility-wise."

My pulse slowed, but my mind spun, wanting to tell him to stop, but my tongue had been struck paralyzed. This was way more personal than the things he knew about me.

"My wife was fine. I wasn't." He studied his large hands, interlocked on the table before him.

"I'm . . . so sorry." And I was. Despite his straightforwardness, Micah had always been a genuine person. The kind of guy you *knew* would be a great husband and father one day. Even the past two days had attested to that.

He nodded, biting his lower lip. "The short story is, more than anything, she wanted her own biological kids, and I didn't want to hold her back."

My heart clenched, instant comradery solidifying in my core. I longed to reach over the table and clasp his fingers. Those for-better-or-for-worse vows hadn't held up for him. And I knew with Ryan, had we gone through with our wedding, they wouldn't have held up for me either.

"She remarried a year after we divorced." His attention slid across the room to the front windows for a moment, then anchored on his plate. "Last I heard, she has five children."

My heart shriveled. I could only imagine the cringy face Jesus must've been making with each of my theories about his divorce. Our past convo came to mind, and I pressed my hand to my forehead. "I'm sorry, so sorry, for how insensitive I must've sounded that night when you'd first visited the café. When I'd prattled on about not wanting children."

With a blink, his stare focused on me, his brows narrowing. "You weren't insensitive. You were being truthful, and you shouldn't have to apologize for that." He surveyed his hands again, rubbing his bare ring finger. "It took some time and a lot of prayer, but I've made peace with how God created me. And I know He doesn't make mistakes."

Swoon! A man talking about God in such an open and reverent way? And a hot man to boot? But my swooning sensation quickly switched gears, Mayté's casserole rocketing up my throat. I clamped a hand over my mouth and bolted for the bathroom.

15

I WOKE WITH A CRINGE that had zero to do with how I felt physically. The ceiling fan in my bedroom hummed a rhythmic whir-
ring, its gentle draft brushing my exposed skin. Taking in a
measured breath, I assessed myself. Traitorous stomach? Tender. Muscles? Achy. Embarrassment level? Off the chart.

The alarm clock on my nightstand read *4:00 p.m.* Hayley
should be home, and Micah should have fled, never to return.
I sighed, shifting beneath the soft covers. The covers Micah
had laundered. I owed him. Big time. I doubted I'd find an appropriate greeting card expressing gratitude for all he'd done
and apologizing for fleeing the room after he'd shared such a
personal tragedy.

I disentombed from the cocoon of my bed, stretching my
back as I stood, and stared at the closed bedroom door. Only
Hayley and Precious should be on the other side. But just in
case, I pulled a bra from my dresser and slipped it on. Especially
since I'd discarded Hayley's hoodie earlier in the bathroom.

Gently, I turned the knob, cracking the door open. The faint
drone of the TV reached my ears, the end of the hallway the
farthest I could see.

"She's not going to . . . I mean . . . Should we take her to the
hospital?" Hayley's worried voice drifted from the main room.

144

My heart clenched.

"Nah," Micah said.

My heart shifted from clenching to sputtering. He was still here.

"She's much better today." Micah again. "She only puked once."

I winced. If only those *Men in Black* memory erasers really existed.

"I knew she'd catch my flu," Hayley said. "She wouldn't leave me alone the entire time I was sick."

"Sounds like you've got a good mom."

No. I screwed my eyes shut, pain striking the back of my throat. *She* had *a good mom with Claire.* I eased the door wider and instantly felt the conviction to stay where I was. *Oh, Lord, not now.* I ground my teeth, one foot in my bedroom, the other in the hall. If only I could see Hayley's face. Was she upset by what Micah had said? It wasn't the first time I'd been linked in a mom reference. People had made the assumption so many times over the years based on our hair color. We'd both stopped correcting people. Learned the hard way it was easier to let strangers assume instead of trying to explain. I hugged my arms to myself. But Micah knew better.

"You know, my mom died when I was fourteen," Micah said.

"Oh. I'm sorry." A sweet maturity coated Hayley's tone. "How'd she die?"

"Cancer."

"Cancer sucks." And gone was the maturity.

Micah snorted. "Yes, it does." A moment passed. "You were young when you lost your parents, right?"

My breath halted in my lungs. I'd never heard Hayley speak to anyone about her parents. I'd always been the one to intercept those questions. Protecting her. At least that'd been my intention. Especially since she'd never wanted to talk about them when I'd brought them up. And all the books and counselors had said not to push. Had they been wrong? Leaning forward, I strained to hear.

"I was two."

"I'm sorry that happened."

"I don't remember them." Hayley's words were nearly a whisper.

God, please let me intervene. The clear sensation to stay put remained.

"All I remember is my aunt Kate. Taking me to the library, church, parades, Papa Noël bonfires, the zoo . . . but not my parents."

Tears blurred my vision. From the conversations we'd had over the years, I wasn't surprised by her declaration. Even the child therapist I'd met with had expressed Hayley not remembering them as a high possibility due to her young age at the time of loss.

"That makes sense," Micah said. "I don't remember anything from that age." All was quiet except for the crinkle of a bag. The distinctive sound of a new bag of chips being opened. Wait. Chips? "Want some?" Micah again.

More crinkling followed. My head tipped back, and I smothered a sigh. Hayley wouldn't eat a thing come dinner.

"In those first years after my mom died," Micah said, "I'd wonder what life would have been like if she were still around."

"Yes!" Hayley bellowed, the relief in her voice clear. "I do that too every so often. It's fast thoughts though. Like wondering how different my life would be." Seconds passed. "It's nice to talk to someone who gets it."

"I bet your school has a counselor you could meet with."

"I know," she huffed. "And my aunt's offered for me to see a therapist. Several times. I just don't feel like I need to. I'm not depressed or anxious or anything like that." A pause. "It's just nice that you understand without being all weird and formal and doctor-y."

My head bowed, tension releasing from my neck. *Thank You, God. Thank you. Thank you.* My relief quickly pricked with guilt. I couldn't help but think of a young Micah. Had he had someone who *got it* to talk to after his mom's death? She'd passed the summer before high school. Other than attending the funeral with Mawmaw and Claire, I hadn't seen Micah until school had started. I'd looked for him every Sunday at church that summer, but he'd never shown. A dull thump emanated from my heart. Though we hadn't been close friends, I should've reached out to him. Done something.

"I feel like I should get mad when friends complain about their parents, but I don't," Hayley said. "My aunt is great. I mean, other than taking forever to get a dog and not letting me ride the streetcar alone. But I think in the end, she's probably a better parent than mine would have been."

Goldilocks. My breathing once again seized at this just-right moment, lightheadedness striking me. I placed a hand on the wall for balance.

"Is that terrible to say?" Hayley asked.

"I don't think so."

Pressing my fingers to my forehead, I pulled in a slow and deep lungful of air, the sensation of a boulder lifting from my shoulders, from my heart. I had a feeling the Lord had known this conversation was as much for me as it was Hayley. *Thank you.* I needed to find a time to thank Micah too.

"She's still not eating. Come on, Precious." Hayley's voice pitched to baby talk. "You need to eat." The sound of the dog's kibble rattling in its bowl followed. "Her food could be gross. Maybe I should give her a Dorito?"

No shot to the brim of my tongue.

"That might make her sick," Micah said. "I had a puppy once who was stubborn to eat."

"What'd you do?"

"I flicked his food across the floor to see if he'd chase and eat it. And he did."

A beat passed.

"It worked!" Hayley exclaimed.

Drying my eyes with the hem of my shirt, I pulled myself together and entered the living area. Hayley and Micah sat on the kitchen floor several feet apart, Precious between them. Hayley gently tossed a piece of dry kibble. Precious chased and pounced on it. "It looks like y'all are playing Hungry Hungry Hippos." Their heads turned in my direction.

Hayley's face radiated pure joy. She threw another morsel of food, and Precious gobbled it up. "Mr. Micah's a genius."

I shifted my attention to Micah, ready for him to jump on that compliment with some witty retort. Or flash me a *Did you hear that?* smirk. Instead, a layer of uncertainty shadowed his face, and he wouldn't meet my gaze. Was he regretting sharing about his infertility? While I'd been sick and sleeping all afternoon, had he been reminiscing his lost marriage? Was that why he hadn't remarried since his divorce? Had all of his love interests bailed on him? Or perhaps his overlong staring at Precious's food bowl was filled with thoughts about his mom's death.

The man needed an easy exit plan. I grabbed another Gatorade from the fridge and settled on the sofa, pulling Mawmaw's afghan over my bare legs. How did one tell someone in a subtle way they could leave? Reaching for the remaining saltines on the coffee table, I unwrapped them. If Micah saw I was better, and Hayley was more than capable of caring for Precious, he'd realize on his own he was free to escape this place and the two redheads who'd reopened his old wounds.

And maybe I'd pull out my laptop and start searching for that perfect greeting card for him. After I checked my email and ensured payroll had been processed correctly. And got a jump start on that SBA loan application for buying the Vieux Carré Café.

Why was Micah still here?

Granted, Hayley *had* cajoled him into staying for a lackluster dinner of canned chicken noodle soup. *Mmm-mmm mediocre.* Micah had added grilled cheese sandwiches, and after, insisted on cleaning the dishes. Hayley completed her homework at the dining room table, while I'd lain on the couch, praying what I'd eaten would stay down. I'd tried to watch TV, but it'd proven impossible. Especially with the sight of Micah in my kitchen, taking care of everything again. Even occasionally helping Hayley with a homework question. I'd basically been rendered useless, and it was . . . nice. Really nice. Like when he'd taken charge at urgent care.

Gratitude had unfurled from within me, and a tension I hadn't realized I'd been holding eased. As long as I could remember, I'd been the one taking care of someone else. Looking out for Claire when we'd still lived at home. Being there for Ryan. Caring for Mawmaw in her final years. Becoming Hayley's guardian. Even my employees and their livelihoods rested on my shoulders too. It'd been luxurious, sitting there, my only job in the moment to eat saltines and hydrate.

But it was now eight o'clock. Hayley was in the shower getting ready for bed. She'd even told Micah good night. And yet he was still here. Playing with Precious on the area rug and watching TV. I finished another glass of water, setting it on the coffee table. Was there more to his infertility talk he'd wanted to share that my puking had interrupted? Was he lonely from Sydney dumping him and needed to be around others?

"You keep sighing." Micah leaned back on his hands, stretching his legs out in front of him.

"Hmm?"

With a lot of effort, Precious climbed over one of his shins and then the other. He gently scratched behind one of her ears. "Have you had enough of me?"

"No." *Puppy poop.* That came out way too fast.

The faintest of smiles tugged at his lips.

"I mean . . . We've basically hijacked your life the past two days. And you've got work tomorrow. Hawaiian shirts to wear. Librarian things to accomplish. I'll be fine."

"You sure?" He moved to rise from the floor.

My heart sank a fraction.

Pushing to his feet, he palmed the back of his neck. "Before I go . . ." His gaze touched on me and slid to the television, then the front door.

Oh, how would he end that sentence? *"Before I go . . . I'd like to reenact carrying you up the stairs again. Especially since you're in clean clothes and don't reek of vomit. Before I go . . . you should know I'm still madly in love with Sydney Dupré and will be until the day I die."*

Precious gnawed his pinky toe. He flinched and squatted, rescuing his wee little piggie from her needle teeth. "Earlier, Hayley and I had a little talk."

"I know. I heard y'all."

His forehead wrinkled. "I wasn't sure if I'd overstepped with anything."

Huh. Was that why he'd seemed off before? "You didn't overstep." I fiddled with the blanket, poking my finger through one of the holes. "I'm actually grateful."

Precious resumed her attack on him, gunning for his big toe. With a reprimand, he again lifted her, his sock snagging on one of her fangs. He gently untangled it. "Maybe you'll stop doubting your parenting skills now."

"Maybe." A huge maybe. Even Julia still questioned her parenting, and her boys were in college. Remembering his conversation with Hayley, my pulse slowed to a dull beat. One thing that there were no maybes about was how badly I'd handled

Micah's mom's death. "I'm sorry I wasn't a better friend when your mom died."

"We were kids." He straightened, cradling Precious with one arm. "And we weren't that close."

"I just . . ." I shook my head. "I should've reached out to you that summer. And then when we returned to school, I didn't know what to say or do, afraid I'd make you feel worse, so I didn't do anything. But I prayed for you and your sister and dad."

"And those prayers were felt."

"Did you have someone to talk to back then?"

He moved to the love seat, the cushions squishing beneath his weight. "My dad sent me and Renee to a few counseling sessions. But it was too fresh. I mostly sat silent through those meetings, numb." He placed Precious on the floor and rested his elbows on his knees. "Looking back though, I can see some good that came from it. It set me on a path that summer."

"How?"

His attention drifted to the coffee table, his gaze distancing a moment. "It was hard to be at home with so many memories of my mom there. I started spending more time at the library. It was free, air-conditioned, and within biking distance. I'd spend all day escaping into fictional worlds. I went so much I got to know the librarian and eventually opened up to her about my mom. I found it easier to talk to her than with a counselor, or to burden my dad or sister."

I drew in a breath, fascination expanding through me. "It's why you became a librarian."

He gave a slow nod, leaning back into the sofa. "I want to be that person for others. Plus, I've always loved books, how they open the world to people."

"Have you helped anyone like you were?"

"Not that I know of. But even if it's just one, it'll be worth it." Precious pawed at his feet, and he bent forward, rubbing her head.

"Based on tonight, I think Hayley could be your one."

He grew still, a small smile spreading across his handsome face. "Perhaps." The dog rolled over, exposing her belly. The hussy. He gave one final rub and stood.

I eased up from the couch, my back muscles still on the achy side but thankfully my stomach holding strong, and followed him to the door.

He slipped on his tennis shoes and motioned to where he'd left the spare key on the kitchen counter. A hint of uncertainty darkened his eyes. "Earlier, you wanted to know what happened with my marriage. I was wondering if you'd go next. You know . . . with Ryan."

"Oh." My mind blanked.

"I mean, not right now. But . . . another time."

I did *not* want thoughts of Ryan looming over me anymore than they already were with his reemergence. With his goal to crush Claire's dream location. With his randomly popping up on me like a hormonal pimple. Plus, after the way Micah had reacted to seeing Ryan that day at the café, I could attain a little more insight into that dynamic.

I held up a staying hand and stepped into the hallway, toward Hayley's closed bathroom door. The sound of running water and her favorite K-pop band emanated. She'd be in there until the last drop of hot water ran out and then move on to dry-ing her hair. Reentering the main room, I motioned for Micah to follow me to the balcony, wanting to put as much distance between the oncoming conversation and Hayley as possible.

While I slipped on my slides, Micah hooked Precious to her leash. He followed me through the living room and out a pair of French doors to the balcony. The mild night air greeted us, along with the light of dusk painting the skies in golden and lavender hues.

Despite the soundproof windows and Hayley's room on the other side of the house, I led us to the right, to the wrought-iron chairs placed outside the French doors to the guest bedroom. I lowered onto one of the seats, the weather-resistant cushion padding my caboose. After being cooped inside all day, the change of environment brought a lift to my spirits. There was nothing like the scene of the grand live oaks lining the road or the distant figure of an army-green streetcar making its way down the center of St. Charles Avenue.

An intermittent flow of traffic kept the street humming. And with another hour to go before closing, the café below us would still be humming as well. Micah took the other chair, releasing Precious to the planked floor. He flipped a switch on her retractable leash to prevent her from getting too close to the railing. The gaps between the iron posts were the perfect size for her to slip through. Something I'd have to keep in mind, and ensure Hayley understood too.

With another glance back toward the doors, I kept my voice low. "The short story is Ryan didn't want to adopt Hayley, and there was no way I wasn't."

Creases marred his forehead, his gaze heavy and brimming with questions. "If you're feeling up to it, I'd like the long version."

A current of wind blew, and the outer branches of the oak trees stirred, as though they were trying to lean in and listen. But it was a tale they knew all too well. One they'd witnessed in those early years with the countless times I'd cried out here after getting Hayley to sleep. Cries full of mourning, exhaustion, fear, loneliness. I pulled in a deep breath of the mossy scent floating on the breeze, thankful to God for His devotion through it all and how I knew He'd carry me through recounting it in this moment.

"Ryan proposed shortly after my grandma's death, when I was twenty-two. At the time it had felt like a lifeline. A fresh beginning after those years of caregiving." My hands curled around my middle. "In retrospect, I could kick myself for not realizing his proposal came on the heels of the reading of Maw-maw's will." I peeked at Micah. "She left everything to me and Claire."

His solemn gaze lingered on my face.

I broke the connection, returning my sights to the view before us while my thoughts flickered to the past. Ryan had tried influencing my and Claire's plans with Mawmaw's inheritance, but we'd quickly become set on the idea of opening the café. And once we'd opened the restaurant, he'd tried convincing us to open a second location right away that he'd run. But we'd stuck to our carefully made plan.

I swallowed, clearing my throat. "We'd been engaged for over six years when it all happened. I'd buried Claire and her husband, became an instant single parent to a toddler, and somehow kept the café running." A junker car rumbled past, its music blaring from the open windows, the noise waning with distance. "With all of that happening, Ryan and our approaching wedding shifted to the back of my mind. Until the night we ended things. One month before the ceremony."

Micah leaned forward, empathy softening his face. If anyone could relate to the loss of a loved one and the unraveling of a deep relationship, it was him.

"In that moment after Ryan left, I could only think of Claire and how relieved I was I wasn't getting married." I glanced at my hands, clenched in my lap, and at my bare ring finger, where an engagement ring had once sparkled. "She was supposed to be my matron of honor, and I couldn't bear to have someone else stand in her place or for her spot next to me to be empty. It would have been excruciating to face that day without her."

The bell on the café's door jingled. A moment later, a couple came into view, making their way down the front path, past the open gate to the sidewalk. I blinked away the sting in my eyes and focused on pushing through this piece of my history.

"Ryan moved out of town and handled canceling all of the

wedding plans." I fingered the hem of my shorts. "A small blessing with all of that mess." A big blessing had been coming to the realization that a huge motivator for him marrying me was my family's money. But with it all sunk into the café, and then facing Hayley's adoption, it still wasn't enough for him. "So instead of wallowing over a broken engagement, I took all the parenting books I'd purchased and compiled a spreadsheet on the milestones of children at each age. Then I tackled researching immunizations and creating vitamin percentage charts."

His lips curved into a slight smile. "That sounds very you."

I shrugged. "Over the months and years, I'd checked those items off. Reassuring myself with every completed item, I could continue doing this."

"And you have."

Comfort spread through me at his words. In the past month, he'd encouraged me more than my parents had in the last decade. "Only by a miracle."

"Did anyone try to challenge you on Hayley's custody?"

I shook my head. "Claire's will was airtight." A valuable lesson we'd learned from Mawmaw and how Mama had contested her will. The sky darkened, the streetlights along the neutral ground flickering on.

Micah studied the leash in his grasp, switching it to his other hand. "It's not my place to say this, but I'm glad you didn't marry Ryan."

"You're not the only one." I gave a rueful smile. "And I'm not surprised to hear you say that based on the stink eye you shot him last month."

"Yeah, well . . ." He ran his hand over his jaw, the stubble bristling. "He was a jerk in high school."

Ryan must've only been a jerk to Micah because as far as I'd known, he was well-liked by everyone. A june bug flew by, popping against the glass on the French doors and falling to the ground. Precious scampered past me to investigate the insect, the leash brushing my legs. "Care to elaborate?"

Micah's gaze flitted from me to the dog. "He used to talk about you . . . in the locker room."

My jaw unhinged.

"The things y'all did."

I held up a hand. "Yup. I got that." Betrayal and embarrassment wound through me. Just when I thought there couldn't be any other terrible consequences from that relationship. "What a jerk." I echoed Micah's previous remark. My pulse pounded, whooshing in my ears. If only I could figure out where he was staying. Or what vehicle he drove. Maybe I'd stuff a banana up his car's tail pipe. Or break in and stash a few crawfish under his car seat. Though I hated to waste the little guys, especially with crawfish season being so short. But they'd be perfect. Their stench growing each day. Or maybe I'd capture Cést Fou and let him loose in Ryan's automobile.

"I never understood why you were with him."

I exhaled a sharp breath, rubbing the Crease. "We all make bad decisions, particularly when we're young and think we know everything." I switched to massaging my neck and concentrating on lowering my blood pressure. "In my defense, he wasn't completely rotten to me back then. He did do some nice things."

Both of Micah's brows arched, his head tipping sideways.

"He was kind to my grandma and Claire." At least, he had been up until Mawmaw's health decline. "And every single Valentine's Day he sent me an anonymous carnation through the high school fundraiser."

Micah snorted. "Did he?"

"He said it was him."

"I helped run that fundraiser each year. He never made a purchase." Micah unwrapped Precious's tangled leash line from around his leg. "But he did take undue credit for a lot of things back then, including one of my history reports that went missing from my backpack senior year."

Hmm. Though he'd never stolen them from me, Ryan *had* used countless papers and projects I'd done, recycling my work from previous years. He'd reasoned me into believing it wasn't a big deal. In college it was simple for him to do since we'd had different professors. And I'd willingly gone along, especially with feeling guilty about Mawmaw's caregiving taking time away from him. And then there'd been the postcollege internship I'd wanted that he'd ended up with. He'd convinced me it wasn't a good fit for me. The muscles at the base of my neck began tensing. Instead of a scarlet *A*, an immense *G* for gullible should've been sewn to my chest back then. At least I'd never let him get his hooks into the café.

"But, hey, people change, right? Maybe he's turned a new leaf since then."

I scoffed, thinking of the Ryan of today. Still not apologizing. Not bothering to ask about Hayley. Snooping around my restaurant. Wanting to destroy the Vieux Carré Café. I was certain his leaf had fossilized when he'd broken my heart.

16

MY LIFE NOW REVOLVED around bird and dog poop. Friday morning had arrived, and I'd just finished hosing off Cést Fou's latest contribution to the courtyard. Next on my list? Disposing of the deposits Precious had left in the side yard. Somehow Hayley had missed them. Part of me wanted to place that doggie doo-doo bag where it would leave a permanent mark on Hayley's brain. Like her pillow. Or phone (if she ever set it down long enough).

Mayté exited the café, descending the steps. The early sun glinted off her black hair. "Hayley and your boyfriend did that while you were under the weather."

"He's not my boyfriend." Though the thought of Micah and Hayley tackling this disgusting deed softened my heart. Maybe I'd let Precious's overlooked manure go this time.

"He should be." She moved into the shade of the live oak, pausing near the fountain. Her gaze lifted to the branches. "My husband wouldn't clean bird caca for me."

I snorted and made my way to the hose reel cart next to the mansion, tucked behind an azalea bush. The shrub's coral blooms dwindled from their latest round of showing off. Bending over, I turned the handle, winding the hose back up.

"I spotted *two* parrots this morning when I came in."

My motions paused. "Two?" Irritation spiked. Wasn't there a verse in the Bible about the fear and dread of humans falling on all animals, including birds? I thrust the wheel with more gusto. Well, it was time for Cést Fou to feel that fear and dread. I finished my task and walked toward Mayté, wiping my hands on the thighs of my yoga pants. I'd planned to slip upstairs, change into business-appropriate attire, and spend the rest of the day in my office, catching up on work. I'd now add in research time on getting rid of nuisance birds.

Mayté cast a glance to the back doors, her lips pressed into a hard line. "I have more bad news. Your ex offered me a job."

My mind blanked and yet hazy thoughts swirled along the borders, just out of reach.

Mayté removed a business card from her pocket, handing it to me.

With numb fingers I held the card, unable to read the ink on the gray background, everything on the little rectangle a blur.

"He wanted to 'compliment the chef' the other day. I didn't want to say anything when you were sick. You know, kicking a dog while it's down and all that."

I slowly shook my head, trying to regain my bearings. Ryan had tried to steal Mayté? Anger flared through my body. He hadn't changed. In fact, he'd gotten worse. This wasn't my college paper on real-world marketing he'd gone after. It was my executive chef.

"He described his place as focusing purely on upscale dinner service. I calmly told him I knew exactly who he was, and he could take his offer and stick it."

The prick of the business card's corner against my index finger registered, and I lifted my attention to Mayté, her last sentence replaying. Mayté's version of calm—eerie calm—combined with her penetrating dark gaze had caused grown men to sweat profusely in her kitchen. It was the reason why she negotiated and ordered all of the café's supplies. Our suppliers never got an order wrong or were dishonest on costs. Hopefully Ryan had felt the heat and got a taste of true loyalty.

"Thank you." I pulled in a steadying breath, the gathering tension releasing, gratefulness to Mayté replacing it. "We've talked about this before, but anything you want—"

"I know." She held up her hand. "I know." Her expression softened. "You'll have to pry my key to this place out of my cold, dead fingers. Plus, I wouldn't want you and Hayley starving to death."

I offered a weak smile and scanned Ryan's business card, the last of the blindsided haze lifting. His name, title, and email address became clear, along with a local phone number and address. My stomach sank. It appeared Ryan was here to stay.

That evening found me back in the courtyard accompanied by my best friend. Our Friday night of beignets and decaf café au lait had been upgraded to include a side order of entertainment in the form of parrot shooting. My weapon of choice? The hose with the nozzle set to *jet*. Julia had arrived toting two locked and loaded Nerf guns. So far the score tallied at humans: 2, parrots: 0. Though our antics hadn't actually touched Cést Fou and his friend, we'd been successful in annoying the feathered fiends into leaving.

I'd finished bringing Julia up to speed on everything. From Hayley's sickness to Ryan's attempt to steal Mayté.

The floodlights from the house illuminated her exasperation. "I can't believe he made Mayté a job offer. Right in your café!"

"I know. A huge part of me wanted to go to his office, find his car, and lace the interior with crawfish." I sighed. "Instead, I started on an application for a federal SBA loan."

Julia leaned forward, resting her elbow on the table. "Much better *and* legal use of your time."

Meh. I wasn't so sure. I'd scoured the online form for some sort of checkbox to mark my submission as urgent, but it looked like I'd have to wait the full ten to twenty-one days for the review to process. I drained the last of my coffee, returning the mug to the saucer with a clank. Perhaps if I called and asked to speak to someone who'd been terribly wronged by their ex, they'd expedite my request with a favorable outcome.

Julia leaned back in her seat. "I was only gone one week. How could so much happen?"

Movement above caught our attention. Julia slowly reached for her Nerf guns. I edged down, picking up the hose at my feet. Lukewarm water dripped from the nozzle, rolling across my fingers. We trained our sights on the tree, scanning the branches.

Darn you, Cést Fou. And darn Ryan. It was one thing to go after the Vieux Carré Café. He didn't know Claire's connection to the place. But my executive chef? That was intentional. What was he up to? Did he have another restaurant already, or was he boldly planning ahead for his future establishment at the Vieux Carré Café? A mosquito buzzed near my ear, and I swatted at it. How could I have been with that man for so long and not realized this deplorable side of him? Had I been blinded by love? Was that a real thing? And if so, there was no way I'd let it happen again.

Micah came to mind. Was he another wolf in Magnum P.I.'s clothing? I needed to consider him with my brain, not my heart, and most definitely not my hormones. A Micah Guidry pro-con spreadsheet began forming. My fingers itched to drop the hose and fetch my laptop.

"There." Julia pointed. "It's just a cardinal."

Sure enough, I spotted the red bird, hopping along a branch. "Maybe it's a spy for Cést Fou." I returned the hose to the ground and dried my hand on my napkin.

"Maybe you're taking this a little too far." Humor twinkled

in her eyes as she set her guns on the table. "Let's talk about how I can't believe you got a puppy. Precious is a cutie."

Hayley had already shown her creature off as soon as Julia had arrived. Micah thought Precious was adorable too. That added another item to his con side. Poor judgment.

"What's going on in that head of yours?" Julia's gaze lasered in on my fingers, rubbing the Crease.

Sighing, I dropped my hand to my lap. "I'm trying to figure out Micah's faults. Now that the truth's out behind his marriage ending, that big red flag is gone."

"Why are you looking for his faults?" One of her brows slowly rose.

Crud. "Because . . . we're friends again . . . and Hayley spends a lot of time at the library . . . where he is."

"Uh-huh." Skepticism shaded her expression, her lips pursing in thought. "Do you have a pro-con spreadsheet on him, and you're hoping to fill the negative side?"

I placed my napkin on the table. "No." *Not technically.* Not yet.

Her smirk confirmed her correct assumption. "He no longer has a girlfriend. That's a pro."

I brushed at a speck of powdered sugar on my skirt. "But he just got dumped, which means his next relationship is a rebound. That's a con."

"Rebound? I think you're looking for excuses."

"It's a valid concern." Besides, with my wary heart, Micah didn't stand a chance. "Plus, I'm on the verge of possibly expanding locations. I barely have enough time to shave my legs, much less date."

"So you're sticking to only being friends?"

"Yes. He's a friend, who's a guy. My only guy friend. Which has me wondering, do friends like Micah and me give each other . . ." Oh, how to ask this without stoking her meddling fires.

She straightened, a spark lighting in her eyes. "Kisses? Neck massages?"

"No!" *Sheesh.* Instead of stoking, I'd tossed on gasoline. "Gifts. Small gifts. That are more like . . . kind gestures."

"Like?"

"He filled up my gas tank."

"Ohhh." Julia practically melted. "I love it when Samuel does that. And a full tank of gas isn't a small gift."

"I know. And I'm pretty sure he won't let me pay him back."

"What if you took him to a swanky restaurant?"

"Nice try, but that's too much like a date."

"Sister, it sounds to me like the past week was too much like a marriage."

My mouth fell open.

Her teasing continued. "That must have been some kiss back in seventh grade. Why didn't y'all start dating?"

I lifted a shoulder, my thoughts shifting back in time. "We kissed on the last day of school. I saw him at church over the summer, but we acted like nothing happened." My attention drifted to the fountain, my pulse slowing. "Then in eighth grade his mom received a cancer diagnosis, and Micah sort of dropped out of sight that year. That summer she passed away."

"Poor Micah."

I nodded. "Then freshmen year I started dating Ryan."

Julia's face scrunched.

"Exactly." I released a humorless laugh. "Love blinded me once. I won't make that mistake again. My heart couldn't take it. And it's not just me a new relationship impacts. I have to think about Hayley and how it would alter her life. Especially with how things between us have gotten so much better." I shook my head. "The safest plan is to stay single."

17

"*THAT GANG OF DUCKS LOOKS LIKE TROUBLE.*" I stared down the cluster of white-feathered creatures several yards away, letting them know they weren't getting the jump on us.

Hayley snorted. "You think all animals are trouble."

Saturday afternoon found us in City Park, making our way through the Old Grove, home to an expanse of live oaks dating back eight hundred years. Hayley ignored the beauty around us, her attention on a trembling Precious, who needed near-constant coaxing to keep moving. The dog sported a purple body harness that could fit a guinea pig and a matching leash. Precious eyed one of the metal crutches supporting a massive branch on one of the trees. Her tail slid between her hind legs, and she released a pitiful whimper.

Hayley scooped her up. "Precious isn't trouble." She peppered her puppy's face with kisses as we continued walking toward our destination.

"Do I need to remind you of the *trouble* I stepped in? In my bedroom? Barefooted? I think that Old Testament decree of an eye for an eye should be utilized, with you having to experience it."

"Jesus did away with that rule."

Out of the mouths of babes.

"Love your enemy and turn your cheek." A hint of smugness shaded her tone.

A grumble rumbled within me. "I know. I know." I also knew it was a hard lesson to follow. Especially when it came to double-crossing ex-fiancés. And people who cut in lines. And smokers who littered.

We approached Bayou Metairie and crossed a stone foot-bridge to Goldfish Island. Surrounded by the murky waters, the smidgen of land was just enough to house two live oaks, several stout palm trees, and one concrete bench. Hayley set Precious down, the dog taking all of two steps away to sniff the dirt.

I sat on the bench, a mere yard from the bridge, placing my purse next to me. Although we were alone on the island, the park bustled with activity. Across the water lay the Peristyle, an enormous open-air pavilion over a century old. With its towering stone columns, the colonnade appeared as if it'd been plucked right out of ancient Greece. A group of teenagers skate-boarded through the oblong structure, while others rested on the stairs enjoying the scenery and cool front that had rolled through last night.

Precious scratched at Hayley's black-and-white-checkered Vans, and she picked up the dog again, taking a seat beside me. "Mr. Micah knows to meet us here?"

"Yes, he chose the spot." I cast my gaze behind me to the footbridge and beyond. No Micah. Just a family of four on bikes pedaling along a paved path. Why Micah had selected this place to brainstorm the next library event, I had no idea. But meeting was a necessity since I'd thought of squat.

I turned around and ran my damp palms down the thighs of my skinny jeans, uncertain about my feelings toward Micah but very certain he would strictly remain a friend. As if to prove my decision, I'd worn a short-sleeved cardigan sweater set. A beautiful deep violet sweater set. Considering he was only a friend, it didn't matter what he thought about my stuffy style. Hayley lowered Precious to her lap, and the dog curled into a ball. "So were you and Mr. Micah like boyfriend and girlfriend back in school?"

Ugh. First Julia, now Hayley. "No."

Her auburn brows rose. "Y'all kissed and weren't even dating?"

Puppy needle teeth. I steered my gaze straight ahead to the view of the Peristyle and the couple walking their rottweiler along the opposite bank. "It's not like I went around kissing all the guys. It was more of a peer pressure thing." I stared at Hayley. "Which is why you should never, ever, ever give in to peer pressure. Not with kissing or more than kissing. Or crack cocaine. Or any kind of dare."

She did a poor job of hiding her smile, her bright blue eyes filling with mirth.

"I'm serious."

"I'll be sure to avoid peer-pressure kissing or more than kissing. And crack cocaine." Her grin turned mischievous. "But only if you tell me what happened with Mr. Micah."

"Blackmailer!"

She laughed, my favorite sound in the whole wide world. It was amazing how God could use the flu and an abandoned puppy to restore our relationship.

"Fine," I mock grumbled. "But I'm going to get your promise in writing."

"I'll text it to you."

I scoffed, shaking my head. *Kids these days.* "There's not much to tell. It was the last day of school in seventh grade, and we were in the library."

"Ew!" Hayley's exclamation jolted Precious. "The *library*?"

"What about the library?" A masculine voice spoke from behind. A voice I recognized.

Sarah McLachlan.

Hayley and I whipped our heads around, and sure enough, Micah stepped off the footbridge, toting a plastic grocery bag. What was he? A Ninja? Had they taught him to walk in stealth mode in those jiujitsu classes he took?

"Nothing!" My hand flew to my forehead, heat rising in my cheeks. "I mean . . . the next library event! That's why we're here. To plan it." Where oh where had the Landry Mask gone?

Precious scrambled down Hayley's legs to get to Micah, landing with an ungraceful thump on the ground. She took off like a shot, her retractable leash raking over me. Hayley stood, skirting the bench, freeing me from the possibility of leash burn. Micah obliged the dog with a thorough greeting, rubbing her tiny, Telly Savalas head.

I fought for level breathing and calm thinking.

Hayley rolled her lips inward, smiling, rocking back and forth, as though she physically couldn't contain what we'd been discussing.

I hurled eye daggers at her.

She smirked.

Micah took a seat, setting the grocery bag on the ground. The Hawaiian shirt he wore indicated he'd come from the library. His gaze moved between me and Hayley, amusement in his features. "I'm certain I'm missing something."

"Nope," I said. "You're not missing anything. Not a thing."

Precious nosed his bag, drawing Micah's attention. For the second time today, I found myself grateful for the animal.

Micah reached down and pulled out the contents, giving Precious another ear scratch in the process. "I brought frozen peas. I thought Hayley might want to feed the ducks."

"Thank you." Hayley eyed the veggies. "But peas?"

He nodded, returning them to the bag. "It's healthier than bread."

Hmm. Thoughtful would have to be added to his pro-con

list. Thoughtfulness toward Hayley *and* ducks. His list was starting to look mighty one-sided. I placed my index finger to the Crease and pressed.

Hayley pulled Precious away from the peas, her gaze on Micah. "Did that squirrel return to the book drop-off today?"

My finger stilled, my brain readjusting to the change in topic. "A live squirrel?"

Micah nodded with a wince. "It wasn't there today. Thank goodness. Poor Nellie's shook up, and she wasn't even the one to find it yesterday."

"Are there normally odd things in the drop box?" I asked.

"I haven't found too many strange items here. Mardi Gras beads, some mail." He leaned back against the bench. "But in Colorado I removed a McDonald's bag filled with uneaten food, a shoe, and some Blockbuster tapes."

"Hmph." I picked a piece of lint from the sleeve of my cardigan. "Must be all the marijuana there that spurred such odd contributions." I directed my gaze to Hayley. "Marijuana is bad for you. It's the gateway drug."

She heaved a full-body sigh with the amount of drama exclusive to thirteen-year-olds. "You've always said cigarettes are the gateway drug."

I pinned her with a stare. "There's lots of gateways. Smoking, vaping, energy drinks—"

A whistle pierced the air, putting us on alert for the park's miniature train headed our way. Hayley stepped on the footbridge for a more advantageous sighting of the ride for kids of all ages.

"Saved by the whistle," Micah murmured.

I turned to him, and he winked at me. Winked! Schooling my features, I conjured the Landry Mask. We needed clear lines in place between us. We would not be flirty friends. We'd be friends, period. It was the most I could offer. All my heart could afford. And the sooner I made that distinction, the better.

I glanced down into my open purse and to the thank-you card I'd gotten for Micah. The friendship wording I'd used within it would be impossible for him to misinterpret.

The red train chugged into view, click-clacking along the thin tracks circling the bayou, botanical garden, amusement park, and Storyland. The conductor pulled the bell's cord, its clang reverberating. A little boy on the train waved to Hayley, and she returned the gesture. The thrum of the motor petered out as the train disappeared.

Hayley meandered back, Precious lagging behind.

Micah kicked his long legs out, crossing them at his ankles. "Have y'all come up with any ideas for the next event?"

Hayley and I slid a look between each other, her guilty face no doubt mirroring mine.

"Slackers," Micah teased. "Lucky for y'all, I did some checking around at other parishes and what their libraries have done."

"Cheater," Hayley razzed.

He chuckled. "Only to use them for inspiration. Jefferson parish arranged books to create a mini-golf course—"

"Veto." I held up my hand. "Flying balls and swinging clubs? I'd like to keep all my windows intact."

"Okay," he said, undeterred. "What about a costume contest based on fictional characters?"

Hayley pulled a face.

"What?" Micah's brows rose, questioning her. "Too lame?"

Her shoulders lifted in an attempt at a polite diss of his suggestion.

"But you dressed up as Susan from Narnia when you were little," I said.

"*Little* being the keyword." Her nose wrinkled. "It'd be pretty cringe to do that now."

"Cringe?" Micah groaned, tipping his eyes to the skies in mock horror.

I couldn't help but smile at their exchange, how at ease they were. How grateful I was to Micah for the way he'd gotten her to open up in such a short span of time. Warmth tingled in my chest, an invisible balloon of appreciation inflating beneath my ribs. Maybe today wasn't the right time to give him that card. Maybe I was overreacting. Maybe we could see what happened. Maybe—

Hayley laughed at Micah, unabashed and genuine.

And realization shot through me like an arrow, deflating my building emotions and muddled thinking. Hayley and Micah had formed a friendship. A positive one in a way I hadn't anticipated. Any romance had too high of a likelihood of ending badly. If Micah and I dated and broke up, Hayley could lose her relationship with Micah, which could in turn affect mine with her.

I gazed at her slim frame engulfed in a black sweatshirt and plaid leggings. Even if she'd been wearing neon colors, the smile on her face right now because of Micah would've been the brightest thing on her. Her bond with him, and me, bore the utmost importance. And I couldn't risk that. I nodded internally, as though my brain were dispatching orders to my emotions and hormones. Ten-hut! Operation Friends Only was officially underway. I could almost feel my vulnerable heart breathe a sigh of relief.

"We could do a destination theme," Micah said. "What's y'all's favorite vacation spot?"

Hayley's smile dimmed, her gaze lowering to the ground.

My gut twisted, heaviness growing within my heart, pulsing weight out through my veins with each beat. I couldn't catch a break today. "We've never been on a vacation."

Micah became unnaturally quiet, and I could only imagine the thoughts running through his head, and how I wanted to silence them with the truth. But I couldn't in front of Hayley.

I cleared my throat. "We've taken day trips here and there." There'd never been enough time for more than that. Or funds available between investing everything in the café and sending

Hayley to a private school. Although Claire and Adrian had had an ironclad will, they hadn't had life insurance.

Hayley's attention shifted to the oak tree behind the bench, and one of its branches that dipped, touching the ground at the shore's edge before arcing slightly over the water. She neared the branch, leaning against it. Precious followed, and Hayley's expression lifted at taking her in. I should've gotten her a dog a long time ago. Twenty dogs. And a hamster.

"Okay." Micah rubbed his hands together as though starting a fire. "If you *could* go anywhere on vacation, where would you go?"

"Hawaii," Hayley said.

I blinked. She sure had whipped that answer out. Guilt pricked my heart again. It took a moment to realize Micah watched me, waiting for my response. Before us, the sun shimmered on the water, and I thought of the screen saver on my computer. Of all the different destinations I longed to visit. Places bragging of God's handiwork. The Grand Canyon, Niagara Falls. My gaze settled on Hayley. "Hawaii."

A tiny sprout of a grin lightened her face.

If only I could make that trip come true.

Micah picked up a leaf from the bench, twirling it between his fingers. "What about a luau-themed event?"

Hayley perked. "Everyone could make their own leis."

"Nice." Micah nodded, letting the leaf drift to the barren ground. "I could bring all the books with ties to Hawaii or the beach."

Hayley shifted away from the branch, moving closer. "We could have beach balls to throw around." She and Micah regarded me, hope in their eyes.

"Beach balls are fine."

"And inexpensive." Micah rested his arm along the back of the bench, his hand stopping mere inches from my shoulder. "The donations I've received can definitely cover that."

His refence to monetary constraints reminded me of my own reality, pushing a real trip to Hawaii further out of reach. I leaned forward, adding distance between his too-close fingers and my body. Picking up an acorn next to my feet, I rolled it around in my palm. Other than the issue of taking that much time off from work, it'd be financially impossible to afford a vacation like that under normal circumstances. But with buying the Vieux Carré Café? My posture slumped, and I let the acorn slip through my grasp, like the reality of that type of trip. We'd have to put it off for quite some time. Possibly to celebrate Hayley graduating from high school. Five plus years away. I winced.

"Kate?"

My attention returned to the present. To Micah sitting next to me, and Hayley carrying Precious across the footbridge, the bag of peas in her other hand.

"You okay?"

"Yup." I pulled in a breath of the moist, earthy scent surrounding us, and straightened my spine. "Never better." I kept Hayley in sight. She walked along the bayou's edge, out of earshot, stopping near a patch of Louisiana iris. Their vivid green leaves provided a beautiful backdrop to their royal-purple blooms.

"You don't have to do that."

"Do what?"

Micah lowered his voice, leaning in. "Pretend everything's perfect all the time."

I swallowed, meeting his gaze. "I know."

"Do you?" His emerald eyes softened.

I fought the impulse to fidget, not wanting to show how correct his assertion had been. Returning my attention to Hayley, I found her tossing a few peas onto the water, several ducks swimming her way. "I believe this past week you've seen firsthand how imperfect my life is." A brisk breeze sailed through, untucking my hair from behind my ear. I left it there, grateful for a partial shield from his penetrating gaze.

He slid closer, bringing the scent of pine and cinnamon. "But it took you having a bad case of the flu to . . . lower your defenses."

To lower my Landry Mask. Which wasn't a wise thing to have done. Especially given how close he was again to making contact with my shoulder. And how much I wanted to shift near and experience his caress.

He moved, the tips of his fingers grazing my elbow in a playful yet purposeful way.

A heated shiver rippled across my skin, and I swallowed, gathering my wits. Friends definitely didn't touch each other like that. Or want their friends to keep doing it. No, once these library events were over, I'd have to put distance between us. In the meantime, maybe I'd gift Micah with a supply of garlic breath mints. Or Pepé Le Pew cologne. But first, I'd leave no room for misunderstandings. I pulled the card from my purse and handed it to him.

A twinkle of surprise lit his eyes. "For me?"

"For you."

He peeled the flap from the envelope back, removing the card. My stomach clenched. A gift card to the Garden District Book Shop slipped out, landing on his lap. He left it, his attention absorbed by the message I'd written: *Friends like you are the best lagniappe.*

His cresting smile paused. A beat passed before he picked up the gift card. "I love this bookstore. This is thoughtful."

"It was the least I could do, especially since you brought my car home from the library and filled the gas tank. Thank you for that." I peered at Hayley, who continued throwing veggies to the ducks, Precious cowering between her legs.

Micah tapped my knee with the card. "Friends, huh?"

"Yes." I met his stare, infusing kind resolve into my words.

"Just friends." There. If a romantic bud existed between us, it'd been officially snipped and now lay decapitated on the ground at our feet.

His gaze altered, as though a spark of determination were igniting.

Oh boy. Either I was reading him wrong, or he wasn't in agreement with the pruning I'd done.

He tucked the card and gift card inside the envelope. "You seem set on that decision."

"I am. I have reasons. Good reasons." I swallowed past my dry throat. "Four of them." Actually, only three came to mind. Hayley, risking my heart, and not having the time to date. Especially with the prospect of expanding locations. But three sounded wimpy and uneven, and I needed the appearance of a concrete case.

"Four." He nodded gravely. "That's a solid number." Something in the way he said it made it sound like he didn't think very much of my four reasons. Easing back, he adopted a casual posture. "What are they?"

I shouldn't have been surprised at his forwardness. This was Micah Guidry after all. The same Micah Guidry who in fourth grade had told our principal she had a huge booger dangling from her nose. And yet here I sat, taken aback. "I . . . I don't need to tell you."

"It's only fair you do." He placed the envelope on the bench between us, confidence and ease in his movements. "And I'll take just two of your reasons."

I scoffed. "You'll take none."

"I held your hair while you puked. That's worth at least one."

I gasped. "I knew you'd use that against me one day."

"I also know about your tabloids."

My eyes widened.

He shrugged.

"Fine. I'll give you one reason."

"I think Bat Boy would agree I deserve two."

I narrowed my gaze. "It's one or none."

With exaggeration, he filled his cheeks with air and blew them out. "You're a hard negotiator." He reached over, holding out his hand to shake.

I eyed his outstretched fingers.

One corner of his mouth quirked. "We're not allowed to touch?"

"No. Or flirt."

"Then I guess kissing's out?"

Fighting the instinct to outright gape at him, I clung to the Landry Mask. But that didn't stop my imagination from wondering just how amazing kissing him would feel. I redirected the awareness rippling through me into faking a fierce glare.

He raised his hands in surrender. "Okay, okay."

Taking a calming breath, I forced my eyes away from his handsome face and to the moss dripping from one of the branches above us.

"So what's *one* of the reasons we can't be more than friends? And I'd like the most important of them."

That was easy. "Hayley."

His brows pulled together, his head slightly flinching.

"If I date anyone, it affects her."

"Obviously. And we'd be careful when it came to her."

Swoon.

Here sat a caring man who wanted to be sensitive to Hayley. A man who wanted to kiss me. That snipped bud on the ground sprouted roots and began burrowing into the hard dirt. *Nope, nope, nope.* "Being careful isn't enough. I don't want her affected. At all. And most certainly not by us dating and breaking up, especially since she likes you so much."

Crossing his arms, he pursed his lips. "We wouldn't break up."

The breath whooshed from my lungs, and I braced my hands

against the bench on either side of my hips. He'd taken the question marks I'd had of his interest in me and replaced them with exclamation marks. Exclamation marks in bold font.

He again lifted his shoulder, all confidence.

I shook my head, regaining my composure. "Well, we'll never find out."

Slowly, one corner of his mouth edged north. "All right, then."

18

A SURPRISE PACKAGE WAITED on the back steps of the café. It was
Monday morning, and I'd just returned from dropping Hayley
and Emma off at school. A yellow Post-it note with my name on
it stuck to the side of a brown paper gift bag. I toted it inside,
greeted by Harry Connick Jr.'s smooth voice flowing from the
speakers and the aroma of freshly brewed coffee. Walking past
the short hallway to my office and the restaurant bathrooms,
I stopped in the main dining room, scanning the space, con-
firming our readiness to open in fifteen minutes. Jonathan and
Penny moved with purpose, Penny ensuring the tables were set
for the first customers of the day, and Jonathan checking the
server station. Meg, the hostess on shift, lined up the menus
at the hostess stand.

"Good morning," I called out. "Do y'all need anything?"

Greetings and *no ma'am*s followed from them, along with
a yawn from Meg.

I approached Jonathan. "How's your mom doing?"

"Better." He wiped down the espresso machine. "Her fender
bender wasn't as bad as we thought. She's got some bruising
and a sprained wrist. Has to take it easy a few days."

"That's great news it's not serious."

177

He nodded, the circles under his eyes hinting at the toll the worry for his mother had had on him. "Thanks for asking."

"If you want to take off to care for her, I can cover your shift."

"Thank you, but I think we're okay."

With everything seemingly in control, I made my way to my office, leaving the door open.

I placed the mystery package on my desk. Peering inside the bag, I found a book and a folded sheet of paper. I retrieved the book, finding another sticky note on the cover with one sentence in a masculine scrawl.

Bat Boy would approve.

I pulled the Post-it off, revealing a red apple held by pale hands. *Twilight?* A laugh broke free, and I shook my head at Micah's ridiculousness.

"What's so funny?" Mayté appeared in the doorway.

I shoved the book into the bag. "Nothing."

She gave me a you're-not-fooling-me look, but didn't press. "One of the fryers is acting up again."

My stomach clenched. "The same one?"

"Yup."

"Is it the thermostat again?"

"Pretty sure. I've put in a service call."

A dull ache began at my temples. This had been the third time in the past six months the equipment had acted up. New fryers typically lasted ten to fifteen years, but I'd purchased this one secondhand to save money. Though buying pre-owned appliances negated extended warranties and factory support, I'd negotiated a guarantee. Unfortunately, that had ended long ago. With all the beignets we made, our fryers were essential, and they needed to be reliable. "Okay." I rubbed the side of my head. "I'll evaluate biting the bullet and purchasing a new fryer or taking a chance on another used one." That trip to Hawaii slipped further out of reach.

"Sounds good." She shifted to leave.

"Hey, can I ask what you were planning for me and Hayley's dinner tonight?"

"Lasagna. I prepped it yesterday. Just have to bake it."

"Can you send Jonathan home with it instead? His mom's out of commission for a few days."

"Sure thing." She disappeared, no doubt heading for the kitchen to give the ailing fryer a swift kick to its shin.

Taking a seat in my leather chair, I pulled the book back out, setting it on my desk. I removed a sheet of white printer paper that was folded in the pages, finding a handwritten note.

Reason #2 for why you won't date me:

☐ I drive a flip-prone vehicle.

☐ You wouldn't be able to control yourself around me.

Another laugh erupted, dampening the qualms of running a business. *Oh, Micah. Why do you have to be so cute? And determined?* I continued reading.

P.S. The balance on the gift card to the bookstore will cover the rest of the books in the series. My sister swears they're addictive.

I snorted and peered into the bag. Sure enough, the gift card to the Garden District Book Shop lay at the bottom. Glancing at the paperback, I wondered if I could return it and reload the money onto the card. It was the right thing to do considering that tank of gas I now drove around on. But how would I give the gift card back to him without actually seeing him? After our convo at City Park this past Saturday, I'd planned to avoid the man until the next event in three weeks. I could mail the gift card or simply leave it on his porch. Nah. Those avenues seemed too predictable.

A lightbulb clicked on in my brain, and a sneaky type of joy slid through me. I bit my bottom lip and my growing smile, knowing exactly how I'd accomplish my task. But first, I'd get my application for the federal SBA loan submitted today, and send up a huge prayer with it.

The next afternoon, I parked on the side street next to the library. The handful of spots in the meager lot had all been taken, which suited me. In keeping with avoiding Micah, I'd planned to text Hayley and have her meet me at the car anyway. Since yesterday, I'd reread his note an embarrassing number of times. And each time I slipped the note into my desk drawer, I'd reminded myself of the pitfalls of romantic relationships. Of the high probability of history repeating itself.

Movement on the property's west lawn caught my attention. There, in the small reading garden, stood Micah at the little free library, opening the glass-paned doors. Today's Hawaiian shirt featured fish in an array of species. An inkling of fondness tugged up the corners of my lips. But then I noticed the slump of his shoulders, his downcast expression. The warm fuzzies that had been building cooled. Without thinking, I exited my vehicle, my focus trained on him.

He glanced over. A hesitant smile crossed his face, then dimmed. He lifted his hand, gesturing me near, and returned to sorting through the books before him.

My heels clicked against the concrete as I followed the path toward him. Carefully trimmed camellia shrubs lined the walkway, their soft pink blooms kissing the air with a delicate fragrance. The walkway deposited me into an area canopied by a live oak. Two benches and the little free library completed the area.

Normally, the enchanting spot would hold my attention,

but not today. No, it remained on Micah. On his glum features and weary posture. Concern for him grew with every step. He appeared so different from the man who'd flirted with me at City Park three days ago. I wasn't even in a relationship with him, and the sensation we were about to be thrown for a loop twisted in my gut.

I stopped several feet away, leaning on my toes to keep my heels from sinking in the dirt. "Everything all right?"

Micah shut the doors on the tiny lending library. "There's something I need to talk to you about."

"Okay." Hefting my purse strap higher on my shoulder, I struggled to keep my mind from taking off in multiple negative directions. I glanced at the library, where Hayley was. Had he discovered something bad about her?

"I didn't think this was a big deal, but . . . in light of what I found out yesterday afternoon . . ." He palmed the back of his neck, his gaze earnest. "It involves why I returned to New Orleans."

My worry eased, and I moved to one of the benches, carefully sidestepping the protruding roots from the oak. I took a seat, setting my purse aside.

"It was to help look after my dad."

The air held captive in my lungs released, more tension slipping free.

Micah's hand dropped from his neck. "I hadn't initially mentioned it, because . . . well, like I said, I didn't think it was a big deal." He paced a few steps away and stopped. "After all, my sister's been here all these years. Cutting his grass, helping him around his house, caring for him when he was sick." The muscles in his back expanded with a full breath. He turned, facing me. "The last time I visited, I realized how involved she's had to be, especially with him not driving anymore. So I decided to move back to give her a break."

The rest of the tightness within me loosened, and another

positive quality filled on Micah's pro-con list. "I'm sure she's grateful to have you here." I studied him, trying to make sense of why helping his dad in those simple ways constituted such seriousness.

"When you were sick, I was going to tell you, but then you'd shared about your grandma. Even though my dad's care was nothing like hers, it didn't seem like the right moment."

My mind snagged on his usage of *was*. And his first words returned to me. *"In light of what I found out."* I leaned forward. "What happened yesterday?"

"My dad sprained his ankle."

"Oh." I could hear the relief in my voice. "That doesn't sound too bad. Is he okay?"

He nodded. "He injured it *so* easily, though—just going down one step—that Renee and I began wondering if something else was at play. The X-ray they took of his leg at the doctor's office showed weakened bones. During the appointment, my dad fessed up to the back pain he's been having and agreed to additional testing."

I fidgeted with the purse strap on my lap. *Oh, Lord, please don't let it be serious. Micah's already been through so much with his mom.*

"We're waiting for the results from a bone density scan, but his doctor said all symptoms point to advanced osteoporosis."

"So it's his bones?"

"Yes." He stared at his shoes. Sunlight snuck through the massive oak's leaves, dappling Micah and the ground around him.

"If it is advanced osteoporosis, are there medications or treatments?"

"There are," he said. "But if it's too advanced, there's no reversing it. It comes down to preventative care."

"I'm sorry this is all happening."

The traffic moving along St. Charles Avenue hummed in the

background, an approaching streetcar adding its own clanking rhythm.

Micah studied his hands clasped before him. "I don't know what the future holds with my dad and what his care may look like, but given what you went through with your grandma, I wanted to be up-front."

I stilled, and a chill pricked my skin at the thought of Mawmaw and those final years. I hadn't been faced with anyone close to me being put in a caregiver role and what that would entail. My shoulders curled forward, uncertainty slowing the breaths in my chest. I lifted my gaze to the oak's thick branches jutting over us. *Lord, please help me have the right heart in this.*

A breeze swept through, bringing the leaves to life. I focused on their rustling and regaining perspective. Micah's potential situation with his father was different from what I'd gone through. And most importantly, it wasn't about me. I took in Micah. His concern not only for his father but his sensitivity toward me. Empathy swelled, overlapping the echo of past fears. I pushed up from the bench and moved toward him. "I'm sorry I painted such a dismal picture of that time with my grandma."

Micah shook his head. "You don't—"

I held up my hand. "Despite how hard it was, I never regretted it." I offered a reassuring smile. "And if it comes to that for you, I have a feeling you won't regret it either. Plus, you have your sister to help."

He made a noncommittal noise. "She's already done enough all these years."

"If it becomes really involved care, you can't do it alone. Not long-term."

Micah nudged a fallen acorn with the toe of his shoe.

"And I hope you know, I'm here too." My stomach gave a mild quiver. "Even if it's just to talk."

His gaze flicked up to mine, and he studied me.

I hoped he saw the truth in my words. Or at least how much I wanted them to be true.

"Thank you." The weight that had been in his countenance seemed to lift. The spark returning to his green eyes.

Every fiber within me wanted to close the distance between us and hug him. Wanted to ignore my vulnerable heart, if only for a moment.

As if he could sense that battle warring inside me, Micah edged closer, the air between us shifting. Building with meaning.

Sarah McLachlan. I glanced at my feet, breaking our connection. This conversation, and Micah setting expectations for what his life may start to look like, felt as if we were tiptoeing out of friendship and into something more. Walking onto a path I couldn't tread. And so I took a step back. Literally. My body smacking into the tiny book house. *Oof.* "Hayley."

Micah darted forward, but I held up my hands, righting myself on my own.

"Hayley." His mouth lifted in a playful smile. "As in one of the four reasons you can't date me?"

"Yes." I winced. "I mean, she's waiting." I grabbed my purse and made my way up the walkway, seeking the safety of the library.

"You know," Micah called after me, laughter in his voice, "I'm still waiting to see which box you check."

For four days I'd managed to avoid Micah Guidry. And that streak came to a screeching halt on Easter Sunday. At church. *Really, Lord? I thought being single was where it was at biblically.* Micah pushed the wheelchair of an elderly man, no doubt his father. My heart pinched, and memories laced with sadness over Mawmaw's final years rolled through my mind. I forced my eyes from the wheelchair to Micah's face. My thoughts lightened, a pitter-patter emerging in my chest.

"Well, well, well," Julia crooned next to me. "Look who switched services."

"Shush," I scolded. "And don't make eye contact."

"Why? You're just *friends*, right?"

"Yes." I cleared my throat and smoothed a hand down the hip of my sleeveless fit-and-flare dress. "Just friends." I hadn't had a chance to tell her about Micah's not-so-subtle hints at the park about wanting to date me, or his surprise gift this past Monday. Based on the meddlesome gleam in her eye, withholding that information had been the correct choice.

"I'm guessing that's his dad," Julia said. "What happened?"

"He sprained his ankle." I also hadn't yet shared with her my convo during the past week with Micah regarding his father.

We stood in the welcome center, against a wall of windows and out of the way of foot traffic. People spilled from the vast sanctuary, some making their way for the exits, others beelining for the free coffee bar. I kept Julia company while she waited for Samuel to finish his undercover security detail. Hayley had already left with Emma and her parents, where they were having a sleepover since they didn't have school tomorrow.

I'd let her choose between a crawfish boil at Julia's house today or going to Emma's. Given the fact Julia's collegiate sons wouldn't be in town (and therefore not in sight to crush on), she'd chosen Emma's.

I scanned the distance to the women's bathroom and eased a step away.

Julia's hand clamped onto my wrist. "What aren't you telling me?"

"Nothing." My response came too fast.

A glimmer shone in Julia's eyes, her grasp tightening ever so slightly.

185

If only I could drink some of that trippy potion from *Alice in Wonderland*, shrink to the size of Precious, and scurry away. "Hi, Micah!" Julia waved at him. And not in a small, polite way. No, she'd fully raised her arm and flailed, as if Micah were an airplane, and she held a bright orange stick, directing him to a gate.

I restrained from stabbing my stiletto heel into her sandaled foot.

Micah's gaze slid between me and my ex-best friend. With a tentative smile, he moved in our direction, carefully weaving his dad through the crowd.

I leaned toward Julia, keeping my voice low. "You're cruisin' for a bruisin'."

She sniffed, and finally released her grip. "I seem to remember you wholeheartedly meddling in my love life last year."

I grumbled, hating her correctness. "There's a distinct difference. I don't *want* a love life." I hazarded another glance Micah's way. His gray slacks and tucked-in white polo highlighted his athletic physique. *Darn you, jiujitsu.* Even ninety-something Marlene Richards, who Julia had nicknamed Miss Hawaiian Tropics due to her lifelong participation in swimsuit competitions, slowed her motorized scooter, her attention channeling on Micah's broad shoulders. Shoulders I had rested my head against when he'd carried me from his Jeep to my bed. Heat spread up my neck, no doubt flushing my face.

"If you don't want a love life, what's the harm in talking to Micah?" Faux innocence coated Julia's tone. "P.S. You're blushing."

"I'm not blushing. I'm hot from these windows and the sun beating down on me." I motioned to the glass behind us, instantly losing my argument. The skies outside boasted fluffy clouds, blocking all direct sunlight.

Julia snickered.

Micah neared, his biceps and forearms flexing beautifully as he steered the wheelchair to a stop before us. "Dad, this is Kate Landry and Julia Reed." He moved to stand beside his father. "This my dad, Gary Guidry."

We exchanged handshakes, and I was pleasantly surprised to find Mr. Gary's grip firm. If it hadn't been for the wheelchair, he'd be the picture of perfect health. "Kate Landry." His attention rested on me. "The one who owns the beignet joint?"

I smiled at his candid description. "Yes, sir."

"It's been years since I've been there." He adjusted the Bible on his lap.

"You're welcome anytime," I said. "My treat."

His cheeks lifted on his kind face. "Thank you. That's a nice offer."

"Very nice." Micah rubbed the edge of his jaw, a mild smirk tugging his lips. Too much flirting infused those two words. He wasn't honoring the rules I'd put in place on that bench in City Park. The scoundrel.

Julia tucked her brown hair behind her ear. "My husband and I are having a crawfish boil this afternoon, if y'all would like to come."

I turned my incredulous stare on Julia and began a con-con list on her in my mind. Double-crosser went in the first spot.

"Thank you, but we have plans with my daughter." Mr. Gary's gaze shifted between me and Julia, and a twinkle overtook his eyes. "Unless y'all like to play poker. Nothing goes better with crawfish than poker."

Micah cut a glance to his dad. "Renee's got a family lunch lined up for us." He turned his attention to Julia. "But thank you for the invite."

My shoulders relaxed a fraction, and I drew in a deep breath through my nose. The last thing I'd needed was an entire afternoon of dodging Micah Guidry within the confines of Julia's house.

Micah scanned the area around us. "I thought I saw Hayley earlier."

"You did." I shifted my purse to my other hand. "She left with Emma. They're having a sleepover."

Micah's sweeping gaze halted, his attention swinging my way and locking onto my face. "Really?"

Whimpering whippets. My handbag slipped from my grasp, plopping to the floor. Why had my tongue added that tidbit? Was an internal mutiny happening? What would be next? My appendix? My heart? Uh-uh. No way.

In a flash, Micah retrieved my bag. "So she's with Emma until tomorrow?" His strong eye contact brimmed with interest.

Clamping my teeth on my traitorous tongue, I gave one brisk nod. He handed me my purse, his fingers purposely grazing mine in the exchange. *Landry Mask! Landry Mask!* That was two of my friendship stipulations broken! In front of his dad! And at church! With our pastor a stone's throw away! Didn't pastors have some sort of sin radar? Or, in this case, a rascal radar?

"Rule breaker," I muttered.

Smile lines fanned at his eyes.

In my peripheral, Julia's sharp attention moved between Micah and me, taking note of every detail. Warily, I turned her way. I imagined a handle cranking in her brain like a jack-in-the-box toy, her thoughts churning and ultimately crafting a devious scheme. Her gaze slowly crept from me to Micah, and as though that final crank had rotated, her mouth popped open. "You know," she said to him, "you could always stop by later for dessert. We're all just going to be hanging out for a while anyway."

Betrayer and *busybody* autofilled on her list beneath double-crosser.

Micah rocked back on his heels. "I may take you up on that."

Julia wisely shifted away from me. "If you give me your number, I'll text you the address."

No. I did not want Julia having Micah's number. Her meddling would know no bounds. "I'll send it to you," I blurted.

One corner of his mouth twitched. "Will you?"

Despite the fire once again blooming in my tattling cheeks, I narrowed my gaze. "Yes, I will."

19

CAJUN SPICES LINGERED IN THE AIR and still tingled my tongue. Today had been ideal weather for an outdoor feast. Overcast skies had kept the temperature mild, and Julia's husband, Samuel, had blended the perfect amount of heat for the food. Several long folding tables had been erected in their backyard, the tops covered with newspaper to make the cleanup easier. Steaming crawfish, corn on the cob, red potatoes, sausage, and garlic cloves had been spread down the middle of the tables for Julia and Samuel's family, friends, and neighbors to gather around and dig in.

I'd eaten next to Julia's cantankerous mother, Mrs. Anne, who complained nonstop about nicotine withdrawal and her latest attempt to quit smoking. The entire time I'd scanned the yard and back door, bracing for Micah's appearance. Rationally, I'd known he wouldn't show until later, but when it came to Micah Guidry, rationality seemed nonexistent. At least I'd been in the right frame of mind to swing by my house and change clothes before coming here. If wearing black was a no-no when eating beignets with powdered sugar, sporting white was a faux pas when feasting on boiled crawfish. I'd donned a cute multicolored polka dot top with cap sleeves, and navy

shorts. Peeling and eating crawfish was a hands-on, messy business. But it was worth it.

After cleaning up from lunch, I'd helped Julia set out the
desserts. I now sat in the back corner of the yard, beneath the
shade of a pecan tree. It was the perfect spot to people-watch
and keep an eye out for a certain librarian so I wouldn't be
taken by surprise. Julia and Samuel had moved to this house last
year after they'd gotten married. With blending their families,
they'd wanted more space. Julia's two sons, from her deceased
husband, attended college out of state but returned home on
breaks and during the summer. Samuel's daughter, Brooke,
also in college, had moved in with them while attending nursing school locally.

Brooke, whom Samuel had received full custody of at birth,
had instantly connected with Julia when she and Samuel had
begun dating. Brooke's own mother had never shown interest
in her life, unless it involved selfish reasons.

Julia approached with a woman in tow. "This is my neighbor
Debbie."

Debbie appeared to be our age. We exchanged hellos, and
it hit me how Debbie was a stark contrast to Julia's ease. The
woman wrung her hands at her middle, her face pale, as though
she stood before a judge, about to be sentenced.

Julia swiped her long dark ponytail off her shoulder. "Debbie
makes the best elderberry syrup for medicinal purposes, and
she's considering selling it."

Ah. Things clicked into place now.

Debbie continued wringing her hands. "Well, I'm not sure.
I'm just thinking about it."

"Mom!" Brooke called from across the yard to Julia.

It wasn't the first time I'd heard Samuel's daughter call her
that, but it still struck me in the heart. And by the budding
emotions on Julia's face, it still struck her right in the heart
too. And it probably always would. I glanced down at my lap,

my stomach sinking. When Claire had died, I'd wrestled with what I'd do if Hayley referred to me as her mom, especially with her being so young. I'd vacillated between correcting her and letting it go, deciding I'd leave it up to Hayley. In the end, it'd been an empty worry since it'd never happened. I swallowed hard, pushing back the disappointment I had no claim to.

"Coming!" Julia called back to Brooke. She placed a reassuring hand on Debbie's shoulder, tossed me a wink, and departed.

I motioned to the chair beside me. "How did you start making elderberry syrup?"

Debbie lowered onto the seat. "Well, it began when my little girl kept having respiratory flare-ups each winter."

An instant connection formed, every bit of my attention anchoring on her.

"I hated to keep giving her over-the-counter meds with ingredients I couldn't pronounce, so I started researching natural remedies and came across elderberries. I tinkered with a recipe until I found the right combination." Her posture eased. "It's worked wonders for her immune system. And I feel this urging"—she held her fist to her chest—"to get it out there and help others with it."

Admiration for this woman and her caring heart welled within me. "Do you think you'd like to open a storefront?"

"Um." Her throat bobbed, and she leaned back. "I'm not sure. I'm making it at home now and giving it to family and friends."

Her story mirrored Julia's. As well as her lack of self-confidence with starting a business. If I'd learned one lesson with helping Julia, it was to begin small, and let God lead the way. "What if you start slow, like selling at a farmers market?"

Debbie's eyes rounded, her pale cheeks yielding to color. "That's a great idea."

"You could also try to place your product with Nancy's Naturals."

The blush in her face vanished, and she gnawed her lower lip. "I love that store, but I'm too chicken to actually approach them."

"Don't be." I leaned forward. "That's how Julia began selling her cleaning products. I bet she'd introduce you to Nancy."

Debbie considered that and sat a little straighter. "Okay. I'll think about asking Julia."

And I would most definitely mention it to Julia. Sweet rightness at that notion encircled my chest. "Just be sure to research your market first, and food safety requirements. And when you do sell your syrup, or anything else you create, do it at a competitive price."

"Okay." Her leg jittered, but her bright countenance confirmed her expanding confidence. "I can do that."

I contained a whoop, not wanting to frighten the skittish woman. "What you're doing is exciting and scary."

"Yes." She gave a full-body exhale. "It's such a relief to talk to you and Julia about this. To people who understand."

That rightness in my chest swelled. "Here." I pulled a business card from my purse. "If you ever have any questions, don't hesitate to reach out."

"Thank you." She glanced at the card and rose. "Thank you so much. It was beyond nice meeting you."

"You too."

Debbie stepped away, brushing past Micah.

The spreading smile on my face halted. *Micah.* The sneaky ninja. Flutters erupted in my belly. He'd switched his pants for cargo shorts, the white polo remaining, indicating lunch at his sister's had been tamer than boiled crawfish. His dazed stare lingered on my face. *What was that look for?*

He approached, lowering onto Debbie's chair. "You like helping people."

I scoffed. "Don't sound so surprised."

"That came out wrong." He lifted his hand. "What I meant to say is you like helping people's dreams come true."

I pressed back into my seat. "Giving advice is hardly making dreams come true."

"I think Julia would disagree. She went into great detail during the last library event about all you did for her business."

"Julia," I grumbled and scanned the people in the yard for her, coming up empty. What else had she gone into "great detail" about when talking to Micah? "She just needed some guidance." And nagging. Lots of nagging. "I had Claire, and we had our grandma's estate to start the café. Most people like Julia don't have that advantage."

He leaned, resting his elbow on the arm rest, edging him closer. "Who else have you helped?"

"Why?"

"Just curious."

I shrugged. "I've given a few seminars for the chamber of commerce. But that was general advice to people likely there for the free lunch."

"Which isn't the same as actually getting your hands dirty and watching someone's small business take off."

I blinked. He couldn't have said it better. The satisfaction I'd had with helping Julia's aspirations come true had been one of the most rewarding accomplishments of my life.

"Have you thought about being a business consultant? Or a mentor?"

"Sure," I deadpanned. "I'll give up the café and start a consulting firm."

"On the side. In your spare time."

"I'm a single parent and the owner of a restaurant. I have no spare time." And even if I did, expanding locations would soak it up. My fingers itched to reach for my phone and check my email for a response on the SBA loan. It'd been less than a week since I'd submitted the application. And the form said it could take up to twenty-one days for them to review it.

"It was just a thought. Especially seeing how much you light up when talking about Julia's cleaning products or when you spoke to that woman."

"Micah Guidry." I layered my tone with mock chastisement, hoping to change the subject. "Were you spying on us?"

"Only you." He shifted his chair closer, our armrests touching. "It's pretty hard to keep my eyes off you."

A bark of laughter erupted from me, and I relaxed, draping my arms on my chair's rests. "That's one smooth line you've got there."

"It's not a line. It's the truth." Not a trace of flirtation lingered in his eyes. No sirree. Just sheer determination.

My throat went dry.

He eased back in his seat, his stare holding, roaming over my face, pausing on my mouth.

Prickles of energy charged the air. With his arm on his chair rest and an inch of space between us, the heat from his body radiated against mine. Moving away felt too much like defeat. Like an acknowledgment that he affected me. His fingers reached across the gap and lightly caressed the side of my wrist. Pleasure cascaded over me, and two words came to mind. The eternal phrase of Uncle Jesse from *Full House*. "*Have mercy!*"

All I had to do was move away. Instead, I turned my arm, exposing the underbelly of the most sensitive part of my skin. He gently traced my blue veins, his fingertips dipping into my palm. I sucked in a breath. What was I doing? I was a grown woman playing the hand-equivalent of footsie in a public setting! This was wrong. On so many levels. And yet reluctance gathered deep within my muscles, holding me still, indulging in the moment. A moment, that when over, would leave me empty. With that sobering thought, I slid from beneath his touch, pressing my tingling arm to my stomach. "I shouldn't have . . . complied like that."

A playful smile tugged at his lips. "I wouldn't call it compliance. If anything, I'd testify you were an accessory in breaking the very rules you put in place."

"Excuse me, Officer Guidry, but I did no flirting. And technically, you did all the touching." I regretted the statement as soon as it flew past my tongue.

Mirth ignited in Micah's eyes, and I rolled my own, shaking my head. I veered my gaze away from him and to safer views, to a bright green pecan husk that had fallen early. I focused on the movement next to it and found a baby crawfish scurrying backward. At least one mudbug always escaped at a boil.

"I haven't seen you around the neighborhood." Micah pumped his arms in exaggeration, mocking my speed-walking technique.

"Oh?" I feigned innocence, even though I *had* adjusted my exercise path to avoid his house. "Are you watching your street 24/7?"

"No. But it goes against how much you like structure and routine."

"There's nothing wrong with structure and routine."

"I also haven't seen you at the library since Tuesday."

I chewed the inside of my cheek. The rest of the week, when retrieving Hayley from the library, I'd remained in the car, with the engine running as though I were a getaway driver ready to flee a heist. The first time Hayley had asked what the rush was, I'd blamed diarrhea. A lie that had churned in my gut until actual diarrhea hit. Lesson learned. The second time I'd had a vendor meeting to discuss replacement options for the fryer. I'd purposefully planned it at a time that wouldn't leave room for dillydallying at the library.

He tipped his head, angling a raised brow at me. "I think it's more than booger books and Nellie's stink eye that's keeping you away."

I knew where he was going with this. Knew and loathed it. I stared at the crawfish, silently imploring it to creep over and pinch Micah's ankle. Just one little pinch.

"And it occurred to me if you weren't interested in dating me, you wouldn't have altered your life to avoid me."

Or one big pinch. With both claws. "I'm not avoiding you." I pushed to my feet.

"Sure looks like it." He motioned at my movement to leave.

"I'm . . . taking precautions. With this crawfish." I pointed to the escapee, or at least to where it'd been.

Standing, he stepped over and nudged the pecan husk with the toe of his shoe. "Making up stories to get away." He tsked. "The only precautions I think you're taking are against falling head over heels for me."

I scoffed. "You think mighty highly of yourself."

"I don't need to think highly of myself. I have evidence." He leaned in, the stubble from his jaw barely grazing my cheek, his mouth almost on my earlobe. "The hand I touched. You're still clutching it to your stomach."

The backs of my knees prickled, my breath shallowing. I purposefully lowered my arm to my side.

He studied my face, satisfaction in his countenance, along with a hint of something else. Desire? "I like it when you blush. When you're . . . you." Stepping back, he breathed in through his nose and released it. Slid his hands into his pockets. "I understand your concerns about Hayley. And I promise, if things don't work out, I won't let that affect my relationship with her."

"Those are the perfect words and sentiment. But despite how hard we'd try, she *would* be affected." I returned my gaze to the pecan husk, hoping my feelings for Micah would wither like the nut's shell soon would.

"Okay. What if we . . . secretly dated?" He gave a slow shrug, a teasing glint in his eyes.

I couldn't help but smile. "Secret dating? That sounds like a headline for the *National Enquirer*." My smile bled away. "Besides, secrets feel too much like lies."

"I agree. Then our only course of action is to talk to Hayley about us dating."

I laughed without humor. "Our only course of action is to remain friends." Which kept Hayley, and my heart, safe.

He rubbed the back of his neck, an almost defiant reluctance taking up residence in his stance.

Julia's tiny terror of a dog, Chewie, charged past us, barking up a storm, cornering the renegade crawfish against the back fence. Chewie wore a doggie shirt that read *Don't pet me.* Appropriate for the unruly canine. The little crustacean squeezed underneath the boards, making a successful escape.

I tossed Micah an *I told you so* look.

He held a hand to his chest. "My apologies I ever doubted you."

Chewie lifted his hind leg and peed on the spot where the crawfish had disappeared. I shook my head. At least Precious was a girl.

"You won't believe what I found in the library drop box this past Thursday," Micah said.

"Another squirrel?"

"No. Something far better. A Ziploc bag containing a gift card for gas and a book-themed travel mug. For the life of me, I can't figure out who it's from."

"Hmm." I rubbed my chin. "Sounds like someone's trying to tell you to fill up your tank, and the mug, and hit the road."

He narrowed his eyes, playfulness softening the planes of his face.

A playfulness I wanted to evade. "Your dad's really nice."

His expression shifted, sobering. "He is."

"How's his ankle doing?"

"Better." He averted his stare. "We're still waiting on the bone density results."

"I'm praying for good news with that."

"Thank you."

Samuel and Wyatt approached, and I eased a step back, grateful for the brothers' interference. Both tall and solidly athletic, they could've been twins. But where Samuel's hair veered to a lighter shade of brown, Wyatt's was nearly charcoal. Another stark difference was the leather eye patch Samuel wore, the result of a permanent injury he'd sustained in service for our country.

"I heard you're a black belt in jiujitsu." Undeniable admiration infused Samuel's tone.

Micah nodded. "And I heard you're both Green Berets."

"Retired Green Berets," Samuel said.

Micah clasped his hand to his wrist. "Thank you for your service."

Samuel dipped his chin.

Wyatt's quiet attention rested on Micah. "What gym do you go to? I've been thinking of getting back into jiujitsu."

And that was my cue to extricate myself from the conversation and put some much-needed distance between me and Micah. I grabbed my purse, retreated past the remaining guests, and found Julia inside, in the kitchen.

She flipped off the faucet at the sink and grasped a dish towel to dry her hands. "I asked Samuel and Wyatt to leave y'all alone as long as possible."

My scalp prickled. Had she seen us playing handsie? I turned my back to her, setting my handbag on the edge of the counter, next to her collection of recipe books. "There's no reason to have done that." Was she about to call me out on my little PDA session with Micah? I moved to the island and began methodically snapping Tupperware lids to the containers of leftovers.

The open space of the area flowed into the living room, where Brooke and one of her friends watched TV. Hopefully their presence would save me from Julia's verbal opinions of Micah and I being a couple.

She leaned her hip against the counter, wringing the towel in her hands. Not the appearance of a brazen matchmaking meddler.

I clasped the lid on a bowl of Creole crab dip. "Everything okay?" Opening the refrigerator, I placed the appetizer inside.

"I need you to remember how much you love me."

My stomach sank, and I shut the fridge, the bottles in the door rattling. "What have you done?"

She motioned for me to follow, and follow her I did, down the hallway to their exercise room. Floor-to-ceiling mirrors covered one wall. Another sported a shelving system filled with free weights in varying sizes. An elliptical machine and a weight bench rounded out the space. Closing the door behind us, she winced. "I had Samuel do a sort-of background check on Micah."

My jaw unhinged.

She raised her hands. "All completely legal."

"And completely uncalled for!" Pulse pounding in my ears, I paced between the window and a freestanding punching bag set up in a corner. Each lap brought me closer to the bag, thoughts of throwing a hard punch becoming more appealing with every pass.

"I couldn't help it. Whenever you talk about him, you light up."

Oy to the vey. Maybe my Landry Mask wasn't so effective after all.

"And then when I saw y'all together at the library event . . ." A goofy grin overtook her face, her fingers interlacing beneath her chin. "There was this *force* between the two of you."

"You've watched *Star Wars* too many times."

"And since I view you as a sister . . ." Her eyes widened, beseeching.

A sharp huff pushed from my lungs. "I can't believe you're trying to mollify me with that."

"Well, I do." She notched her chin, all the while radiating a mischievous glow.

I shook my head. "You're more like your mama than you think."

"If I were my mama, I'd have been spying on Micah myself."

I pointed to the door. "Sending your Green Beret husband to do it is just as bad."

"You're right. You're right." She reached for a puddle of resistance bands resting next to a workout ball and began untangling them. "Don't you want to know what he found out?"

"No. No, I don't." The irritation raking through my veins didn't want to hear another word from Julia on what she'd done. On the line she'd crossed. I moved to the window overlooking the backyard, my gaze zeroing in on Micah as though I were a heat-seeking missile and he were my target. He still talked to Wyatt and Samuel. If Samuel had allowed Micah into his house, and around his wife and daughter, that had to be a positive sign, right? That he hadn't found anything horrible from Micah's past? Or was it a Green Beret strategy to keep enemies close? What if Micah had really relocated from Colorado for nefarious reasons?

I turned from the window to face Julia. "I changed my mind. But for the record, I want to state what y'all did was wrong with a capital W."

Her gaze drooped to the floor. "You're right. And I vow not to do any other Green Beret things ever again." She slowly met my stare, one of her brows raising. "Unless you ask me to."

"Thank you. Now, what did Samuel find out?"

A smile the size of the Superdome spread across her face. "Nothing."

My shoulders sagged, and I turned, not wanting her to witness how relieved I was.

"See!" She pointed at my face in the mirror.

Darn you mirrors!

"That right there! I was right to do a little digging."

"I'm only relieved for Hayley's sake. And besides, a little digging involves a shovel. You used a backhoe. And dynamite and—"

"And since nothing came up on Micah, I can now proceed with what I want to talk to you about."

I frowned at my best friend and the sharp turn in our conversation.

"A couple of weeks ago, you mentioned Hayley as a reason not to date him."

Pooping parrots. Dropping my butt to the weight bench, I crossed my arms. "I seem to remember you being extremely gun-shy about dating because of your boys."

Her head cocked. "That was different, and you know it."

My arms slipped free of their hold. She was right. Her boys had been old enough to know and remember their father, and be traumatized by his passing. So many emotional ramifications had entailed, which later included the possibility of Julia dating again. Thankfully, they'd worked through those issues.

"I understand you don't want to risk damaging Micah and Hayley's relationship now that she's opening up to someone. But if things don't work out, you and Micah are both adult enough to have an amicable split." She lowered onto the bench next to me. "Especially knowing how it could affect Hayley. And especially with what you told me about Micah's past and his heart for helping kids with loss."

Again, she was right.

"You've only considered the negatives to dating Micah when it comes to Hayley. What about the positives? If she's opened up to him so quickly, imagine how much more that would happen if he was a larger part of her life."

I studied my toes peeking out from my wedge sandals, uncertainty dithering in my core.

"He's obviously a caring person. He jumped in with both feet to care for you, and by extension, Hayley. Plus, he has a good relationship with his sister and dad."

The mentioning of his father highlighted another concern for Hayley I'd battled all these years. I caught a glimpse of myself in the wall mirror, rubbing the Crease, and dropped my hand. "Part of me has always wondered if there's a father-figure hole in Hayley's heart."

Julia winced. "I know exactly how you feel. That was a big worry for me with the boys too."

A worry she'd had that had been validated. My neck bent, and I pulled in a deep breath that did nothing to alleviate the tightness surrounding my heart. "Other than worrying about Hayley, I'm not sure if *I'm* ready. If I ever will be."

Julia curled her arm around me in a side hug. "Well, one thing we do know, it's like everything else in your life, you need to give this over to God."

20

FOR THE NEXT WEEK, life returned to normal. I hosed bird poop in the mornings and resumed speed walking my regular route. Though I'd braced myself to encounter Micah as I exercised past his house, that didn't happen. I'd expected him to be waiting on his peach porch, ready to toss a flirty comment my way. But no. Not even his garbage can was out on the wrong day for me to razz him about. An itty-bitty kernel of disappointment wedged in my gut. I'd considered texting him, just to see how his dad was, but hadn't wanted to appear prying.

Not wanting Micah to have the satisfaction of thinking I purposely avoided him, I'd also gone into the library to pick up Hayley. Though he hadn't been there, Nellie's stink eye sure had. I'd reasoned Nellie's outright dislike of me as the cause of my dampened mood. But on the ride home, Hayley had talked nonstop about the library event planning she and Micah had done before he'd left that day, asking my opinion about a limbo pole. We'd spent the rest of the night chatting and looking up more party ideas.

Sunday had rolled around with no sighting of Micah at church. Maybe he'd gone back to attending at the other service time. That kernel of disappointment festered in my belly the remainder of the day, all night, and into the next morning. I pulled into my driveway after bringing Hayley and Emma to school and killed the engine. Was Micah avoiding *me* now? I exited my car and entered the courtyard through the iron gate, the metal squeaking. If he was dodging me, then . . . great. I nodded to myself, my steps and heartbeat slowing. That would make our situation easier. For me, it'd be like Micah had never returned. Well, except for him being a listening ear for Hayley. This was ideal. I was having my cake and eating it too. My stomach churned. Rotten tofu cake.

The last thing I'd said to him was a remark about filling up his gas tank and hitting the road. And that was after insisting our only option was friendship. It'd been said in jest, but still. My steps slowed even more. He'd left that Easter crawfish boil without saying good-bye. Samuel had said he'd received a phone call and apologized for leaving abruptly. If it had been an emergency with his dad, wouldn't he have come and told me? Maybe it'd been Sydney Dupré who'd called. They could've gotten back together. I halted next to the crepe myrtle, its tiny leaves budding at the tips of its branches. It'd make sense that Sydney would realize the record-breaking catch she'd released into the water and try to reel him back in.

My mouth popped open. What if I'd been his rebound after all? Or really, half a rebound, considering we hadn't dated. With my head feeling too heavy for my neck, I continued on, walking past the fountain. No more flirting or secret gifts or playing handsie. A storm cloud of disappointment hovered above me. Despite my efforts, Micah Guidry had gotten into my system. And now I found myself in withdrawal. Complete with a shaky heart and whirling mind. See? This was why I'd been thinking with my brain since Ryan had left me. Why I'd kept my walls up when it came to men.

My gaze shifted to the back stairs of the café. To a shiny

silver gift bag waiting on the top step. My breath caught, my fingers tingling around my car keys. *Easy, girl*. It could be from someone else. After all, last time Micah had used a plain brown bag. This one even had white tissue paper sticking out of it.

Bottling the hope rising in my chest, I set my purse and keys on the porch railing. I reached past the tissue paper, grasping soft material, and pulled out a shirt. A Hawaiian shirt with Twinkies on it. I laughed. With each exhale of amusement, my wild imaginings of Micah boomeranging to Sydney Dupré vanished. Just like that, this ridiculous shirt had injected me with a dopamine hit. A Micah-high I wasn't sure I wanted to come down from. And all too quickly, truth settled over me. Micah had become important to me. And I didn't want to only be friends. *Pitiful pit bulls*.

Movement inside the café snagged my attention. I should head to my office and start my workday. Payroll awaited. As well as examining bank statements, updating the daily business review from the weekend, and later, showing the courtyard for a potential wedding. I'd also be obsessively checking my email for a response on the SBA loan. Instead, I left the bag on the steps and headed to my prayer spot.

Lowering onto the small bench, I pulled in a deep breath of the cypress mulch layering the gardens. "Lord, I need wisdom." I folded the Hawaiian shirt on my lap. "With Micah and the Vieux Carré Café. And with purchasing a new or used fryer." I fidgeted with the belt of my navy, A-line dress. "I know you've resurrected bodies and restored them. What about industrial kitchen equipment?"

An earsplitting screech pierced the air, and a green parrot swooped toward the café's steps.

Cést Fou!

The evil creature landed on the gift bag, its wings and tail flapping.

"No!" I jumped to my feet and charged forward, waving Micah's shirt. "Shoo! Shoo!" Cést Fou's massive wings pumped, lifting its body, the silver bag grasped in its talons. Feathers fluttered out with every attempt to flee. I'd heard birds were attracted to shiny objects but hadn't believed it until now.

"Thief! Thief!" I closed in on him, ready to smack him with the Twinkie top. He released the bag and flew up to the lowest branch on the live oak, more feathers floating down in his wake. I slung the shirt over my shoulder and ran for the hose. Turning the spigot to full blast, I grabbed the nozzle and darted back. The storage wheel cranked behind me as I tore up to the tree with my water gun a-blazin'. I met the beast's beady eyes. "'Say hello to my little friend.'" I squeezed the trigger, the nozzle already set to jet. Water dribbled out. "What?" I glanced back and found a kink in the line.

Channeling Indiana Jones, I whipped the hose, trying to straighten it. "Not today, Cést Fou." I growled the words, whipping the hose again. Success! Water shot from the nozzle, and I aimed it north, chasing the feathered menace from branch to branch. It swooped over me to the crepe myrtle and back to the oak, then back to the crepe myrtle again. Water rained down on me, but I didn't care. I was sick of this bird. Sick of cleaning its poop every morning. Sick of thinking of having to clean its poop every morning.

Finally, he arced high in the sky and flew off toward the Mississippi River, a smaller parrot joining him. I released my grip on the nozzle, my arm dropping to my side. Where in the world had that one come from? Was it the same one Mayté had seen? Was that villainous bird putting a gang together?

"Cést Fou!" Mrs. Adélaide's outraged voice came from behind.

I ducked and jerked around, expecting to hear a gunshot or two.

"He's still here." Her empty hands planted on her hips. Thankfully, her little body wallet was strapped across her torso. It appeared she hadn't found a purse enormous enough to bring her gun.

Thank You, Lord. I let out a huge breath, grateful for not having to deal with a gun-toting Cajun French grandma. "It's fine, Mrs. Adélaide. I've got it under control." My toes squished in my heels. My favorite red heels. Darn that bird.

Mrs. Adélaide examined me, from my dripping hair to the hem of my soaked dress. Her lips pursed as her penciled-in brows rose above her thick glasses.

I lifted the soggy Twinkie shirt from my shoulder and took in the courtyard. Water dripped from the trees. The assaulted gift bag lay drawn and quartered across the steps. Drenched tissue paper was strewn all about, along with green and white feathers. And there on the ground lay the gas gift card I'd given to Micah. It must've been at the bottom of the bag. That sneaky man.

"Take heart, *cher*." Mrs. Adélaide's smooth accent glided over the endearment, but then she shook her fist to where Cést Fou had disappeared. "Dat bird won de battle but not de war."

⊹&—♪⊹

Two days later found me once again violating the library's drop box policy. Using another Ziploc bag, I'd tucked the gas card Micah had returned to me inside it, along with a T-shirt that read *Jiujitsu. Because you might run out of ammo.*

⊹&—♪⊹

I hated glitter. And it was everywhere. In every size and color. In the shape of seashells and starfish. And it seemed fitting for this beach-themed library event because, like sand after a trip to the Gulf Coast, I'd no doubt be finding these menacing specks for a long time to come. Micah had shown up with the contraband, insisting it would be a hit with making the leis. The only hit concerning me was my heart knocking against my ribs at the first sight of him in nearly two weeks. That Hayley, who'd stood next to me, would hear the pounding. Thankfully neither of them had noticed. And Micah had been right about the demon dust. The children had been enthralled with the craft project, proudly wearing their creations.

We were in the final stretch of the event, the courtyard resembling a tropical hullabaloo. Before the party had started, Hayley and Emma had toilet papered the lower branches of the oak with colorful streamers. Their laughter had made for a cute video I would cherish. Kids now darted through those hanging decorations, hopped up on Capri-Sun and sand-dollar sugar cookies donated by a bakery. Hawaiian music played through the outdoor speakers, and beach balls randomly sailed through the air. A fake fire pit Micah had put together occupied one side of the space, beside a borrowed limbo pole.

The entire afternoon Micah had kept his distance. Not one single flirty look. No sneaky touches. Nothing. He was honoring my wishes because of Hayley. And it made him even more attractive. Especially with watching the comradery between them grow. Micah Guidry was a Hawaiian shirt–wearing double-edged sword.

"If you sigh any louder, you're going to bust a lung." Julia, who'd volunteered again, sat next to me at the arts-and-crafts table. Her lei was a tribute to LSU with purple and yellow foam flowers alternating around her neck. "The kids are thrilled, and the café's still standing."

"Both excellent points."

"Is all your groaning because you're still battling your feelings for Micah?"

I scoffed. "I've got plenty of other issues swirling through my head right now. Scheming ex-fiancés, the future of my business, and that SBA loan. The fact I'm going to have to call my mother at some point." The luau-themed playlist started over for the millionth time. Pitching forward, I rested my elbows on the table and rubbed my temples. "There's also my newfound hatred of the ukulele."

"The first three are doozies I'm already praying about," Julia said. "But the fourth . . . Why don't you go to your office for some quiet time? I'll keep an eye on everything."

I lifted my head and glanced over to Hayley, who was gathering the younger kids for story time. She would read for fifteen minutes and then lead the kiddos in a game of limbo while the preteens took their turn at who could hula-hoop the longest.

"Go on." Julia fluttered her hand, several flecks of glitter shimmering on her arm.

"I reinstate your title as best friend."

"When had I lost it?"

I widened my eyes and reduced my voice. "Micah's background check."

She shrugged, unabashed, and again motioned for me to skedaddle.

I shut myself into my office and closed the blinds. Despite the melee on the other side of the window, silence ruled in here. Soundproofing was a blessing we'd splurged on during renovations. Claire's office off the kitchen had gotten the quiet treatment too. I lowered my bottom to my chair and my head to my desk. Fifteen minutes. For fifteen minutes I'd think of nothing. Or at least try to think of nothing. Penny and Mayté were here, so the café rested in good hands. *Stop! Stop thinking!*

A knock sounded on the door.

And there went my alone time. Straightening with a weary grumble, I smoothed my hair. "Come in."

The door cracked open, revealing Micah's concerned face. I pushed to my feet. "Everything okay?"

"Yeah." He stepped in, closing the door behind him. "Julia said I should check on you."

"Julia." I hissed her name and rounded my desk. "You can go back out and inform her that her beignet privileges have been revoked."

One side of Micah's mouth curved, a spark lighting in his eyes. "Why don't I have any privileges?" His voice dropped on the last word, and he eased a step toward me.

Fire spread across my skin at his undertone. My ire at Julia shrunk, right along with the size of my office and the amount of air in the room.

"I did get you that stylish shirt." He gestured to the Hawaiian Twinkie top a smidge too big for my frame. I'd worn it unbuttoned and classed it up as best I could with a silk camisole and fitted capri pants. He edged closer, that spark in his eyes glinting with something resembling mischief. Maybe even kissing mischief.

No. Say something snappy. Something to press pause on this moment. On a moment that could very well turn into a kiss. You're not prepared. Your breath isn't minty fresh. You haven't made out with anyone in over a decade. What if kissing is done differently nowadays?

He lifted his hand to my face, and I instinctively took a step back. He chuckled. "You have glitter on your cheek."

"Oh." Okay. Maybe this wasn't a kissing moment.

"May I?"

I nodded, keeping my mouth closed, uncertain of my breath, racking my brain for the last thing I'd eaten. A grilled shrimp salad for lunch. *Ugh.* Shrimp was not the stuff of romance. Wait! A peppermint! Julia had offered me a peppermint not too long ago. *Hold up!* Had she planned and prepared me for this moment? What a meddling matchmaker!

Carefully, Micah's index finger wiped my cheek, and he held the renegade speck of glitter up to me. "See?" A sparkly gold starfish dotted the tip of his finger.

"For the record, I did tell you glitter was a bad idea."

His lips quirked, and his eyes scanned my face. "From where I'm standing, glitter was an excellent idea. There's another one." He pointed to my neck, his gaze questioning, silently asking permission.

In answer, I lifted my chin up and to the side, granting him better access.

He shifted closer. With the lightest of touches, his fingertip and thumb slowly brushed the hollow of my throat. Once. Twice.

My knees buckled a hair, and I resisted the urge to close my eyes, to savor the intimacy of this moment. Perhaps glitter wasn't so bad after all.

"Got it." His voice was a gravelly rasp. He straightened but didn't move away.

I stared directly ahead, at his neck, then dipped my gaze to the first button on his shirt and the glimpse of defined chest muscles peeking out. His warm breath fanned against my forehead, slow and steady. My own went in the opposite direction, picking up speed, right along with my pulse. The few inches of space between us charged with energy. We were like one of those lightning balls I'd had as a child. The strikes of light zapping out where it sensed heat and touch. If he found another piece of glitter on me, I would combust.

"Micah?" I whispered.

"Yes?"

I worked to swallow past my dry throat. "You must . . . cease and desist."

A chuckle, low and sexy, vibrated from him. "Cease and desist?"

Tipping my gaze up to meet his, I nodded, the movement only highlighting how close we were. How had I never noticed those flecks of burnt orange in his sage eyes?

With a blink he straightened, defusing the energy charging between us. His brows drew together, sincere regard in his features. "Do you want me to leave?"

I breathed in through my nose, supplying much-needed oxygen to my brain. *Did* I want him to leave? A resounding *no* echoed through my mind. My qualms about avoiding more than friendship with him shrank. Here stood a caring man who I liked a lot. And what was the harm of one little kiss? Licking my dry lips, I gave a slow shake of my head, my nerve endings tingling, as though they reached out for him.

A soft smile covered his face as we both closed the gap between us. I edged up in my flats, and he leaned down. And with a tenderness I hadn't expected, our lips met and held for a breathless moment. His hand cupped my face, his fingers sliding across my jaw, sending a sizzling current along my skin. His other hand moved to my waist. The kiss continued in a perfect, unhurried rhythm. My hands found their way to his chest, his rapid heartbeat below my fingertips belying the control in his gentle movements.

Our breaths mingled with the give and take of affection. My fingers stretched into the back of his soft hair, and a shudder rocked his body. His hand trailed a blaze of heat from my jaw, down my neck, to the edge of my shoulder. Longing unfurled within my core. His mouth left mine, leisurely skimming against my skin to the sensitive spot beneath my ear.

Goldilocks.

He eased back. "Did you say, Goldilocks?" Amusement coated his husky tone.

The romance bubble I'd been in popped. Warmth, having

nothing to do with desire, swept across my face. I opened my eyes and found delight in his.

A knock rapped at the door.

With a gasp I startled, releasing my death grip on Micah's shirt. *Gracious.* When had that happened? I wiped my mouth with the back of my hand, my attention swinging to the door. Hayley. I knew it would be her. A knot looped and tightened in my stomach. Being caught playing seven minutes in heaven was not the way I wanted to talk to her about my interest in Micah.

"Katherine?" My mother's voice punctured the air.

My lungs exhaled a puff of relief. Never had I thought I'd be thankful to hear her sharp tone. "My mom," I panic-whispered to Micah as I glimpsed the doorknob. Unlocked. That woman would have no qualms about marching right in. I tamed my locks, straightened my Twinkie shirt. *Oh, the Twinkie shirt.* That knot in my gut tightened. Mama would have a field day with my ensemble.

She knocked again. "Katherine?"

"Just a moment." I glanced at Micah.

He hadn't moved. And neither had the delighted expression on his face. His hair was mussed from my fingers. His Hawaiian shirt too. And he was seconds away from coming under Mama's cutting scrutiny.

"Can you straighten up?" I motioned to his hair and shirt.

He obliged, a crease puckering between his brows.

Closing my eyes, I took a calming breath, then another, willing the heat in my cheeks to subside. I gave Micah a once-over, sent up a prayer, and opened the door.

Clatter from the bustling café and Mama's disapproving face greeted me. Her attention momentarily shifted to Micah, and in an instant, her expression smoothed, the Landry Mask sliding into place. That didn't stop her critical gaze from raking over me, from my no-doubt swollen lips to my beige flats. "Katherine, you've forgotten your manners."

I flinched at her scolding and hated myself for it.

Mama's mauve-colored lips slightly tipped up. Her regard slid from me to Micah, where she began her silent scrutiny of him.

Reluctantly, I retreated a step and motioned to him. "Mama, this is Micah Guidry. Though it's been a long time, you may remember him from Mawmaw's Mardi Gras parties."

She entered, wearing a lavender satin blouse and cream slacks. Her heels struck the wood floor with quick, sharp jabs—like her opinions. She held out her manicured hand to Micah.

He took it. "It's nice to see you again."

"You as well."

"We need to return to an event we're hosting." I ushered them from my office, closing the door. "I'll be out in a second," I said to Micah.

Something akin to disappointment flitted across his features. He tipped his head to my mother. "Ma'am." And with that, he left us in the hallway.

Mama's forehead furrowed. "What does he think of Hayley?" Her inflection portrayed Hayley as baggage.

A simmer began in my blood, and I literally clamped my teeth onto my tongue.

"I hope you control yourselves when in her presence. The last thing she needs is thinking sleeping around is okay."

The simmer turned to a boil. *Be calm. Don't sink to her level.* "We're not sleeping around." Though technically, he had slept on my couch when I was sick.

Mama sniffed. "What does Hayley think of you dating?"

Dating? *Hoo boy.* Is that what Micah and I were doing now? I rubbed the Crease. It's not like I could explain to my mother

I wasn't sure. "She doesn't know. And I'd appreciate it if you didn't mention any of this to her."

Mama's eyes gleamed.

Holding a neutral reaction, I internally winced at giving her the upper hand. Such a rookie mistake.

She fingered one of her diamond stud earrings. "I won't tell her, but I want something in exchange."

I fought a sigh. Of course she would. The woman would've made a perfect career politician.

"Stop rubbing between your brows," she chastised. "You'll come to dinner next Saturday night. It *will be* the last Saturday of the month, after all." And there was the jab about missing March's dinner.

I lowered my hand, my breaths coming in a little easier. Okay, her request wasn't horrific.

"Hayley doesn't have to come."

Even better.

"But Micah Guidry does."

Sarah McLachlan.

"Deal?" Her haughty expression resembled a poker player who held four aces.

I sighed, folding my puny pair of deuces. "Deal." All I could do now was get her out of here lickety-split. The last thing I needed was her catching sight of the function in the courtyard, which hopefully she hadn't noticed on her way to my office. "What are you doing here anyway?"

"Such a pleasant greeting for your mother." Her attention dipped to my shirt, her face twisting. She reached out and felt the fabric of my top. "Is this a joke?"

I shrugged away from her.

Her brows gave a prissy lift. "We were having lunch with Ryan, and he suggested swinging by."

My muscles tensed. "Why would you have lunch with my ex-fiancé?"

"We keep in touch." She straightened the cuff of her sleeve, avoiding eye contact.

They keep in touch? "Come on." I stepped toward the front of the café, directing her vision away from the rear French doors. "I'll see you back to your table." And ponder the fact my parents maintained a relationship with Ryan. The man who'd abandoned me.

"Oh, we don't have a table." Her mouth pressed into a tight line. "Ryan brought us through the courtyard entrance."

Dread rolled through me in one deep-sweeping wave. Like a horror scene switched to slow motion, I turned and glanced through the windows of the French doors. There stood Ryan, next to the fountain, with Daddy.

This wasn't a coincidence. No way, nohow. Ryan had picked this moment on purpose to bring my parents. The library event being held here was public knowledge. I'd even let Micah put a flyer on the hostess stand. And since Ryan knew my financial situation, he'd have known my most likely source for a loan for the Vieux Carré Café would come from my parents. Who hated disorder and unprofessionalism.

I pushed through the doors and became engulfed in a ukulele solo and the not-so-solo yelps of children darting all around in what appeared to be a game of hula-hoop tag. One of the kids' hoops goosed Daddy, and he jumped, his face flaming. Ryan tried his best to contain a laugh. The snake.

Hurrying down the stairs, and avoiding collision with one of the hula-hoop hoodlums, I ignored Ryan, focusing on my father. "Hi, Daddy." I motioned him to the side exit. "Why don't we go this way?"

He followed me for all of three steps before becoming entangled in the streamers hanging from the tree. He swatted at them as if he'd walked into a spider web.

I glanced back and found Mama trailing us. A beach ball careened her way. She held her designer handbag like a shield, as though she were a gladiator in the Coliseum fending off lions.

I scanned the party for backup and discovered Julia using a first aid kit, tending to a little girl with a scraped knee. Plump tears tumbled down the child's cheeks. Micah intervened between two preteen boys having a heated argument. Where were their guardians? Had they been the drop-and-dash parents Micah had mentioned earlier? Emma lowered the limbo pole to the cheers of the preschool group. Where had Hayley gone to? And had someone turned the music up?

Mama reached us, pressing a hand to her chest. "Are you running a business or a daycare? I can't believe this is what you're doing with this space. With this investment."

One of the boys Micah spoke to swung at the other kid. Using Mr. Miyagi speed, Micah blocked the punch.

"Rat!" Mama's bloodcurdling scream punctured the air. "Rat!"

Shrieks erupted, and people darted everywhere, some running for the porch, others lunging for seats like a life-and-death game of musical chairs. Several kids splashed into the fountain for protection.

Mama clutched Daddy's arm, utilizing him to catapult herself onto a nearby table, knocking cups over, spilling drinks. She pointed wildly to the ground. "There! There!"

I peered toward where she gestured and found Precious, sprinting straight for me, Hayley a few steps behind, holding the dog's unattached leash.

"Rat!" Mama yelled, clutching Daddy with one hand.

A huge white glob plopped onto Daddy's shoulder. And another hit the top of his head. He discharged a round of expletives and rushed for the exit, leaving Mama stranded on the table.

I glanced to the tree and spied Cést Fou. Meeting its beady eyes, I made a solemn vow. *This. Means. War.* My enemy flew off, and my gaze met the face of my other nemesis. My molars ground together, red tinting my vision. Ryan radiated self-satisfaction. Maybe he'd lose that smirk if I swiped the bird poop from Daddy and rubbed it in his face. He slipped his hands behind his back, confidence in his posture. *Landry Mask. Landry Mask. Don't show him your weakness.* Turning my back to him, I took in the bedlam before me. Nothing, absolutely nothing, could make this moment any worse.

The back doors to the café swung open, and Mrs. Adélaide shuffled out, toting an enormous purse.

21

THANK YOU, LORD, *that Saturday's event didn't end with a Cajun French grandma discharging her firearm.* Monday morning found me in my office, praising God for the second day in a row. And also thanking Him for Julia. At the sight of Mrs. Adélaide and her gigantic purse, Julia had sprung into action. Being gun proficient, she'd carefully taken hold of Mrs. Adélaide's bag. We'd then ushered the woman into my office.

Julia had removed a huge revolver but discovered no bullets in the chamber. Mrs. Adélaide explained she was going to wait until she'd had Cést Fou in her sights before loading the gun. Julia asked Mrs. Adélaide if she had a concealed-carry permit, and she'd proudly produced it. But upon review, Julia revealed the license had expired. Mrs. Adélaide had been shocked, and since she didn't have a holster to open carry it safely, she'd asked Julia to drive her promptly home so she wouldn't be breaking the law another minute. They'd left, and I'd come to the realization if Mrs. Adélaide was able to renew her permit, or get a holster, I'd have to be firm in telling her she couldn't bring her gun here again. Between her, a vengeful parrot, and a renegade fryer, how much drama could one restaurant have?

Wendy, a newly hired waitress, knocked on my open door. "I'm pretty sure there's a food critic here."

"What?" I slipped my heels on and rounded my desk.

She nodded, her black curls bouncing. "He took a picture of the menu and ordered way more than he can eat. He's taken pictures of his food too."

Curiosity mixed with anticipation, and I motioned for Wendy to lead the way. I followed her slim frame, smoothing my indigo top and gray pencil skirt. It wouldn't be the first time we'd had a food critic here, though it hadn't happened in quite a while. I stifled a groan. Of all the days for Mayté to be off. Our sous chef ran the kitchen today.

"It looked like he was taking notes," Wendy said. "At first I thought he was texting, but I snuck a peek over his shoulder, and it was definitely a notes app. He's the only person in the sports room."

"Thanks. I'll take it from here." I made my way through the main dining room, my lips pinching at only half of the tables being occupied. Sunlight poured in the front windows, the aroma of fried dough mixed with savory breakfast meats filling the air. Stopping at the sports room's entrance, a fist of icy dread punched my core.

Ryan.

He just sat there, his head bending over his phone.

I couldn't move. Couldn't breathe. My mind raced, cataloging some of the partially eaten dishes covering every square inch of his table. Apple-smoked bacon beignets with a honey-pecan glaze, Bavarian cream–stuffed beignets, eggs Benedict beignets with a brown-sugar cream sauce. And then I considered Wendy's observations of him taking pictures and notes. It didn't make sense. He was planning to open an upscale dinner-service-only restaurant. Unless . . .

He glanced up and had the gall to appear amused. He lifted both hands in a playful gesture of being caught.

I fought the urge to grab the fork from the plate before him and stab that gleam right out of his eye.

He eased back in his seat, sliding his phone into his pocket. "I decided to go another route with my new restaurant. You pointing out the downfalls of changing the Vieux Carré Café's ambiance got me thinking. You've done so well here with what you're doing. And you obviously feel strongly about expanding to the French Quarter."

Flashes sparked in my vision, and my hands trembled at my sides, anger building within. I was like a shaken can of coke, ready to explode. But I had patrons just behind me, and I couldn't jeopardize my business by making a scene. I unclenched my aching jaw and endeavored to keep a tremor from my voice. "Why are you doing this? Being so . . . so—"

"You think you're the only one who had their well-planned future pulled out from under them?"

My breath whooshed out. "This is all some big revenge because I adopted Hayley?"

He snorted, shaking his head. "Everything's always personal with you. That's not the future I was talking about."

My gaze drifted around the room, working through his words. His professional future? Was he referencing the times he'd disagreed with my and Claire's plans for Mawmaw's inheritance and the café? Pressure built within my head. Back then he'd never offered true help. Not until the café had successfully opened. And even then, he'd only wanted us to get a second location up and running for him to manage. I scoffed, and motioned to the food before him, stepping forward. "It makes perfect sense, you doing this. You've never had a unique idea in your entire life. Not in high school or college or when we were engaged. And certainly not now."

His smirk remained. "Thanks to you, I've never needed to."

Because I'd been so gullible and allowed him to use me. The cruel blow struck right to my heart.

He removed his credit card from the server's billfold, stood, and ambled past me.

Distantly, I heard the bell on the front door jingle. I pulled in my first full breath since laying eyes on Ryan, and slunk into one of the chairs at his table.

I contemplated each of the delectable creations before me. It would be a double blow. Ryan attempting to copy Mawmaw's and Claire's lovingly crafted recipes *and* peddling them from the place that had been Claire's dream.

No. Not today, Ryan Comeaux. Not ever.

Muscles tightening in readiness, I pushed to my feet. With determined steps, I made my way back to my office. I'd call the Small Business Administration to once again check the status of my loan application. Then I'd formulate a backup plan. Because there was no way on God's green earth Ryan was going to win.

The next evening, Hayley, me, and Precious met Micah at Lucy's, a restaurant at the corner of Tchoupitoulas and Girod. To Hayley's delight, Micah had suggested the eatery in the Warehouse District as the perfect spot to discuss the next library event because of the outdoor seating that welcomed dogs. I wasn't complaining. It was the perfect distraction from waiting for the SBA to return my call.

We now occupied a sky-blue picnic bench on the sidewalk, laminated menus in hand. The second-floor balcony provided the ideal amount of shade from the evening sun. Thankfully, no one had yelled *rat* at the sight of Precious. Not yet, anyway. The bald puppy sat on Hayley's lap, trembling at every vehicle that drove past. Hayley soothed the dog as she studied her menu. Precious wasn't the only one feeling apprehensive. Micah and I hadn't seen each other since Saturday, or had the chance to talk about that knee-weakening kiss we'd had.

But despite that powerful kiss, I wouldn't foolishly risk my heart again. The sucker punch of Ryan's visit yesterday still ached. Deeply. No, I'd think rationally. Gather the answer to the final question lingering in my brain about him: his breakup with Sydney Dupré. Julia had labeled my rebound worry an excuse. But I couldn't help the need to clarify. The *why* of their relationship ending had been like a gnat, my mere swats allowing it to circle back and keep biting. I was ready to squash it. But with Hayley here, the task was impossible.

I slid my sunglasses to rest atop my head. "How's your dad doing?"

From the other side of the table, Micah's gaze rose to mine. "Much better, thank you. He's out of the wheelchair and graduated to a cane."

"That's great." I reached for one of the waters the waitress had dropped off when we'd taken our seats. "Have y'all gotten the results from his test?" The ice in my glass clinked as I moved it in front of me.

He nodded, his expression dimming. "It's what the doctor suspected, advanced osteoporosis."

I pressed my lips together with a wince. "I'm sorry to hear that. From what you said before, the goal is to be preventative, right?"

"Right. He's started two prescriptions and physical therapy. These next few weeks, they're teaching him exercises he can do at home to strengthen his muscles and balance."

"Sounds like a solid plan."

He glanced at Hayley, who sat beside me, completely absorbed by texting on her phone. His attention shifted back to me. "The doctor warned us how brittle his bones are. Even something as minor as bending over wrong or coughing could cause a fracture. And with his ankle weakened . . ." A muscle twitched in his jaw. "With this condition, a fall at his age doesn't have the best odds of recovery."

My heart clenched. "What's your sister think of all this?"

"She wants to cover my dad in Bubble Wrap and move him to a retirement center with 24/7 care." The humor in his voice fell flat.

"How do you feel about that?"

"I just want what's best for him. Physically, mentally. And right now, he's not speaking to Renee since she made that suggestion, so I'm going along with what he wants. The last thing we need is him getting injured and not telling anyone."

"I believe your dad has a little stubbornness in him. Just like my grandma."

He sighed. "Yeah."

"If there's anything I can do to help—"

"There isn't."

I straightened, meeting his stare straight on. "But if there is, I hope you'll tell me."

He gave a noncommittal nod.

I hoped his declining my help didn't stem from when I'd shared about Mawmaw. My gut twinged with guilt over how raw I'd been in that moment. "I know the things I said before about my grandma, but . . ." I worked against the pressure crowding my throat. "This is a completely different situation." *God, please let it be different.*

A bittersweet smile whispered across his features.

Cheers erupted from inside the restaurant, and Precious released a mournful wail, snapping Hayley's attention from her device. Through the windows lining the side of the building, I spied all of the TVs tuned in to the Pelicans' first NBA playoff game of the season.

Hayley set her phone on the table. "We should make our courtyard dog friendly for customers. It's an untapped market."

I gawked at her. "An untapped market?" Who was this child?

"I think it's a cool idea," Micah said, his countenance lightening at the change in topic.

"Of course you would," I mumbled.

"Most people love their dogs." Hayley shot me a look. "And they like to have a place to take them. Remember all those dogs at PetSmart?"

"Yes, I do. And I clearly remember one of those dogs lifting a hind leg and peeing on one of their employees. There would be dog *business* on my brick pavers."

Hayley shrugged. "There's already bird poop."

"Not helping," I scoffed.

"We could have one of those dog poop stations and ensure the owners pick their poop up. And have special treats for the dogs."

"I don't know." Micah set his menu aside, a teasing expression forming. "That's just giving them more ammunition for pooping."

A couple walking by turned their heads our way. I leaned forward, my ribs pressing against the wood, and reduced my voice. "Will y'all please stop mentioning *poop* at a restaurant?"

"Gourmet dog biscuits," Hayley said, undeterred. "People would pay for treats like that."

I sighed. "I'm not asking Mayté to make dog food. Plus, I don't want people in my backyard at all hours, where we come and go from our home."

"Oh." Hayley's brows pulled together.

Micah rested his elbows on the table. "What if you treated it like a special event and opened the courtyard to dogs once a month?"

I nailed him with a glare.

"Or once a week!" Hayley's tone pitched. "Like every Saturday."

I swung my attention to her. "Most of my special events are on Saturdays." I struck the end of my straw against the table, pushing the paper down.

"Then Friday evenings," she huffed, and snuggled Precious to her chest. "And I'll help the entire time."

"Ha!" I pulled my straw free and shoved it into my drink. "You mean you'll play with the dogs the entire time."

"I'll clean up after them, supply water." She kissed Precious's forehead, right above the creature's tennis ball–sized eyes. It was a wonder the dog didn't tip forward all the time from the weight.

I wadded the paper wrapper from my straw, squeezing it between my fingers. "We're supposed to be talking about the next library event."

A motorcycle flew by, earning a honk from the vehicle it illegally passed. Precious whined, clawing up Hayley's neck in an attempt to hide in her auburn hair.

"We could do a dog-themed party." Hayley's mouth gave an impish curve as she readjusted her hold on the animal. "There's lots of dogs in fiction. And everyone could bring their pets."

"Great." I'd said the word as though replying to my gynecologist's suggestion of scheduling my first routine mammogram.

Another round of whoops and cheers burst from the inside customers.

Hayley maneuvered from the bench and stood, handing me Precious, ensuring the dog's leash looped around my wrist. "I'll be right back." She headed inside, either to use the bathroom or to pick the restaurant manager's brain about Beignets & Books' untapped market. Holding the trembling lump of skin, I exhaled a sigh, my gaze catching on Micah. His attention already rested on me, a knowing glint in his eyes. I licked my dry lips and fidgeted with Precious's leash. Now would be the perfect time to scratch off the last item on my Micah list.

"Do you want me to hold her?" He inclined his chin to Precious.

"Thank you, but no."

He reached across the table, petting the dog, his fingers purposefully grazing mine. The sneaky cuddler.

My nerve endings stirred, heat tingling beneath my skin. *Nope.* I would not be a public handsie hussie a second time. I shifted away from him, and he retreated with a chuckle, grasping his drink. The tendons in his forearm flexed, and I followed the movement up to his bicep. Precious had calmed under his affection, while my heartbeat had kicked up a level. Against my will, I sensed my attention pulling to his face. I braced for that flirtatious twinkle in his eye, but when I met his gaze, I observed something else instead. What could only be characterized as . . . earnestness.

Hoo boy. I scanned the sidewalk for our waitress. It turned out I wasn't quite ready to remove that last barricade from my heart easing on down the relationship road. My pulse quickened, and I found myself grateful for Precious to shield my chest. I had no doubt my pounding heart visibly beat right through my top.

Lips parting, his brows rose with a soft, questioning gaze. "Kate." His tone wrapped my name in tenderness.

The playful, roguish side to Micah, I could handle. It felt safe, heart-wise. But when he cast that serious stare on me, one that spoke of promises. Promises that could be broken when you least expected it. Well . . . unlike my face, my heart didn't have a mask. Which validated why I'd only thought with my brain since Ryan. Maybe if I didn't go all in with my entire heart, I'd be okay. I took in his olive-hued eyes. My leg jittered beneath the table, my heel lightly tapping against the concrete. Maybe I could bear giving him twenty percent of my heart.

"How much longer are we going to dance around this?" He motioned back and forth between us.

Or fifteen percent. I fidgeted with the tags on Precious's collar.

"Kate?" His voice was a whisper.

"Why did you and Sydney break up?"

He straightened, his forehead furrowing.

I swallowed past the lump in my throat. "I don't want to be a rebound."

Our waitress appeared. "Sorry it took so long. Things are super busy inside with the game. Are y'all ready to order?"

Where were you five seconds ago, missy?

Micah turned to her. "Can you give us another minute?"

"Sure." She retreated, leaving us alone.

He scratched the back of his neck. "Is rebounding even still a thing?"

"Isn't it?" I lowered Precious to my lap, and she curled into a wrinkly ball. "Of course, what do I know?" I mumbled to my silverware roll. "I haven't dated in a decade."

"You haven't dated anyone since Ryan?" Undeniable surprise coated his tone.

My spine stiffened. "I've been busy. You know, single parent, running a business."

One side of his mouth quirked. "And yet you have time for me."

Which would dwindle with opening another location. Something I'd need to talk to him about. Precious shifted to stand on my lap, her paws digging into my thighs with surprisingly pointy force, as though she walked on chopstick stilts.

"*I* broke it off with Sydney." He clasped his hands over his menu. "I realized at that first disastrous library function my attraction to you was more than physical. My childhood crush had returned with a vengeance."

He'd only spoken three sentences, and yet it was a monumental amount of information to process. His words pinged through my mind like the little metal ball in a pinball machine.

"*I broke it off with Sydney.*" Ding!

"*Childhood crush.*" Boing!

I lightly touched my forehead.

"When I brought Sydney home that afternoon after the event, I told her I thought we were better as friends. The next time I saw you, nine days later, when you put on my shirt at the library during the tornado, I knew."

My head tilted, my mouth slowly opening. "Knew what?"

He rubbed his hands down his thighs, his cheeks reddening the teeniest, tiniest little bit. "Not to sound like some cheesy romance, but . . . I knew I was going to pursue you."

Swoon.

He lifted a muscular shoulder. "Taking care of you only solidified that."

My stomach fluttered while my mind raced, trying to make sense of his declaration and failing. "But . . . you watched me puke. In your Jeep. You know about my horrendous periods. And Bat Boy. I'm cardigan sweaters and spreadsheets and routines. You're . . ." I motioned to the flamingos he wore. "Goofy shirts and lame jokes and unpredictable."

"We're more than those things." His voice had softened, adopting a longing tone.

My belly flipped. I shifted Precious and her pointy paws to the bench, then crossed my arms and tried to conjure the Landry Mask. Maybe if I only offered him half of my heart, that would be okay. But only half. "I'm planning to open another café in the very near future. That's going to soak up all my extra time."

"I'll take whatever you can give."

Have mercy. "I'm serious about how busy I'll be. For a long time. A long, long time."

His brows rose in challenge. "I'll take whatever you can give."

My leg jittered again. "I'm not going to wear bookish T-shirts and throw glitter parties."

A rascal smile spread across his face. "Haven't you heard opposites attract?"

I scoffed. "We're not a Paula Abdul song. I'm too stuffy for you."

"I kind of think you're just right for me." He crossed his arms, mimicking me. Except his motion only highlighted his biceps.

Goodness. I averted my stare.

Micah continued. "You forget I've had a front-row seat at how caring you were growing up. With your grandma, Claire, even Ryan back in the day. And now Hayley." He uncrossed his arms, leaning forward. "You don't let a lot of people in, but the ones who you do . . . That's where I want to be."

My breath caught in my chest, my heartbeats slowing. The problem was, I wasn't sure I could ever let him in like that.

The next morning, I returned from bringing Hayley and Emma to school and found a surprise waiting. Propped against the back doors to the café was a single pink carnation wrapped in tissue paper. I neared, taking in the flower, noting the deep crimson edges of the petals. My lips parted in recognition. It was the exact coloring of the carnations I'd anonymously received every year in high school through the Valentine's Day fundraiser. A gift Ryan had always taken credit for.

Oh, Micah. Wonder swept through me, tingles surging from my brain, carving a path straight to my heart and taking a chisel to the walls there. He'd been serious about having that child-hood crush. All those years, it'd been him. I couldn't remember him dating anyone seriously back then. And he'd never shown interest in me, other than our kiss in seventh grade. Unless he had, and I hadn't picked up on it because I'd been with Ryan. Slowly shaking my head, I lifted the flower and found the gas card taped to the back of the tissue paper.

22

RIDING THE STREETCAR WASN'T FOR ROOKIES. The next day after school found Hayley and me on one of the army-green cars running St. Charles Avenue. I was considering allowing her to ride the public transportation to and from the library. *Considering* being the key word.

We'd boarded and made our way down the center aisle. Wooden benches for two lined the walls, their slatted backs reversible, permitting riders in groups of three or four to sit facing one another. Being a late Thursday afternoon with nothing touristy going on in the city, only half of the car was occupied. Next week would herald a different story with Jazz Fest. For eleven days, music-loving tourists and locals from surrounding parishes would fill New Orleans, and the café, for the annual New Orleans Jazz and Heritage Festival.

Hayley followed me to the last set of seating on the right. With the bench before it vacant, she slid the back so we sat across from each other, each of us next to an open window. I'd hoped this outing, and the prospect of a little more freedom, would soften what I aimed to talk to her about. I fidgeted with my purse strap. The constant rocking of the car only increased the gurgle in my stomach from the coffee I'd downed before we'd left. I should've known better, but I had wanted the caffeine comfort.

I pitched my voice over the clunking of the streetcar's compressor. "What do you think of Mr. Micah?"

Her gaze slid from the iconic views of the oak-lined street to me, a slight pucker gathering between her auburn brows. "That's vague."

"Is it?" I kept my tone light and adjusted the pull-down canvas shade above my open window, returning it all the way up.

Air streamed in, whipping Hayley's long hair. "Do you want my opinion of him as a librarian, a general human being on the planet, or as your boyfriend?"

"He's not . . ." I tucked my own flying hair behind my ears and strove for an unaffected demeanor. "He's not my boyfriend."

Over the intercom, a computerized voice announced an upcoming stop.

Mischief twinkled in Hayley's eyes, so reminiscent of Claire. "But he wants to be. And so do you."

I stiffened, the boards in the seatback pressing into my spine. "Why would you think that?"

She pulled a face. "I'm thirteen. Not some naïve ten-year-old. I have eyes, and I see the way y'all look at each other."

"And how is that?"

The brakes squealed, the car coming to a halt. A passenger lugging several plastic grocery bags made their way down the aisle to the back doors and exited. We accelerated, the whizz and hum of the motor growing louder, the vehicle returning to its rhythmic rocking.

The hint of a smirk played across Hayley's features. "He watches you when you're not looking, and you watch him when he's not looking." She gave half an eye roll. "So childish."

Childish? My lips pursed. "Mind your manners, missy."

"Sorry," she mumbled and pulled a rubber band from her

wrist, wrangling her hair into a ponytail. We passed another streetcar traveling in the opposite direction, our conductor waving at them. Hayley glanced at her phone and shoved it back in her cross-body purse. "As a librarian, Mr. Micah's book recommendations are solid."

Debatable. The man had, after all, given me a copy of *Twilight*. Though I hadn't even cracked a page of the paperback, so maybe that was an unfair judgment.

"As a human being in general." She shrugged. "Precious likes him."

I held in a snort.

"He's easy to talk to. And I've never seen him litter when he could have. Or curse. Not even when a toddler throwing a tantrum chucked a book and nailed Mr. Micah in his man parts."

"What?"

"Oh yeah." She nodded, straightening in her seat with a smile. "Jacob was there and said that definitely called for cursing."

Jacob, Emma's brother. The likelihood of him being Hayley's last-minute ride home from the library gave me another reason for wanting to have a backup plan for her transportation.

"As your boyfriend . . ." She crossed her arms, leaning back all casual-as-you-please. "I think you should give him a chance."

The tension that had been building within me eased. "So you'd be okay if I went on a date with him?"

"Sure." She lifted a shoulder, returning her sights to the window.

My gaze drifted to the sign on the wall, noting the streetcar's standing on the National Register of Historical Places. Next to the coffee still gurgling in my gut, an odd combination of anticipation and uncertainty churned. I was stepping into an unknown era. Rubbing the Crease, I tried to think rationally. It didn't have to be a full step. I could ease one toe in at a time. And pull it out any moment. My heart could handle that. Right?

Hayley picked at her fingernail polish. The color hued the darkest of purples, one shade away from black. "But if y'all get serious, you need to warn him about Grandmother and Grandfather."

My head tipped back with a groan, and Hayley raised her brows, giving me a *That's right* look.

Growing up, Micah had had enough glimpses of my parents at Mawmaw's Mardi Gras parties to form an opinion. And again when I'd been sick and at the last library event. Still, I'd have to properly forewarn him about my parents sooner rather than later. Because I was supposed to bring him to dinner. In two days. Now that Hayley knew about Micah, I could cancel. But I'd made a deal. And Mawmaw had always quoted Ecclesiastes, teaching us to keep our vows.

Our destination approached, and I nudged Hayley with my foot. "You need to pay attention. I won't always be with you to make sure you get off at the right stop." I pulled the thin metal wire running atop our windows, signaling the conductor we wanted to exit. The streetcar slowed, the brakes squealing. I stood, keeping one hand on the seat for balance, and motioned with my other hand for Hayley to follow. We made our way to the rear. With the green light over the back doors giving the all clear, I stepped down to them. "You have to push good and hard." I shoved the doors, holding them open for Hayley, lest they swing back and knock her slight frame down. On the return trip home, I'd make her be the one to fight them. If I were a betting woman, I'd give her fifty-fifty odds.

We spilled out onto the neutral ground, and the streetcar continued on its way. I cast my gaze across St. Charles Avenue to the library. And to Micah in his Jeep, pulling away from the small parking lot. *Strange.* He was supposed to be working until the library closed. Did one sizzling make-out session qualify me for asking his whereabouts? We hadn't even been on a date. Or defined our relationship as a relationship.

See? This was why the last decade of my life had been easy. What was I doing opening a can of worms at this point in my life?

I'd been granted a reprieve. That evening, Hayley and I had been eating Mayté's tamales and talking about the café's expansion, when Mama's *Jaws* ringtone had interrupted us. Per usual, I'd let the call roll to voice mail. And per usual, I'd slowly chewed an antacid while belatedly listening to her message. Except this time, good news had poured from her lips. She'd moved our dinner back a week. *Thank You, Lord!*

I now walked the wraparound porch on the second floor. With the sun waning, and the sky transitioning to darker shades, the later hour had cooled the air. I'd pulled on a long-sleeve flannel over my T-shirt and shorts, and held one of Julia's Nerf guns, scanning the trees for Cést Fou. To aid in my vigilance, and deter the feathered nightmare from taking up residence on my property at night, I'd repositioned the floodlights to shine on the trees. Hayley was in the shower, using every last drop of hot water, and Precious snoozed in a ball on the living room rug.

The scent of freshly cut grass wafted up, and I rotated my neck and shoulders, trying to ease the aches. I'd mowed the lawn and weed whacked today. Since I'd started cutting the grass again this past month, the lawnmower had been persnickety when starting up. As if it too, like the café's fryer, were putting me on notice. My posture wilted at the thought of another added expense right now.

"Name one good thing" filtered through my thoughts in Mawmaw's voice. How many times had she asked me and Claire to do that on this very porch when in the dumps over something? I closed my eyes and tuned out the traffic noise, concentrating on the breeze rustling through the leaves of the

great oaks. One good thing was Hayley's positive reaction to the idea of Micah and I dating.

Opening my eyes, I redirected my attention to my phone, my finger hovering over his name. Flutters erupted in my stomach, as though I were in junior high and calling a boy for the first time. Before I could chicken out, I hit dial and listened to several rings carry over the line.

"Well, hello." Surprised delight filled his tone.

I actually felt the smile spreading across my face. "Hello." I bit my lower lip, turning the corner from the side of the house to the rear. "What are you doing?"

"I'm on my way back from jiujitsu."

"And did you beat anyone up in your little karate lesson? Like a third grader?"

He snickered. "You clearly need to come to one of my classes. What are you up to?"

"Not much. I'm on the balcony, keeping an eye out for that vile bird." My gaze swept the oak for movement, my finger tightening on the toy gun's trigger.

"Any sightings?"

"Not yet, though he left his calling card this morning." I continued walking, looking down on my prayer nook, where I'd spent extra time today. Although I hadn't sensed any certain direction from God with my business troubles or Micah, I had peace in talking to Him. In knowing He heard me. And cared. I pulled in a breath. There was no going back after this. "I talked to Hayley. About you."

"And?" The playfulness from his tone vanished.

My gaze skimmed over and down to my neighbor's yard, and the colored lights shimmering in his pool. "According to her you're a solid librarian, don't curse when socked in your man parts with a book, and she thinks I should give you a shot at dating."

His exhale carried over the line.

A small lump of emotion gathered in my throat at his relief over Hayley's consent.

"I bet Precious liking me had everything to do with her approval."

My heart softened at how well he already knew Hayley. How he'd slid so easily into our lives. Yearning to see him in this moment ignited in my core. Maybe I'd ask him to come over. Maybe—

"For the record, I did curse when that kid threw the book," he said. "I just did it very quietly. That happening isn't what I signed up for with my job."

I tensed, as though a bucket of ice had been dumped down my shirt. A sharp memory of Ryan pierced my mind. His words so long ago on the night he'd left. *"This isn't what I signed up for."* Caution, cold and jagged, bit into me, warning me against falling too hard and fast. Against the past repeating itself.

"Kate? You still there?"

I cleared my throat, dislodging what felt like wedged icy shards. "We . . . we need to take things slow."

"I had to wait twenty-seven years to kiss you again. If we go any slower, I may be too old to remember who you are."

A blip of warmth breached the chill that had submerged me. I turned the corner, bringing me back to the view of St. Charles Avenue. My steps slowed, and I found myself reluctantly grateful for the curveball I was about to throw him. Or, really, test him with. "There's one other thing. My parents want us to come to dinner next Saturday."

"Can you hold on a second?"

"Sure." Silence carried over the line. I stared at my phone's screen. Had he really just ended our convo at the mention of my parents? My hand holding the phone collapsed at my side. "Well, that's a big fat F," I mumbled. "In bold red ink." That ten percent of my heart that had opened to Micah shrank.

The clunk and clang of a streetcar drew my attention, its

lone center headlight slicing through the inky dusk. Although I couldn't blame Micah for not wanting to be around my parents, they were connected to me. Like cutting the lawn and battling fire ants, they were inevitable.

"Hey." A masculine voice came from behind.

I whirled, a gasp lodging in my lungs, and pulled the trigger on the Nerf gun. An orange foam dart shot out, hitting Micah square in the chest before plunking to the floorboards.

"Sorry." He held up his hands, laughter breaking free.

I clutched my phone to my breastbone, my pulse pounding in my ears.

"Didn't mean to scare you." He slid his own cell into the pocket of his track pants and reached down, picking up the dart. A gentle tease radiated in his expression. "Didn't you say you wanted to take things slow? I'm all for going to that dinner, but officially meeting your parents seems like a giant step."

His big fat F upgraded to an A-. "Says the man who's stalking me." I set my phone and the Nerf gun on a side table nestled between two patio chairs.

"It's not stalking when you tell me exactly where you are." He neared, the shadows giving way, revealing a red mark beneath one of his eyes.

My stomach dropped. "What happened?"

"Oh." He waved me off. "I got elbowed in class. It happens."

"That's going to leave a bruise." I chewed the inside of my cheek, examining the injury. "Will it be gone by next week?"

"Probably. It's not a big deal."

"But it will be to my mom." I fought the impulse to rub the Crease, crossing my arms instead. "Good impressions are everything to her."

"Are you forgetting last Saturday? Now, whether it was good or not . . ." He lifted a shoulder.

Ugh. He was right. I screwed my eyes shut, snippets of that day playing through my mind. Mama interrupting our kiss.

She and Daddy witnessing Micah break up a fight. Shaking my head, I opened my eyes and found Micah staring at me. He hooked his thumbs into his front pockets, and his smile bent into a flirty curl. Those earlier flutters in my belly returned, and my jaw unclenched, my frustration defusing.

He drew himself up to his full height, his T-shirt slightly stretching against his chest. "You're really sexy when you're agitated."

I scoffed. "You should watch me reconciling my bank accounts." *And had he called me sexy?* A vehicle with a shot muffler rumbled down the street, and in my periphery, I caught sight of the lampposts along the neutral ground flickering on.

Micah neared, an air of certainty in his movements. And with every step closer, my irritation inexplicably waned. Stopping before me, he reached for my hand, sending a million tingles across my skin from the simple touch.

I pulled in a lungful of air and stared up at him. "I know you probably think I'm overreacting. It's just . . . my mom doesn't need something else to pick on me about."

He grew still, his brows drawing together. "From what I've seen and heard from you and Hayley, I'd say trying to please her is a lost cause." His thumb caressed the top of my hand.

Slowly, I nodded. "But I feel like I should try. Maintaining some semblance of a relationship with my parents was important to Claire. She was the one who started our monthly dinners with them after Mawmaw's death as a sort of olive branch."

With a concerned tilt to his lips, he considered me. "Even olive trees can run out of branches."

I tried and failed at a smile, only managing a nod.

His solemn gaze leveled on me. "I'm not going to let anything ruin dinner with your parents."

My heart pitter-pattered at his sincerity.

A mischievous smile curved one edge of his mouth. "I'll even iron my fanciest Hawaiian shirt."

A puff of laughter escaped me.

His fingers entwined with mine. A perfect fit.

Goldilocks.

Gently, he squeezed my fingers. "So, Hayley's good with us?"

"She is," I whispered.

His other hand lifted, cupping my face, his calloused thumb brushing against my cheek. "And you're good with us too?"

A heated shiver dashed down my spine, nearly vanquishing the last of the chill from that long-ago memory of Ryan. Throat too dry to speak, I nodded.

Smile lines creased the corners of his eyes, his gaze earnest and smoldering. He leaned down, his lips tenderly meeting mine. Unlike our previous kiss, this one held a note of gravity. Of intentions. Of a declaration. Longing unfurled within, stretching and reaching. Hoping to find steady ground.

Don't make me promises you won't keep.

Don't use me.

And if I fall in love with you, don't leave.

23

"I'M READY TO STEEL MAGNOLIAS THIS BIRD."

Julia lowered her coffee cup to the table, right next to her Nerf gun. "Fireworks are illegal to shoot privately in New Orleans. A lesson my mom learned the hard way."

A long-withering sigh pushed from my lungs.

She patted my hand. "I'll get you the contact info of the guy who removed the bats from my father-in-law's house. He may be able to help."

It was Friday evening, and Julia and I sat beneath the covered porch at the back of the café, indulging in our weekly carb binge. Normally we resided under the oak tree when dining outside. But normally, I didn't have a merciless parrot with perfect aim wreaking havoc. That morning, when I'd brought Precious downstairs to do her business because Hayley had woken late, I'd done a double take at the courtyard.

Snow in New Orleans was something I'd only witnessed three times in my entire life. And during those instances, the white stuff had barely stuck to the ground, so I'd known I wasn't walking into a winter wonderland. No, I was sidestepping poop landmines. Even the fountain and the table and its four chairs

242

had been accosted. It'd taken all morning to hose and clean everything. To drain the fountain and fill it back up again.

Pouring salt into my wounds, I'd finally received word from the Small Business Administration. I hadn't met the requirements for acquiring a loan. The value of Mawmaw's mansion was a blessing in many ways, but a curse with grants and government loans since it counted against my business worth. I'd channeled my frustration into scrubbing every nook and cranny of the fountain and finalizing my next move.

But here and now, Julia and I caught up on our week, her delight over the developments with Micah clear.

She rested an elbow on the table. "It says a lot about Micah that he didn't lead Sydney on. Plus, I don't think you need to worry about feeling awkward around her. She didn't give the impression they were serious."

I scanned the trees.

"You know, for a woman in a new relationship, when everything's supposed to be all exciting and fun, you seem to be on the subdued side."

The beignets in my stomach churned at the oncoming conversation. "My SBA loan application was rejected."

The lines marring her forehead disappeared, and she eased back in her chair. "I'm sure you're disappointed, and I hate that for you, but I'm relieved. This entire endeavor, and how rushed it's been, hasn't sat right with me."

I bit the inside of my cheek, studying the new freckle on my wrist. If only I had a dollar for every freckle on my body. It would be the gift that kept giving.

"What aren't you telling me?"

I cut a quick glance from her to the table and to my lap, where I smoothed my napkin.

She straightened in her chair. "Spill it, sister."

I straightened, matching her chutzpah. "I have a plan D."

Her head tipped back with a groan.

"I'm not ready to wave the white flag."

Crossing her arms, she stared me down with the same expression I'd seen her give her boys on multiple occasions, like when one of them had borrowed her car and returned it on empty. "If Ryan weren't a factor, would you be this bent on this property?"

If I answered too hastily, her mom-glare would only continue. I pulled in a breath through my nose and squirmed in my seat. *Would* I still be pursuing the Vieux Carré Café if Ryan wasn't involved? I thought back to when I'd first stood outside the place, waiting for Trisha, how mixed my feelings had been. Want versus need teeter-tottering in my gut. How those feelings had changed abruptly with Ryan's appearance, my rear end thumping hard to the ground on the want side. Especially in light of this past week. "Ryan's planning to copy Beignets & Books."

Julia blanched. "Can he do that?"

"Pretty much. At least, to a certain extent. I caught him here Monday, conducting his own little research session. If he wins, he'll have Claire's dream location and be using her and Mawmaw's recipes. Well, recreations of them."

"That man is rotten." A beat passed, her gaze turning reflective. "But if he doesn't get the Vieux Carré Café, what's to keep him from doing that anyway? Surly there are other properties out there."

"Not in the French Quarter."

She slid me her mom-look. "Aside from his lack of ethics, I can't help but think this is your way of getting back at him for how he mistreated you."

Heat flushed my skin, my hands balling into fists beneath the table. If only the Landry Mask worked with Julia. If only she didn't know me so well. "Ryan is a part of the equation. There's nothing I can do about that. Or him trying to copy my café. But the fact remains it's still Claire's dream location at stake." My eyes stung. "I *can* do something about that."

Empathy radiated in her steady eye contact, and her throat bobbed, as though she were choosing her words with care. "If Claire had remained on this earth longer, who's to say her dream wouldn't have shifted to another location? Or something else altogether? And wasn't y'all's carefully laid out plan to wait another six years before expanding?"

My chin trembled, and I slid my gaze away from hers, away from the truth she'd spoken. How many times had I stared at that plan, framed and hanging on the wall in my office? We'd given ourselves a five-year break after the courtyard renovation prior to another year of gearing up again.

"Have you been praying on this?" Gentleness layered her tone.

A dull ache began throbbing in my head. "Of course."

"And listening for direction?"

"Yes." I rested my elbows on the table, massaging my temples. "And I'm not hearing anything."

"Maybe you need to give it more time."

I dropped my hands. "I don't have the luxury of time. There's a countdown clock ticking over my head that ends July Fourth."

"But it won't end there." Her voice brimmed with compassion and caution, matching her expression. "If you win what's probably going to be a bidding war between you and Ryan, you'll then be faced with the monumental project of opening another restaurant. Is that something you want to take on right now?"

The ache in my head amplified to pounding. What I needed was two Advil and a café au lait. With a shot of espresso.

"This doesn't sit well with me." Julia placed a palm to her chest. "It's too hurried. Sometimes, I think the enemy wants us to rush-rush-rush. To stay busy and stressed, which leads to bad decisions."

"But I don't see anything wrong with doing everything I can for this opportunity. I may not even get the property."

"True. I just don't want all of your free time gobbled up again, especially when things have improved with Hayley."

My heart clenched. Our relationship *had* gotten so much better the past month.

"And now you have Micah in the mix. How are you supposed to grow a relationship with him?"

"Micah and I are taking it slow."

She tossed me a dubious glance. "So what's plan D? Asking your parents for a loan?"

A slight weight lifted from my heart with the shift away from talking about the tender, personal areas of my life. "They were actually plan C, and they'd be the clean option. But I can't do that. I couldn't stand to be beholden to them." Besides, after the luau there was no way Mama would invest.

"Then what are you going to do?"

I squared my shoulders, drawing on my reserves of strength. "It's a two-pronged approach. I'm going to do a big push for booking special events, which means gaining security deposits, which in turn means solidifying incoming cash flow. I'm also putting together a solid business plan based on expanding locations and will begin looking for a silent partner."

She touched the base of her neck, her head tipping sideways. "I wish you could peek inside my brain right now, at how hard it's spinning."

"It's not going to be difficult, just time-consuming."

She pulled another mom-face.

I shook my napkin out, a few powdered sugar remnants falling to the floor, and placed it atop our dirty dishes. "How are things going with your cleaning products?"

She cocked an eyebrow. "Real suave with the subject change."

I wrinkled my nose.

"I'll let it slide for now." A smile tipped her lips, a glint igniting in her stare. "Nancy's Naturals increased their last purchase order."

Joy burst through me. "Of course they did!"

"And Wyatt is such a whiz with technology. He's creating a website for me to test how online sales would be and that whole process." Her face glowed with delight and possibility.

My heart swelled at how far she'd come in gaining confidence. "Ah! I love it!"

She laughed lightly. "You sound exactly like Samuel and the boys."

"If you need help, let me know."

"I will." Her grin tapered, and she reached across the table, squeezing my hand. "I wouldn't have made it to this point without you." A sheen covered her eyes.

Emotion swept through me.

"Oh," she straightened, blinking her unshed tears away, "Debbie, the woman you met at the crawfish boil, she's decided to sell her elderberry syrup at the Crescent City Farmers Market."

Sweet satisfaction curled in my chest. "That's wonderful. I'd given her my card but hadn't heard from her, so I was wondering."

"She about died when she discovered all the legal stuff involved. The licenses and tax certificates."

"And general liability insurance."

Julia nodded. "I'm helping her with it as best I can." She tucked her long brown hair behind her ear. "It makes me wonder how many people with a dream are overwhelmed by the legal and business items and give up like I had." Her gaze, filling once again with emotion, held on mine. "Thankfully I had you."

"Stop trying to make me cry." I dabbed the corners of my eyes with my knuckles.

She chuckled and sniffled, wiping the tip of her nose with her napkin. "Sorry. It just has me wishing for a program to help people like me and Debbie. Something broken down. Like those FOR DUMMIES books. Except even more basic."

"Like a how-to-get-started class."

"Yes! Because that first step is super intimidating."

The notion quickly took root, little shoots of possibility sprouting. "The first session could be people talking about their ideas."

"Brilliant!" She scooted to the edge of her seat. "Goodness knows it was hard for me just to talk about my cleaning products. I felt so inadequate."

"It could be something like a business-idea support group."

Julia's eyes rounded, and her head bobbed. "That would've been so helpful to me all those years ago."

Different class topics bloomed through my brain, my pulse picking up. "And how much fun would it be to use your products as an example? A real-life success story to infuse true encouragement."

She stilled, her mouth forming in the shape of an O. "That's even better. See? This is why you'd be so good at heading up a program like this."

Reality dropped like a guillotine, severing the path my mind barreled down. My spine wilted. "I don't have time for something like that, especially not now." My scampering heartbeat slowed, and I picked at the coral fingernail polish on my thumb. "It's a great idea." I peered at Julia. "What if you did it? You could use the courtyard as a place to gather."

She scoffed. "I'd be in the class as a student. You're the one with the know-how." She perked. "What if you charged people to attend? And offered an online version? You could put that money toward the new restaurant."

I shook my head with a weak smile. "It'd take too long to pull something like that together. I'd need a legit curriculum to charge people, and that would take time and resources. Plus, people may not show up. It's too risky right now with the July deadline I'm on." I brushed the specks of nail polish from my lap. "At least Debbie has you. And please remind her I'm only a call away."

"I will." The excitement from her voice had plunged, along with her expression. "And I understand. Maybe someday when things slow down again for you."

A chasm of emptiness opened between that possibility and reality. I rubbed the Crease. If I did purchase the Vieux Carré Café, that would be a really faraway someday.

24

THE DREADED DINNER WITH MY PARENTS had arrived. I sat in Jazz Fest traffic on the interstate, creeping my way to my parents' house in Old Metairie. Thankfully I'd added in enough time to account for the congestion I now sat in. Hopefully Micah had done the same. Although we'd wanted to ride together, I'd attended a function for an organization specializing in destination weddings in New Orleans. With that time constraint, it made sense just to meet at my parents'.

I eased my foot off the brake, crawling forward. To my left, the green metal rooftops of Xavier University contrasted against the pink and orange tones in the sky from the setting sun. My gaze returned to the bumper of the vehicle in front of me, the events of the past week playing through my mind.

Death had come to the café. And unfortunately, it hadn't been Cést Fou. The deep fryer that had been on its last leg had finally given up the ghost, and Monday had yet again held on to its title as evilest day of the week. Instead of working on the business plan for my potential silent partner, I'd spent the morning haggling over a new fryer. The bright side was that the appliance had been in place in time for the Jazz Fest rush that had begun Thursday. The dark side was the debt that had been added to my shoulders and credit score, looming heavy ever since.

Something gold glinted on the dashboard. I bent forward, my seatbelt pulling against my torso. A fleck of glitter in the shape of a starfish. How in the world had that gotten in here? A bubble of lightness broke through at the thought of Micah. I hadn't seen him since last Saturday night. He'd brought over two bags of groceries, he and Hayley making shepherd's pie while I'd sat at the kitchen table, registering for every viable networking event I could attend up until July Fourth. My smile faded. The most lucrative function for this week had been yesterday evening, which meant I'd had to bail on my beignet date with Julia.

The Airline Drive exit came into view, and I eased onto it, sailing the rest of the way. I pulled into my parents' driveway and killed the engine. No sign of Micah. I pulled two packets of travel Tums from my purse. One for each of us to get us through the evening. I'd already put a serious dent in my roll on the drive over.

I glanced at my cell. *6:51 p.m.* Dinner started sharply at seven. *That's fine.* He would pull up any second now, and we'd stroll up to my parents' door together with minutes to spare.

I turned in my seat, looking up and down the street. What was that old saying Mawmaw had always used? A watched pot never boils? I faced forward. *Stop being ridiculous. He'll be here. He knows how important this is.* Each night this week we'd either texted or spoken on the phone, Micah assuring me he hadn't acquired a black eye or broken nose at jiujitsu.

6:53 p.m. The backs of my knees began sweating. I checked my device, ensuring the ringer was on. Although Mama irritated me to no end, I didn't want to give her anything else to hold over my head. Our tumultuous bond already hung by an unraveling thread, especially since our last meal with her picking on Hayley.

251

Hayley. I opened the tracking app on her phone and found her pulsing dot at home. She'd offered to come tonight—talk about self-sacrificing—but I'd declined. If Micah couldn't handle the full force of Mama, better to know now than months or years into our relationship.

6:55 p.m. Popping another Tums, I sucked the sugarcoating, glad I'd splurged for the more tasty candy version. I swiped my finger across my phone's screen and selected my favorites shortcut to call Micah.

The front door to the house swung open, Mama emerging. *Sarah McLachlan.*

I shoved the Tums in the pocket of my full skirt, pulled my keys from the ignition, and grabbed my purse.

Mama moved onto the walkway, wearing a cream sheath dress with three-quarter-length sleeves. Beige pumps and her signature nude panty hose completed her ensemble. Her critical expression swept the driveway and street.

Exiting my car, I couldn't help but scan the road too, my stomach sinking a little deeper. I placed my keys in my purse and ensured my sleeveless lavender top was tucked perfectly in at my waist.

"You're alone." She skimmed my outfit, her eyes narrowing the slightest bit at my legs. Probably because I wasn't wearing vile panty hose.

"I had a function to attend, so Micah and I agreed to meet here."

"And he knows dinner is at seven?"

"He does."

She sniffed. "So much for punctuality."

I shifted from one heel to the other. Unfortunately, I couldn't disagree with her in this moment. And it wouldn't aid to point out he'd been punctual the times he'd met up with me and Hayley. An SUV drove by, lifting my hopes, only to keep going. What seemed like a cloud of doom floated in, hovering over me.

I shot Micah a quick text, asking if he was okay. Had he been an unreliable wolf in sheep's clothing those other occasions?

Mama turned for the door. "We're not waiting out here for him like some backwoods porch hounds."

I followed, breathing in her trail of Chanel perfume. My belly churned, and I popped another Tums. In the foyer, I set my purse on a side table and slipped my phone into my other pocket.

Mama continued on, her pumps clicking against the marble floors. "We're having appetizers in the parlor."

Okay. That was good. It'd give Micah extra time. Missing appetizers wasn't nearly as bad as arriving late to the actual dinner, especially if he brought flowers for Mama like I'd suggested. I chewed the final bit of antacid. We entered the parlor, a palette of whites and creams, a room screaming no children lived here. A room Mama hadn't allowed Hayley in until last year. And even then, she'd watched her like a hawk, as though Hayley would produce a pack of markers and go wild.

Daddy stood from a pearl-hued wingback chair, holding a whiskey glass. His white button-down and tan slacks blended with the room. Mama loved color cohesiveness. Goodness knew she probably still set his clothes out every morning. His gaze swept from Mama to me, then to the empty space behind me, his forehead creasing. "He's not coming?"

"He's on the way." I crossed the off-white Persian rug and kissed Daddy's smooth cheek, catching the scent of aftershave and liquor.

Mama made a big show of lifting her arm and staring at the watch on her wrist. "My bet is he's not coming."

The Tiffany & Co. clock on the fireplace mantle read six fifty-nine. "He'll be here." *Lord, please let him make it. And if there's an emergency happening, please let everything be okay.* I took a seat on the antique settee upholstered in cream fabric. The coffee table between us held a serving tray of what resembled canned cat food smeared on crackers. Pâté. I inwardly cringed.

Mama moved to the built-ins surrounding the fireplace, adjusting an ivory vase. "Better to know exactly the type of man he is now rather than later."

"If he's late, there's a logical reason." I slipped my hand in my pocket, running my fingers along the roll of Tums. Only one remained in my pack. "I don't understand the rush to meet him anyway."

"I want to get to know the man you were hurling yourself at in public."

My breath whooshed out. "I wasn't hurling myself at him. We were having a private conversation in my office." I peered at Daddy, who'd retaken his seat, studying the drink in his hand, bowing out of the discussion. *Big surprise.* I pulled on the Landry Mask. "Need I remind you I'm an adult, and I make my own choices."

"Need I remind you Hayley is a minor, and my granddaughter, and it's my responsibility to ensure she's not exposed to untoward things."

A cold tingle broke across my skin. "Hayley is *not* your responsibility."

"It still stands she shouldn't be around inappropriateness." She clasped her hands before her, superiority in her posture.

I hauled in a slow breath, eased to my feet, and approached the back windows overlooking their landscaped lawn and garden. *God, please help me from throttling my mother. You and I know the truth, and that's all that matters.*

Daddy pushed to standing, carrying his empty glass to the cocktail cart.

I unpeeled my last Tums, sticking the antacid in my mouth.

"What are you eating?" Mama asked. "Candy? Do you realize how rude that is?"

Daddy poured himself another scotch.

Mama tsked. "Though I suppose what's really rude is your new boyfriend keeping us waiting."

Heat spread up my neck. I chewed and swallowed. "You make it sound like I have a different guy every week." I pointed my finger to the coffered ceilings, also painted white. "Let the record show Micah Guidry is the first man I've dated in over a decade."

Mama rolled her eyes. "Don't be so theatrical."

"Well," Daddy said, "I guess Ryan was right."

My hand fell to my side. "What's that supposed to mean?"

Mama tugged at one of her sleeves. "He warned us."

I gave a slow blink. And another. "First of all, why are y'all still in touch with him?"

"He's been in our lives since you were teenagers." Daddy returned to his seat, easing into it with a slight groan. "We see his parents from time to time at different functions. It makes sense to catch up with him every once in a while."

I scoffed. "Does it? Don't you remember what he did to me?"

Mama shot Daddy a glance.

"What was that look?" I neared, stopping behind the antique settee.

"It's nothing." Mama lowered onto the other wingback, primly crossing her legs at her ankles.

I grasped the wooden trim on the sofa. "It's something."

"Honestly, Katherine, can't we have one dinner in peace?" Mama smoothed a crease on her dress.

I outright stared at her. "Are you actually giving Ryan a pass for what he did to me?"

Mama released a sigh. "He'd already seen how involved you were caring for your grandma those final years of her life. Did you expect him to play second fiddle to Hayley too?"

My grip on the edge of the settee tightened, disbelief cutting through me. "You're giving me whiplash. One minute you're concerned with Hayley being around 'inappropriateness,' the next you're referring to her as less important than Ryan."

"No," Mama said. "We've always desired the best for you *and* Hayley. That was why we wanted custody of her. For her own sake and for yours, so Ryan would stay. You can hardly blame him for leaving."

My head spun at the outrageousness of her words. Of her defending him. If she couldn't see him for the jerk he was in the past, maybe she could in the present. "Can you hardly blame him now for wanting to copy my café? For wanting to steal Mawmaw's and Claire's recipes?"

Daddy flinched. "That can't be right."

"Oh, but it can. Did he tell y'all why he's back in town?"

Mama fingered her necklace. "To open another restaurant for Paul Rodgers."

"To take the location I want. The place Claire loved. He plans to imitate Beignets & Books. I have a long list of how he used me in the past, and now he's back, doing it again."

A crease formed between Daddy's brows. "Is this the same property you mentioned the last time you were here? The one in the French Quarter?"

"Yes." I loosened my hold on the settee.

He studied his drink, tipping his glass one way and then another.

My phone dinged with a new text. I pulled it from my pocket.

MiCAH
An emergency came up with my dad. I'm so sorry.

My heart sank to my stomach.

KATE
Is everything okay? Do you need help?

MiCAH
He fell. From what I can tell, it's not bad.
Waiting to see if anything swells or really starts
hurting. Renee's out of town, so I have to be
here. Please apologize to your parents.

KATE
Of course! Don't worry about dinner. Let
me know if you need anything. Sending up a
prayer.

"Well?" Mama asked.

I returned my phone to my pocket, grateful I still had Micah's pack of Tums. "Micah sends his apologies. There's an emergency with his dad."

Daddy lowered his glass to his knee. "What kind of emergency?"

"His dad had a fall."

"A fall?" Mama's skeptical tone grated.

"He has osteoporosis," I said. "A simple fall can be very damaging."

"John Causey's mother had advanced osteoporosis." Daddy's somber gaze turned inward. "In the end she required near-constant care with a live-in aide."

Mama's eyes narrowed on me. "What kind of osteoporosis does Micah's dad have?"

Chin up. Chin up. "Advanced."

"Does he have an aide? Or the ability to get one?" Her brows notched higher with each question.

"No. And no. Or at least, I'm not sure."

The crow's-feet around Mama's eyes tightened. "So Micah has a fulltime job, and he's also caring for his father? Has he asked you to help?"

"No."

"Not yet." She shot the words back. "Oh, Katherine. It's like your grandma all over again. You'll be trapped. How do you expect to have the time to open another restaurant while being dragged down by this man and his ailing father? Plus, your responsibilities to Hayley, which are already lackluster."

She'd done it. Pushed my Hayley button. My vision tunneled on Mama.

She adjusted the watch on her wrist. "Your grandma trapped you and so will this man."

I gritted my teeth, my hands curling into fists at my sides. "I loved Mawmaw. I wasn't trapped with her."

"Really," she scoffed. "Changing her diapers? Bathing her? Rearranging your life around her?"

I unclenched my jaw. "At least you don't have to worry about me doing those things for you."

Silence exploded at the full meaning behind my statement. Mama raised her chin. "Nor would I want you to." She adjusted her sleeves. "I think we've had enough drama for the evening." She stood, motioning toward the dining room. "Let's eat and keep the conversation to polite topics."

Daddy did what he'd always done best. He quietly followed her.

I rotated on my heel, purposely digging it into the rug, wishing I had gum stuck to the bottom of my shoe. Dessert had better be phenomenal to stick this night out.

Last night I dreamed of Mawmaw. A reliving of one of the more delusional moments she'd had toward the end. Anger had filled her wheezing words, along with a Kleenex box that flew past my head, followed by a remote control that had connected with my nose. Like in real life, it had started when I'd tried changing her diaper one evening. Our daytime caretaker had departed, and Claire had been on a date with Adrian.

I'd awoken with a jolt and tears in my eyes. Not wanting to return to sleep, I'd reread my last text exchange with Micah, grateful Mr. Gary was fine and his fall hadn't resulted in any noticeable damage.

Five hours later, I sat in church between Julia and Hayley, rubbing the Crease, unable to concentrate on the sermon. I blamed the nightmare on Mama. Since leaving my parents' last night, my row with her had played on repeat. What chafed worst of all was that there was some truth in her words. Between being a single parent and running the café, I was already stretched thin. Opening a second location right now was an ambitious venture that would stretch me even thinner. And then I'd gone and added Micah to the mix.

I was like a juggler. Keeping two balls in the air had been manageable. Hayley and the café. Adding a third ball with another location would be more challenging. Then somehow, Micah had slipped in, adding another ball to the rotation. And I shouldn't be contemplating Mr. Gary's future care, but there his ball loomed in my periphery, waiting to be thrown in. I had no idea how I'd handle it. Or if I even could emotionally.

Julia had said the beginning of a romance was supposed to be exciting and fun. So far I'd experienced a lot of uncertainty and a few good kisses. Scratch that. "Great kisses," I muttered, pressing the Crease a little harder.

Julia glanced my way, her own crease puckering.

I shook my head and remained tightlipped the rest of the service.

⚮

Hayley and I arrived home and found Micah sitting on the back steps to the café. Lightness at witnessing his smiling face pulsed through me with each heartbeat. And the fact that he was here, and not with his dad, reiterated good news on that front.

With the restaurant closed on Sundays, all was quiet except for the water cascading from the fountain. A bouquet of wilted cream roses wrapped in paper lay on the table. No doubt the ones meant for my mom.

"Your dad still okay?"

"He is." Micah pushed to his feet. "He's currently at home watching *The Sting.*"

I chuckled. "He really does like poker, doesn't he?"

"You have no idea." He slid his hands into the pockets of his shorts. "I wanted to apologize again for last night. If—"

I raised my hand. "If you say you're sorry one more time, I'm going to sock you in the gut."

Hayley snorted. "Worst apology acceptance ever."

"Because it's not needed." Movement from the live oak pulled my attention north, my muscles clenching. A blue jay hopped along a branch. I relaxed. There'd been no signs of Cést Fou since the morning of the winter wonderland. Maybe he and his flock had contracted a bird flu, and they'd all flown off and died somewhere. Or he'd somehow sensed the wildlife specialist coming tomorrow.

Hayley cocked her head at Micah. "My grandmother's really going to hate you now."

A deep sigh pushed from his lungs. "I'm aware."

"Here." I handed her my keys, purse, and Bible, and made a shooing motion.

With a teasing grin, she took the stairs, letting herself inside.

"So . . ." Micah edged a step closer.

I held up my finger.

Predictably, Hayley reappeared, carrying a squirming Precious down the stairs. The wrinkly dog gathered pets from Micah and me, then proceeded to do her business. Hayley scooped the pup into her arms. She shot a mischievous glance at Micah. "Don't worry about my grandmother. She hates everyone." With a chuckle, she disappeared inside.

I smothered a sigh. At least Hayley knew it wasn't personal when it came to Mama's behavior. I took the steps to the covered porch, moving out of the sun, and out of sight from Hayley if she happened to be spying from the second-floor windows.

"How do I make it right with your parents? Should I bring those to your mom today?" He cut a glance to the roses.

"Bring her wilting flowers? Not a good idea. Besides, she doesn't deserve them."

He eased onto the porch, leaning against a column. "How was last night?"

Sharp tension slid into my muscles. "I'm not ready to talk about it."

"That bad, huh?"

I nodded, kneading the back of my neck. How could I tell him how truly awful Mama had been? I definitely couldn't mention the opinions she'd voiced about Mr. Gary.

He pushed from the column, moving closer. "I've missed you. Seems like forever since I actually saw you."

A flutter stirred in my belly, the tension within me lifting. "It's only been eight days."

One corner of his mouth tweaked. "Look who's keeping track."

My face warmed, and I rotated, grasping the porch railing, facing the courtyard.

He came up from behind, and gently, his fingers draped my shoulders, his hands gliding down. "I like it when you blush." The huskiness in his voice vibrated through me like a delicious caress, the heat from his body pressing through the fabric of my dress.

Taking a steadying breath, I turned toward him.

He straightened, studying my face, his expression shifting to uncertainty. "You sure you don't want to talk about what happened last night?"

I opened my mouth. Closed it. Shook my head.

Tenderly, he kissed my temple. "Do y'all have plans for lunch?"

"Turkey sandwiches."

Pulling his phone from his pocket, he checked the time. "Come on." He tugged my hand. "We can do better than that."

Fifteen minutes later found the three of us at the French Market, an open-air structure squeezed between the edge of the French Quarter and the Mississippi River. It was a combination of farmers market and eatery, with walk-up food stands featuring burgers, seafood po'boys, sweet and savory crepes, and snowballs. And for those tourists more daring culinary-wise, alligator was served a myriad of ways. Thankfully, we hadn't had to wait long for one of the few round metal picnic tables to open.

We settled in, and I dug into my caprese crepe, savoring the warm mozzarella, tomato, and basil. The background noise of slow, steady traffic from the surrounding streets combined with a plethora of conversations from those in the market. My attention caught on a nearby vendor table. They sold handmade jewelry and had a sign propped on an easel touting their items as perfect Mother's Day gifts.

Mother's Day. Ugh. I swallowed my bite, my appetite dwindling. Next Sunday brought the annual holiday that loomed heavy in two opposite ways. The first being Mama. Long ago I'd given up trying to find a card for her that wasn't a complete lie. I'd opted instead to have flowers delivered with a generic note. This year, I doubted that would even happen, or if I'd send anything to Daddy for Father's Day.

The second heaviness to Mother's Day was Claire. I gazed across the table at Hayley, who devoured her BLT crepe. Her big blue eyes absorbed our vibrant surroundings. People meandering with their purchases held in plastic bags, vendors haggling with shoppers over things from T-shirts to handcrafted tchotchkes and elaborate Mardi Gras masks. Next to me, Micah steadily ate his fried oyster po'boy, keeping an eye on the happenings around us. I took comfort in his presence. That I wasn't alone with Hayley in such a chaotic environment.

My sights once again caught on that Mother's Day sign. I lowered my crepe to my paper plate. After Claire had died, I'd secretly cried through the first few Mother's and Father's Days, mourning Hayley's loss afresh. When she'd started school, I'd ensured her teachers were aware of her situation. And each year, before any in-class Mother's and Father's Day projects began, I'd gently prepare Hayley for it. Give her the opportunity to talk about her feelings and also give her the choice to do a different class activity or spend that time in the school library.

Hayley had always chosen to stick to the same projects as her classmates, and came home with the gifts she'd crafted. Hand-painted coasters, a trivet stamped with a fleur-de-lis pattern, a paperweight by way of a mini mason jar filled with colorful layers of sand. She'd given them to me, for both holidays, and I'd oohed and aahed over them. Telling her how much her mom and dad would've loved them. How much *I* loved them.

A truck horn blared on the road next to us, momentarily garnering everyone's attention. The vehicle rumbled on its way, and a street performer playing a saxophone transitioned the area to smoother melodies.

Once Hayley had hit fifth grade, she'd told me we didn't need to have the annual prep talks or do anything special on those days. And so I'd honored her request. Treated those two Sundays a year as any other Sundays. I'd still sought opportunities to organically bring Claire and Adrian up, and reassure her it was okay to talk about them. But she never really wanted to contribute to the conversations or showed much interest.

With Micah, though, it was different. He never shied away from talking about his mom. And sitting here with him, knowing his past with her, my heart ached for another reason.

I reached for my tea, taking a cool, cleansing sip through the straw, and turned my attention to him. "Do you do anything special for Mother's Day?"

He casually shook his head, finishing his bite. "Not anymore." He reached for a napkin from the pile I'd set at the middle of the table and wiped his mouth. "The first few Mother's Days my dad, sister, and I made it a point to spend the day together, but it was hard. Felt too forced. And once I moved to Colorado . . ." He lifted a shoulder. "I just spend some time on those days thanking God for the years I had with her."

"That's sort of what I do," Hayley said.

I stilled.

"I mean, the thanking God part. I thank Him for her, that I was born, and for my aunt."

"That's so nice." I somehow managed to string the words together, emotion rapidly building within me.

She cast a glance to me, the hint of an uncertain smile forming, and returned her focus to Micah. "I do the same on Father's Day." She took a swig of her canned Barq's and continued eating, as if she hadn't just shaken my world in the best way possible.

An overpowering wave of elation washed through me. But knowing how Hayley was, and not wanting to make a big deal out of her revelation, I had to hold it together. Play it cool.

Micah reached beneath the table, his hand finding mine. He gently squeezed my fingers, passing strength to me I didn't know I needed until that very moment. Silence stretched, needing to be filled, but I couldn't speak for fear I'd start blubbering. I glanced at Micah, and his returning expression shifted from pleased to what I could only describe as awkward concern. And yet I still couldn't tamp down the geyser of joy building throughout my chest and expanding up my throat. His handsome face blurred as unshed tears invaded my vision. I clasped his hand like a vise.

"Um . . ." He straightened. "For Father's Day, we get together for my dad." His voice pitched unusually loud, no doubt to distract Hayley from noticing my overemotional reaction. "Even when I lived in Colorado, I made the trip in. Yup. We'd gather at my sister's place. Eat lots of food. Play cornhole, poker."

I sucked in my unshed tears like nobody's business and eased in a calming breath.

Thankfully, a woman with a massive dog walked past, garnering all of Hayley's attention. The lady stopped several feet away at a wooden cart filled with watercolors of different New Orleans scenes. She began perusing.

"Can I?" Hayley jutted a thumb in the dog's direction, already rising from the table.

I nodded with a smile.

Micah and I watched Hayley ask the woman if she could pet the dog, and then proceed to lavish love on the animal. I rested my head against Micah's shoulder, holding his hand with both of mine. He'd rescued me. In a poignant way I hadn't expected. "Thank you for that."

He placed a kiss to my forehead. "You looked like you were about to burst. I guess that was all new info."

"It was." I straightened with a sniffle, pulling myself together. "It's nice that you flew in each year for Father's Day. I'm sure going to all that trouble meant a lot to your dad."

"It did." He dragged in a heavy lungful of air and released it. Nudged his plate aside, ignoring the remains of his lunch. "It also helped to be distracted on that day, because . . . you know." A sliver of woe crossed his profile.

My stomach dropped. *Oh, Micah.* Why hadn't the impact of his infertility and failed marriage, diminishing his hopes of being on the receiving end of Father's Day, crossed my mind before? "That's had to be hard for you, year after year."

"It was in the beginning, when I first found out. And especially with the divorce. But it's gotten easier with time." The usual playful glimmer in his green eyes had dimmed, and I found myself earnestly wishing for a way to bring that spark back. He cleared his throat. "So what do you do for Mother's Day? Seems like a hard day, between Claire and your mom."

I returned my gaze to Hayley. The beast of a dog had rolled onto his back, Hayley laughing as she rubbed its belly.

"Well, with my mom, I just send flowers. Back when Claire had started our monthly dinners with my parents, we'd decided to give ourselves off holidays with them to make it more bearable."

265

A crease formed between his brows. "So for all the holidays it's just you and Hayley?"

I nodded, tucking my hair behind my ear. "Unless we get together with Julia and her family."

He considered that, taking a sip of his bottled water.

Hayley returned, plopping onto the bench. "Precious is going to be so jealous when she smells that dog on me." She drained her Barq's, the breeze from the ceiling fans toying with her hair.

I resumed eating my crepe.

Micah downed the rest of his water, casually scanning the area around us before returning his attention to our little group. "Since this is my first year living here again, for Father's Day I'm planning to host a full-out BBQ for my dad. My sister and her family will be there too."

Hayley maneuvered her long locks into a ponytail. "Could we come?"

I blinked. It was the first time Hayley had wanted to make plans for that day.

"Of course," Micah said.

I blinked again. He'd answered with no hesitation. As if Hayley had asked if he knew how to tie shoelaces. That was a big step. Introducing our families to each other. Especially on such a bittersweet day for Micah. And although he'd steadily been in our lives for almost three months now, we'd only been officially dating eleven days. Eleven! "Hayley, you can't just invite us to his family gathering."

"Sure she can." Micah collected mine and Hayley's trash, placing it atop his. "I'd love y'all to be there. Precious too."

Hayley threw a victorious smirk my way. Like she hadn't just smashed the fast-forward button on my relationship with Micah.

25

CÉST FOU'S DAYS WERE NUMBERED. The next afternoon I exited the back of the café, heading to pick up Hayley and Emma from the library. I walked past a trap net erected on the courtyard ground. Parrot treats, which resembled Fruit Loops, covered the trip wire. That morning, the wildlife specialist had arrived eager to get to work, impart parrot-specific facts, and charge a hefty fee.

He presumed my nuisance to be Quaker parrots. These creatures easily lived thirty years, granting validity to Mrs. Adélaide's claims. I'd learned this type of bird was territorial and defecated as a means of marking their turf. That explained the amount of poop. I'd also learned a fee would be charged with each capture and relocation of a parrot to a wildlife sanctuary in northern Mississippi. That explained the burning sensation that had started in my gut.

I'd paid for the initial assessment and setup with the company credit card. Normally I paid the card off every month, but between the new fryer and now this, I wasn't sure if I'd be able to swing that full payment. Especially with wanting the bank account to appear as robust as possible in case I got a nibble from a potential investor.

Pulling onto the library grounds, I slowed to a stop before the carriage house occupying the rear corner of the property. Its front barn doors had been slid open. Back in the day it had housed horses. Now it served as a spot for the library to sell old books once a month. Volunteers, including Hayley and Emma, kept it organized and running. Hayley appeared in the entranceway and held up her hands, indicating they'd be ten more minutes.

I continued on to the line of parking spots next to the repurposed mansion, parked beside Micah's Jeep, and entered the library.

He peered up from the reception desk, his expression gliding into one of pleasure.

My pulse quickened. Goodness, he was handsome.

A playful smile spread across his face as he stood. "How may I help you, Miss Landry? Are you looking for anything in particular?"

I set my purse on the counter, resting my elbows next to it. "I was wondering if you had a book on library etiquette."

He chuckled, tossing his pencil atop a notepad. "Really?"

I scanned the area, ensuring our privacy. Standing on my toes I eased forward, lowering my voice. "I'd like to know if library kissing is appropriate."

His jaw slackened, a spark igniting in his jade eyes. He perched sideways on the lower portion of the desk, leaning in. "Are you speaking of past library kissing or future library kissing?"

"Definitely future." I let my arms fall, bringing my hands within touching distance.

He reached, one of his hands covering both of mine. Ever-so-faintly, his thumb brushed back and forth, the gleam in his eyes turning hungry. "Are you trying to get me fired?"

Biting my lip and my growing smile, I edged down from my toes, putting more space between us.

Still toying with my fingers, he used his other hand to tug at his collar.

My gaze flicked to his Hawaiian shirt, complete with a fleur-de-lis pattern in purple, green, and gold. "You're a little late for Mardi Gras."

"Yeah. It was accidentally sent to my old address and finally rerouted here. If you like, I can order you a matching one for next year."

My heartbeat skittered, having nothing to do with his touch grazing underneath my wrist. "Next year, huh?"

"Yes." He held my stare, squeezing my hand. "Next year."

Hayley plopped her book bag on the counter.

I startled.

She gave a pointed look to me and Micah. "Old people flirting is gross."

Micah dramatically widened his eyes and slowly released my fingers, lifting his hands as though Hayley aimed a gun at him.

She rolled her gaze to the ceiling, all the while combating a smile.

I bit back a chuckle and nudged her elbow with mine. "Where's Emma?"

"In the bathroom."

"Before we were so rudely interrupted by the PDA police . . ." Micah shot a teasing glance at Hayley.

She smirked and unzipped her book bag, rummaging through it.

He continued. "I was thinking about starting a Mardi Gras party tradition like your grandma used to have." He tapped the counter in front of Hayley, garnering her attention. "Every year your mom tried a new beignet creation."

Her gaze shifted between us. "I've heard a few stories about those parties."

Gratitude swelled through my chest at his attempt to connect

Hayley to the past in a positive way. "Do you remember in eighth grade when she stuck gummy worms in them?" I asked.

"Yeah." He cringed, straightening from the desk.

"What a disaster. Those poor worms oozing out."

"Those poor worms? Poor me!" He pointed at himself. "I actually ate one."

Hayley smiled, and my heart lightened. It wasn't a full toothy grin, but I'd take any encouraging reaction to the mentioning of Claire. The door behind us opened, and an elderly man entered.

Micah watched the guy disappear into the periodicals section. "Instead of beignets, which I'd either burn or start a grease fire with, I'd make my mom's seafood gumbo."

Gorgeous, caring, and he could cook. He was like a slot machine, all the bars spinning around and lining up for a jackpot. But . . . gambling never ended well. Not for the person betting, anyway.

Hayley's face tipped over her phone. *Sigh.* At least we'd had some interaction from her.

"I bet your dad would love that," I said. "Getting to eat your mom's cooking again. How's he doing today?"

"Um . . ." Micah's attention fell to his desk. "Better." He gathered several sheets of paper, straightening them into a pile.

My scalp prickled. "You sure?"

"Yup." He gave a half smile and slipped the papers into a file folder.

I reached across the counter, stilling his motions.

His head tipped sideways. "I promise. He's much better." He opened a drawer and dropped the folder in. "Did you ever hear from that lady at the crawfish boil?"

My thoughts tumbled to a stop. *Well, that's random.*

He took in my expression and shrugged. "Just popped in my head."

Needing an evasion tactic, I dug through my purse for my keys. "Julia and I were actually talking about that woman the other week." I peered at the clock on the wall, and then to the back of the library, where the bathrooms were. *Come on, Emma.*

Hayley glanced up from her phone. "Mrs. Julia thinks Aunt Kate should teach a class for people too scared to start a business."

Sarah McLachlan. I fumbled my keys, gawking at her.

She shrugged. "I overheard y'all from the balcony when I came to bring Precious out."

My mind returned to that evening. With us sitting beneath the first-floor porch, we wouldn't have seen her lurking up there. And we certainly hadn't heard her open the door. I pressed my tongue against a back tooth. "You must've been taking your sweet time coming down those stairs."

The edges of her mouth curled, mischief sparkling in her blue eyes.

I'd have to start putting a bell around her neck. "Next time you will make your presence known."

"Yes, ma'am," she mumbled.

Returning my focus to Micah, I found a wide grin on his face. Too wide. And a glint in his eyes. I narrowed my own.

He scratched the back of his ear. "I think you teaching a class like that is an excellent idea."

I scoffed. "I can't."

"You can. It could be held here at the library, once the repairs are done. I'd handle spreading the word, getting everything scheduled. We could even record it and make it available for download."

My headshaking slowed, my gaze drifting around the room. It would be so much easier with someone else heading it up. Plus, the library's resources with marketing and reaching more people. But I'd still have to come up with a curriculum. And the time for it all. My headshaking ramped back up again. "I can't."

Micah studied me in a way that caused my skin to itch.

"I don't have the time for it." I raised my brows for added measure.

"All right." He lifted his hand, letting the topic fade. "What are y'all doing for dinner? Want to take Precious to Lucy's again?"

Hayley perked, lowering her phone.

My belly sank. "Not tonight. I've barely got enough time to drop Emma off and get Hayley home and settled before heading out."

The disappointment on their faces made my heart twist. *All of this extra work is temporary.* Unless I actually acquired the Vieux Carré Café. Then there'd be a round of renovations, getting the place up and running, and splitting my time between two locations. My phone chimed, and I tensed at the all-too-familiar calendar alert notification, reminding me I had an hour until my next meeting.

Micah, now accustomed to the alert, inclined his chin toward my purse. "What's on the schedule tonight?"

I lowered my finger from pressing the Crease. "A venture capitalist networking event."

His face puckered, and he turned to Hayley. "Is she speaking English?"

"No." Hayley sighed. "It's a form of business-ese. Get used to it."

⸙

The following two weeks flew by. For the sake of being home at night with Hayley, and being able to make it to all of her end-of-school-year functions, I'd begun participating in daytime luncheons to push special events for the café and sniff out investors. Which meant delaying unfinished café tasks to complete at night and on the weekends, along with finalizing the new business plan. Despite needing to order more business cards, I hadn't had any bites for a silent partner. But I had made connections that resulted in two corporate party bookings.

The only times I'd seen Micah were when picking Hayley up from the library and at church. Thankfully, other than walking a bit wobbly with a cane, Mr. Gary looked good.

Not looking good was the fact that extra caffeine had done little to put a much-needed pep in my step. It was Monday morning, and I was in my office finishing payroll. The muted clinking of silverware and muffled conversations drifted down the short hallway to me. I gave two long blinks, the computer screen before me still bleary despite the espresso I'd chased my café au lait with. Doubts about continuing at this pace had started creeping in this morning when I'd smacked the snooze button on my alarm clock.

A knock sounded at my open door, Micah filling the space.

Unexpected glee at his presence chased my weariness. Maybe I needed to see him every morning instead of increasing my caffeine intake.

Wearing shorts and a plain T-shirt, he paused next to a guest chair. "I'm about to make a grocery run for my dad and thought I'd pop in to say hi."

I pushed to my feet. "I'm glad you did."

Mayté abruptly stepped into the room, shutting the door behind her. "Can we talk?"

"Sure." Confusion shaded my tone.

Micah glanced between us. "Should I . . . ?" He motioned for the door.

Mayté lifted a staying hand. "This won't take long." We were in the post-breakfast lull, but the clench in her jaw indicated she wasn't enjoying the break. "Corey put in his notice."

"What?" I deflated into my chair, my arms dropping over the sides.

Micah's forehead furrowed, and he retreated, standing next to the filing cabinet in the corner.

Mayté crossed her arms over her white chef's coat. Her stiff posture radiated control, but the fire in her eyes spoke volumes about losing her sous chef.

"Please tell me it's not to work for Ryan." After learning of my thieving ex's plans to copy the café, and considering he'd tried stealing Mayté, we'd assumed he'd go after our sous chef next. We'd preemptively talked to Corey weeks ago.

She gave one sharp nod. "It is."

A shock of cold exploded through my chest, splintering out with jagged edges.

Mayté continued, "He's supposed to work in their Atlanta restaurant and move back when they open the location here, as their executive chef."

The iciness within me surged to heat. I pushed up from my chair, my muscles quivering, and paced the length of the small room, my heels clicking against the floor. Ryan already planned to copy our menu. *Click-click-click.* Of course he'd want our sous chef to make stealing our recipes easier. *Click-click-click.* He was taking an employee I'd found, invested in, and trained. *Click-click-click.*

"I told him it's risky," Mayté said. "That they don't even have a place here yet." She expelled a heavy sigh. "He said it's a sure thing."

"A sure thing," I grumbled, striding past the window again. "What if we offer him the same position if we open another location?"

Mayté shook her head. "He's not ready to be a head chef. And frankly, I don't want him in my kitchen anymore. I've got no room for disloyalty."

Think, Kate. Think. Forcing myself to pause, I pulled in a deep breath and dropped my hand from rubbing the Crease. "Ryan could go after everyone at this point. We need to have an all-hands staff meeting."

"I agree," Mayté said. "I'll get it scheduled."

"Thank you."

She left, closing the door behind her.

My gaze floated to Micah. He took me in, concern edging his eyes.

"I've known for the past month that if Ryan gets the Vieux Carré Café, he's planning to turn it into a beignet restaurant and try to copy our menu."

Micah pushed off the wall. "Can he do that?"

"Yes. And considering he'll now have my sous chef, it's that much easier."

"Are your recipes trademarked or . . . copyrighted?"

I massaged my throbbing temples. "Recipes aren't protected works."

"What can we do?"

Pain struck the back of my throat, the tendons in my chest tightening. "There's nothing I can do about him stealing our menu and employees, but I can stop him from having Claire's dream location." My line of sight connected with the signed napkin Claire and I had framed all those years ago. I drew near, standing before it, my heartbeats slowing.

"What if we grab lunch in a few hours and talk all this through?"

I turned, taking Micah in. Part of me wanted to fall into his arms, if only for a minute. Just to stand there, being held and breathing him in. But Ryan's continual blows reverberated, stirring my old sense of caution. The one that had kept my heart safe all these years. Was I falling too fast for Micah?

"Kate?" He stepped forward, his brows pulling together.

I snapped back to the moment. "Can't. I'm meeting with my CPA. She's doing me a favor, squeezing in an assessment of my business plan." My phone dinged with a text, and I lifted it from my desk, checking the screen. "That's actually her. Asking to move our appointment up, which barely allows me to finish payroll." And most certainly would push back creating the next staff schedule. Well, beggars couldn't be choosers.

Hurry-hurry-hurry pulsed through my veins. I rounded my desk, lowered onto my chair, and moved the mouse, waking my computer.

"Then maybe we can meet for a late lunch?"

I shook my head. "I've got a showing this afternoon for a possible wedding." With a wince, I shifted my gaze to the window and the courtyard beyond. I needed to disassemble the parrot trap and hide it before the potential clients arrived. And ensure there wasn't a speck of poop in sight. *Darn you, Cést Fou.*

"What about dinner?"

I texted a positive response to my CPA. "Um . . ." *Hurry-hurry-hurry.* "Maybe. If we stay in. I need to catch up on some stuff from the café."

The undertone of a smile brushed his lips but nowhere near reached his eyes. "Just let me know."

My heart pinched, or really, it was more of a tear. "I will."

The next night after the café had closed, I gathered with my employees in the main section of the restaurant. Everyone except Corey had shown up. Mayté had ended his employment yesterday, right after our discussion.

Some stood around the perimeter of the room, others sat at the tables. I took up my position next to the hostess stand, everyone's attention resting on me. Though I held the Landry Mask in place, my insides quivered. Oh, how I wished Claire were here to help shoulder this burden.

Mayté calmly made her way through our employees, coming to a stop before me. Determination loomed heavy in her gaze, and she lowered her voice just for me. "You've got this, because God has you."

Emotion flooded my throat. *Lord, thank you for Mayté.*

She moved to step away, but I lightly grabbed her hand, silently asking her to stand with me. I released the touch, and she slid beside me, notching her chin high and placing her hands behind her back.

And Lord? Please give me the right words in this moment.

"Thank you all for coming. I'm going to keep this brief so you can get on with your closing duties or returning home. I'm not sure how many of you are aware of this, but I've discovered Paul Rodgers's partner is scouting a location here for his next restaurant."

Dead silence filled the room. Not a single murmur or reaction.

"Okay," I said lightly. "I guess everyone knows."

Chuckles and bobbing heads followed.

I loosely clasped my wrist before me. "I'm guessing everyone also knows this man has approached at least two of you, offering employment."

Another round of nodding from most of the employees.

"I'm not here to influence your decision if he does approach you," I said. "I just want you to be aware of the facts."

Some of the workers who sat in chairs leaned forward.

"Number one." I held up a finger. "They don't have a location yet, which means nothing's stopping them from changing their minds and pursuing a restaurant elsewhere. Nine months ago, Paul Rodgers planned to open a place in Chicago and pulled out at the last minute." I had Mayté to thank for that nugget of information.

Mutters spread throughout the group.

I brandished a second finger. "Number two—"

Jonathan raised his hand.

I gestured for him to speak.

"With respect, we don't need a second reason," Jonathan said. "Or a first. I don't see how anyone would trust the guy after what he did to you and Hayley."

Cowering Chihuahuas! I was not intending to bring my personal life into this.

Murmurs of "Truth" and "That's right" erupted. It seemed everyone also knew my history with Ryan. *Just peachy.*

Mayté stepped forward, raising her hands. "We don't need to get into personal details here."

Jonathan straightened from leaning against the opening to the music room. Behind him, the cardboard cutout of Harry Connick Jr. came into view, along with Mrs. Adélaide. *What in the world?* We'd closed fifteen minutes ago. Had she not realized it? She sat at a table, sipping from a coffee cup, a book open before her. It was too late for her to be walking home alone. I'd have to give her a lift after the meeting.

Jonathan placed a hand to his chest and pitched his voice to the room. "This job *is* personal for me. Miss Kate looks out for me and my family."

My nose pricked.

"Ditto!" Tara, one of the prep cooks, spoke up. "I look forward to coming here. It's a positive space for me, one I don't have at home."

A stinging sensation struck my eyes. I cast a glance at Mayté and found pride blooming in her features.

Penny stood from her chair. "There's no way I'd jump ship, especially not from someone who's been loyal to me. Who cares. Who wants to help us advance in life." She turned to the group. "How many of you has Miss Kate helped with completing college and grant applications?"

Several hands lifted.

My vision blurred. Where was that Landry Mask?

One of the line cook supervisors, Marcus, also pushed to his feet. "Plus, they don't skimp on pay and benefits. Or put up with slacker employees. I've worked lots of other kitchens. This one's legit."

More and more workers added their opinions, their acclamations filling the room, and my heart.

26

THE SMELL OF FREEDOM AND SALAMI floated in the air. Today had been the final day of school. No more carpooling, getting Hayley up and out the door in our morning rush, no ensuring she stayed on top of her homework, and no last-minute projects involving mad dashes to Walgreens for posterboards.

We were celebrating with Micah tonight over dinner at our place. It had been three days since I'd seen him. Since Ryan stole our sous chef. With my and Hayley's southern regions being at war, neither of us had wanted to venture out. Especially me, after I'd unexpectedly covered two waitressing shifts today. Pizza had been delivered, and I'd slid the boxes into the oven to keep them warm until Micah arrived. Look at me using the oven!

Hayley snuggled with Precious on the sofa watching an old episode of *Monk*. Despite my heavy eyelids, I sat before my laptop at the dining table, making last-minute revisions to my new business plan based on the feedback from my CPA. Tomorrow held another venture capitalists' event, and the hope of plan D still being a success. A deep yawn ripped loose.

My phone rang, Micah's name appearing on the screen, and I answered. "Hey."

"I can't make it." Concern infused his tone.

I stiffened. "What's wrong?"

"My dad rolled his ankle. He can't put any weight on it, and it's swelling."

I scooted my chair back and stood. "Where are you?"

"About to leave his place and head to Touro."

The closest hospital. The one I'd taken Mawmaw to so many times. Placing a hand on the table, I steadied myself. I'd known stepping into this sort of moment was coming. I'd been praying steadily over it. I just didn't think it would arrive so fast.

"Umm . . ." My gaze sailed to Hayley, who'd paused the TV, her attention on me. Thank goodness she could be left home on her own. "I'll meet you there."

"No. There's no need. I just didn't want y'all waiting for me."

"Are you sure?"

"Positive. I'll call you later, okay?"

An automatic pinch of relief hit, and I hated it. "Okay."

He disconnected, and I lowered to my chair, opposing emotions vacillating. The past warring with the present.

Hayley rose from the sofa. "What's going on?"

"Mr. Gary hurt his ankle. Micah's taking him to the hospital."

"So it's not serious?"

"Doesn't seem to be." A slight lie for her sake, especially considering Mr. Gary's condition. *Lord, please don't let it be serious.*

She set Precious to the floor and ambled through the kitchen, helping herself to the pizza. Precious shadowed her every move, her nails pitter-pattering against the wood.

I returned my attention to the Word document and the final tweaks I needed to make. But all I could focus on was the handful of times I'd been in the Touro ER with Mawmaw. Sitting in freezing exam rooms. Her lying there, pale and fragile. The beeping of the monitors. Waiting-waiting-waiting for test results or to talk to the doctor.

Name one good thing.

I pulled in a breath, my back leaning against the wooden chair. I'd had Claire. During those ER visits, we'd clasped hands in the hallway and prayed. Drank horrible hospital coffee. And cried on each other's shoulders when we'd been told it was time for hospice. But we'd done it all together. I rubbed the tip of my nose, blinking myself into the present. Micah's sister would be with him. He didn't need me. *Although* . . . I bit my lower lip, my pulse hastening. From what he'd said before, I wasn't sure. He'd been adamant about giving Renee a real break from caring for their dad.

God, what do I do? I haven't stepped foot inside that hospital since . . . I screwed my eyes shut. This wasn't about me or what I could handle. *Right, Lord? And I have Your strength to draw on.* I nodded to myself and closed the screen on the laptop with a decided click. "I'm going to the hospital."

I was a blur of movement, shoving my feet into sneakers, grabbing my purse, and hurdling out the door and down the stairs. At the landing, I screeched to a halt. A lump of green feathers flailed in the trap net. My audible gasp echoed through the courtyard. After three weeks, we'd gotten one! From the smaller body size, I knew it wasn't Cést Fou, but I still counted it a victory.

Adrenaline surging, I retrieved my phone and called the wildlife specialist number I'd been given. "Hi!" My breathlessness nearly shouted the word. "This is Kate Landry from Beignets & Books. We caught a parrot. In one of your traps."

"Okay." The person who'd answered clearly wasn't as excited. "I need you to keep an eye on it until we can get someone there."

My pounding heart sank. "Do you know how long that'll take?"

The sound of a drink being gulped carried over the line. "Hmm, a couple hours? Our on-call agent is picking up a gator in Mandeville right now. He can swing by after."

"He's going to bring an alligator here?"

"Don't worry. It'll be restrained in the back of his truck."

Tension wound through my shoulders, coiling up my neck. I bullied the Crease. There was no way I could leave. Not with Hayley upstairs alone and an alligator on the way.

"I need to forewarn you, since this is after hours, there's going to be an extra charge."

I huffed my bangs from my eyes. Of course there was.

Saturday arrived, along with a warm front heralding the return of full humidity and higher temps. Not-so-perfect for today's outdoor library event. Also not ideal? The theme. Dogs in literature. Attendees were encouraged to bring their friendly, sociable canines. When Hayley and Micah had settled on that premise, a tiny ache had begun in the depths of my eye sockets.

Keeping my thoughts from spiraling over my courtyard being overrun by animals was the uplifting news reaped from yesterday's venture capitalist function. I'd finally scored interest from an investor and had been offered a private meeting to further discuss my business plan. Unfortunately, due to a tight schedule involving the investor going out of the country for the summer, they could only meet this morning at ten. Not the best timing with the library event starting at one but still manageable.

Before leaving, I'd helped Hayley prepare the courtyard. We'd moved the parrot trap and hauled out the event tables from the storage shed, setting one up with dog treats donated by library patrons. Another would hold human treats. Similar to the last two events, we'd also set up an arts-and-crafts table. Dissimilar to the last two events, we'd arranged a doggie poop station, complete with waste bags and a lidded trash can. I'd showered, changed into my most professional skirt suit, and darted out the door, ensuring I arrived for the meeting fifteen minutes early.

With my pulse galloping, I'd checked in with security at the front desk of a Poydras Street skyscraper. The guard had told me to "get comfortable," and man oh man, had he been right. I'd waited in the lobby for two hours, pacing, stewing, calculating the absolute latest I could leave and still make it back to the café. At noon I'd been brought up to the fortieth floor and sat through another hour of the investor complaining about a recent venture before getting to my business plan. In the end he'd wanted way too much equity and had too little respect for my time in keeping me waiting because he'd had "a late start" to his day. If that meeting was a precursor to a working relationship with the man, I'd pass.

With a heavy and irritated heart, I sped home and rushed through the courtyard gate, stepping into what looked to be an after-party for the Westminster dog show. Canines in various shapes and sizes darted here and there, their lighthearted barks filling the air. Kindergarteners through preteens, along with their parents, meandered through the space, everyone with smiles on their faces.

Micah stood on the back porch, speaking to a woman holding a tiny poodle. Yesterday morning I'd dropped off beignets and café au lait at his house for him and his dad. By the time Crocodile Dundee had shown up the night before and carted off the parrot, Mr. Gary had been released from the hospital. His previous mild ankle sprain had graduated to small tears in his ligaments, and he'd been relegated back to a wheelchair. They'd headed straight to Micah's. It turned out his rental had an ADA-compliant addition built on the rear of the house. A type of mother-in-law suite. It was one of the reasons he'd chosen the place over his other options.

Hayley and Emma oversaw a game of cornhole on the side stretch of grass. Mrs. Adélaide, who'd taken a keen interest in regularly visiting the courtyard since Cést Fou's appearance, sat in a grouping of chairs, reading a *Clifford the Big Red Dog* book to several children. She hadn't yet renewed her concealed-carry permit, so I hadn't had to worry about her toting her revolver.

My gaze moved to the crafts table, surprise parting my lips. Julia praised a little girl as she finished her construction-paper slinky dog. The child skipped to her dad, proudly showing her work of art. Julia waved at me, her hand connected to Precious's leash. The dogs in the courtyard had to be on leashes, a must to ensure they didn't escape via the wraparound porch and out the front gate if a café customer left it open. A temporary safety fence had been erected on the side lawn, giving the four-legged creatures a free area to roam.

I approached Julia, setting my purse and leather business portfolio on a clear spot on the table, grateful today's activity didn't involve glitter. "I didn't know you were coming." I checked the folding chair before lowering onto it. Precious immediately scratched at my legs, and I lifted her to my lap.

Julia passed the leash handle. "Hayley texted last night, asking if I could help."

"Oh." That stung. I rubbed Precious's ear. "Well, thank you. I'd planned to be here sooner, but my appointment ran late."

"Was this appointment part of plan D, or have you moved on to plans E, F, or G?"

"Har, har. I'm still on plan D. It was a meeting with a potential investor."

Julia reached across the table, gathering a pair of rogue googly eyes, returning them to their rightful bin. "How'd it go?"

I gave a thumbs-down.

Her face scrunched. "Sorry."

With a shrug, I let my attention wander, needing to focus on better things. A terrier snatched one of the beanbags from the cornhole game, a boisterous round of laughter erupting from those nearby. Hayley ran after the thief. On this side of the safety fence, a boy lost his hold on his Labrador and shrieked. The dog beelined for the treat table, snagging a Milk-Bone and gobbling it, giving the kid enough time to grab its leash. Precious curled into a ball, closing her eyes and tucking her nose beneath her back leg. How she could nap in the midst of this melee was a mystery.

Several feet away I spied a puddle of liquid on the brick pavers. "Please tell me that's spilled juice."

Julia followed my line of vision, her lips pursing to one side. "It certainly could be."

A beagle on a retractable leash approached the puddle, sniffed, and promptly squatted over it. My head tipped back. "And Hayley wants to open the courtyard to dogs on a weekly basis."

"Speaking of Hayley . . ." Julia's brows lifted, and she began cracking her knuckles, a telltale sign of her nervousness.

Oh no.

Her expression softened. "What happened to you being a part of these events to get closer to her?"

My belly clenched. "I was a part of it." I ran my finger over the purple stitching of Precious's body harness. "Sort of. I helped set up before I left and tried to be back in time."

"I know you did. But from the way Hayley was talking, other than today, you haven't been involved."

"Well . . ." Perspiration gathered along my skin, and I shrugged out of my suit jacket, careful not to jostle Precious. "She and Micah handled this one."

"I got the impression she didn't just mean this event."

Oof.

Julia scooted her chair closer. "She said when you're home, you're always on your laptop. And it's not for fun."

"Spreadsheets can be fun," I mumbled, folding and draping my jacket over my purse, keeping it out of reach from wandering dogs.

She studied me, her forehead creasing. "I'm worried about you."

"Why?"

"Hayley also said you're not eating as much."

Shock struck, sharp and searing. My gaze drifted to Hayley, who handed a beanbag to a little girl. It appeared her teenage attention span had expanded well past her phone and Precious. And I shouldn't have been surprised, considering she'd picked up on me and Micah before there even was a me and Micah. "I tend to lose my appetite when I'm stressed."

"I know, which is why I'm bringing it up."

The backs of my thighs began sweating. I readjusted Precious. For not having hair and being a little speck, she sure radiated a ton of heat.

"What I'm about to say isn't a complaint. It's out of love." Sincerity shone in her features, her gentle tone. "You've canceled on our weekly beignet date the last four Fridays."

I could feel the Crease puckering. Had it really been that many times?

"And the last few weeks at church, I've noticed a change. You're distracted, and you've got this going on." She motioned under her eyes. "Which makes me think you're not sleeping."

Heat prickled up my neck. "I'm sleeping."

Her head tipped sideways. "Hayley said you're sleep talking. A lot."

Sheesh. When had Hayley become the mouth of the South? I pinched my white blouse at my ribs, pumping the material to get the air flowing.

"Mumbling about income statements and comparative data."

I winced, releasing my shirt. It seemed the dreams about pitching my business plan hadn't remained inside my brain. Which made sense. I always dreamed more when stressed. Plus, I hadn't had time to exercise the past few weeks to help release that tension. Between the networking functions during the day and keeping up with café responsibilities at night and on the weekends, something had had to give.

My phone's calendar alert chimed, jolting me and Precious. I leapt for my purse. What was I supposed to be doing now? Had I forgotten something?

"Steady, girl." Julia leaned forward, pulling her phone from her back pocket. "That was me." She shot me a look, tapped her device's screen, and set it on the table. Her vision shifted to my business portfolio, her eyes narrowing. She reached, pinching the corner of a protruding sheet of paper, tugging it free. It was the list of plans and tasks revolving around the purchase of the Vieux Carré Café.

My heart skittered to a stop.

"'Annihilate Ryan'?" She held the page up, pointing at the header at the top. "I knew it. You're running yourself ragged, and for what? To beat your ex?"

I snatched the page from her, returning it to the folder, earning a glare from Precious for all of the jostling. "Ryan stole our sous chef this week."

"*What?*" Her head quickly drew back. "I'm so sorry to hear that."

I absently rubbed one of Precious's ears. "Regardless of Ryan, if you look at this analytically, all I'm doing is taking the plans Claire and I made and moving them up, ensuring we get her dream location. Sticking it to Ryan is lagniappe."

She tossed me her mom-look. "Sister, I think you're fooling yourself. From where I'm sitting, it seems you're letting Ryan dictate your actions. Or really, reactions. Why are you giving him that control?"

I bristled.

"Do you honestly need to open another restaurant now? Or ever?"

The enormous head of a husky poked between us, its hot breath panting on my arm. It gave Precious a sniff and was pulled away by its owner. I plucked the white fur it had shed on my gray skirt.

Julia brushed several hairs from her black shorts as well. "If this truly is about Claire and the roles were reversed, wouldn't you want her to be happy over keeping business plans y'all created a lifetime ago?"

"Of course I would." I plucked another hair with a little too much gusto, flicking it to the ground. "But this *will* make me happy."

Julia expelled a deep sigh, concern etched in her features. "Will it make Hayley happy?"

Everything within me stilled.

"Your relationship with her has gotten so much better. It'd be a shame to lose that. And if *she's* telling me how busy you've been, asking me to step in today, that's saying something."

Eyes stinging, I searched for and found Hayley. My heart beat heavy in my chest.

Julia laid her hand atop mine. "I know you've been praying on this."

"I have. And asking for His will to be done."

"And possibly ignoring His will?"

The heat accosting me since arriving dissipated, a chill slipping in. I slid my hand from her grasp.

"What if all of these roadblocks are God's way of answering you? From that wild bird wreaking havoc, Ryan's reemergence and shadiness, the grant and SBA loan getting denied, the fryer breaking, and today's meeting being a bust?"

A brick of disappointment stacked on my shoulders with each setback she'd named, and I tried to ignore the burning in my throat.

Julia offered a hesitant smile. "Just because God says *not now*, doesn't mean *not ever*."

27

JULIA HAD GOTTEN UNDER MY SKIN. Her blunt words lurked like an underground pimple refusing to fully surface. Growing bigger and more tender with each of the six days that had passed. Especially her insight with Hayley. Plain and simple, I'd been cut to the heart. So much so I'd skipped half of this week's networking events and experienced an odd withdrawal from all the hurry-hurry-hurrying I'd been doing the past five weeks.

It was now Friday morning, and after being pulled from my office to deal with a disgruntled customer, my concentration had been shot. I headed through the back doors for my prayer spot in the courtyard. I should power through my next task, but the world wouldn't crumble if I didn't update our social media accounts with today's new content. And at the very least I could do it tonight.

My thoughts paused, remembering what Hayley had told Julia. This past week I'd started waiting until Hayley went to bed to catch up on work. Which meant even less sleep. I pressed a fingertip below my eye, knowing Julia was right about my lack of slumber. If I did purchase the Vieux Carré Café, I'd have no choice but to work evenings and nights to keep up with the hectic duties of running a restaurant. Scratch that. Running two restaurants. Where would that leave time with Hayley? Or even Micah? My heart sank.

Vivid green caught in my periphery vision and I turned, finding a motionless lump beneath the trip net. A hushed gasp escaped my lips. Cést Fou? Slowly, I tiptoed toward the mound of feathers. With its wings tucked in, and lying on its stomach, only its back showed. It had the size and color of the feathered monster, but I couldn't see its face. That distinct mark of bright teal on its cheek. Was it dead? Had the net induced a bird heart attack? I scraped my bottom lip between my teeth. If only I had a stick to poke him with. Glancing about, I came up empty. I could fetch the rake or a broom, but that would involve retrieving the keys to the shed, which lay all the way upstairs. I inched closer, hovering over its body, catching the teeniest sight of its teal stripe.

My mouth fell open. So it *was* Cést Fou. After three months of the stress and aggravation he'd inflicted on me, I had him. It was over. Except . . . the euphoria I'd anticipated in this moment somehow rang hollow. It seemed odd to see him like this. With his eyes closed. Still and lifeless. The other parrot we'd captured had flailed under the net. Had that bird been Cést Fou's mate? Had Cést Fou willingly allowed himself to be captured in order to be reunited? Or come here and died of a broken heart at missing his partner? I placed my hand to my breastbone, a slight twinge cramping my heart. I hadn't meant for Cést Fou to die. Leaning closer I surveyed the bird, hoping for a sign of life. That maybe Cést Fou could have a happily ever after with his mate at that sanctuary. Goodness knew *I* wanted a happy ending. I wouldn't want Micah ripped out of my life, not when—

Cést Fou's eyes popped open, and his head whipped around. The demon bird screeched, flapping against the netting.

I screamed, jumping back. Had it been playing possum? Executing one last act of meanness? "Evil! You're pure evil!"

Another shriek pierced my eardrums.

The back door to the café swung open, Mrs. Adélaide emerging, sans her purse. "You got him!" She pumped her fist in the air, the sagging skin beneath her arm jiggling. "I can't believe it." She held on to the railing, taking the steps one at a time in her orthopedic sandals.

With my pulse pounding, I made a quick call to the wildlife specialist, informing them of the capture.

Mrs. Adélaide neared, sizing up the thrashing bird. A scathing string of Cajun French poured from her lips, ending with a hiss.

I disconnected from the call. "The trapper's on his way. He's going to relocate him to Mississippi, where he took the other parrot."

"Dis bird needs to be relocated to Hades."

"Mrs. Adélaide!"

"'Tis true." She purposefully stepped on a shed feather, as though stomping out a cigarette.

I tipped my sights to the tree branches above. "How many parrots have you seen at your place? I'm hoping this will be the last of my bird woes."

"*Deux*." She held up two fingers.

"Thank the Lord." My shoulders relaxed, and a euphoric release of tension unfurled from my core. I hadn't felt this good since . . . well, that luau kiss Micah had surprised me with. And so, with the parrot thrashing several feet away, I called him, cutting off his hello. "We captured Cést Fou! And Mrs. Adélaide said she's only ever seen two parrots at her place, so I think we're in the clear!"

"That's great," he said. "But I can't talk."

I sobered. "Oh, I'm sorry. I didn't mean to interrupt anything."

"It's fine. I just need to check on my dad. He's not answering his phone."

"I can do it." The rightness of my offer settled over me, like when I'd brought breakfast to Micah and Mr. Gary the morning after his ER visit. "Do you have a spare key hidden somewhere outside?"

"You don't need to."

"I have nothing to do except wait for the wildlife guy to come haul Cést Fou away. And I can ask one of my employees to keep watch."

"I'll watch him." Mrs. Adélaide rubbed her hands together, a gleam in her eye. "If it tries to escape, I'll snap its neck."

I flinched, doing a double take of the woman. *Gracious.*

"I've got it," Micah said. "I'm already leaving the library." A vehicle door slammed in the background, and an engine roared to life. "If I need help, I'll let you know, okay?"

"Okay."

He disconnected.

My arm fell to my side, frustration clouding my thoughts. I certainly wouldn't be holding my breath on him asking for help. This past week I'd felt an internal nudge to pop in on Mr. Gary while Micah worked. But when I'd offered, he'd shot me down. Was his reluctance based on my history with Mawmaw? Or was it his own guilt over the years his sister had been solely caring for Mr. Gary? Either way, I wasn't quite sure how to broach the topic with him.

⚶

Sunday afternoon arrived. After eating sandwiches with Hayley, I'd cut the grass, and she now helped me tend the gardens in front of the café. Or I should say, she mostly followed the butterflies, snapping pics of them with her phone. Ever since she was a toddler and had discovered the delight of butterflies, I always made sure to plant flowers that attracted them.

Sporadic traffic flowed along St. Charles Avenue, mingling

with the more routine trundling of the streetcars. Kneeling on a gardening pad, I reached between a cluster of bright pink pentas, finding the base of a weed and gently pulling it free, releasing the scent of cypress mulch. The low-maintenance azaleas framing the house had finished their blooms, now providing a green backdrop to the heat-hardy flowers.

I added the weed to the growing pile of offenders and swiped my forearm across my brow, knocking my sunglasses and hat in the process. With our fair complexions and not wanting to expand our collection of freckles, Hayley and I both donned sun hats and had slathered our arms and legs in sunscreen. Hayley, ever the protective dog mom, had rubbed a layer of sunblock on Precious, citing that she'd read an article about dogs getting sunburns.

Though the front gate was closed, Precious remained on a retractable leash attached to a yard stake. We hadn't wanted to take a chance with her tiny body squeezing through the fence posts. A sprinkler fanned back and forth on part of the lawn, and I couldn't help but think of when Hayley was little, playing in the water while I'd weeded. She'd worn princess swimsuits and squealed when the sprinkler caught her by surprise. A bead of sweat ran into my eye, and I blinked it away, along with the treasured memory.

"I'm going to take Precious up," Hayley said. "I think she may be getting overheated." She unhooked the pup and carried her, disappearing down the side stretch of lawn between us and our neighbor.

Weather permitting, I tried to do maintenance like this on Sundays when the café was closed. I reached for another weed, carefully maneuvering around a honeybee going to town on a bundle of sweet alyssum. Those bees were always working. Which reminded me. Tonight, after Hayley went to sleep, I'd finish the next staff schedule. With summer here, the next few months' schedules would be harder to maintain with people taking off for vacations. And the bigger hit of the college grad-uates moving on to other jobs altogether. I needed to start recruiting for their replacements, which always started with asking my most trusted employees for recommendations.

"Hello," a feminine voice called out.

I turned, leaning back on my haunches, and found a familiar woman outside the entrance gate. "Hi." I pushed to my feet, my back and leg muscles aching, and headed up the walkway. "I think I saw you at the last library event held here."

"Yes, I'm Regina Claiborne." She appeared to be in her fif-ties and was dressed as though she'd come from church. She gingerly rested her hand atop the locked gate. A necessity on Sundays to keep people from wandering in and around the property.

"Kate Landry." I removed my gloves, wiggling my sweaty fingers, granting them a momentary reprieve. "I'm sorry, but we're closed on Sundays."

"Yes, I didn't realize until now." She motioned to the *Closed Sundays* sign hanging on the gate.

"It's no problem." With a slight wave, I moved to step away.

"Actually, I came by to see you."

"You did?" I pinched the neck of my T-shirt, using it to wipe my cheeks and, hopefully, remove any mascara sweat trails.

"I'm the regional branch manager for the New Orleans Pub-lic Library."

Slowly, my hand lowered. So she hadn't been a parent attend-ing the last function but Micah's boss? Why hadn't he told me?

"I wanted to thank you for your help in keeping the spring events going." A car with its windows down and bass thump-ing slowed, pausing our conversation. It turned at the corner, its noise fading.

"You're welcome," I said. "But it was all Micah's doing. He truly loves his job, and helping the kids." *And I'd love for you to hire him permanently and keep him at Hayley's library.*

Regina chuckled, her crow's-feet deepening. "You don't need to talk him up to me. We're over the moon with what he did having the events here. It's kept our patrons involved and actually increased foot traffic through his branch in the children's demographic. And now he has his sights on reaching more adults too."

He did?

Regina's amber eyes lit. "He's spearheading a new adult educational program, starting the series with you teaching an introductory business class."

My pulse and body stilled while my mind raced. I must've heard her wrong. Maybe I'd been in the sun too long.

"I can't thank you enough for how generous you've been with your café and your time. And now to have this on the horizon." She beamed. "We're all thrilled."

A burning pain swelled in my throat, my breaths barely slipping past. Where was the Landry Mask?

"You know, when Micah first interviewed for the temporary position, we'd told him he'd need to really wow us to consider taking him on permanently, and that's exactly what he's done. Between the success of the spring events and now this adult education program, he's a shoo-in for branch manager if the head librarian doesn't return. But in all honesty, I'd like to steal him for my office."

I could only stare, struggling to hold the Landry Mask in place, grateful for my sunglasses.

She took a step back. "Thank you again for all of your support."

I managed a fake smile and cool nod. Mama would've been proud.

Regina made her way down the sidewalk, vanishing from sight.

A wave of lightheadedness struck, and I pinched my lips to keep them from trembling. Wounded betrayal spiraled through me. The déjà vu of history repeating itself. Of being used. My palms stung, and I glanced down. Found my nails digging into my skin. And on the ground, my gloves. A hot tear slid down my cheek as I reached for them.

In a fog, I retraced my path toward the café. Tossed the gloves and picked up my phone resting on the front stairs. I pulled up Micah's number and paused. *Lord, how do I handle this?*

With a sigh, I sank onto the top step, grateful for the shade.

If our roles were reversed, wouldn't I want Micah to give me the benefit of the doubt? I didn't know this woman, other than her job title, that she owned a poodle, and that she apparently waved a *Team Micah* flag. But then again, how would Regina Claiborne even know about the introductory business class unless Micah had proposed it? Eyes stinging afresh with tears, I slid them shut.

My mind rewound over the past few months. How Micah wouldn't have been able to save the spring events apart from the use of my courtyard. And everything Regina mentioned about his job security and possible promotion were things that couldn't have been accomplished without me and my café.

Heart thudding dully in my chest, I stared at my phone, wondering if texting him would be better than calling. I could choose my words carefully. Read and pray over what I said before clicking *send*. The last time I'd talked to Micah was Friday, when I'd called to check on Mr. Gary. It seemed Micah had overreacted to his dad not answering his call. Mr. Gary had simply been napping. They hadn't made it to church today, or the preceding Sunday for that matter. Soon as this morning's service had let out, I'd messaged Micah, offering to pick up lunch. I'd thought it'd be a lift for Mr. Gary, especially since he'd been so sociable the times we'd been around him. But Micah hadn't responded.

In fact, my previous texts to him had gone unanswered. A puff of air whooshed past my lips, and I lowered my phone to my lap. How was I supposed to work this current problem out if he wasn't responding to the other issue already growing between us?

28

I WAS GOING OLD SCHOOL. No phone call to Micah or text. I was an adult, and I'd handle this situation like one. I would talk to him face-to-face. Going even more old school, I'd walked to his house, needing the extra time to order my thoughts. With every step, I'd battled a myriad of emotions swirling in my gut. Glancing at the bottled water in my hands, I wished it were Tums.

I entered his front gate, similar in style to the one bordering the café, and took the steps up to his porch. Indecision struck, my finger hovering over the doorbell. What if Mr. Gary was napping? I didn't want to wake him. A bead of sweat escaped from my hairline, trickling down the back of my neck. Forming a fist, I knocked on the mint green wooden door and eased back. A sparrow caught my eye, its little body hopping along the blooming branches of the crepe myrtle on Micah's sliver of lawn.

The door opened, and he appeared, clearly surprised. A layer of scruff graced his strong jaw, testifying to his being off work yesterday. His attention dithered on my sun hat, one corner of his mouth hitching.

I removed my sunglasses. "Can we talk? Alone?"

His rising smile fell. Before stepping out, he flipped a switch, the porch ceiling fan beginning a wobbly rotation. He shut the door behind him. "I'm sorry I haven't texted you back, it's just . . ." He scratched his cheek, his fingertips bristling against his stubble. His apology died midair.

It was the perfect transition to discussing one of the two items I'd come here for. But my old wound of being used burned in my chest, begging for relief, one way or another. I took a few steps across his narrow porch, passing two chairs, and licked my lips. Salt lingered on my tongue, and I wasn't sure if it stemmed from sweat or my earlier tears. "Regina Claiborne dropped by my place."

Micah's head tipped, a question forming on his face.

"She caught me out front gardening and started talking about you. How you had to 'wow'"—I air quoted the word— "them to secure a job. Is that why you originally came to me, asking to use the café?"

"No." His direct gaze sharpened. "That had nothing to do with it. I only wanted the program to continue for the kids."

Considering his unique and intimate history with the library, I believed him. A droplet of sweat rolled between my shoulder blades, all the way to my lower back. "Did you look for another venue, or did you only ask me?"

His intense stare weakened, his Adam's apple bobbing. "I only asked you." He lowered onto one of the chairs, resting his elbows on his knees. The fan's momentum increased, toying with his hair. "It seemed perfect. You had the space, a personal connection to the library with Hayley. And most of all . . ." His eyes rose, meeting mine. "It was nice to be around a friend. Then *really* nice once we became more than friends."

My heart geared up to swoon.

But I was a Landry. And we did not allow emotions to cloud rationality. "And what about the adult educational series you're starting? The one beginning with me teaching a class? A class I told you I can't do."

He straightened, blinking rapidly, his mouth falling open. "That's not . . . I mean . . . Regina spoke out of turn. I only used you as an example of my vision."

I pointed the water bottle to where I'd come from. "Are you sure about that? Because she was just at my place, thanking me for volunteering to kick it all off."

"It's a misunderstanding. One I'll clear up." Sincerity coated his features, his tone.

But Ryan had always seemed sincere too. I yanked off my hat. Fresh air kissed my perspiring scalp, doing little to extinguish my ire.

Micah rubbed his forehead. "I promise this looks worse than it is."

"Really?" I scoffed. "Because to me, this looks like history repeating itself."

He eyed me like an out-of-towner trying to peel boiled crawfish for the first time.

I dropped my hat upside down on the other chair, tossed my sunglasses on it, and turned toward his front lawn. The bottled water crackled beneath my strangling grasp. "Too many times I willingly sat by while Ryan used me in high school and all through college with papers and projects. And now he's back and doing it on another level." I gave a slow shake of my head. "Then I find out today about you." I unscrewed the water, downing the last of it, balancing the empty container on the railing.

"This isn't fair." Micah's low, rough voice drifted over my shoulder.

"You're right. It's not." I faced him, crossing my arms, my skin grimy from sunscreen and sweat.

"No." A line puckered between his brows. "I mean it's not fair that you're comparing me to Ryan." Slowly, his eyes widened, his head tipping back. "And you've been doing it all along." With a soft snort, he pushed to his feet and took two steps, grasping the railing with both hands.

From where I stood, I was justified in that comparison. That old "fool me once" saying wasn't a cliché for nothing.

Except for the fan's breeze stirring Micah's hair, he remained eerily still, his expression contemplative. "This is more than today, with you thinking I've purposely used you. Which I haven't." His gaze anchored on his Jeep parked at the curb. "I've been waiting for the woman who kissed me during the luau like her life depended on it to return. We haven't spent a lot of time alone together, but when we have, there's this . . . barrier. Like you're not all in." A vein pulsed at his temple. "And with you bringing up Ryan, it now makes sense."

My arms loosened their stiff hold. I hated that he was right on that front. That he'd noticed my cautious heart.

His vision dipped to the lawn, the afternoon sun catching on his lashes. "It's unfair for me to pay for his mistakes."

It was like I'd stepped on a landmine, the truth of his words erupting, ricocheting within me. I hadn't thought of it that way. Of my hesitation in our relationship resulting as a punishment for him. A heated tingle broke across my face, my throat growing thick. "You're . . ." I struggled against the lump of shame. "You're right . . . and I'm sorry." I glanced at my tennis shoes, willing my feet to move toward him. But his closed-off stance gave me pause and made it impossible to pull in a normal lungful of air. "It's difficult for me to be vulnerable in that way."

"I know." He sighed. "It's hard not to let your past control your present." An almost imperceptible shake of his head followed, and his tone lowered. "And I think you have that happening in more ways than just Ryan."

That pulled me up short. "What do you mean?"

The tendons in his forearms flexed with his hold on the railing, and his eyes slid shut, his head bowing. Was he praying? Straightening, he drew in a deep breath and released it, then trained his gentle gaze on me. "I think your past with Claire is affecting you too."

I gaped. Had we been on a daytime talk show, the audience would have gasped, and possibly thrown in an *oh no he didn't*.

His hands shot up. "Please, hear me out. I'm speaking from experience. And concern."

Unable to meet his earnest stare, my attention slunk to the black-and-gold Saints logo on his T-shirt.

"You're so bound to that plan hanging on the wall in your office. And the Vieux Carré Café. They keep Claire involved. And believe me, I get it." He splayed his fingers across his chest. "I went through that with my mom."

My heart clenched, and I mustered the strength to focus on him again.

"When I'd graduated high school, the last thing I wanted was to move away. But that's what I'd talked about with her, all through her treatments. The University of Colorado had been her alma mater. And so I went. I wasn't happy, but I stuck it out because of her. Because of this . . . sense of duty."

Sense of duty. Oh, how his words pierced my soul, ringing true to what I'd felt for decades. To Mawmaw and later Claire.

"On graduation day, I realized that wasn't what she would've wanted for me. Sticking out life for the sake of conversations we'd had when I was only a kid in junior high. It was a bitter pill to swallow." He slid his hands into the pockets of his basketball shorts. "I'd hate for you to get through the goals you'd made with Claire and regret what you gave up to achieve them."

Heaviness bled into my bones. I pushed my damp bangs away and rubbed the Crease. Hadn't Julia mentioned something similar before? Or maybe not. These unexpected revelations and twists in our conversation had left my mind mushy, with too much to process. I screwed my eyes shut.

"It's just something to consider. Something I felt led to share." His warm fingers brushed against my face, tucking the hair that had escaped my ponytail behind my ear. His touch lingered.

I leaned into his affection, opening my eyes and taking him in. I'd been wrong to hold back my heart with him. Had I also been mistaken to take his boss's words as valid? Especially when they didn't match the person I knew Micah to be?

On the other side of the street, a lady wearing neon-pink knee socks walked a German shepherd. The dog sniffed at Mardi Gras beads lying in the gutter and continued on.

Micah's other hand lifted, his thumb brushing my cheek. "Do you believe me about Regina? That it's not as it appears?"

I fought against a tremor in my voice, in my heart. "I want to."

Something akin to determination lit in his eyes, and he gave a slight nod.

"There's one other thing I want to talk about. Your dad."

That spark in his gaze dimmed, his caress slipping away. He retreated to his seat.

"You never want to talk about him." I retrieved my hat and sunglasses from the chair I'd placed them on, lowering next to him. "And you don't want me helping with him."

He ran his palms down his thighs. "Your time has been stretched so thin, I didn't want to take what's left away from Hayley."

Well, that sucked the wind right out of my sails. "I'm sorry about how busy I've been."

He gave a dismissive wave. "You'd warned me about that, re-member? And other than taking up more time, I haven't wanted my dad's situation put on you."

I fidgeted with the brim of my hat. "You spoke from experi-ence before, with your mom. Now it's my turn." That earlier swirling in my belly returned. "I'm going to have to be involved with your dad. You're going to need support. At the very least, emotionally . . . and at some point, physically."

His gaze turned toward me, uncertainty coating his features. "And if it's too much for you?"

"I don't think it will be." And I'd continue praying it wouldn't. "Besides, I believe there's a little line in the Bible, instructing us not to worry about tomorrow." There were also lots of proverbs about being foolish. I could only hope I wouldn't fall into that category again when it came to trust and falling in love.

29

TO HAVE A GOOD FRIEND, one needed to be a good friend. And since I'd practically ghosted Julia the past month, I'd made sure to keep our beignet date the Friday after she'd called me out at the dog-themed library event. She'd brought me up to speed on her happenings, and I'd filled her in on everything, including Cést Fou's capture.

Due to Julia and Samuel scoring tickets to a Pelicans' game, we'd postponed last night's rendezvous to this morning. And for the sake of ensuring Hayley didn't overhear us, we'd made a ten-minute drive to the Audubon Riverview Park (a.k.a. the Fly). Up and over the levee we'd gone, dipping down into the space buffering the Mississippi River and Audubon Zoo.

A to-go box that had held steaming beignets now sat empty on our bench. Before us lay the Mighty Mississippi, the edges of its waters lapping the bulkhead only two yards away. Julia had eaten in silence as I'd divulged my chat with Micah's boss and subsequent convo with him.

She lowered her café au lait, resting it atop her leg. "Do you believe him?"

I gazed at the river, the murky water bobbing and weaving, mirroring my thoughts. "I feel like I'd be a fool if I did. I mean, the evidence seems clear, right?"

"It does. Though I could see why he wanted to hold the events at the café to spend more time with you." The crease along her forehead smoothed. "It's sweet."

"It is." I finished the last sip of my now tepid coffee and stuck the cup in the cardboard beverage tray. A breeze arose, stealing the scent of chicory and replacing it with damp earth and algae. "But how can I disregard what his boss said about me teaching that class?"

The wind intensified, tossing Julia's ponytail. She unwrapped it from her neck. "Did you interact with her at that library event? Maybe she's a scatterbrain. Oh! Or a conniver. She knew you didn't want to do the classes but hoped to manipulate you into them because she knows you're dating Micah, and you wouldn't want to hinder his career. Micah looking good makes *her* look good to her boss."

"That's diabolical." I brushed my bangs from my eyes.

"People in this world are known to do shady things."

The echo of a referee whistle sounded, and I turned. On the other side of the road, one of the soccer fields hosted a rugby game, a thin crowd lining both sides. I returned my gaze to the river. "One thing I'm sure of. He was right about me comparing him to Ryan."

"Give yourself grace. It's hard not to do that, especially with the way Ryan treated you. How he's still treating you. It's a tender area."

"I know but still." A tugboat chugged along, maneuvering to the shipyard on the opposite bank.

Julia picked at the cardboard sleeve of her to-go cup. "If you can't trust Micah, that's not a solid foundation to build a relationship on."

"And there's my struggle." I bent over, reached for an oyster shell, and chucked it into the water. "I don't sense that user vibe from him."

She set her coffee in the drink tray and pulled her phone from the thigh pocket of her running pants. She swiped and tapped at her cell, then held up the device. "Neither do I."

Unforeseen joy struck me at the picture filling the screen. Micah stared at me, adoration in his eyes. I glanced at Julia and back to the phone. "You're a sneaky one." Taking in his sincere features, warmth ballooned in my chest, lifting my heart. Based on our clothes, the candid occurred at the library luau. Before the kiss and chaos had ensued. "He's been supportive of everything I've been doing. Hasn't complained once about how busy I've been. And look at how great he is with Hayley. Plus, caring for his dad." I texted the pic to my phone and returned Julia's cell.

She stuck it back in her pocket and reached into the open box between us, pinching a clump of powdered sugar and dropping it in her mouth. "Have y'all even been on a date yet? Just the two of you?"

I winced. "No."

Her brows rose. "If your heart isn't in it all the way, it's not going to end well for either of you. Or Hayley."

"I know."

"Before we part ways today, we're going to pray on it."

"That'd be nice."

"Okay." She straightened, dusting powdered sugar from her fingertips. "Catch me up on the Vieux Carré Café. Are you still on the hunt for a silent partner?"

My stomach twinged, and I pulled in a deep breath that held a hint of waterlogged wood. I studied my wrist on my lap, the spray of freckles on my forearm. "Ever since you gave me that smackdown about ignoring God's will, it's given me a different perspective to consider. And coupled with Micah sharing about college and his mom . . ." I shrugged.

"I bet that wasn't easy for him, knowing you could've taken it the wrong way and gotten angry. It shows he put his concern for you above his own neck."

"Sort of like what you did with your smackdown talk."

"It wasn't a smackdown."

"I'm pretty sure I saw 'Macho Man' Randy Savage peeking around the corner, ready to be tag teamed in."

Smile lines fanned at the borders of her eyes, and she directed her gaze to the water. An enormous black-and-red tanker moved upstream at eye level. "What Micah said, is that how you feel? Duty bound to the plans you and Claire made?"

I nodded against another gust of wind, unsticking the hair caught across my lips. "It's this weird sensation of wanting to complete the goals we'd set but also dreading when they're done because then . . . it's over." A hollow weight slid into my bones, and I hugged my arms to myself. "Everything I'd planned with Claire is finished. I guess that's why I jumped on the Vieux Carré Café so hard. It was another link to her. To having more things to achieve in that specific space she'd daydreamed about."

Julia angled toward me, resting her elbow on the back of the bench. "Claire left you with something far better than business goals and her musings of the Vieux Carré Café. She left you with Hayley."

An ache gripped my heart, and my eyes pricked. "When I'd first gotten the news of Claire and Adrian dying in that accident, I thanked God Hayley hadn't been with them." I wiped my nose with the back of my hand. "And not for her sake, but my own."

A glossy sheen swept Julia's eyes. "That's exactly what I'd thought, too, when Mark died. I trusted in God that for whatever reason, it was best for Mark to go home to heaven. And I'd praised the Lord for leaving me the boys."

Sniffling, I pulled two tissues from my purse, handing her one. *Thank You, Lord. For bringing Julia into my life all those years ago, precisely when I needed her.* Closing my eyes, I gave in to the peace of the moment. To the breeze swirling, the lapping water, and the cherished friend sitting next to me. A rustle broke in, and I opened my eyes to a white egret landing along the bank nearby.

Julia fiddled with her tissue. "If you'd been the one to die, do you think Claire would've deviated from those plans y'all made? It's a lot of burden for one person to shoulder, especially with raising a child. She may have stretched that timeline or abandoned it altogether."

"Maybe." That same thought had occurred repeatedly when exhaustion from running the café and parenting had set in. The egret stalked along the river's edge, its sharp gaze scanning for prey. I couldn't help but think of Ryan and how he'd had a similar predatory gleam in his eyes the last time I'd seen him. "I'd just really hate for Ryan's plans to succeed."

"What's it been since he left you high and dry? Eleven years?"

I nodded.

"That's a long time to hold a grudge." She folded her Kleenex into a square, and then an even tinier one. "Perhaps Ryan's return is God's way of letting you work on your forgiveness of him, so you can move on. *Truly* move on."

I scoffed. "How can I forgive him if he's not sorry?"

Her expression gentled. "You don't need an apology from someone to forgive them. And believe me, in this case, forgiving Ryan isn't for him. It's for you."

⸬

For the next ten days, I wrestled with Julia's suggestion of forgiveness. Although I hadn't made peace with the idea of pardoning Ryan, I had come to the conclusion I couldn't continue the hectic schedule I'd been on. I'd pulled back my efforts. And it was oddly freeing.

It was a Tuesday, and I'd just shown the courtyard for a wedding anniversary, which I'd successfully booked. One beneficial aspect with all the networking was the increase in catered events, which meant extra income on the horizon. I'd have the new fryer paid off in no time and be in a position to schedule the painters to redo the porch ceilings.

I sat in my prayer nook, the afternoon sun streaming through the oak's branches, lighting on the pavers that had blessedly remained poop free since Cést Fou's apprehension. As a result of drastically cutting back on business functions, I'd caught up on work, leaving my nights open for Hayley, intentionally spending time with her. We'd begun watching the old movies Mawmaw had introduced to Claire and me, and on a few occasions, Micah had joined in.

On Father's Day, after church, we'd had lunch at Micah's house, meeting his sister and her husband and two teens. It'd been an easy gathering, getting to know everyone, seeing Micah with his family. That layer of vulnerability that had coated my heart steadily thinned. My run-in with his boss still weighed on him, and he'd mentioned searching for a different position, but I'd reassured him it was fine. All the little and big things he'd done for me and Hayley, and also reflecting on the boy I'd grown up with, led me to believe Micah Guidry was trustworthy.

I braided my fingers over my skirt. *Lord, I don't understand everything that's happened in my life, and I don't just mean the past few months. But I trust You. Please help me be wise in all areas. Hayley, Micah, the café.* Ryan came to mind, and a shard of resentfulness surged. My hands slid, curling around the edge of the bench. *I know I should pray for him, but it's hard.* Rolling my shoulders, I squeezed my eyelids together, wrestling with what I wanted versus what was truly right. *I don't know if I can forgive him, or how, but I think I'm willing to try.* Posture hunching, I stared at an acorn lying sideways next to my heels. *And, God, if You see fit, it'd be great if You kept Ryan from getting his cheating hands on the Vieux Carré Café. Amen.* I tipped my head back, wrinkling my nose in apology, thankful God loved me in spite of myself.

The *Magnum P.I.* theme song rang from my phone, signaling it was Micah. I smiled as I answered. "Hey."

"Are you in the middle of anything?" His tone exuded unease.

"What's wrong?"

"My dad called. He knocked his walker out of reach and can't get up from the sofa."

"I'm on my way." I darted across the courtyard and up the steps into the café, heading for my office.

"I hate to ask." The struggle in his voice was clear. "But I'm about to go into a meeting, and can't get a hold of Renee."

I grabbed my purse and rushed back out. "I'm leaving the café now."

I'd found the hide-a-key rock where Micah had told me he'd left it and let myself in the side door, depositing myself into the kitchen. "Hello! It's me, Kate!" I infused chipperness into my tone, masking my worry. "Micah asked me to drop in." Hopefully Mr. Gary didn't like to lounge on the sofa in tighty-whities.

"I'm in here." His voice came from an open pocket door to the right. When I'd been here on Father's Day, this door had remained closed.

I quickly made my way down a short, wide hallway. The sound of a television intensified as I entered a large space styled as a bedroom and small den. And there Mr. Gary sat on a loveseat. Blessedly, fully clothed. His walker lay askew on the floor. "Hi, Mr. Gary!" Taking in the easy situation before me, my smile turned authentic.

"I'm sorry you had to come." His cheeks mottled red, and he pointed a remote at the TV, switching it off.

"I'm not." I moved closer, dropping my purse on the couch and setting his walker upright. "This is a wonderful change of scenery since I've been stuck at work all day."

"Micah told me not to sit here when I was alone, that the cushions were too soft and would be hard to get up from, but . . ."

"But you're a wee bit stubborn?" I winked.

A rueful smile tipped his lips. "I am. And look where it's gotten me. Next time I'll stick to that." He inclined his chin to a nearby wooden chair abutting a sturdy end table.

I stood in front of him, planting my feet and offering my forearms, like I had so many times with Mawmaw. He latched on, and I carefully helped him stand. Once he was stable, I reached for the walker.

He gripped it with both hands. "I think you've done this before."

"I have."

"I'm glad my son's dating a woman with experience."

I chuckled. "Please don't go telling your friends that."

He gave a hearty laugh, his eyes twinkling. "Now that I'm upright, I'm heading to the can." With a firm grip on his walker, he steadily shuffled toward an opening set in the back wall next to his bed. No doubt an ADA bathroom.

On the drive over, I'd asked Micah about bathroom assistance, and he'd said his dad managed fine on his own since he'd graduated out of his wheelchair again. Not wanting to be a lurker, I retrieved my purse and retreated to the kitchen, keeping alert for any crashes or calls for help. With every moment of silence that passed, the tension that had wound through me the past five minutes released. In all of the hustling over here, I hadn't had time to think about those darker days with Mawmaw. I'd been solely focused on getting to Mr. Gary. That old fear hadn't had a chance to take hold of me. And it wasn't hooking its claws in me now. *Thank You, God.*

"You still here?" Mr. Gary called out.

"Yes, sir." I pushed off the doorjamb and moved farther into the modest kitchen. The entrance to the dining and living room lay on the other side. I peeked through. If I only had two words to describe the space, I'd go with rustic charm. Pine floors and the identical planks on the tall ceilings. On one side, a moss-green sofa set sat before a simple entertainment center. Across from where I stood lay a farmhouse dining table, an exposed brick fireplace, and French doors leading to a deck.

My gaze slid to the fireplace mantel and the line of books stretching the surface. C. S. Lewis, Tolkien. Bright orange caught my attention, my lips parting. A Nerf dart. The one I'd shot Micah with? I hadn't noticed it when we'd been here two days ago. Those last dregs of worry floated away.

Mr. Gary's shuffle-thump neared with his approach, and he reached the space faster than I'd expected. A smile graced his face. "Thanks again for coming, but you don't need to stay."

I glanced around, genuinely not ready to leave and struck by the fact that it felt right being here. A stark contrast to what I felt at all of those networking events. "Um, I thought I'd hang out, if that's all right. Hayley's at her friend's house, so . . . would you like some coffee? I'm not much of a cook, but coffee I can handle."

"How about coffee and a game of poker?" He motioned to the breakfast nook, and the deck of cards on the table.

I smiled. "It's a deal. Though I should warn you, my grandma taught me how to play." I raised my brows with an air of haughtiness. "Penny ante."

His eyes lit. "My kind of lady. I wanted to play on Father's Day, but Micah and Renee wouldn't let me."

"Are they any good?"

"Terrible." He moved toward a chair and eased onto it, using his walker. "How about we play for something interesting?"

"Like?" Even I heard the leeriness in my voice. Had I unwittingly walked into a gambling trap?

"If I win, you owe me an order of beignets once a week for a month."

I puffed a laugh. "Okay."

He smiled, cutting the deck of cards. "If you win, you get my BBQ pit."

My stomach mini heaved. For several reasons. The greatest of which was the eyesore outdoor grills were. "Oh no, I couldn't."

"Sure you could. I play for stuff like this all the time. I lost my old record player to my grandson." He shrugged. "One of the speakers is busted, but I'm certain he can fix it." He shuffled the cards. "Before that, I lost my big screen TV to my daughter. Of course, it had started randomly turning on and off on its own, but it still worked."

My lips pursed. What ailed his BBQ pit? Missing grills? No hood? I held up my hand. "I can't. Beignets for a BBQ pit isn't a fair trade."

"I think it's fair."

And I think you're trying to offload useless items from your house. "I don't cook."

"Perfect! Grilling isn't cooking." He pointed behind me. "Coffee's in there."

With a smothered sigh, I turned to where he'd indicated and opened a drawer, grabbing a bag of grounds. My gaze caught on what lay on the counter before me. A sheet of paper dotted with crumbs and a coffee ring stain, heralding the Jefferson Parish Library logo. I fumbled the bag. Micah worked for Orleans parish. Jefferson was our sister parish to the west. Smaller, but still a part of the greater New Orleans region. The header on the page read, *Job Description: Programming Specialist Librarian.* A lump of shame plopped into my stomach and sank-sank-sank.

"Find it okay?" Mr. Gary asked.

"Yes, sir." Oh, I'd found something all right.

For the next hour and a half, I'd slipped off my heels and sat in the kitchen with Mr. Gary, drinking coffee, trying to lose at poker, and trying not to think about that paper on the counter. A plethora of scenarios ran through my mind. Had Micah told his boss I wasn't on board with teaching those classes, and she'd given him the boot? Or had he and Mr. Gary planned an elaborate scheme for me to come here today, find that job description, and think better of Micah's intentions? I glanced at Mr. Gary. I didn't think he had it in him to be a true schemer, especially with the unclever way he tried to unload his BBQ. And honestly, I sensed to my core Micah wasn't a schemer either.

The side door creaked open, and Micah appeared. He wore dress slacks, a button-down with a tie, and he held a matching jacket. A complete suit. Despite how devastatingly handsome he looked, that lump in my stomach sank deeper. He'd either been to a funeral or a job interview. And I knew the answer.

He scanned his father from head to toe and moved to me, his assessing gaze remaining on my face. He placed his keys and a black folder on the counter, and cleared his throat. "How's it going?"

"Your girl here's a card sharp." Mr. Gary laid his cards facedown on the table beside his dwindling poker chips. "How'd your meeting go?"

I fidgeted with the top button on my short-sleeved cardigan set. *Meeting or job interview?*

"Good, I think." Micah hung his coat on a peg next to the door.

My attention dwindled to the pair of kings in my hand I needed to discard. *Good* as in he'd be starting all over again with a new library system? That the relationships he'd begun with his patrons would end? That he'd be leaving Hayley's beloved branch? Taking a position that put more miles between him and the parent he cared for?

Mr. Gary reached for his walker.

I fought the instinct to help. The last time he'd gotten up, and I'd offered my arm, he'd patted it and told me he was fine. I gathered our cards, setting them atop the deck.

"I'm going to watch the news." Mr. Gary eased to his feet, his attention on me. "If I don't see you before you go, thanks again."

"Any time."

And with that he shuffle-clomped away, pausing to shut the pocket door behind him.

Micah set his hip against the counter, studying me again. "You okay?"

"Yes."

He scratched his chin, his brows lifting.

"Truly." I widened my eyes for emphasis. "I think because it all happened so fast, and . . . it's hard to explain. It was just a strangely nice experience." I picked up the mugs from the table and brought them to the sink. "I'm glad you called."

His expression eased, his arms loosening at his sides. "Then I am too."

I turned on the faucet, filled the cups with water, and shut the tap off. "How'd your job interview go?"

His mouth pulled to one side in adorable awkwardness. "Suit gave it away, huh?"

"And the job description you left." I motioned to it.

He followed my line of vision, wincing. "I was waiting to see how the first interview went to tell you. That was today."

"You don't have to get another job."

His gaze held on to mine, and his throat bobbed. "I don't know how else to make it clear I didn't use you."

My heart swelled. Here stood a good, good man. A self-less man. And I'd been a fool to think otherwise. To even consider comparing him to Ryan. Two steps in my bare feet, and I wrapped him in a hug, pressing the side of my face to his chest. "You don't need to do anything. I'm sorry I didn't fully believe you before. And I'm sorry I let my past get in the way."

His arms enveloped me. Strong and secure. And forgiving. "It's okay." He nuzzled my hair, placing a kiss to my temple.

I closed my eyes, breathing in a trace of his aftershave and savoring what felt like a new beginning. *Thank You, Lord, for this sweet gift. That I didn't ruin it.* Basking in the comfort of his embrace, I could only think of how Micah's life could've taken a drastic turn if not for his firm faith. The loss of his mother at a young age had irrefutably shaped him. He'd chosen not to be angry with God but to help others like he'd been helped. And the loss of his marriage and his inability to conceive. He could have turned bitter. Shaken his fist at the Lord. But he'd leaned *into* God. And God had seen him through. Gratefulness expanded within my chest, pressing against my ribs. I slid my hands between us and smoothed my palm down his tie. "It's smart to see what else is out there, in case Mrs. Gail returns or Regina changes her mind."

"Gail's not coming back. She officially resigned yesterday."

I lifted my head. "So her job is yours?"

He gave a restrained nod.

A relieved puff of air flew past my lips. "Then take it! Unless you'd rather work in Regina's office."

A crease deepened along his forehead. "I don't want any doubts between us."

"I promise you"—I lightly tugged his tie—"there aren't."

An easy smile stretched his face, the skin at the corners of his eyes crinkling. "Then I'll stay where I am. I like it there. A lot. And it's close to home."

I pulled in a long, almost-victorious breath and released it. "Today was a good day."

A soft chuckle vibrated through him. "You having to come rescue my dad equals a good day?"

"Knowing I can. And knowing you'll ask me when you need help. And also realizing, with all of my heart, I trust you."

His expression softened, and he traced a fingertip along my cheek. "Then today was a *very* good day." His voice held a rough scrape of emotion.

And in that moment, my heart became his.

30

NOT ALL KISSES WERE CREATED EQUAL. Especially where Micah Guidry was concerned. For the past three days, since he'd walked me to my car after leaving his house, I'd contemplated that truth. He'd sent me off with the tenderest farewell that played through my brain at the most mundane times. While brushing my teeth, trailing an acceptable distance behind Hayley and Emma at the Riverwalk mall, and now, as I updated the daily business review.

Two figures appeared in the open doorway of my office. I glanced up and found my parents. A spike of unease shot through me. I jammed my feet into my heels and stood. "Everything okay?"

"Yes," Daddy said. Sporting a periwinkle polo and tan slacks, he gave the impression of having golf on his schedule today.

Mama, in a skirt suit and panty hose, gave the impression of sucking on a lemon. "Everything's fine."

I made a show of looking behind them. "Didn't bring Ryan with you this time?"

Mama sucked a little harder on that lemon.

"No," Daddy said. "Though he is part of why we're here."

Wariness prickled up my spine. I imagined a lengthy spool

of yellow-and-black caution tape rolling out before them. "Can I get you anything to drink? Or eat? The lunch rush is over, so it wouldn't take long."

"No, thank you," Daddy said.

I gestured toward the two guest chairs. Daddy shut the door, and Mama, oddly quiet, took a seat, lowering primly onto her chair. I did the same, folding my arms atop my desk. How strange. It was the first time all three of us had been in my office.

Daddy moved to the framed business goals, his face softening the slightest bit, no doubt at seeing Claire's signature. "You were right about Ryan."

I blinked. And pinched the inside of my elbow. Not dreaming. Was I having a stroke? I focused on my arms. Wasn't one of them supposed to be tingling? Or was that only for a heart attack?

Daddy slipped his hands into the pockets of his pants. "Two months ago, Ryan asked us to partner with him and that celebrity chef, Paul Rodgers, on a French Quarter property."

Whoa. It was a good thing I was already sitting.

"He'd said it was for an upscale restaurant," Daddy continued, "and that Paul Rodgers wanted local backing on the project. It wasn't clear to us Ryan was interested in the same location as you until you specifically mentioned it. Ryan also neglected to inform us of his number of failed projects. It's horrendous what our private investigator discovered."

I sat there, mouth agape, so many things clicking into place. Ryan reconnecting with my parents, his Chicago restaurant falling through.

"More recently, our private investigator overheard Ryan bragging about stealing your key employees and your café's concept."

I shook my head, my tongue pushing at the back of my teeth. "Technically, he's only gotten one employee."

Daddy lifted his hand. "The Landry name has been long

associated with this house and your business venture here. Your reputation in the local industry is top-notch, and we refuse to stand by and allow Ryan to use what you've accomplished."

Mama fingered her diamond tennis bracelet. "We want to loan you the money for the Vieux Carré location."

My heart thumped against my ribs, and I pinched the inside of my elbow again. Good and hard. Staring at them in equal measure, I mentally weighed their current words to their past actions. They hadn't cared before when I'd told them what Ryan had been up to. Judging by Mama's overall quietness and the sourpuss expression breaking through her Landry Mask, something overtly sensitive was at play. "What else did your investigator overhear Ryan saying?"

Mama tensed.

Daddy's cheeks reddened, and he stepped to the window, studying the view with great interest. "A few derogatory remarks about your mother, but nothing of consequence."

Ha! So there it was. Her pride had been jabbed, and now she sought revenge.

Mama leveled her gaze on me. "We'll lend you the funds with certain conditions."

Of course. And now I knew I wasn't dreaming. Strings were always attached with her.

Ever so slightly, she shifted in her seat. "We want to be partners in the new location."

I practically sensed the ground shaking from Mawmaw's bones rolling in her grave.

"We also want both locations open on Sundays," she said.

The blood flowing beneath my skin began a low simmer. She'd always despised that aspect of the café. Could never understand it.

"And you'll stop doing the lawn maintenance." Mama's chin rose. "Janice Freemont said she saw you mowing the grass. That's ridiculous and embarrassing."

The simmer bubbled, but I projected a firm calmness instead of yielding to my instinct to reach for a pointy object. I was an adult. I had control. My gaze strayed to the pencil holder on my desk, filled with all sorts of sharp writing utensils. I tucked my hands beneath my thighs. "What's ridiculous is the cost to pay someone when I can do it myself."

"Well," she scoffed. "With our backing, you can afford for someone to do those things from now on."

The fire in my veins ebbed. Giving up cutting the grass in the dead heat of summer marked a definite perk.

She picked a piece of lint from her skirt. "We also want to reinstitute our monthly dinners."

Oof.

Mama glanced at her watch. "With the property going on the market in less than two weeks, we need to get our partnership agreement settled. Our attorney will be sending you a contract to review." She motioned toward Daddy. "Let's go. I've got a hair appointment, and you have a tee time."

They left as abruptly as they'd arrived. I hadn't even had time to stand and show them out. Had the last five minutes happened? The scent of Mama's Chanel lingered, answering the question.

One thing was for certain, Micah was receiving an invite to tonight's beignet date with Julia.

⊹⊱——⊰⊹

A librarian, a maid, and Harry Connick Jr. joined me at a table for four in the music room of the café.

Micah pointed to the life-sized cardboard cutout. "Is Harry really necessary?"

"Harry is always necessary." I patted his hand atop the table. "Get used to him."

The café had just closed, the staff working to clear the main dining area and other rooms, leaving ours for last. Julia and I had our usual order of original beignets before us. Micah had chosen the daily savory special. Three delicious beignets topped with slow-cooked, apple-braised pork debris and tasso cream sauce.

Julia sat on the edge of her seat, her eyes holding too much excitement for a woman drinking decaf. "Are y'all making things official?"

"What?" I snapped upright in my chair, feeling my eyes bulge. "No!" I glanced at Micah, expecting a dazed expression. Expecting him to have possibly vanished. He simply watched me, a trace of humor on his face. I glared at Julia.

One of her shoulders lifted. "What'd you expect me to think when you'd told me he'd be here tonight, and you had something big to discuss?"

She had me there. "My apologies for the confusion." I smoothed a napkin on my lap, collecting myself from her slight detour. "My parents have offered to loan me the money for the Vieux Carré Café."

It was Julia's turn to wear a shocked expression, and it quickly morphed into wariness.

Micah stared at his plate, quietly absorbing the revelation.

Julia eased back in her seat, crossing her arms. "What's the catch?"

I filled them in on my parents' conditions. Again, Julia's concern shone clear in her countenance. And again, Micah remained quiet. I took a sip of coffee, giving them a moment to wrap their brains around this new twist. On the other side of the wall dishes clattered, along with a chair being dragged and muffled conversations from the staff.

Julia's thoughtful gaze leveled on me for a prolonged second. She picked at one of her beignets, as though carefully pondering her words. "My advice is to play it forward. Think about how involved they'll be and for how long."

I nodded, a speck of the tension I'd carried since this afternoon releasing. "I could negotiate stipulations, as far as their roles and percentage of ownership. And buyout options." My attention swung to Micah, who hadn't even touched his silverware yet.

He leaned, resting his elbows on the table, a crease lining his forehead. "I'll support you, no matter what you decide. But I agree with Julia. Play it forward. Once you start on this road with them, there's no going back."

"Thank you." I offered him a hesitant smile, unsurprised by his encouragement considering how supportive he'd been the past few months. The weight on my shoulders receded to a more tolerable level.

"What's your gut telling you?" Julia lifted a beignet and took a bite, powdered sugar falling to her plate.

"I'm not sure." I turned my cup on its saucer, the ceramic scraping. "The fact I'm not overly excited says a lot."

"It's a serious decision," Micah said. "And commitment."

I pointedly met his stare, arching my brow for added measure. "I'm not afraid of commitment."

"Good to know," he murmured, one edge of his mouth tipping north.

⚬—⚬

The hope of a Twinkie and a tabloid had been my focal point for the past seven hours. I'd filled in for a waitress who'd called in sick, and I was grateful for the busy Saturday shift to be over. For the chance to relieve my aching legs. Thankfully, Mayté was on duty and would handle the official closing, including locking up the cash in my office safe and setting the alarm. I stepped through the back doors into humid air. The landscape lighting in the courtyard cast a golden glow, and the fountain sparkled, its rhythmic cascade of water adding a layer of sound to the night.

"Kate."

I whirled, a scream building in my lungs.

To my right, Ryan casually leaned against the house, the overhead light pouring a yellowish hue over him.

I pressed a palm to my galloping heart. "What are you doing here?"

"I wanted to talk."

"And you thought lurking in the shadows was the place to do that?"

He motioned toward the café. "I stopped in a little while ago but didn't stay. I saw you working and decided to wait back here."

I hadn't noticed him. Of course, tonight had been nonstop.

He pushed from the wall, taking a step closer.

I remained next to the doors, refusing to budge an inch.

"I talked to your parents earlier."

Ah. So that explained his visit.

"They made it clear they're ready to pay whatever it takes to purchase the Vieux Carré Café." He searched my face.

I held strong to the Landry Mask, adding a slight smirk for funsies. "I can't believe you tried to partner with them."

His chin lowered, and he stared past his slacks to his loafers. "I can't believe you *are* partnering with them."

Did I enjoy the look of defeat on his face? Yes. Yes, I did. Should I tell him I hadn't accepted my parents' offer yet? I internally shrugged. A small part of me wondered if this was the moment I'd been waiting for. That he'd finally apologize. Maybe he needed a little prompting. "Life has thrown crazier curveballs my way."

He shook his head. "You mean Hayley, right?"

I remained silent.

He paced several steps away, then back, his footsteps heavy and reverberating. "It always comes back to Hayley with you." His voice raised a notch. "We agreed we didn't want kids. You didn't want them." He gestured toward me. "I didn't want them." His hand thumped his chest. "It was why we were so perfect for each other."

I concentrated on the fountain's peaceful babbling, such a contrast to this long-overdue moment. "It still wouldn't have worked between us for one huge reason that had nothing to do with Hayley." I took in his frustrated features and swiped my limp bangs from my eyes. "We didn't have a shared faith. We didn't have God at our core." The past few months with Micah had made that blindingly clear.

"You had plenty of God for both of us." His smirk had me briefly wishing for Cést Fou's return. For Ryan to experience the winter wonderland treatment.

"I was naïve to believe that. I was also naïve to believe you'd love me enough to stand with me through anything."

His head tipped forward with another shake, a muscle in his jaw flexing. "Neither of us wanted children. Did that change for you at some point during our relationship?"

"No." A mosquito buzzed my ear, and I swatted it. "But then Claire died, and everything changed."

"Oh, I know." He drew in a sharp breath and released it. Paced another short distance.

I motioned toward him and his peeved state. "You're the one who chose to leave. You didn't love me enough to stay."

"You didn't love me enough to keep your promise we weren't going to have kids."

I stilled, my stomach clenching. "What was I supposed to do? Let my parents raise her?"

He scoffed, his face contorting. "Your parents never even factored. As soon as we found out about Claire and Adrian, I knew you'd want Hayley."

The truth of his words settled over me, and a bittersweet smile escaped, taking the bite out of our conversation. "And I knew you wouldn't."

With his gaze anchored on me, he answered with a shrug.

The irritation that had been steadily building within slipped away. My weariness from a long day and this unexpected encounter struck, my sore legs and back muscles pushing to the front of my mind. I rubbed the Crease. "Why did you come here?" Because it sure hadn't been to apologize.

"If this French Quarter deal falls through for me, I'll lose my job."

My hand dropped to my side, a jolt of energy zipping up my backbone. "You came to me for what? Expecting me to roll over and let you have everything? This isn't some postcollege internship." A vague ringing echoed in my ears. "You went after my executive chef. You stole my sous chef. You plan to copy Claire's and Mawmaw's recipes."

"Those things are all business." He gave another flippant shrug.

Heat flashed through my body, and I wondered if Micah's jiujitsu classes taught how to rip someone's shoulders off. Slowly, and one at a time. "Get out." My tone was lethally calm. "And don't come back here again."

After one last imploring look, he made his way down the porch steps and across the courtyard to the side gate.

For the second time in my life, I watched him walk away. The me of eleven years ago had been shattered. Now I only felt relief. And gratitude. I sank down to the top stair, my muscles moaning, and tipped my gaze to the faint stars twinkling between the branches of the live oak. "Thank You, Lord, for sparing me from a life with that man." I wrestled with the conviction twisting through my core. "I don't know if I'm doing this right, but I want to forgive him. Please help me to. Please change the desires of my heart to want what You want."

After another moment of letting my heart and thoughts drift in prayer, I trudged upstairs, unlocked the door, and was met with silence. "I'm home." I peered into the hallway to our bedrooms and found Hayley's door shut, light leaking from the bottom. No doubt Precious was curled in bed with her while they watched anime on YouTube. Hopefully not the cartoon with the psychotic morphing dog. We didn't need Precious getting any ideas.

My stomach growled, reminding me I'd missed dinner. After retrieving a Twinkie and one of Mawmaw's old tabloids from my room, I returned to the kitchen, placing them on the island. The cover of this edition of *Weekly World News* claimed a new Elvis sighting. I snorted.

After grabbing a bottled water from the fridge, I rooted through the pantry for the peanut butter and sliced bread. Dropped them on the counter and opened a drawer for a knife. Normally any sounds emanating from the kitchen resulted in Precious magically appearing, her enormous eyes beseeching. And if she was in Hayley's bedroom, she'd scratch the dickens out of the door to get out. I paused from lathering a slice of bread with peanut butter and tipped my ear. Nothing.

I moved to Hayley's door and knocked. "Hayley?" Turning the knob, I eased the door open, only to find the room empty. Dread rolled through me, and I swayed. Her school backpack, the one I'd been nagging her to clean out the past month, was missing, the contents dumped on the floor in a chaotic heap of old notebooks, worn pencils, and scraps of paper.

"No," I gasped. *This isn't happening.* I dashed through the rest of the house, room by room. No Hayley. No Precious. Standing in the kitchen, my pulse whooshing at my temples, my gaze fell to the counter, where we kept Precious's body harness and leash. Gone.

"Hayley!" I yanked the front door open and darted outside, jogging the wraparound porch, scoping the area below, calling her name again and again into the dark of night. Nausea swirled, bile licking up my throat. A kidnapper wouldn't have locked the door behind them, right? Or bothered with stealing her yappy dog too. Taking Precious for a walk this late was against the rules. And Hayley wouldn't have brought a back-pack. My mind spun. Had she run away? Why?

I pulled in a wheezing breath, skidding to a halt. My thoughts flipped back to when Hayley had eavesdropped on my convo with Julia when we'd been on the first-floor porch. Where Ryan and I had been. Had she overheard us? I yanked my phone from my pocket and checked our tracking app. Instead of her pinging dot, I found a notice. *Location permissions off.*

"No." I ground out the word and called her. Landed straight into her voice mail. Fingers sweating, I shot her a text and dashed downstairs, my cell in a death grip. Flying into the café, I saw Jonathan standing in the dining room with a broom in his hands. My chest heaved with quick shallow breaths. "Have you seen Hayley?"

He shook his head.

I threw the café's bathroom door open. Empty. Rushed toward the kitchen, pushing through the swinging door. Everyone stilled, taking me in. My wild gaze scanned the space. "Anyone seen Hayley?"

No's all around.

I darted out the front door, the bell dinging, Jonathan on my heels. We ran the perimeter, unshed tears pressing hot against my lids. By the time we'd circled back, Mayté and the rest of the crew lingered on the lawn. Jonathan sprinted through the entrance gate, scanning the sidewalks.

"Lord, please," I whispered, a tremble rocking my frame.

"Fan out." Mayté barked the order. "Cover the surround-ing streets." Her small, firm hand touched my back. "Call her friend's mom."

"Right. Yes." With shaking hands, I rang Emma's mom and waited while she asked Emma and checked Emma's phone for texts. Emma was clueless to Hayley's whereabouts. With spots dotting my vision and pain shooting across my chest, I discon-nected and dialed 911.

31

TIME DRAGGED AS I WAITED for the police to show. Emergency response times in New Orleans had only worsened the past few years with the loss of officers to surrounding parishes. My call after them had been to Micah and Julia. Micah arrived within minutes and began examining all of the entry points, wanting to rule out foul play despite my theory.

Mayté and the rest of the staff continued searching the neighborhood. Julia and her husband, Samuel, arrived too. Julia's pale, tear-streaked face mirrored mine. Samuel had set right back out, driving the streetcar line. A fresh wave of overwhelming fear had crashed over me at that realization. Hayley, now an experienced streetcar rider, could be miles away.

Micah emerged from Hayley's bedroom, worry pinching his expression. "I think you're right that she left on her own. Did you check your security camera footage? They'll let us know when she left, confirm it's not a kidnapping, and which direction she went."

I shook my head, placing a hand to my queasy stomach. "They haven't worked for over a year."

Julia's brows pulled together. "They do work. At least that's what Wyatt had told me. Back in March, when he'd fixed your internet for that library event, he'd checked all your systems, noticed the cameras weren't working, and restored the connection. I thought he'd told you."

"He only said he'd restored everything. I didn't realize . . ." A sliver of hope cracked through the wall of darkness surrounding me. I rushed downstairs and into my office, Micah and Julia trailing. On my desktop I entered my password and maneuvered the mouse, pulling up the two video feeds. One aimed at the front yard of the café, the other an angle of the courtyard. That camera had been set up on a corner column to capture the back door of the restaurant and the bottom portion of the stairway to our residence. With trembling fingers, I maneuvered through the courtyard footage first. Images of me and Ryan, and me starting up the steps. Within seconds, Hayley came into view, exiting the stairs. My breath whooshed out. "She must've been hiding on the side of the porch, waiting for me to go inside."

Hayley cradled her backpack, which no doubt held Precious. She beelined through the courtyard and out of sight. The tightness in my chest eased. She hadn't been kidnapped.

"Thank You, Jesus." Julia's whisper carried over my shoulder.

I clicked on the other feed, showing the café's front. I matched up the timeline from Hayley leaving the courtyard and pressed play. From the side street, she appeared, darted across St. Charles Avenue, and caught a streetcar just as it pulled up to the stop. My heart thudded dully beneath my ribs. "She could be anywhere."

Julia called Samuel, telling him what we'd found.

Micah quickly kissed the side of my head. "I'm heading out in the direction she went." And he was gone.

A strange numbness settled over me. I rose from my desk and drifted down the hallway into the main dining room, my movements heavy and sluggish. "Lord, please," I murmured to the empty space.

"Why don't you sit down?" Julia asked, pulling out a chair at one of the tables.

I hadn't realized she'd followed me. I gazed through the front windows to the spot where Hayley had gotten onto that streetcar. How much of that talk with Ryan had she overheard? Tears blurred my vision. Where were the police? Why was it taking them so long to arrive? I swiped my cheeks and glanced at the clock above the kitchen entrance. Twenty minutes had passed since calling them. I gave a slow blink, staring at the hour and minute hands. That couldn't be right. It seemed like an hour, at least.

What if someone on the streetcar had taken advantage of Hayley? Or schemed at this very moment to? I'd watched *Sound of Freedom* and wept at how easily children were abducted and never seen again. I screwed my eyes shut, my chin trembling. *God, please control my thoughts. Be Hayley's shield. And mine.*

Julia's voice broke into my reverie, and I tried focusing on her. Focusing on anything other than the panic hooking its claws into me and trying to drag me into an abyss. With her phone pressed to her ear, she met my gaze. "Micah thinks she may be at the library."

The library. My knees buckled, and Julia wrapped her arm about my waist, helping me to a chair.

"He's nearly there." A long pause followed as she listened, chewing her thumbnail. "He's pulling into the parking lot. Says there's a light on in the carriage house."

My breathing shallowed, my fingers and toes tingling. *Please, Lord. Please.*

Julia smiled, tears tumbling over her lashes. "She's fine. Totally fine."

Hayley had refused to come home, so Samuel offered to drive me to the library. I'd notified the police before leaving, and Julia stayed behind, getting ahold of Mayté, who contacted our employees still out searching.

Samuel pulled his enormous black truck in front of the carriage house, his headlights cutting across Micah, who stood in the open entranceway, where one of the barn doors had been slid back. In his arms, he cradled Precious.

I exited on rubbery legs and headed toward him. Precious's rat tail wagged.

Micah's pallid and worn face could rival any father who'd been scared to death by the disappearance of their child. And I loved him for it. He managed a partial smile, his eyes glossy, and motioned me in.

I stepped through, air conditioning swathing my clammy skin, and took in the space crammed with old bookshelves of various colors and sizes. Exposed brick painted white matched the wooden slats on the tall ceiling. The scent of paper and mildew greeted me, along with Hayley's red, tear-streaked face. Wearing an oversized graphic tee and shorts, she sat on a folding chair, arms crossed, radiating defiance.

Micah moved outside, sliding the door shut behind him, giving us privacy.

I eased forward across the concrete floor, dying to hug her and fuss at her for shaving ten years off my life.

She sniffled and roughly wiped the tip of her nose with her wrist. "You don't want me." Her quiet voice shook.

"That's not true. I've always wanted you."

Her cheeks flushed, and her voice grew stronger. "I heard what y'all said. I ruined your life."

"No. You made my life immeasurably better."

She rolled her eyes and stood. Moved to a small wooden table piled with books, angling away from me. Despite notching her chin, her thin shoulders curled forward.

The emotional strain of the last hour was fast catching up, heaviness seeping into my bones. Unfolding another chair, I placed it next to the one she'd abandoned and lowered onto it. "How much of that conversation did you overhear?"

"Enough." She flung the word like a dagger and busied herself with moving books from one stack to another.

"But obviously not all of it." I sighed, rubbing my aching temples. "I wish you had."

Her petite frame turned a little more my way, her profile revealing a frown. A window unit softly hummed in the background.

God, please give me the right words. I clasped my hands on my lap and gathered a steadying breath. "When I was younger, I didn't want kids."

Hayley's stare whizzed to mine, and she grew still.

"I never had that . . . pull to motherhood." I studied my intertwined fingers. "I think it had a lot to do with my relationship with my parents." My gaze rose to hers. "But then you were born, and when I held you for the first time, you were so small and precious." The tenderness of remembering that moment spread through my chest, chasing my weariness. "You looked like the last doll in a nesting set. And something tugged on my heart. Before that point, I'd never felt that way toward anyone else's baby, and I've never felt it since." I lowered my hands, realizing they pressed to my breastbone. "Two years passed, and your hold on me that entire time grew like wildfire. But as far as having children myself, that feeling never changed." My mouth grew drier and drier. "But then your parents died, and I knew, with everything in me, I wanted you." My voice rasped, and I gritted my teeth, my fingers curling into fists atop my thighs. "That I would fight anyone who tried to lay claim to you."

Quick as a blink, Hayley landed in the seat next to mine, her face to my neck, her thin arms wrapping around me.

Thank You, God. Again.

We both shook with silent tears and shuddering breaths. I

smoothed my hand across her auburn hair, swiping the strands from her wet face and tucking them behind her ear. Gently, I rocked us back and forth, like when she was little.

"I'm sorry I ran away," she blubbered. "I feel awful for scaring you. And Mr. Micah."

"Good," I said dryly.

She sniffled a laugh and straightened.

I reached for a box of Kleenex on a nearby shelf. She pulled two, and I took one. I blew my nose and relaxed against the seatback, lifting my eyes to the whirling ceiling fans. Gratefulness, thick and sweet like pure cane syrup, coated me.

"I don't remember my parents." Hayley's voice sounded a smidge stronger than a whisper.

Oof. I turned in my seat, facing her.

"I feel like I should, and it makes me a terrible person that I don't."

My heart tweaked, and I draped my arm across her shoulders. "You were only two."

She fidgeted with her tissues, now rendered into limp wads. "But I should remember something."

"I don't recall anything from when I was seven, much less two. Maybe it was God protecting you." I gave her arm a light squeeze.

Her lashes, dark and spikey from tears, fanned against the tops of her cheeks. "Did I grieve? Or something like it?"

"Did you grieve?" My tone oozed playful teasing. "You had insomnia for months after their death and only slept in spurts." Only God's grace had gotten me through that time of sleeplessness and keeping up with Hayley and the café. "Every time you woke, you asked for Mama and Dada."

"I did?" Her voice pitched, a sparkle glinting in her bloodshot blue eyes.

I nodded, the corners of my mouth drawing up, and released my hold on her, swiping a late-arriving tear.

She settled against her chair with a small smile, appearing as though that cane syrup poured over her as well.

The chirping of a cricket inside the room pierced the silence. I glanced at Hayley and found her own mini crease puckered between her brows, contemplation clear in her features.

She picked the polish clean from her thumbnail and peeked up at me. "For a long time now . . . I've wanted to call you Mom."

My eyes blurred, along with a soul-deep stirring in my heart.

"But I felt guilty about it. That you'd be hurt because of how much you miss her."

I struggled with the thickness in my throat and took hold of her hand. "If you want to call me Mom, I'd really, really love that."

A full smile bloomed across her face, and she leaned, resting her head against me.

I wrapped both my arms around her and closed my eyes. Pulling in an expansive breath, wonder swelled through me at the good I was already witnessing from tonight's maelstrom of drama. *Lord, You sure do work in bizarre ways.*

Hayley's slender hand rested on my forearm, her dark violet nail polish a stark contrast to our fair skin. "What do you miss most about her?"

What a perfect gift her question was. To ask about Claire on her own. If a heart could burst from grinning, I knew mine was in this moment. "She was my best friend. We were partners in everything. Growing up with our parents, we understood each other like no one else could. It was like we were a team in dealing with them."

"That's how I've felt about their dinners all this time. That we were in it together."

"We *are* in everything together." I let go of her and leaned back, catching her gaze. "But as your parent, it's for me to take care of you. Not the other way around."

Her attention fell to the wadded tissues on her lap, her mini crease making another emergence. "What about those dinners with Grandmother and Grandfather? Do you think we'll start doing them again?"

My spine withered. *I* certainly would, if I agreed to partner with them. It would be one of the items to cave on in lieu of opening the cafés on Sundays. "If we do, it'll be up to you to decide if you want to go." And I would forewarn my parents no comments would be made about Hayley's appearance or grades. I could even add that as a formal stipulation to our partnership contract.

"I only dressed up for them so you wouldn't get in trouble."

An easy smile touched my lips. "Whenever we go, we'll both dress how we want to."

She perked. "My favorite ripped jeans?"

"How about we start with regular jeans and work up to those?"

Tonight God had shown me what mattered most, and it proved humbling. I leaned against the doorjamb to Hayley's bedroom, watching her sleep. Light from the hallway poured in, illuminating the steady rise and fall of her breaths, and Precious snuggled to her side. The alarm clock on her nightstand read one in the morning. We'd been home for hours, and I should've been in bed too. But rest wouldn't come. With each passing moment, clarity on two specific subjects had banished my emotional and physical exhaustion, keeping slumber at bay.

The first, unsurprising, was Hayley. How many times had Julia spoken about the importance of teen years? With Hayley on the cusp of what could be a challenging season, it didn't sit right to start on a new and all-consuming business venture. What had felt right were the past few weeks of cutting back on networking events and the extra, intentional time Hayley and I had spent together.

The second matter, also unsurprising, was Claire, and how we'd crafted our restaurant goals. Praying and fasting over them. How we'd received certainty about moving forward with those plans. Why was I doubting that now? Why was I trying to rush the timeline God had made clear to us? Why hadn't I treated this opportunity with the Vieux Carré Café the same way? Instead of praying and truly listening, I'd run headlong into my selfish desires. My old, sinful nature wanted control. But time after time, God had proven His ways were perfect for me.

A rich and familiar peace expanded within my core, and a soft smile crested my lips. Tomorrow I would decline my parents' offer and let my real estate agent know I wouldn't be bidding on the Vieux Carré Café.

I padded down the hallway, slipped beneath my cool sheets, and rested my head against my pillow. Breathing in the crisp scent of laundry detergent, a third aspect came to mind. Micah, and how I'd have more time for him and be able to support him with his dad when he needed it. Every muscle within me relaxed, my body sinking into the plush mattress. My eyes drifted shut not out of exhaustion but deep satisfaction. *Thank You, Lord.*

32

THE NEXT AFTERNOON I found myself caught by a jazz funeral procession. Very fitting since I was on my way to pay my last respects to the Vieux Carré Café.

I stood on the slate sidewalk, taking in the glossy black carriage hearse pulled by two gray horses. It rolled past at a gentle pace. A full brass band, including drums, strolled with the funeral goers, filling the air with a swinging rendition of "I'll Fly Away." Those following on foot wore black, some waving white handkerchiefs, others bobbing decorated second-line umbrellas, and still others dipping regular umbrellas up and down. Despite the loss and tears, those mourning also radiated joy, seemingly knowing the heavenly destination of the loved one they'd lost.

The direction of the procession indicated the mourners headed to the St. Louis Cemetery, five blocks away. I prayed for those walking past, that they would have the peace flowing through my veins. God's inexplicable peace that made no sense. But I knew not to question or prod at it. Just to float in the precious gift from above.

With the last of the funeral gone by, I crossed the street and stood before the one-story building that had consumed my life the previous four months. That in some ways, I was ashamed to admit, had become an idol. It would officially go on the market in nine days. Behind me, the occasional vehicle drove down the narrow, one-way road, leaving exhaust fumes in their wake. Being a lazy Sunday afternoon, the normal hustle and bustle in this area had eased to more of a trickle. Unlike the last time I'd stood here, my reflection in the dingy glass of the front doors now gave the appearance of a woman sure of her next steps, and happy to take them.

A shadow moved inside, and I startled. Someone meandered along the back wall, near the antique bakery display case. I pressed right up on the glass inlaid in the wooden door, cupping my hands to my eyes. The lights flickered on, revealing Mrs. Adélaide.

What in the world?

She stared at me, the excitement on her wrinkled face giving the impression she was not surprised to find me leering through the windows of the long-closed French pâtisserie.

I inhaled in understanding, my hand covering my parted lips. Her Cajun French heritage. This French bakery. The fact she'd become a regular customer at Beignets & Books around the same time as the Vieux Carré Café closing.

She shuffled across the tiny black and white hexagonal floor tiles and opened the door.

My fingers dropped from my face. "You own the Vieux Carré Café?"

"*Oui.*" She waved me in with a chuckle. "Though now, it's jus' the structure."

I nodded robotically and entered, disbelief sputtering through me. Like last time, the stale air held a trace of espresso.

"Still. I like to come and allow the place to breathe from time to time." She left the front door wide open and moved past me to the old French doors leading to the side courtyard.

I awoke from my stupor. "Please, let me. When I was here

before, they stuck." My heels clicked against the tile, emitting a light echo. With a gentle shove, I opened both doors and took a step outside, still trying to grasp this odd turn of events.

"*Merci.*" Mrs. Adélaide lingered in the doorway, taking everything in, from the large courtyard to the building across the street. The second and third floors there boasted charming wrought-iron railings. Such a quintessential French Quarter view.

My gaze lifted to the huge southern magnolia standing sentinel over the space. "You'd said Cést Fou had taken up in your magnolia tree long ago." I'd assumed it was the magnolia at her home.

She nodded and motioned grandly to the area, the skin beneath her arms wobbling. "Half of my seating was out here. Imagine having to come out each morning and clean this. I had to cover the tables and chairs every night. Such a mess."

No wonder she hated that bird so much.

For a moment she closed her eyes, taking in and releasing a deep breath. "Other than letting some life inside, I was stopping by to say good-bye."

"So was I."

Her brows drew together behind her thick glasses. "My agent told me you were one of the parties interested."

"I was. But I can't afford it. And if I could . . . the timing's not right."

Mrs. Adalaide's expression became reflective, and she slowly retreated indoors.

I followed and moved toward the gem of the empty room, running my fingers across the bakery case. Not a speck of dust resulted from my indulgence.

"Are you sure you won't put in an offer?" Mrs. Adélaide wrung her hands over her soft middle. "You're such a good business owner. The way you pitch in. Bussing tables, unclogging toilets, encouraging your employees . . . caring for them. You could jus' sit in your office and distance yourself, but you don't." Her expression turned earnest. "And you care for your mawmaw's place. Take such tender care of it, inside and out. Dat's the kind of person I want taking care of my place."

My cheeks warmed. If Mrs. Adélaide expressed so much praise, I knew I'd done Mawmaw proud too. And Claire. I pressed my lips together, tamping down my growing smile. "Thank you for your lovely words." I laid a hand to my heart. "They mean more than you could know. But I'm certain I can't open another location right now. It's not where the Lord's leading me." My attention lingered on the curved ceiling, trailing one last time to the French doors. The moment had arrived to let this property go. And it was well with my soul to do so. "I'll be praying God's will with who does get this place and peace for you with that decision."

Mrs. Adélaide's mouth twisted, and she studied me. It seemed perhaps it wasn't so well with her soul to have me out of the running. But goodness knew there would be interest outside of Ryan. My parents would probably buy the building and sit on it, merely to exact their revenge on him.

A tiny prickle of worry had my gaze sliding to the side. "Would you be open to selling me the bakery display? Unless you plan to keep the piece for yourself, I think it'd be a wonderful addition to Beignets & Books."

"*Oui.*" The wrinkles bracketing her mouth and eyes deepened with fondness. "I would like dat."

Mr. Gary's gaudy BBQ pit sat in the middle of my beautiful courtyard. Making the metal monstrosity somewhat bearable was the incredibly hot man standing before it. Micah tended the grill. Despite only half of the burners working, smoke billowed, and flames sizzled the meat. Thankfully the eyesore would remain hidden behind the shed when not in use.

Micah had insisted that on the Fourth of July, one needed to indulge in hamburgers and hot dogs, along with potato salad and baked beans. I'd quickly volunteered to provide the baked beans and had just come from upstairs with them. The serving bowl, covered in foil, was warm in my hands.

With Renee and her family spending the holiday out of town, we were a small gathering of four. And since Mr. Gary couldn't handle the stairs to my place, we were dining down here. If the summer heat proved too much, we'd head inside the café. But thankfully the skies had been overcast. Hayley and Mr. Gary sat at the table, a deck of cards between them. Today began her first lesson in poker. I smiled, not only for their budding relationship but also because I'd instituted a chip-only betting rule.

Micah turned from the grill, a long metal spatula in his hand. "Look at you cooking." The amount of flirtation in his voice was shameless.

I set the beans on the table. "I'll have you know I used two kitchen appliances."

Hayley snorted. "I don't think a can opener counts as an appliance."

Mr. Gary chuckled, rearranging the cards in his hand.

The back door to the café yawned open, Mrs. Adélaide appearing, dressed as though she were Uncle Sam's wife. "I thought I saw some people back here."

With a smile I approached, taking the steps up to the porch. "Happy Fourth of July."

"To you too." She waved at everyone, a set of red, white, and blue bracelets jangling on her wrist.

"Would you like to join us? We've got plenty of food."

"*Merci*, but no. I have plans. I jus' stopped by to say I decided not to put de Vieux Carré Café on de market."

I blinked, every coherent thought tumbling from my mind. "I . . . I don't . . . understand. Why?"

"Sometimes de timing's jus' no' right." She winked. "I decide to wait for de right person to buy."

"Oh, Mrs. Adélaide." My stomach sank, and I wrung my hands. "I'd hate for you to miss this opportunity." Ryan dropped into my mind, the dots connecting to what this meant for him and the loss of his job. A smidgen of compassion arose. "I don't even know if I'll ever expand to another location."

"Dat's for true." She reached across the space between us and patted my arm. "Only God knows what de future holds. You see, I been praying for a long time on what to do wit' dat building and got tired of waiting on God. So, thinking I know best, I put it up for sale. Well"—she chuckled lightly—"dat obviously didn't sit right wit' God, and He's let me know." She tapped her fist to her chest. "So now I wait." Her gaze turned heavenward, her eyes practically sparkling behind her glasses, matching her grin. "He'll show me what to do wit' de building in His perfect timing." And with that, she left.

I stood, my mouth agape, watching her retreating form through the glass in the door. Gently, a euphoric type of wonder whispered over me. *What are You up to, Lord?*

"Mom!" Hayley called out. "Food's ready."

Breath catching, joy expanded through my heart, nearly bursting through my ribs. "Coming." With a smile as vast as the Mississippi, I was certain I floated down the steps. I took a seat next to Micah, and he said grace over the food spread before us. As Hayley and Mr. Gary busied themselves making their plates, I leaned toward Micah, my mouth to his ear. "I love you, Micah Guidry."

He pulled back just enough to gaze at me, a smile on his lips. He pressed a kiss to my cheek and lingered. "I love you, Kate Landry."

Hayley made a gagging noise. "Y'all promised no PDA."

Laughter rang around the table.

For so long, I'd thought my dreams were planned, framed, and hanging on a wall, ready to check off one at a time. But my true dream had been a part of my heart before I'd even realized it was there. And my heart wanted a life centered on God's peace, with Hayley, and now Micah. Anything good that came after that would be God lagniappe.

EPILOGUE

MARDI GRAS DAY HAD ARRIVED. The three sets of French doors in Kate's living room lay open for friends and family to easily meander through. Outside, the Krewe of Rex made their way down St. Charles Avenue. Inside, laughter, conversation, and the scent of fresh beignets and seafood gumbo reigned.

Kate and I stood on the porch, talking to Julia and taking in the view. Purple, green, and gold banners draped the balcony railing. On the street below, thick crowds lined both sides of the road. Paradegoers waved their arms and shouted at the floats rolling by, the masked riders tossing beads, doubloons, and plastic cups.

"Your first Mardi Gras off since the café opened," Julia said to Kate. "How does it feel?"

Kate raised her hand, as though in church and praising the Lord. "It feels wonderful."

Penny ran the café today in her newly appointed role as assistant manager, which had freed up more time for Kate. And with that extra time, she now considered teaching an introductory business class at the library. I'd never seen her eyes light up so much when talking about something, other than Hayley.

347

A double-decker float rode by, some riders hurling beads like pro baseball pitchers. Several snagged on the limbs of the live oaks.

Kate's hand dropped with a groan.

"Don't worry." I nudged her with my elbow. "I'll help you cut them down tomorrow."

She snaked her hand around my arm to my bicep. "Just when I thought I couldn't love you more." Her fingers squeezed. "And since you won your dad's partially working tree trimmers, we'll get those beads down in no time."

I couldn't stop my chuckle.

"How's your dad doing?" Julia asked.

"Really great." And it was a relief to mean those words. Five months ago, he'd broken his foot and been admitted to a rehabilitation center for recovery. That facility resided within a retirement community Dad had instantly connected with, especially with several of his friends already living there. He'd moved into an apartment and promptly started a poker club. Once a week, I picked him up to have beignets at the café and play cards with me, Kate, and Hayley. For chips only.

On the flip side, Kate had not returned to the recurring dinners at her parents' home. However, her father had started stopping by the café on the mornings of what would have been Sad Saturday. Last month had included me and Hayley for the first time. I'd been prepared to step into a protective role, but it hadn't been necessary. From what we understood, Kate's mom wasn't aware of the breakfast gatherings.

"Oh!" Julia pulled her phone from her back pocket. "Let me snap a picture of the three of y'all before I forget." She hurried off for Hayley, who sat at the kitchen table, playing a raucous game of Uno with Emma, Mayté, Brooke, and Samuel. Corralling Hayley toward us, Julia's expression radiated pure joy. "Y'all are so cute dressed in the same shirt."

Hayley and Kate exchanged a knowing look. I'd bought

them Mardi Gras Hawaiian shirts to match mine. Upon opening the gifts last night, they'd reacted with teasing jokes at the purple, green, and gold fleur-de-lis pattern. I'd reasoned they were perfect to take on their Hawaiian vacation this summer. With extra income from all the events Kate had booked, they were all set for their dream trip. To my surprise, when I'd arrived this morning, they'd both been wearing them. The sight had caused an unexpected swell of tender affection to wash over me.

Julia held up her phone, gesturing us together. She grinned so much, her chin trembled.

Kate and I flanked Hayley for the shot, our arms wrapping around each other. Emotion struck me hard at the family-like image being captured. With the picture over, Hayley darted back inside.

"Text that to me," Kate said to Julia as they headed indoors too.

I remained on the balcony, needing a minute to compose myself. Turning my gaze to the parade, I gripped the railing and found I couldn't focus on the partying before me. I couldn't concentrate on anything except the wonder coursing through my veins. The last time I'd stood on this spot on Mardi Gras Day, I'd been eighteen and heavyhearted. My college choice that fall would take me to Colorado. To a place I didn't want to go. Away from my family and friends. Away from Kate, who I'd had a longtime crush on. But I'd gone and made a life there. And lost a marriage. And found God.

The few romantic relationships I'd had since my divorce hadn't felt right. Too shallow or unbalanced, or missing something I could never quite put my finger on. I'd been like a boat, drifting, wary to anchor. That first day Kate had walked into the library, something had clicked. I'd known she had a genuine heart. Had witnessed it growing up. Then I'd gotten to know her as an adult and a parent. Observed that caring side of her, now amplified. And then there was Hayley. My throat grew thick, and I blinked, turning my sights to the clear skies above the treetops.

That longing I'd had for so long of a little family of my own . . . Tears smarted at the backs of my eyes, and I worked to swallow. Pulled in an expansive breath, and released it. That night when I'd found Hayley safe at the carriage house, I'd dropped anchor, knowing with them was where I belonged. I never thought I'd end up with two redheads and one ugly dog. But God had known. I'd trusted Him, and He'd steered me exactly where I needed to be.

Kate appeared next to me and leaned her head against my shoulder. "I'm glad you restarted Mawmaw's Mardi Gras party tradition."

"Me too." I slipped my arm around her, pressing a kiss to her hair, inhaling her addictive scent of vanilla and citrus.

Her fingers intertwined with mine, and she straightened, mischief twinkling in her blue eyes. With a wink she tugged me to follow, my pulse kicking into second gear. We turned the corner of the porch to what had become our make-out spot when Hayley was home.

My thumbs caressed her soft cheeks, brushing the freckles there I'd come to adore. Her gaze brightened with expectation, and I leaned in, working a slow, savoring kiss across her lips. She swayed. I shifted my hold to her hips, gliding my fingers to her lower back. She grabbed fistfuls of my shirt, pulling herself against me. Need expanded, electricity snapping beneath my skin where her touch lingered, where her body pressed to mine. Taking a reluctant breath, I rested my forehead on hers. Chest heaving, she stared at my mouth, her fingertips grazing the stubble on my jaw.

Releasing a low growl, I eased away, breaking all contact between us. "Anyone could easily find us here." I imprisoned my hands in my pockets, not trusting myself.

She bit back a smile, straightening her shirt. "It wouldn't look so bad if I had a ring on my finger."

My brows arced, and I shot her a teasing smirk. "Are you proposing to me?"

"What if I was?" She played along, lifting her chin in mock challenge, bringing her plump lips closer to mine.

My resolve broke, my hands returning to her waist, toying with the belt loops on her jeans. "Where's *my* ring?"

Her nose crinkled. "I'm sure I could find something to make do."

With a building grin I tugged her near, nuzzling her neck, breathing in her sweet aroma and warmth. "How about a bread tie?"

She shivered, and her throat bobbed. "Precious's collar?"

Smiling against her skin, I reached into my pants pocket and retrieved the engagement ring Hayley had helped me choose last month. I slid to my knee, holding the ring up. "How about we try this proposal again?"

AUTHOR'S NOTE

I took the liberty of combining two places of interest on St. Charles Avenue to create Hayley and Micah's library: the Milton H. Latter Memorial Library and the W. P. Brown Mansion. There's an intriguing history behind the Milton H. Latter Memorial Library and its charming carriage house, and how the mansion was donated to the public library system. But the unique Brown Mansion and its stunning Romanesque architecture have long held my attention as a "castle" in New Orleans. So with the leeway writing fiction provides, I united the two estates into one.

DISCUSSION QUESTIONS

1. One of the themes in *Kate Landry Has a Plan* is forgiveness. Kate has a hard time forgiving her ex-fiancé, but through wise counsel and her faith, she finds a way to do it. Have you had a similar situation where you struggled to forgive someone? Did you rely on your faith to help you through it?

2. Kate and Micah's story trope is opposites attract. Did you relate more to the type A personality of Kate or the laid-back personality of Micah?

3. This author is known to love writing romance, especially those early moments in a budding relationship. What was your favorite scene in the book that involved Kate and Micah?

4. Did Kate's past with being a caregiver resonate with you? Have you been a caregiver or known someone who has?

5. This story has a unique aspect in the characters being more mature in age than what is typically found in inspirational romances. Did you enjoy reading about characters in their forties? Did you find any big differences between these characters and others you've read about who are younger?

6. The author incorporates distinctive secondary characters in her stories. Did any of the supporting characters in *Kate Landry Has a Plan* stand out to you? Why?

7. There's quite a bit of humor in this story. What's one of your favorite lighthearted moments?

8. New Orleans is such an iconic city. Did any particular scenes in the story stand out to you because of the location?

ACKNOWLEDGMENTS

Steve, Steve Jr., and Alex—thank you for being supportive all these years and for putting up with my scattered brain when it's in writer mode.

Momma and Nancy—thank you for also putting up with my writer brain. Sorry for penning another romance. ☺

Rachel Scott McDaniel—I'm forever grateful to God for bringing us together. When we first met, I thought I'd hit the jackpot in finding an amazing critique partner. It didn't take long to realize God had much better plans for our relationship. Thank you for being my friend and soul sister, and thank you for always making my stories stronger. I'm especially grateful for your suggestions for Micah being a hunky librarian and digging deeper into the caregiver aspects. I love how your genius brain works.

My prayer warriors: Rachel Scott McDaniel, Deborah Clack, Joy Tiffany, Crissy Loughridge, Amy Watson, Katie Powner—ladies, I dearly thank God for you. Your prayers and support have helped carry me through the hardest parts of my life. Thank you.

Jessica Sharpe and Kate Deppe—y'all are the best editors a girl could ever ask for. I'm beyond grateful for your guidance on this book. This story is so much better because of your talent and insight. Thank you.

Bethany House—I still can't believe I've written two books with my dream publisher! I wish I could thank everyone individually. The skills, organization, and attention to detail in every department are outstanding. Thank you for making the publishing process easy and fun. Special shout-out to Raela Schoenherr, Rachael Betz, Lindsay Schubert, Joyce Perez, Anne Van Solkema, and Genevieve Smith.

Bob Hostetler—thank you for being my agent. The past six years have been an amazing and wild ride.

Readers—There aren't enough words to express how grateful I am to you. Thank you for your grassroots support in spreading the word about my debut, *Julia Monroe Begins Again*. Each of your encouraging notes, social media posts, and reviews have been lovely gifts I'll always cherish. I hope you've enjoyed this second book in the series, and that the Lord will uplift your hearts through it. If you wouldn't mind leaving reviews for this book at your favorite spots, that would be so helpful. Thank you!

JULIA MONROE BEGINS AGAIN

With her two boys off to college, forty-year-old Julia Monroe intends to expand her cleaning business in New Orleans, but God seems to have other plans. Samuel Reed, the ruggedly handsome Green Beret who broke her heart more than twenty years ago, has returned to town, and he's determined to win her back.

IN HINDSIGHT, SCHEDULING MY FIRST routine mammogram on my fortieth birthday may not have been a wise choice.

I sat in the empty waiting room of the New Orleans Women's Clinic, clipboard on my lap and pen in my hand. A fountain wall dribbled to my left, trying to emit calmness and having the opposite effect on my bladder.

I sailed through the beginning of the patient form: name, birth date, address. The next section, though . . . My pulse slowed as I read the question of my relationship status. *Single* and *married* were the only options. Where was the *widowed* box? And why did they need to know this information? Did my marital situation really impact my breasts? Well, maybe it did. Today would be the first day in ten years my North American regions had seen this much action.

With the paperwork completed, my gaze swept the pamphlets on the end table. Colonoscopies and mammograms and colorectal screenings, oh my! Didn't they want women to willingly return to this place? There should be *People* magazines, a coffee bar, and one of those mall masseuses set up in the corner.

The fountain continued calling to my bladder as though it were the Pied Piper. I'd already scoped the reception area for a bathroom and had come up empty. Curse that café au lait I'd had on the drive here. Of course, that was what having two babies did to you.

My boys. The urge to text them distracted me from the call of nature and the impending doom of being squeezed like an orange in a juicer. My youngest had started his first year of college in North Carolina at the same university where my oldest was now a sophomore. They had each other and my in-laws, who lived fifteen minutes from the campus. Those two reasons, and the fact that they had full scholarships, made the distance between us somewhat bearable.

"Julia Monroe?" A nurse in pink scrubs stood next to the back door, a folder in her hands.

I pushed my self-dyed brown hair from my shoulder and grasped my purse.

"Are you a healthcare worker too?" She motioned to my black scrubs, ironically appropriate for today.

"Oh. No, I'm a maid."

She nodded. "I bet the last thing you want to do when you get home is clean."

If I had a dollar . . . A forced chuckle matched my smile.

⚜

"I can't believe you put Harry in mourning clothes." I shook my head at the life-sized Harry Connick Jr. cardboard cutout and my friend Kate Landry, who owned Beignets & Books. The eatery operated within a historic house handed down through her family. The tourist and local hotspot nestled on the edge of the neighborhood known as the Garden District. Each room on the first floor held dining tables and shelves brimming with well-loved books ready for perusal on everything New Orleans.

Kate, also dressed in black, took a seat across from me at the round table for three. "Since you wouldn't let me throw an official over-the-hill party, I had to make do." She set a plate of fresh beignets on the black tablecloth spread before us. Powdered sugar drifted from the dish, dotting the fabric. Matching streamers mummified our chairs.

"I'll be sure to return the favor when you hit forty."

"I plan to stay in my thirties forever." Kate rubbed her index finger between her brows, smoothing a crease she'd recently become obsessed with.

The rest of the establishment was empty of customers, Kate's business having closed half an hour ago. The murmur of voices, laughter, and dishes clattering drifted from the kitchen at the back. Smooth jazz music piped in through the speakers.

We were breaking the cardinal rule of not wearing black while eating these confectionary treats, but considering the occasion, spilled powdered-sugar stains could be overlooked. I sank my teeth into a puffy square-shaped pastry. Soft sugar dusted the crispy outside, giving way to a melt-in-your-mouth tender middle. This week's food cheat had been worth the wait.

Kate's sideswept auburn bangs cascaded over one eye. "Do you know what I realized today?"

"That you need to get Harry a kilt for when St. Patrick's Day rolls around?"

A smile unfurled, bringing a sparkle to her blue eyes. Grabbing a packet of raw cane sugar, she ripped the paper and added the crystals to her mug. "Other than that."

"What?"

"With the boys gone, it's like you're really single again."

"I've been single for a decade." I placed the last bite of beignet into my mouth and sagged back in my chair in ecstasy.

"I know that." She poured decaf coffee from a French press, stirred her brew, and rested the spoon on her saucer. "But now you don't have the boys to take care of or to keep you from going out. Have you thought about dating again?"

"Have you?" I boomeranged the question, raising my brows for good measure.

Kate tucked her bobbed hair behind her ear. "What about Hayley?" She had adopted her niece when her sister had died around the same time as my husband.

"She's eleven with internet access. I think she knows adults date. Where is she anyway?"

"Spending the weekend with my parents. And nice try, but I know you're *stal-ling*." Kate sang the last word.

Grumble, grumble. My attention wandered past Harry's soulful eyes and beyond the front windows. Lampposts dimly lit the neutral ground of St. Charles Avenue, and a streetcar stuffed with passengers glided along its tracks. "Why would I want to pretend I don't belch or pass gas? Or worry about shaving my legs?"

"You shave your legs."

"Only for church and not in the winter." I raised my mug, eyes lifting to the ceiling. "Thank You, Lord, for knee-high boots."

"I'll toast to that." Kate lifted her cup too. "But I've read that people who had great marriages have a higher likelihood of happily remarrying." Her head tilted. "Is it because of Mark?"

"No." A feeling of sorrow descended, having nothing to do with the mentioning of my departed husband's name. Time, counseling, and God had shepherded me and my boys through our abrupt loss via a car accident. "Mark would've wanted me to move on."

I busied myself with pouring coffee I had no interest in drinking. If there was one thing life had taught me, it was that if you loved someone—one way or another—they could be taken from you, and I didn't have the strength to go through that kind of pain again.

Rebekah Millet is a double Selah Award, Cascade Award, and ACFW First Impressions Award–winning author of contemporary Christian romance novels. A New Orleans native, she grew up on beignets and café au lait, and loves infusing her colorful culture into her stories. Her husband is an answer to prayer, who puts up with her rearranging furniture and being a serial plant killer. Her two sons keep her laughing and share in her love of desserts. You can connect with Rebekah through her website, RebekahMillet.com.

Sign Up for Rebekah's Newsletter

Keep up to date with Rebekah's latest news on book releases and events by signing up for her email list at the website below.

RebekahMillet.com

FOLLOW REBEKAH ON SOCIAL MEDIA

Rebekah Millet - Author   @RebekahMillet   @RebekahMillet

More from Rebekah Millet

With her two boys off to college, forty-year-old Julia Monroe intends to expand her cleaning business in New Orleans, but God seems to have other plans. Samuel Reed, the ruggedly handsome Green Beret who broke her heart more than twenty years ago, has returned to town, and he's determined to win her back.

Julia Monroe Begins Again
Beignets for Two